**(The wartime memories of a Devon policeman, 1938 - 1946)**

# TAKE COVER

**(The wartime memories of a Devon policeman, 1938 - 1946)**

**Written by Edward TRIST**

**Compiled by Simon DELL, MBE**

**FOREST PUBLISHING**

**(In association with the Devon & Cornwall Constabulary)**

First published in 2001 by FOREST PUBLISHING, Woodstock, Liverton,
Newton Abbot, Devon TQ12 6JJ



**British Library Cataloguing in Publication Data**

A catalogue record for this book is available from the British Library.

ISBN 0 9536852 3 3

**Forest Publishing**

Editorial by:
Mike and Karen LANG

Typeset, design and layout by:
Simon DELL, MBE

Checking and proof-reading by:
Wendy BRAITHWAITE and Peter SURCOMBE

Printed and bound in Great Britain by:
Peter HOWELL & Co, The Printing Press, 21 Clare Place, Coxside,
Plymouth, Devon PL4 0JW

I.T. support provided by:
Julian MILDREN, *'THE COMPUTER DOCTOR'*, 32 Willow Road,
Bishopsmead, Tavistock, Devon PL19 9JH

# CONTENTS


Foreword ..... 7

Preface ..... 8

Introduction ..... 9

1 An ambition fulfilled ..... 11

2 The June 1938 intake ..... 19

3 Our introduction to the force ..... 29

4 Training and pay ..... 37

5 The ubiquitous Ralph Hare ..... 39

6 Ex-Sergeant Philip Prowse - The storeman ..... 47

7 Paignton ..... 51

8 Honiton ..... 63

9 The day war broke out ..... 71

10 Newton Abbot ..... 79

11 Flying duties in the RAF ..... 93

12 Return to the force ..... 97

13 Foot and mouth disease at Morebath ..... 107

14 The Plymouth air raids ..... 109

15 Return to rural policing ..... 113

16 Moretonhampstead and Dartmoor ..... 115

17 Highweek ..... 127

18 Dawlish ..... 137

19 Teignmouth ..... 147

20 Bampton ... 153

21 Tiverton ... 165

22 The wives ... 171

23 In conclusion ... 179

Index ... 185

The headquarters of the Devon Constabulary, seen in about 1930. This building was known as 'Constabulary Barracks' and was situated next to Exeter Prison. By the late 1930s, however, new headquarters for the Devon Constabulary had been constructed within the city of Exeter which, incidentally, had its own police force, and the building was taken over by the prison service for use as administration offices.

*Devon & Cornwall Constabulary Museum archives*

# FOREWORD

It must surely be to the police officers of Edward Trist's generation that we who serve in today's police service owe a debt of immeasurable gratitude. Based upon their efforts and dedication we enjoy the proud reputation of the British police service, one which police throughout the world can only envy. That reputation was hard won, particularly when the country was in the grip of the threat of invasion and facing the very real possibility of the destruction of everything that our society stood for.

It was the police officers in those challenging years from 1939 to 1945 who gave their 'all', maintaining not only everyday law and order, and occupying themselves with the routine and often mundane aspects of police work, but also dealing with the horrors and the reality of policing a country under constant enemy threat, attack and bombardment.

It is now over 60 years since a young Constable Trist joined the Devon Constabulary. Only he and his colleagues know the reality of policing a country during those war years, when every shadow or dark country lane presented a potential hiding place for an unseen enemy. They, too, are the only ones to know the real hardships and privations that officers suffered, and have truly earned our respect and admiration.

This book tells Edward Trist's story and that of his colleagues and friends during those troubled years. I am sure that much has been omitted by his self-effacing modesty but, through it all, it is clear to see that the courage, humour and sensitivity of police officers has changed little in all these years. It is those of Edward Trist's generation, sadly now declining in numbers, who will always remain in our hearts as members of the constabulary family and whose memory will last long after ours has faded. We owe them much.

**Sir John Evans OSt.J, QPM, DL, LL.B**
**Chief Constable**
**Police Headquarters**
**Exeter**
**May 2001**

# PREFACE

Whenever a group of police pensioners meet there is one core of agreement. No matter how each individual may have been the odd man out in his actions and opinions when serving with his erstwhile colleagues, definitely, yes most definitely, we were the lucky ones to have been in the Devon Constabulary in the pre-amalgamation days. We reminisce about just how good - how enjoyable - our service years were compared with the present. But were we so fortunate? Was life so enjoyable? Did we really have such great careers with our fellow officers? Perhaps a few anecdotes of our 'halcyon days' might put things into perspective.

Having attained the age when it is difficult to recollect what was eaten at yesterday's breakfast, I humbly beg the reader of this collection of memories forgiveness for any mistakes discovered. With the passage of time the memory plays strange tricks, and over 60 years have passed since I joined the Devon Constabulary. It would be quite remiss of me if I failed to record the kindness and interest shown by contemporaries and others, without whose encouragement the following pages would not have been recorded.

They include Brian Estill, former curator of the force museum, Irene Haysom, 'Larry' and Nancy Hurrell, ex-Chief Inspector 'Reg' Perryman, Paul Richards of *Exeter Micros Ltd,* whose expertise recovered nearly 60 pages so painstakingly tapped out and apparently devoured by my ancient Amstrad computer, John Slater, who worked so hard to keep it from such bad habits, Mrs Marie Reid and my wife, Mary, whose patience has been sorely tried by my interminable questions about names and dates. She has consistently given encouragement when disasters occurred.

Actually sitting down and typing my memoirs followed a chance conversation at the force pensioners' day a few years ago. A serving constable was bemoaning the fact that he had been ordered to stand by newly-issued items of equipment exhibited for the information, and bewilderment, of us pensioners. Apparently the officer wished to be engaged on anything but that particular duty, and was not averse to stating to all and sundry how irksome his task was. Later, when visiting the force library, I was laughingly assuring the librarian, Jane Lashbrook, that the constable did not know what really frustrating duties were, but that he could quickly learn if he asked any of the pensioners discussing the riot gear and weapons etc. in his charge. All would have quoted examples of what they had suffered and accepted in their years of service. Quoting a few personal experiences had Jane enquiring if I had recorded them and "If not, why not?" - "Otherwise they will be lost for ever". Any of Jane's colleagues will confirm that she is extremely persuasive, allegedly being able to 'charm the birds from the trees' - hence this attempt to describe the work pattern of Devon Constabulary policemen in the pre-war and wartime years.

Finally my thanks to the Chief Constable, Sir John Evans, for his interest and kindness in agreeing to take the time to pen the foreword, and for enlisting, on my behalf, the expertise of Simon Dell, a policeman of a more modern age and the author of other policing books, who has turned my manuscript into a publishable format, and has kindly donated photographs from his, and the force museum's, extensive collections to illustrate this book.

**Edward Trist**
**Shillingford St. George**
**May 2001**

# INTRODUCTION

When a serving police officer receives a telephone call from the office of his Chief Constable it is, perhaps, quite reasonable for him to fear the worst, and start to imagine that all past misdemeanours, however trivial, had eventually caught up with him. You can, therefore, understand my relief that it was merely a request to go and meet a retired policeman who lived in a small village not far from headquarters at Exeter, to discuss his memoirs that he had written. Having written three books on the subject of policing history, I didn't consider this too onerous a task and readily accepted. 'Ted' Trist, I was told, was a former detective inspector and a rather 'sprightly' octogenarian who had retired from the force in 1964. Having just collected my 22 years long-service medal that year, and considering myself no spring chicken, I fully expected to find a frail old man, quite probably bent double with a hearing trumpet attached to his ear! Still, with almost 20 years' experience as a community constable, and used to taking tea with police pensioners, I was quite adept in talking loudly and stifling the odd yawn or two.

The day came for my visit and I arrived at the chosen hour at Ted's home. The door was answered by a lady who I assumed might be his daughter. I introduced myself and enquired if he was at home (where on earth I expected to find a frail old man in his mid 80s other than at home escaped me, but it seemed polite at the time!). I was then invited in and met the lady's husband (probably Ted's son, I thought). I almost fell off my chair when this gentleman, who I guessed was in his late 60s, introduced himself as Edward Trist! From that moment on he had me enthralled with tales of policing in a very different service to the one that I had joined over 20 years previously, and this visit was the first of many such encounters with Edward and Mary, his charming and equally youthful wife.

His manuscript had been a 'labour of love', extending to over 80,000 words, painstakingly typed, and recounting almost every detail of his varied career which spanned the war years and continued up until his retirement from the force in 1964. I had always considered myself lucky indeed that my own tutors in my early years in the force had been men who had joined when high-necked tunics were the order of the day and a ride in a police car was almost unheard of. Men such as 'Long-John' Russell, 'Barnie' Pawson and 'Pete' Telling; constables with stories that I never tired of hearing. Yet I was now meeting a man who was from a generation of policemen before even *my* tutors had left school! And what stories he had to tell me - some which brought tears of mirth rolling down my cheeks, some which were downright wicked and many which proved to me that some things never change and that the depths of human deprivation were being explored even then.

I was asked if I could "do something" with his massive manuscript, and after much discussion and several visits to enjoy Mary's kind, and never-ending, hospitality we decided upon producing this book, an abridged version of his work, with some photographs thrown in for good measure. Over the ensuing months of getting to know Ted and reliving his service, how fortunate I considered myself not to have been through the horrors of policing a county during wartime, but quietly jealous that I had not been a member of the intake of 1st June 1938. I am just pleased to have known him, and to have taken some small part in preserving his accounts before they were lost for ever. We invite you to share them, and simply to wonder at what had to be left out!

**Simon Dell, MBE**
**Police Constable**
**Tavistock**
**May 2001**

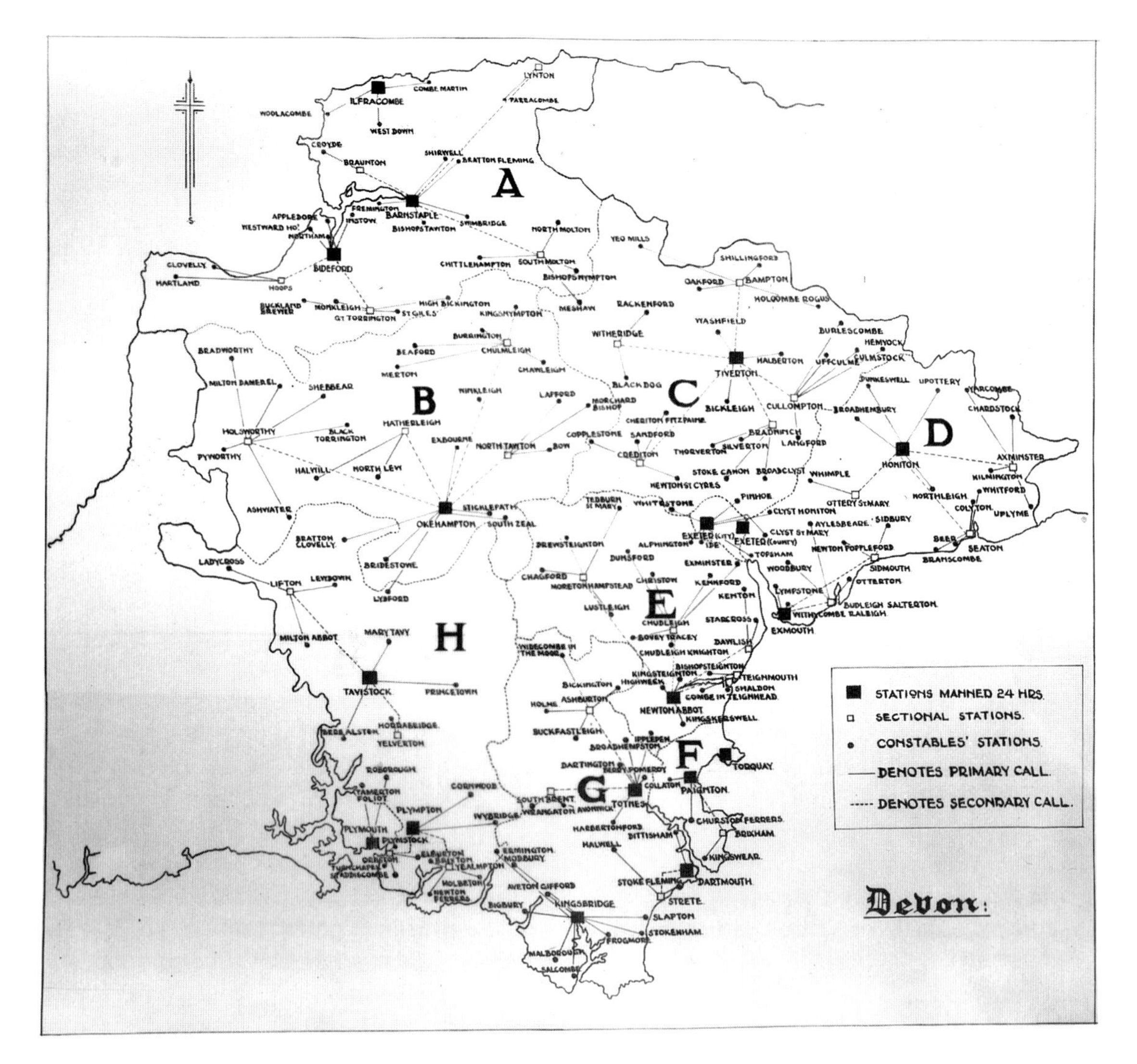


***A MAP OF THE DEVON CONSTABULARY AREA.***

*This map of the area of the Devon Constabulary, dated about 1937, shows the location of the country beat stations as well as section stations where sergeants would have been located. It was produced to identify lines of communication between stations within the force area and shows how remote some of the smaller rural beats were at that time. Some constables were many miles from their neighbouring colleagues and even further from their own sergeants and inspectors. With only pedal cycles available for transport about their beats they relied totally upon the community which they served for support and assistance until reinforcements from other, equally isolated, stations could arrive. The section sergeants at that time were also obliged to cycle during the performance of their duties, which included travelling around their section areas and supervising their constables in the more remote parts of the force.*

*Devon & Cornwall Constabulary Museum archives*

# CHAPTER 1
# AN AMBITION FULFILLED

Where to begin? Perhaps 1937 is a good starting year. I was a shop assistant in Plymouth and regularly met a fellow worker, 'Jack' Smith, after work on Saturday nights. Jack finished at 8.30pm and would wait for me until my shop closed at nine. I was, however, marking time in my job, having been promised favourable consideration when reapplying to join the United African Trading Company to work on the Gold Coast. But I had just learned that only applicants already serving in the U.K. with the Unilever Group were eligible to go to Africa when 21, others not until they were 22. At 20 this seemed a long way away and caused me to reconsider my plans and think seriously about my long-held thoughts of a career as a policeman.

Jack remarked that he had been trying to join the police service for some time but, despite daily exercises, was under the required 36-inch minimum chest measurement. He had been making regular visits to the Devon Constabulary police station at Crownhill but had been unable to persuade the interviewing sergeant (later superintendent), Edgar Eddy, to allow him to take the entry examination.

On the following morning (Sunday) at 10 o'clock I was at the Crownhill station expressing my life-long ambition to be a policeman, but was quickly told that I was too short - I was devastated. It was agreed that 5 feet 10 inches was the required minimum and, when grudgingly permitted to stand in stockinged feet against the measurement stand, you can imagine my delight when I was found to be a 'little over five ten and a half'. My chest, being over 36 inches, was also satisfactory, so I was duly seated and given tests in dictation and arithmetic. Neither was over-demanding: a single spelling error in 'accommodation', which I gave only one 'm', has resulted in that word, whenever seen, to be carefully checked to this day!

*The former Devon Constabulary station at Crownhill, near Plymouth - long since demolished - pictured in about 1960.*

*Courtesy of Plymouth City Museums and Art Gallery Collection*

Leaving the police station with physical and educational standards deemed acceptable, I optimistically thought that it was just a matter of days, perhaps weeks, before I would be in the force. This idea was shattered when I was notified of further requirements before I could be considered as a suitable applicant. It was a formidable list, including holding a driving licence for a car as well as for a motorcycle (not too common in 1937), being able to swim a minimum of 50 yards in normal clothing, having had a recent vaccination against a number of specified infections, holding a recently awarded St. John's Ambulance certificate and also being able to furnish the names of two acceptable householders as referees.

After obtaining a provisional driving licence, I bought an ancient A.J.S. motorcycle and, with just a few minutes instruction, took it onto the highway. Meanwhile, my brother-in-law had allowed his Austin 10 to be maltreated and said that he thought I should take the test before the gearbox was wrecked. So, with the driving test passed and the ambulance certificate obtained, there was only the vaccination to be undergone, and my 70-year-old doctor did this as he had always done it since commencing in practice in the 1890s. He held the blade of his penknife over a spirit lamp and, when satisfied the blade was sterilised, scraped a portion of my upper arm, broke a phial of vaccine onto the bleeding arm surface and, after a moment or so, covered the wound with a plaster. Basic, but so effective. Within a day I was flat on my back with an arm swollen double, and remained in bed until having to attend the interview and medical examination at the force headquarters in New North Road, Exeter.

It was necessary to take the 7am train from Plymouth North Road railway station to ensure being on time for the interview. By the time that I had arrived at Exeter St. David's, at 8am, and walked to the town centre, my earlier post-vaccination loss of appetite had disappeared. Ravenous, I breakfasted in Deller's Cafe, Bedford Circus - two poached eggs on toast and a pot of tea, costing 1/5d, such rash expenditure being considered justified on such a special day *and* in such a splendid eating house. Deller's was truly a magnificent restaurant, good food served by charming, pretty waitresses in pleasant surroundings. A three-piece orchestra played popular light music from 11am to 2pm and from 4pm to 6pm each weekday. The premises were lost when Exeter was blitzed in 1943, the victim of one of Hitler's 'Baedaker' air raids. It was a sad loss to Exeter and certainly no other Exeter restaurant, in my opinion, has since equalled Deller's for their decor, standard of food and service.

At the force headquarters I was fortunate in being interviewed by a kindly, true gentleman, the Assistant Chief Constable, Mr Frederick Hutchings. He was understanding and went out of his way to put me, a very nervous candidate, at ease.

The next trial was the medical examination, conducted by two Exeter doctors. Almost immediately one drew attention to the hitherto unknown fact that I was becoming flat-footed. The other doctor explained there would be a lessening of the foot arches because we candidates were bigger, heavier men than the average, adding: "But look at that arm, there's no doubt the vaccine has been ingested!" So thrilled were they with 'that arm' that the flat feet were forgotten. The days in bed prior to the medical examination had probably also helped in improving the diminished arches, so it can be said that the long put-off vaccination changed my life. I was told to report to headquarters at 10am on 31st May, for reception prior to commencing official duties on 1st June 1938.

Upon arrival, our new career started at a hectic pace. There were 26 men making up the Devon Constabulary intake, later to be joined for training at our headquarters by other constables who were joining neighbouring Westcountry forces. These officers were William Firebrace and Stanley Powell, who were joining the Exeter City Police along with

Stanley Edwards and Ronald Botheras, who were recruits in the Tiverton and Penzance borough forces respectively.

***The Penzance Borough Police, July 1939.*** *Constable Ronald Botheras is pictured in the third row, second from the left. This group photograph, showing the entire force, was taken outside the Penzance borough headquarters at St. John's Hall in the town. As can be seen, the uniform of this much smaller force differs greatly to that of the larger Devon Constabulary.*

*Devon & Cornwall Constabulary Museum archives*

The Devon Constabulary recruits were met by our 'sergeant major', one Inspector Charles Webber, 'Charlie' to all recruits from 1931 to 1939. He allocated us lodgings at various nearby houses by alphabetical order of our surnames, resulting in Jack Smith and me being sent to number 29 New North Road, where we shared a bedroom with a window just feet from the prison's perimeter wall.

After introducing ourselves to our new landlord, and depositing our suitcases, we hurried back to headquarters to be immediately whisked off to the 'Nisi Prius' court at Rougemont Castle. (The Nisi Prius court, incidentally, was the higher civil court at that time, presided over by a high court judge.) Awaiting us was Colonel Ellicombe JP, the very model of a military gentleman, who patiently heard us all swear that we would: *"Well and truly serve our Sovereign Lord, the King"*. He stressed the importance of the duties that we were undertaking and just how much the nation at large depended upon us to protect its citizens from dire perils and even anarchy. He ended by congratulating us and wishing us well in our newly-chosen careers. Undoubtedly, he inspired the majority of us.

***The Tiverton Borough Police,*** *prior to its amalgamation into the Devon Constabulary in the January of 1943. Rear row (standing, left to right): Special Constable Bennett (a retired inspector from the Metropolitan Police), Constables Frank Harding (not to be confused with the Frank Harding of the Devon Constabulary who is mentioned in this book), Stanley Edwards (as referred to previously), Bill Stuckey, Sid Badcock (later an inspector in the Devon county force), Arthur Chidgey and Jack Squires, and Special Constable Morrell. Front row (seated, left to right): Acting Sergeant Bill Land, Sergeant Frank Galpin, Chief Constable Mervyn Beynon, Sergeant Frank Williams and Constable Cyril Richards.*

*Fred Williams*

Marching back to headquarters via Rougemont Gardens saved us from being seen by too many members of the public, our attempts at marching being pretty pathetic and certainly such as would not have commended us to the worthy Colonel! Charlie then issued us with our official 'collar' numbers, requiring the first use of numbers 472 to 492 in the history of the Devon force. Our colleagues from the smaller borough and city forces, who were being trained with us, had been issued with their own individual collar numbers by their own force, and were not part of the Devon Constabulary's numbering system. Whilst we did not appreciate the fact at that time, this meant that prior to June 1938 there had been a maximum of 471 constables and sergeants, supervised by fewer than 30 senior officers, covering every duty and commitment that occurred in the county with the exception of the areas policed by Plymouth city, Exeter city and Tiverton borough officers. Many of these duties have now been hived off to separate, expensive organisations.

***Inspector Charlie Webber,*** *with a group of recruits at headquarters in 1937. Rear row: Constables Dennis Stocker, John Wakeham, Bill Cheek and unknown. Middle row, standing: Constables Bill Stone, Harry Williams, Harry Adams, Percy Ferris, Don Cowling, unknown, unknown and Ron Honeywill. Front row, seated: Constables Alfie Coker, Ron Ferris, Rupert Hardwell, Charles Medland and George Webber, Inspector Charlie Webber and Constables Stan Thorning, Freddie Brooks, Edgar Burnell, Eddie Tapley and unknown.*

*Rupert Hardwell*

It was taken for granted in those days that the police should prepare and present the evidence in all cases at petty sessions and juvenile courts, control traffic at fixed points and deal with parked vehicles, undertake all responsibilities relating to the 'Diseases of Animals Acts' (including market supervision duties), interview both juvenile and female victims in alleged sexual and assault offences, and control traffic and crowds at sports and other public-supported events. Police station cleaning and manning of the charge office were also duties that were considered as highly desirable, for any man allocated to do them was regarded as fortunate indeed. In addition, the typing of all reports was carried out in off-duty hours.

Another duty accepted as the norm in 1938 was the checking of private houses when the owners were away. A register was kept in the charge-room of every police station, and residents would report dates of absence, keyholder and other necessary details. The night and early turn constables noted the details and checked the properties on their beats. Before going off duty details of the time and the property checked during the tour of duty had to be entered in the register. Failure to make the visits, especially if the house was broken into, or a false statement of visits, could result in dismissal.

Traffic lights were being gradually installed at various urban crossroads within the county and presented yet another duty undertaken by the beat constables, namely switching on the lights shortly after 6am, checking that all signals were in working order and, when necessary, replacing any burnt-out bulbs. This required the use of a stepladder, so constables very quickly found out where there was a friendly shopkeeper or householder from whom one could be borrowed.

At each road junction controlled by traffic signals there was one pole with an enlarged base which provided a container for the mains switch and a storage place for replacement bulbs. Invariably there would be at least one burnt-out bulb to be replaced each day.

It was one morning in 1940, when making the bulb check at the traffic lights at the junction of The Avenue and Kingsteignton Road in Newton Abbot, that I saw a familiar figure approaching. It was a local mentally-handicapped man who, for some reason, strongly disliked policemen, mouthing unknown words and glaring through his pebble-thick spectacles whenever he passed a uniformed constable. For my part, I always greeted him with a cheery reference to the prevailing weather, usually causing him to hasten away muttering 'unpleasantries'.

On this particular morning I was at the furthermost point from the mains switch pole. Upon seeing me, he began throwing baleful glances and muttering at me whilst his constant companion, a large lurcher dog, literally pulled him along, tugging at a length of rope being used as a lead.

I had left the door at the base of the pole open and, upon seeing this, 'our friend' jerked the rope lead. The dog obligingly halted, half turned, cocked a leg and projected a stream into the switch area. There immediately occurred a truly electrifying event; the dog emitted a most painful yelp, leapt high in the air and then rushed off towards Kingsteignton at high speed, the rope lead trailing behind him, while his bewildered master stood transfixed looking at his hand, apparently hoping to find in its palm some explanation for the actions of his pet!

Hurrying over to him, I berated him for his wicked action in encouraging the dog to urinate into the base, telling him what an excellent conductor of electricity water is and that he could have caused the death of the animal. However, I doubt if my lecture did anything to improve the man's knowledge of electricity or his sentiments towards policemen, though his later perambulations with the hound apparently never included that particular road junction again.

Unilateral parking orders were in force in most towns and in a number of villages. Again, it was the lot of the early turn beat constable to change the heavy cast iron half-flapped signs. The flaps indicated *'Parking Permitted This Side On Even Dates'* which was covered by dropping the half-flap indicating *'Parking Permitted This Side On Odd Dates'*. The dropping or lifting of the plates also required the use of 'borrowed' steps, except on the part of very tall officers who were able to reach up and move the flaps as the dates required. At Newton Abbot, Constable 'Clem' Ryder, being over six and a half feet tall, had no difficulty with these signs, but most of us, rather than regularly having to ask for the loan of steps, carried a short fork-ended stick which we used for releasing the holding catch and for pushing up or easing down the flap as required.

Torquay Directory

SOUTH DEVON·JOURNAL

Phone 2830 · Telegrams: "DIRECTORY" TORQUAY

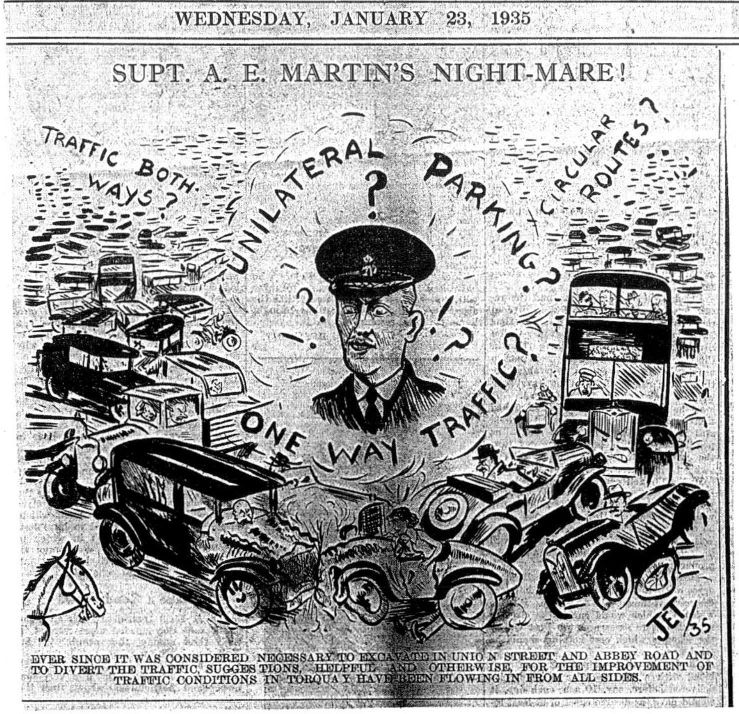

WEDNESDAY, JANUARY 23, 1935

SUPT. A. E. MARTIN'S NIGHT-MARE!



EVER SINCE IT WAS CONSIDERED NECESSARY TO EXCAVATE IN UNION STREET AND ABBEY ROAD AND TO DIVERT THE TRAFFIC, SUGGESTIONS, HELPFUL AND OTHERWISE, FOR THE IMPROVEMENT OF TRAFFIC CONDITIONS IN TORQUAY HAVE BEEN FLOWING IN FROM ALL SIDES.

*Courtesy of The Torquay Directory and South Devon Gazette*

***The June 1938 intake.***

*In this photograph the class of June 1938 is seen in the grounds of Rougemont Castle in Exeter, where the 'Nisi Prius' courtroom was used as a classroom for the recruits. Those shown are:*

Stan Ledbrook

Stan Coldridge

Alfred Christophers — Leslie Banks

Sidney Bray — Ronald Lee — John Elliott

William Firebrace (Exeter City Police)

Ernest Bob Southcott

Richard Jack Smith

William Tom Pill — Frederick Windeatt — Stanley Powell (Exeter City Police)

Kenneth Harvey — Percy Norman Rose

Reginald Fear

Stan Edwards (Tiverton Borough Police) — Edward 'Ted' Trist

*Photograph courtesy of Edward Trist*

# CHAPTER 2
# THE JUNE 1938 INTAKE

The 26 men making up the Devon County intake were a mixed group - clerks, engineers, farm workers, shop assistants, a bus conductor, a gas-fitter and a postman. They were:

Leslie Banks. He had served in different parts of the county prior to joining the R.A.F.V.R. in 1941, when police officers were permitted to volunteer for flying duties, but only as observers or pilots. After obtaining his 'wings' he was commissioned, and attained the rank of squadron leader. 'Les' took his demobilisation papers in South Africa in 1945 and remained in that country.

Richard 'Dickie' Bennett. He was one of a number of Plymothians in our group. Dickie served at Barnstaple and Newton Abbot before being called into the army in 1942. He served in the Royal Artillery in North Africa and throughout the Italian campaign, having landed with the U.S. forces at Anzio. In Florence, in 1945, he transferred to the Army Special Investigation Branch, serving mainly in Trieste. Sadly, Dickie's parents both died during air raids on Plymouth. He returned to the force in 1945 and was stationed at force headquarters, where his shorthand expertise was fully utilised in the Central Criminal Investigation Department, under Detective Superintendents William Harvey and 'Harry' Langman, and then in the Motor Patrol Department with Superintendent William Doney. He was promoted to sergeant, and then to inspector, in the clerical department, retiring in June 1964 whilst in charge of the clerical office at Totnes. He died in June 1997.

Sidney Bray. He became a lieutenant in the army after being called up in 1942, and after his demobilisation he served most of his police career in the Newton Abbot 'E' division. Whilst stationed at Kingsteignton he was affectionately dubbed 'the sheriff' and never lost this nickname. He moved to Newton Abbot on promotion to sergeant, and after retirement worked in a local solicitor's office until his untimely death in 1981, when in his early sixties.

Alfred Christophers. Alfred was an ex-Grenadier Guardsman, and after completing his training went out to his first station on 24th September 1938, but for some reason, long since forgotten, he resigned on lst October!

Stanley Coldridge. After a comparatively short period on routine foot patrol duties he transferred to the Motor Patrol Department, in which he remained for his police service. During the war years he served in the army, in one of the guards' regiments, attaining the rank of sergeant. After retirement he started, along with his wife, what proved to be a successful driving school at Paignton.

John Elliott. He completed his training but resigned very shortly after commencing beat duties in his first station.

Leslie Evans. Unique in pre-wartime, 'Les' was appointed a detective constable in his first year of service. He was called into the army and received a wound to the leg, and thereafter had a slight limp. On demobilisation he reported back to the force and was interviewed by the then Assistant Chief Constable, A.E.Martin, who stated that the force could accommodate "only 100% fit men". Les accepted this decision with good grace and used his undoubted talents in starting what proved to be a most successful business.

Reginald Fear. He was one of the oldest men in our group and served most of his career in the C.I.D., mainly in the Totnes and North Devon divisions. He was detective sergeant at

Barnstaple when he retired and subsequently founded a private investigation business, which he ran successfully until shortly before his death, in 1997.

***The 1938 intake - 20th June 1938.***

*Stan Coldridge John Elliott*

*Stan Ledbrook Ben Muckett Ken Harvey Alfred Christophers Sidney Bray*

*Fred Windeatt Stan Edwards*

*Les Evans*

*Leslie Banks William Firebrace Reginald Fear Percy Norman Rose Frank Harding Frank West*

*Photo courtesy of Frank Harding*

'Stormy' Gale. Undoubtedly he had a forename, but was only ever called 'Stormy', which, in his case, was most apt. During our training period he managed to be in every scrape and prank in which we were involved, always admitting his responsibility to Charlie when our misdemeanours came to light. Prior to joining the Devon force Stormy had been serving in the Palestine Police, where he had been wounded by an Arabian rifle bullet. After his convalescent period in England he had decided against tempting fate by returning to the Middle East, so joined the Devon Constabulary instead. It was Stormy who, characteristically, worked out his own system when on 'county postman' duty. On this duty we had to collect the post satchel from headquarters at 7am each weekday and ride on the 'county cycle' to the sorting office in Bonhay Road, Exeter, to collect the mail and duly deliver it to the chief clerk. Stormy worked out on his first day as 'postman' that if he went directly from his lodgings to the sorting office he could have an extra half an hour in bed. Unfortunately for him, his ruse came unstuck on the Wednesday, his third day on that job, when the chief clerk saw Stormy sauntering along New North Road without the 'county cycle' *and* without the official satchel, but with the collected mail under his arm. He was quickly told that the tried and approved system was the only acceptable method! After completing his training he served in several county stations before transferring to the Exeter city force during the war years. I have only recently found out, from a quite unexpected source, that Stormy was actually christened Eric Francis.

Frank Harding

***Left.*** *Frank Harding, photographed at the well-fortified front door of Okehampton police station. As a divisional headquarters it was naturally assumed that Okehampton station would be a target for enemy bombing raids.*

***Right.*** *Frank Harding, photographed at home during a brief leave period whilst he was in training.*

Frank Harding

'Frank' Harding. The son of a Devon Constabulary constable who was then stationed at Clyst St. Mary, Frank had just completed his apprenticeship as a motor engineer when he successfully applied to join the force. He was called into the army in 1942 and took part in the subsequent invasion of Italy. The destroyer conveying his group was torpedoed and Frank survived by swimming five miles to the Italian shore, unfortunately behind the enemy line. He was befriended by local peasants and worked in the fields with them for some weeks, suffering several close encounters with German raiding parties before successfully passing through their lines to reach allied troops; a battalion of American infantrymen, who kitted him out and armed him. Within a few hours of his transition from fugitive to uniformed soldier, the area that he and his new-found colleagues occupied suffered exceedingly accurate pattern-bombing by

American Flying Fortresses! Just nine men emerged from this attack unscathed, comprising Frank and eight Americans. After working for days helping the injured and burying the dead, Frank was able to get a lift to rejoin British troops, with whom he remained until the capitulation of the enemy in Italy. After the war Frank served until 1968, when he retired from Okehampton station with the rank of inspector. After a further career at County Hall dealing with road traffic black spots and checking the roadworthiness of school buses he again retired, but was incapacitated through ill health from 1993 until suffering a fatal heart attack in January 1997.

Kenneth Harvey. After completing his training, Kenneth served in several stations as an unmarried constable, before being called up, in 1942, to serve in the Royal Marines. He attained the rank of captain, acting major. On demobilisation in 1945 he did not return to the force, but, instead, became an enquiry officer with the national grid. After his retirement he was last known to be living in Malaysia.

Stanley Ledbrook. Stanley served as a beat constable in various North Devon stations until his call-up in 1942, when he served in the Royal Corps of Signals, becoming an expert in radar. After the war he returned to the force but soon resigned and subsequently started a television and radio business. Much later he became an usher at Cullompton magistrates' court, prior to retiring to Dawlish.

Ronald Lee. The son of a Walsall borough detective sergeant, Ronald was the baby of our intake, being just 19 years old. He was called up in 1942, commissioned and attained rank of acting captain, seeing service with the Royal Artillery in France, Belgium, Holland and Germany, until returning to the force in 1946. He spent most of his career in the C.I.D., serving at Newton Abbot, Honiton, Barnstaple, Tavistock and Exmouth. He was eventually promoted to the rank of detective inspector, and retired at Exmouth in 1968 after having served 30 years. During that time he was awarded the Chief Constable's commendation on six occasions.

*Ann Lewis*

***Left.*** *Arthur Lemon, photographed early in his service, at Buckfastleigh races in 1938.*

***Right.*** *Bill Lewis, also seen in 1938 at the Buckfastleigh races.*

*Ann Lewis*

Arthur Lemon. Arthur came from the postal service into the force. In 1941, whilst stationed at Okehampton, along with Constable Trevor Moss, he rescued Flight Sergeant Price, R.A.F., from a blazing Hampden aeroplane which had crashed at Folly Gate whilst on a training flight. The six Polish airmen aboard all perished in the flames. During the war he received an army commission, returning to the force after demobilisation, and was subsequently promoted to sergeant and then inspector. He was later appointed staff officer to the Chief Constable, Colonel Greenwood, in his capacity as Regional Police Commander (South West) Designate. Arthur represented Colonel Greenwood at a number of departmental meetings and oversaw the formation of the inspectors' course for police war duties at the police training college at Falfield, Gloucestershire.

William 'Bill' Lewis. During our training months Bill was the man everyone turned to when any object was required. A piece of string, even a knife to cut it with, a screwdriver or a bottle opener; Bill would dig into one of his many pockets and, inevitably, produce whatever was asked for! Most of our intake group possessed snapshots taken in the Rougemont Castle grounds or whilst we were cleaning the force van in the exercise yard (usually there would be five to fifteen of us in the photograph), but no one has a picture of Bill posing with us. The reason was simple; he was operating *his* camera and using *his* film for the benefit of the rest of us. Bill served at Newton Abbot and then in several other stations before being called into the army in 1942. He returned to the force in 1945, and was promoted to sergeant in 1957. He retired in 1964 to take holy orders, serving in a number of Devon and Cornwall parishes before retiring from his second career.

*Ann Lewis*

***Left.*** *Constable Bill Lewis, pictured in about 1957, just prior to his promotion.*

***Right.*** *Sergeant Bill Lewis, photographed at Tiverton just prior to his retirement and taking holy orders.*

*Ann Lewis*

***Constable Clifford Moore** with Sergeant Climo of Hoops station, pictured on 4th February 1948 near Bucks Mills in North Devon, following the rescue of a stranded bullock from a ledge on high cliffs. Also in the photograph, on the left, is Inspector T. Crook of the R.S.P.C.A.*

*Devon & Cornwall Constabulary Museum archives*

Clifford Moore. Probably the most popular man in our group, he was equable, ever smiling and hard working, besides being conscientious in every respect. He served his whole career on uniform foot patrol duties at Paignton, Barnstaple, Sidmouth, Ottery and also at Branscombe, where his wife died in 1943. Clifford was then transferred as a 'single man', living on the stations at Barnstaple and Braunton. His eyesight was badly affected by experiences that he suffered whilst on relief duties in Plymouth during and after the blitz. This resulted in his failing the armed services' medical when called up. He then served for ten years at Bickleigh, near Tiverton, during the whole of which period he was acting sergeant (unpaid) for the Tiverton section. His 'reward' was a commendation from Colonel Greenwood, the Chief Constable, for his "conscientious and sympathetic assistance in instructing and guiding probationary constables". He retired in 1968 to live in Tiverton, where he had been serving as sergeant.

Benjamin Muckett. 'Ben' was posted to Newton Abbot as his first station and then had periods at Barnstaple (just six weeks) and Torquay (nearly two years - which would have been longer had it not been discovered that he was courting a Torquay girl, resulting in an immediate transfer, with just two hours notice). He was then posted to Paignton, and it was there that he married in the November of 1941. His army call-up came in the October of the following year; his active service included the fighting at Arromanches and right through to Hamburg by May 1945. After being demobilised in the following September, he served at Paignton on patrol duties until being transferred to the C.I.D. early in 1948. Ben remained at Paignton until he was promoted to sergeant and transferred to Torquay in 1957. He later served in charge of Sidmouth and then Ottery St. Mary sections until retiring in 1966. He then commenced a second career in the magistrates' courts offices of East Devon, becoming assistant to the Clerk to the Justices at Ottery St. Mary; then in charge of the fines and maintenance departments for the Mid Devon courts until, shortly after being awarded his certificate of competency to conduct courts, being promoted to principal assistant. Since his second retirement, in 1980, he has lived in Sidmouth.

***Constable Ben Muckett,*** *seen at Buckfastleigh races 20th August 1938.*

*Ann Lewis*

***Kenneth Reid,*** *photographed in about 1967 in the uniform of an inspector of the Devon and Exeter Police.*

*Jim Thorrington*

William 'Tom' Pill. The third of the four sons of Superintendent Morley Pill of the Cornwall Constabulary, Tom was a 19-year-old solicitors' clerk when he joined our group in 1938. It was thought on his arrival that his redoubtable father possibly gave him an edge over the rest of us, and certainly Mr Pill senior left Charlie in no doubt that great things were expected of this recruit, but Tom had so many attributes of his own that such pressure was unnecessary. He was an all-round sportsman, educated, had beautiful handwriting, and was already steeped in police procedures and law, and so had a head start on us all. The weekly papers set for him by his father, throughout his training and probationary years, also ensured that he maintained his early lead. He served both in the uniformed branch and in the C.I.D., retiring with the rank of chief superintendent, the highest rank achieved by any member of our group. Tom died in 1997.

Kenneth Reid. After six months in his first station at Cullompton, 'Ken' arrived at Newton Abbot in April 1939, where he courted and, in 1941, married the local beauty queen. They were fortunate in finding a vacant flat, and remained in Newton Abbot for a few months until a married station became available at Clyst Honiton on the perimeter of Exeter airport, a prime target for the Luftwaffe! Ken was called up in 1942 and served in the army until he was demobilised in 1945, with the rank of corporal. He then had a number of stations, including Sandford, which, like Clyst Honiton, had no electricity, indoor water supply or bathroom, followed by transfers to Salcombe, Moretonhampstead, Dartmouth, Tavistock and Torquay before retiring with the rank of inspector in 1968 to take a post as security officer with a building supplies company. Ken, who died suddenly in July 1972, had two sons, one of whom, Keith, joined the Devon and Cornwall Constabulary and had many years in the C.I.D., including some six years in the Regional Crime Squad from 1989 to 1995, when he retired.

Sidney Richards. After uniform beat work, Sidney volunteered for flying duties but later transferred to the army. After the war he returned to the force and served mainly in East Devon, retiring in 1968 whilst serving at Honiton, where he lived until his death in 1996.

Percy 'Norman' Rose. Transferring to Devon from the Metropolitan Police, he was comparatively experienced and found the training period to be a pleasurable exercise. When called up, he was commissioned in the army. On returning to the force, after the war, he was mainly engaged in clerical duties, retiring with the rank of inspector.

Richard 'Jack' Smith. After leaving headquarters in September 1938, Jack was posted to South Molton, where he lodged with a baker. When off duty he loved assisting in the bakehouse and especially in sampling the confections as they left the ovens. The result was that when he was transferred to his second station this man, who was accepted, although unable, at that time, to reach the minimum chest measurement, was a giant with a 44-inch chest! Later he transferred to, and remained on, motor patrol duties until called up, when he obtained a commission in the Royal Navy, being skipper of one of the landing craft on 'D' Day. After demobilisation in 1945, he returned to the force, resuming motor patrol driving duties in the 'F' (Torquay) division, which he continued until retiring in 1963. Remaining in Torquay, he became a court bailiff and also founded a private enquiry agency which he ran until his untimely death at the age of 51.

***Photograph of the 1938 intake at headquarters.***
*Standing, left to right: Frederick Windeatt, Edward Trist and Ernest 'Bob' Southcott, and sitting, left to right: William 'Tom' Pill and Richard 'Jack' Smith.*

*Edward Trist*

Ernest 'Bob' Southcott. He was the younger brother of Constable (later Superintendent) 'Jack' Southcott. Bob was a big man in every way - over 6 feet 2 inches tall, with huge hands and feet, in keeping with his previous calling as a stonemason - who found classroom work tedious and volunteered for any, and every, job that would get him out into the fresh air. Prior to being called up in 1942 he was uniform beat constable in the 'D' (Honiton) and 'A' (Barnstaple) divisions. He became a member of the military police, serving in the Special Investigation Branch. In 1946, after hostilities had ceased, he interviewed a Polish army deserter who had a fearsome criminal reputation. The prisoner had been searched but had, somehow, concealed a weapon on his person with which he stabbed Bob to death.

Irvin Edward 'Ted' Trist. (The author of these memoirs.) I left school in 1933 and joined the merchant navy before taking shore employment as a shop assistant. I then joined the Devon Constabulary in 1938 and my first stations were at Paignton, Honiton and Newton Abbot. After a brief wartime spell in the R.A.F. I returned to the force when deemed 'medically unfit for flying', and resumed police duties at Newton Abbot, having temporary transfers to Morebath and Hemyock before serving at Moretonhampstead, Highweek, Dawlish, Teignmouth, Bampton and Tiverton. At Tiverton I was appointed detective constable in 1947 and married Mary in 1948. Our daughter was born while we still lived at Tiverton, in 1951. Following a promotion to uniformed sergeant, I was transferred to Paignton in 1953, and attended the police college the next year. I later transferred to Totnes as detective sergeant in charge of 'G' division C.I.D., and was promoted to detective inspector in 1960, when 'G' division took over Paignton, Brixham and Kingswear from 'F' division. After some considerable thought I left the service in 1964 and took over the managership of a haulage company in Exeter, where I remained in the haulage industry until eventually retiring in 1982.

'Frank' West. Frank was a motor engineer before joining the force and served all his career on uniform beat and country patrol duties. From 1942 to 1945 he served in the army, being demobilised with rank of corporal. He retired to the Barnstaple area.

Frederick Windeatt. The oldest man in our group, 'Fred' was exempted from call-up but volunteered for flying duties and served as flight engineer on Halifax bombers. He was commissioned and attained the rank of flying officer before he was demobilised and returned to the Devon force in 1945, when he was subsequently promoted to sergeant. After retirement he became security officer at Dartington Hall, near Totnes. Fred died in 1986.

***Constable Frank Harding,*** *pictured in the August of 1938 at headquarters on an A.R.P. exercise in front of the boundary wall which separated headquarters from the adjacent prison grounds. It was the duty of the recruits to brush down the yard every Saturday whilst in training.*

*Frank Harding*

*The recruits assembled gas masks from components which were stored in the old recruit dormitories - small cell-like rooms which were situated at the rear of the headquarters building, overlooking the nearby prison wall. Here the intake is engaged in 'fatigues', which were performed every Saturday whilst in training - although the donning of gas masks for the photograph was in high spirits as opposed to a requirement of duty!*

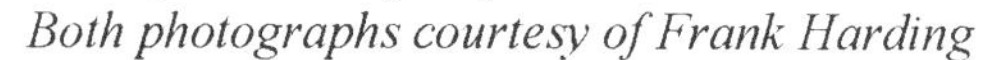
*Both photographs courtesy of Frank Harding*

# CHAPTER 3
# OUR INTRODUCTION TO THE FORCE

Now officially accepted as constables, we were then lectured at some length by Charlie in respect of how heavy a burden we had undertaken, exactly how we must behave and, above all, just how swift and terrible the punishment inflicted upon any of us would be for failing to uphold the high reputation of the Devon Constabulary.

We were left in no doubt just how important and responsible were the duties which we would shoulder during our service, and we were told that the headquarters building was the nerve centre of the force. It was, therefore, something of an anti-climax when two constables of some three hours standing were instructed to leave the room and report for duty at 10pm to "man the telephone until relieved at 6am". It transpired that these 'veterans' would be in sole charge of the 'nerve centre' and would record messages and deal with any callers to the building.

In the event of an emergency they were to call Mr Hutchings (the Assistant Chief Constable) from his quarters in the building. Fortunately, for their peace of mind, nothing transpired during their vigil requiring them to decide whether or not to awaken that very senior officer. Today it is hard to believe that eight night hours could pass without a single serious incident being reported to the focal point of all police activities in the whole of Devon (except for Plymouth city, Exeter city and Tiverton borough, who still had their own police forces at that time), but that was the case in those seemingly 'halcyon' days.

***The Chief Constable, Major L. Morris*** *MC, on the occasion of a visit by King George VI and Queen Elizabeth to Dartmouth in 1939. Major Morris is seen to the right of the photograph and a young Princess Elizabeth is also pictured in the royal party.*

*Devon & Cornwall Constabulary Museum archives*

The senior officers of the force were: Chief Constable, Major L. Morris; Assistant Chief Constable, Mr F. Hutchings; and the Chief Clerk, Chief Superintendent J. Salter (promoted to that rank on the day we arrived). His clerical staff were Inspector R. Garnish, Sergeant Talbot and Constable Carnegie, all based at headquarters, as were members of the Central Criminal Investigation Department, headed by Detective Superintendent A. West. Nearby, at Mont le Grand, the motor patrol supervisors had their office and garage. In 1938 they were headed by Sergeant Hammond, with Constables Doney and Climo. A Home Office-approved expansion of that department in 1938 resulted in their promotion to inspector and sergeants respectively, in the last quarter of that year.

Until 1938 constables had been recruited into the department mainly because they had trained as motor mechanics or bus drivers before joining the force. Their actual driving skills were fairly elementary, as was quickly discovered when the newly-promoted motor patrol sergeants commenced passing on the lessons they had learned at Hutton Hall, the driver training school. Apart from the Motor Patrol Department, there were eight territorial divisions. They were:

**'A' Division**, which had Superintendent E. Parr and Inspector W. Johnson at Barnstaple, with Inspector F. Rendell at Bideford. Superintendent Parr made a point of interviewing all constables on arrival in 'his' division, with an invariable opening gambit being: "This is the 'A' division, and I aim to maintain its position as the 'A1' division of the county". (Quite wrongly, in my opinion, he always claimed 'A' was the premier division over 'F' division!) There were section sergeants at Appledore, Barnstaple, Bideford, Great Torrington, Hoops, Ilfracombe, Lynton and South Molton, overseeing constables in country stations at Bishopsnympton, Brayford, Braunton, Clovelly, Combe Martin, Croyde, Fremington, High Bickington, Instow, Monkleigh, Northam, North Molton, Parracombe, St. Giles, Sherwell, Swimbridge, West Down, Westward Ho! and Woolacombe.

**'B' Division**, which had Superintendent P. Melhuish (later Assistant Chief Constable) and Inspector R. Annett at Okehampton (telephone number 35). Section sergeants were based at Chulmleigh, Hatherleigh, Holsworthy and Okehampton; supervising country station constables at Beaford, Black Torrington, Bradworthy, Bridestowe, Bow, Exbourne, Halwill, Kingsnympton, Lapford, Merton, Milton Damerel, Morchard Bishop, Northlew, North Tawton, Pyeworthy, Shebbear, South Zeal, Sticklepath and Winkleigh.

***Kingsnympton police house.***
*Devon & Cornwall Constabulary Museum archives*

**'C' Division**, which had Superintendent F. Barnicott at Cullompton (telephone number 15) and Inspector R. Hulland at Crediton. Section sergeants were stationed at Bampton, Bradninch, Crediton and Cullompton, with country stations manned by constables at Bickleigh, Black Dog, Broadclyst, Cheriton Fitzpaine, Copplestone, Culmstock, Halberton, Hemyock, Holcombe Rogus, Langford Green, Meshaw, Newton St. Cyres, Oakford, Pinhoe, Rackenford, Sandford, Shillingford, Silverton, Stoke Canon, Thorverton, Uffculme, Washfield, Whitestone and Yeo Mills.

**'D' Division**, which had Superintendent J. Marshall at Honiton (telephone number 3) and Inspector R. Holmes at Exmouth. Section sergeants were at Axminster, Exmouth, Honiton, Ottery St. Mary, Seaton and Sidmouth, with beat constables stationed at Branscombe, Broadhembury, Chardstock, Clyst Honiton, Clyst St. Mary, Colyton, Dunkeswell, Lympstone, Membury, Newton Poppleford, Northleigh, Otterton, Sidbury, Topsham, Uplyme, Upottery, Whimple, Whitford, Withycombe Raleigh, Woodbury and Yarcombe.

**'E' Division**, which had Superintendent F. Coppin and Inspector V. Crook in the Newton Abbot police station in Union Street (telephone number 18), and section sergeants based at Chudleigh, Dawlish, Moretonhampstead, Newton Abbot and Teignmouth. Country stations were at Chagford, Christow, Combe-in-Teignhead, Drewsteignton, Dunsford, Exminster, Highweek, Ide, Ipplepen, Kennford, Kenton, Kingskerswell, Kingsteignton (then said to be the largest village in England), Lustleigh, Shaldon, Starcross and Tedburn St. Mary.

***Left.*** *Superintendent F. Coppin of the 'E' division. His son, Eric, was also a constable in the Devon Constabulary, stationed at Ladycross police house, which was situated between Launceston and Bude, but just within the county of Devon.*

**'F' Division**, which had Superintendent A. E. Martin (known by all as 'A.E.M.') in charge of the senior division in the county. With him, at Torquay, were Chief Inspector A. Drew, Inspector E. Stone and Detective Inspector (later Assistant Chief Constable) W. Harvey, whilst at Paignton was Sub-Inspector W. Hutchings. Section sergeants were at Brixham, Paignton and Torquay. There were just four 'country beat' stations in the division, situated at Brixham, Collaton, Churston Ferrers and Kingswear. In addition to having the sole chief inspector and the one and only sub-inspector in the force, 'F' division had the only detective inspector, plus four uniformed sergeants in Torquay on beat patrol supervision. Then based in Market Street, Torquay, divisional headquarters was a Victorian building in which the occupants worked under poor conditions in small, dark offices more in keeping with Dickensian times than the norm expected in 1938.

***Above.*** *Assistant Chief Constable A.E. Martin at his desk at headquarters in 1940.*
***Below.*** *Assistant Chief Constable Bill Harvey, in the centre of the photograph, at the opening ceremony of Lifton police station in 1963.*
*Both photographs courtesy of the Devon & Cornwall Constabulary Museum archives*

***Right.*** *Evangeline Booth of the Salvation Army, pictured outside the entrance to Torquay police station with two constables in about 1943. On the rear of this photograph the inscription reads: "Commander Evangeline Booth at Torquay police station, where she was arrested with other members of the Salvation Army 37 years ago for playing their instruments in the streets on Sunday".*
*Devon & Cornwall Constabulary Museum archives*

**'G' Division**, in Totnes, which had Superintendent T. Milford and Inspector Tothill housed in probably the worst divisional headquarters in Britain. The building still stands, situated directly behind the parish church on the ancient Totnes Ramparts, and is well worth a visit to see the conditions under which the Totnes-based officers then worked.

So bad were the conditions in both the Torquay and the Totnes stations that it was necessary for new stations to be built during the darkest days of the 1939-45 war. Leaders appeared in the national press expressing strong criticism of materials and men being diverted from war work at such times, but the building continued and the new stations became operational, Totnes late in 1943 and Torquay in April 1944.

The construction of both stations gives ample evidence that they were built when enemy air attacks were a constant threat. At Totnes the basement consisted of a reinforced concrete ceiling with immensely thick walls, strong enough to offer almost complete protection, even from a direct hit by any of the high explosive bombs then used by the enemy.

The Torquay station, similarly, was almost bombproof - at least for the chosen few. The top floor consisted of four flats occupied by married police officers' families. Above was an apparently normal roof, but the flats had concrete floors of two feet thickness, giving almost total protection to the occupants of the offices below - the senior officers!

**Totnes police station c1923.** *Officers of the 'G' division pictured outside Totnes police station.*

*Ken Northey*

The occupants of two of these flats were Detective Inspector (later Detective Chief Inspector) Cyril Luscombe and Detective Sergeant George Roper.

Cyril died in 1998, since when I have learned that his father, John (who served between 1901 and 1926), and Cyril (who joined in 1934) had, by coincidence, been allocated the same 'collar' number, being constable 403.

The division had section sergeants at Ashburton, Dartmouth, Kingsbridge, Strete, South Brent and Totnes, with constables at Ashburton, Aveton Gifford, Avonwick, Berry Pomeroy, Bickington, Bigbury, Broadhempston, Buckfastleigh, Dartington, Dartmouth, Dittisham, Frogwell, Halwell, Harbertonford, Holne, Kingsbridge, Malborough, Modbury, Salcombe, Slapton, Strete, South Brent, Stokenham, Totnes, West Alvington, Widecombe-in-the-Moor and Wrangaton.

***Berry Pomeroy police house**, situated in the old toll-house at the junction of the main road from Totnes to Paignton with the lane leading into Berry Pomeroy village.*

*Devon & Cornwall Constabulary Museum archives*

**'H' Division**, whose superintendent was 'Daddy' Smith at Crownhill with Inspector A. Newberry at Tavistock (telephone number 17). Section sergeants were at Bratton Clovelly, Crownhill, Lifton, Plympton (where the new divisional headquarters was being built - to take over from Crownhill police station - and destined to be fully operational by mid-1939), Tavistock and Yealmpton. Constables were stationed at Bere Alston, Billacombe, Bratton Clovelly, Brixton, Cornwood, Crabtree, Crownhill, Elburton, Ermington, Holbeton, Honicknowle, Horrabridge, Ivybridge, Ladycross, Lewdown, Lifton, Lydford, Mary Tavy, Milton Abbot, Newton Ferrers, Oreston, Plympton, Plymstock, Princetown, Roborough, Staddiscombe, Tamerton Foliot, Tavistock, Turnchapel, Yealmpton and Yelverton.

***Left.*** *Superintendent S. Smith and Sergeant 'Josh' Jewell, pictured outside the front door of Crownhill police station in the late 1930s. At that time Crownhill was policed by the Devon Constabulary, but was taken over by the Plymouth City Police just after the war in the late 1940s.*

*It was Superintendent Smith who took charge of the Devon Constabulary reinforcements that attended the 1932 Dartmoor Prison mutiny. A few years after this photograph was taken Sergeant Jewell also rose to the rank of superintendent.*

*Mrs Jean Creber*

***Below.*** *The National Identity card (with police endorsement) belonging to the 'H' division Ladycross constable, Eric Coppin, the son of Superintendent F. Coppin of Newton Abbot.*

*Eric Coppin*

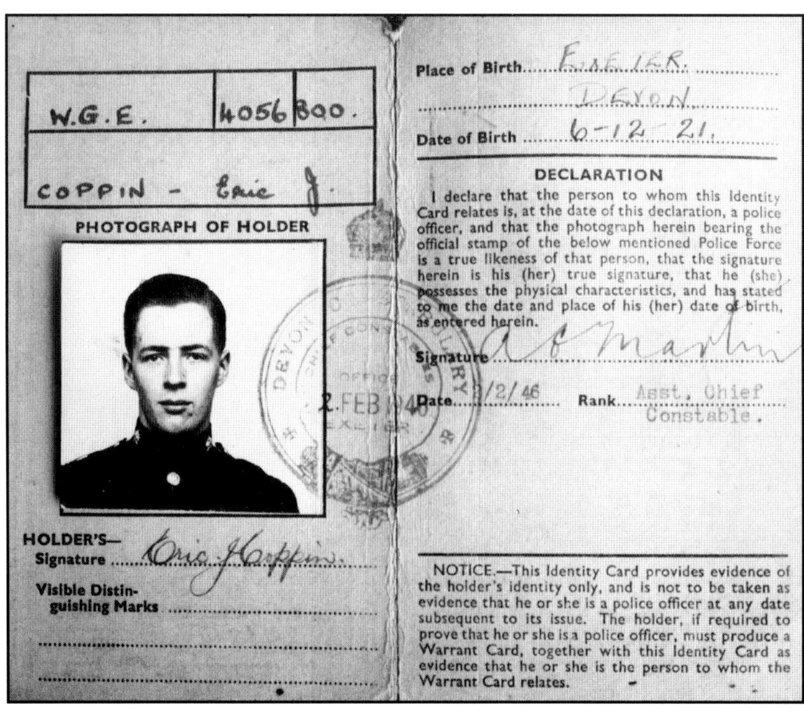

W.G.E. | 4056 | 800.

COPPIN - Eric J.

PHOTOGRAPH OF HOLDER

HOLDER'S— Signature Eric J Coppin.

Visible Distinguishing Marks

Place of Birth EXETER.
DEVON.

Date of Birth 6-12-21.

DECLARATION

I declare that the person to whom this Identity Card relates is, at the date of this declaration, a police officer, and that the photograph herein bearing the official stamp of the below mentioned Police Force is a true likeness of that person, that the signature herein is his (her) true signature, that he (she) possesses the physical characteristics, and has stated to me the date and place of his (her) date of birth, as entered herein.

Signature A F Martin

Date 2/2/46 Rank Asst. Chief Constable.

NOTICE.—This Identity Card provides evidence of the holder's identity only, and is not to be taken as evidence that he or she is a police officer at any date subsequent to its issue. The holder, if required to prove that he or she is a police officer, must produce a Warrant Card, together with this Identity Card as evidence that he or she is the person to whom the Warrant Card relates.

# CHAPTER 4
# TRAINING AND PAY

Training started in earnest on the second day. Because of our numbers it was necessary to find a classroom large enough to accommodate us. Certainly there was no such space available at headquarters, where cell-like offices were occupied by senior officers, and the uniform and stores department was buried deep in the lower basement. The dormitories, which in earlier years had housed the trainees and single constables stationed at headquarters, had been gutted and were gradually being filled with the various components required to make up service-type gas masks and other air raid precaution equipment, as mentioned earlier.

We were ordered to report at 9am at the 'Nisi Prius' courtroom in 'The Castle', where, for the remainder of our time at Exeter, we endured the training methods of Inspector Webber. Our first instruction was to break off, visit Messrs Wheaton's stationery shop in Fore Street, Exeter, and obtain two training manuals - *Moriarty's Police Law* and *A Police Constable's guide to his daily work*, the total cost being about 18 shillings and causing temporary financial difficulties to several of us.

Charlie's system was to have each class member read a page or so from one of the manuals. He would then enlarge upon the text before dictating, at breakneck speed, his version of the printed word. We, in turn, were required to rewrite the numerous pages that we had scrawled throughout the day in 'fair hand' in one of the several exercise books with which we had been issued, this was to be done in our lodgings that same evening and be subject to spot checks the following day.

Charlie had slavishly copied the voice and mannerisms of his predecessor, the last training officer in the force to be officially designated 'sergeant major' - the one (and only) Superintendent Arthur Martin, who, in 1938, was commanding the Torquay division. Unfortunately Charlie lacked the depth of experience that Mr Martin had acquired, resulting in some of his dictated notes later causing a few of us to be the butt of 'charge office humour' and embarrassment.

Our training weeks, on the whole, were an enjoyable period in our police careers, with a few incidents which inevitably are recalled when two or three of us meet. On one hot mid-July day Charlie entered the classroom and boomed out: "Hands up any of you men skilled in horticulture". The classroom was airless, the studies boring, and about 20 hands shot up. Four lucky men were selected, and learned that they were to tidy the gardens fronting the headquarters building. Kitted out in blue overalls, they commenced forking over the garden soil with their uniformed inspector standing behind them watching their efforts.

In 1938 the headquarters building was that dingy brick edifice on the eastern end of Exeter Prison - it is now part of the prison, a rather shabby, featureless property comprising administrative offices. Despite the closeness of headquarters to the prison, the gardeners were quite surprised when one of two ladies passing by remarked in far from subtle tones: "Look at them there. They're nothing but boys. I wonder how long they've got to do". Charlie immediately stepped forward and replied: "They all have the same sentence, ladies. With good conduct, 30 years". As they hurried off, one lady was heard to say: "Oh my gawd, what can they have done? Such nice looking boys, too!".

The first month passed and it was pay day at last! Our gross pay was £3.2s per week. Until 1936 it had been £3.9s, but in the nation's efforts to rise out of the financial depression a scheme had been devised by the Chancellor of the Exchequer for all wages to be cut by 10%, and this had been accepted by workers with very little complaint and certainly with no threats of striking or working to rule! As well as suffering this 10% reduction in pay we had to endure other significant deductions for superannuation, sports association and hospital aid, so our final monthly nett pay amounted to under £11.

On our first pay day in the constabulary one of our group, whilst carefully stowing away his wages, spoke to his neighbour, who gave a fleeting smile. The eagle eye of Charlie saw the change of expression and demanded: "What's the joke, Constable Harvey?" He replied: "Nothing, sir. Just a remark of Constable Smith's".

Jack was immediately ordered to his feet with Charlie demanding to know what was so funny, adding: "Speak up man, we could all do with a laugh". After assuring Charlie "It was just a remark, nothing really, sir", the constable, now standing stiffly to attention, added: "I said I'd just as soon have the deductions as the pay, sir. It was only a little joke". We then saw the 'sergeant major' come out in our instructor, literally roaring at the abject figure before him: "If you don't like it man, *GET OUT, GET OUT*, I say. I've a hundred men waiting for your job!". Sadly that was true; in 1938 the Devon Constabulary had no recruiting problem - in fact, it had no recruiting officer!

The board and lodge obtained for us by Inspector Webber cost £1.4s per week - if circumstances made it impossible to obtain such services at this price the force paid the additional amount charged, but this rarely occurred. The only exception was in the case of a single constable transferred to the Torbay 'F' division during the summer months, when accommodation was at a premium.

Doubtlessly our landlords and landladies were Charlie's eyes and ears. There was little that we did that he did not become aware of. A couple of us had dated two young ladies working at Marks and Spencers. Having rushed our writing-up of our day's notes, we were standing awaiting their passing out of the staff exit of the store. To our consternation who should saunter up and stand on the opposite pavement but Charlie. Next morning we had to endure a lengthy, oblique reference to the incident, warning us all of the dangers of becoming involved with 'Kitty Farley's' when we should have been in our lodgings with heads deep in our *Moriarty's*.

Tom Pill had also met a young lady and took her on a boating excursion on the canal. But, whether he was too daring or too inexperienced, he somehow ended out of the boat and in the water. Needless to say Charlie made the most of this incident, referring to it time and time again.

***Left.*** *A photograph from a contemporary training manual being used during the 1930s for police recruit instruction, on point duty and traffic control methods. The text accompanying the picture instructs:*

*"No.1. To halt a vehicle approaching from the front, extend the right arm and hand at full length above the right shoulder, with the palm of the hand towards the driver of the vehicle.*

*Where two vehicles are approaching by converging roads, and only one is to be halted, the constable should face towards the driver of the vehicle to be halted, to show clearly that the signal is intended for him".*

*(Little do many modern-day police officers realise that the well-known 'number one stop sign' got its name from this instruction manual as it was the first, or 'number one', instruction in the book.)*

*Devon & Cornwall Constabulary Museum archives*

# CHAPTER 5
# THE UBIQUITOUS RALPH HARE

In addition to the various senior and other officers based at force headquarters there was one man who probably had the greatest influence over us in all matters apart from our actual training. He was the imposing Constable 235 Ralph Hare, who had joined the force on 26th June 1919 and with 19 years' service, could, perhaps, be excused if he worked off his frustrations on us! He was general handyman and the driver of the county furniture lorry. One of his duties, and one in which he took particular pleasure, was to ensure that we recruits maintained the highest possible standards of cleaning, polishing and scrubbing of every part of the premises, including the drill yard, stairways and cellars.

***Working party of recruits - late 1920s.*** *The practice of recruits having to do fatigues had been with the force since the previous century. Constable 'Sid' Pollard, the officer in uniform seen to the right of the group, was stationed at Roborough, near Plymouth, during the war years.*

*Mrs Jean Creber*

***Fatigue party 1930.*** *Whilst in training all officers were required to perform fatigues under the direction of Constable Ralph Hare.*

*Devon & Cornwall Constabulary Museum archives*

Each weekday the general tidying, sweeping and dusting of the offices was carried out by the two night-duty recruits, but Saturday was *the* day and we were entirely in the hands of Constable Hare. With no classes for us to attend, he kept us working the whole morning, always with the threat of having us return in the afternoon if our efforts were not to his satisfaction. The wooden floorboards of the passageways had to be scrubbed, the brown coloured linoleum in the offices had to be washed and then polished, whilst the old, *extremely* old, and well worn, office furniture was treated as genuine 'Chippendale', with particular attention being given to the rails and frets of chairs and to the back edges and back legs of desks. Constable Hare would run his finger along ridges, even behind and under shelves, and woe betide any recruit who had missed any portion of the skirtings, picture rails or other dust-gathering part of an office, and no matter where we were Constable Hare seemed to be immediately behind us, ubiquitous indeed!

The trainees from Exeter, Penzance and Tiverton forces were excused these fatigues, it being stated that they were obliged to report to their respective Chief Constables and detail the programme of training they had received during the preceding days. How we envied them, and how they delighted in informing us of how short a time of their priceless Saturdays had been taken up in presenting their verbal reports.

Cleaning one of the basement passages, we found that it was filled with a number of sacks and files of papers. Constable Hare sternly warned us not to touch anything but merely to clean around them. We later learned that the items were exhibits and statements which had been presented at the then recent trial of two men accused and convicted of murdering Constable Potter at Whimple in January 1938. This terrible incident had become a virtual legend within the force.

One of the men, Stanley Martin, had been found guilty of murder and sentenced to death, later to be commuted to life imprisonment, whilst his confederate, Leslie Downing, had been found guilty of 'office-breaking' and sentenced to 12 months imprisonment.

Constable Potter had suffered several office-breakings at Whiteways Cider premises on his 'patch' and had made arrangements with the cider company's manager to have access to the offices in order to keep watch in the hope of catching the offenders. So keen had been the officer that no one should have knowledge of his efforts that he had not even informed his wife or son before leaving the police house, but even more unfortunate was that he had gone out without his truncheon.

The office in which he had hidden had been broken into by Martin and Downing. He had challenged them and, whilst Downing had turned and made good his escape, Martin had lashed out at the officer, leaving him unconscious before he had also run away.

In 1938 it was not unusual for a police officer to continue enquiries or keep observation for long periods beyond normal duty hours, so Mrs Potter had not been unduly worried when her husband failed to return home. It was not until about 3am that she had raised the alarm and it had been a further two hours before Constable Potter was found lying bleeding and unconscious. He had then been rushed to hospital, where he had died two weeks later. The delay undoubtedly contributed to his succumbing to the injuries inflicted by Martin.

A public subscription was opened on behalf of the widow, to which Messrs Whiteways contributed most generously, and the sum raised was sufficient to buy a house for her in Whimple, where she lived until 1992. Then, when aged 93 years, she decided to join her grandchildren in Canada, but the trauma of such a move so late in life possibly put too much of a strain upon her as she died a few months later.

One further matter linked with Constable Potter's death has been noted on a number of other cases; that is the almost inevitable return to home ground by felons after completion of lengthy terms of imprisonment. When Martin was released, in 1950, he returned to Whimple and lived there for the rest of his days. With all the world to go to, I have always found it inexplicable that such men should return to the one place where their past misdeeds are known to everyone and where, in the main, they are despised and often ostracised.

With the trial finishing in March 1938, the case was very much in the mind of Charlie when we commenced training, with hardly a day passing without some mention of the regulation concerning carrying 'accoutrements whenever and wherever an officer is carrying out police duties'.

As already mentioned, another duty which fell to the lot of the Devon recruits was being the 'postman'. In addition to making a 7am collection of the incoming mail from the G.P.O. sorting office, this involved missing morning classes and riding around the Exeter area on the 'county cycle', delivering constabulary mail to sundry offices.

This important activity resulted in the force saving postal charges, at that time 1½d for a letter not exceeding two ounces in weight, and was our first introduction to the rather penny-pinching attitude permeating the whole force, and the clerical staff in particular.

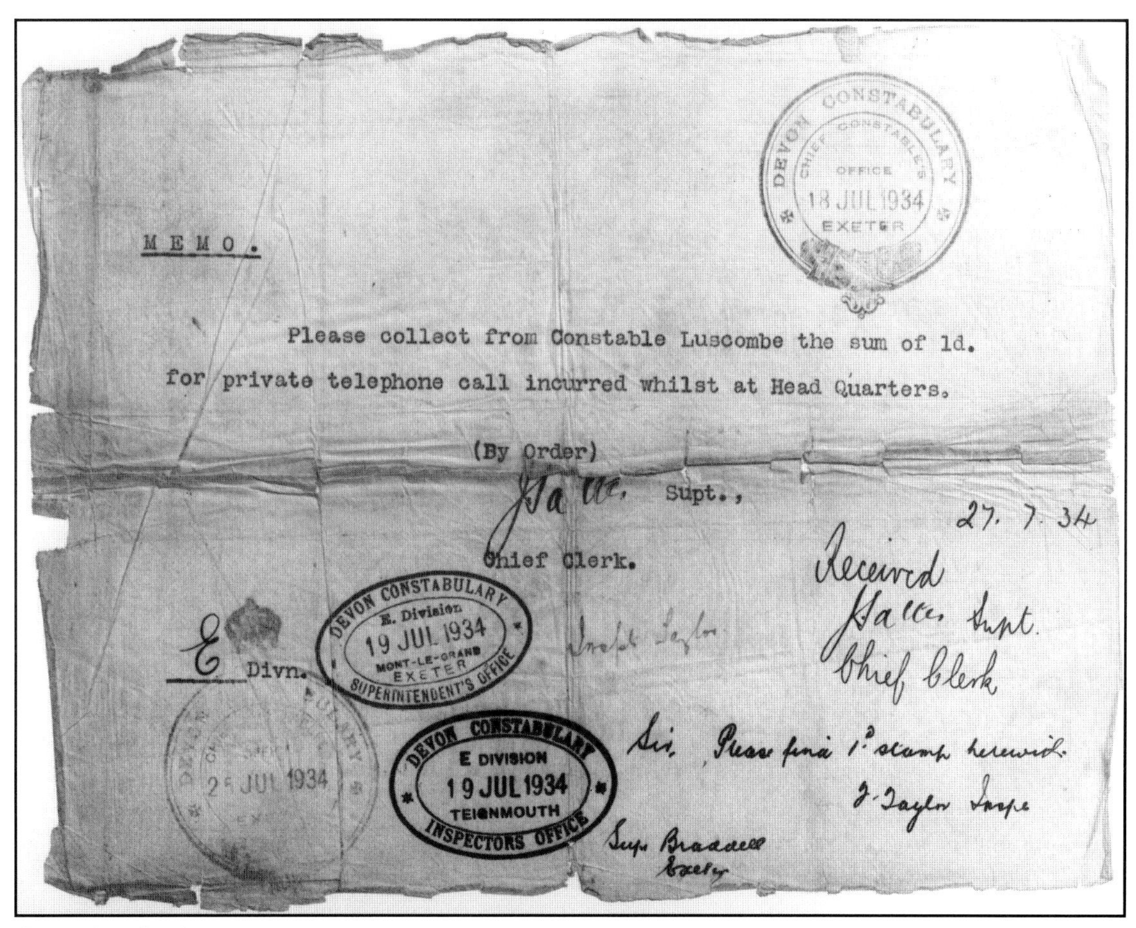

DEVON CONSTABULARY
CHIEF CONSTABLE'S
OFFICE
18 JUL 1934
EXETER

M E M O.

Please collect from Constable Luscombe the sum of 1d.
for private telephone call incurred whilst at Head Quarters.

(By Order)

Supt.,

Chief Clerk.

E Divn.

DEVON CONSTABULARY
E. Division
19 JUL 1934
MONT-LE-GRAND
EXETER
SUPERINTENDENT'S OFFICE

DEVON CONSTABULARY
E DIVISION
19 JUL 1934
TEIGNMOUTH
INSPECTORS OFFICE

27. 7. 34
Received
Supt.
Chief Clerk

Sir, Please find 1d stamp herewith.
J. Taylor Inspr

*Constable Cyril Luscombe's one penny telephone bill, which must surely have cost considerably more than one penny to process!*

*Devon & Cornwall Constabulary Museum archives*

We were introduced to this duty on our second day but it was not until later that we learned that no one below the rank of inspector was permitted to use a new envelope, other ranks being required to "carefully slit open all incoming mail envelopes for reuse with economy labels".

Some years later, when collecting a prisoner from the West End metropolitan police station, I saw a banner on the noticeboard reading "DEVON, GLORIOUS DEVON", below which was a line of envelopes bearing one, two and even three of our economy labels!

Training continued in the warm summer days and, with our instructor's lectures being delivered in a monotone, eyelids began to remain closed for longer periods than mere blinks until Charlie's voice suddenly rose to a higher level as he uttered the dreaded words: "Back to the exercise yard you men. I can see you need waking up".

A smart march from Rougemont Castle to New North Road at least indicated that our training in marching and deportment had borne fruit. At headquarters we quickly changed into gym shoes, shorts and vests before being issued with heavy broomstick length drill poles and commenced 'pole-drill'. This involved rapid movements of the poles with rigid arms, forward, above head, backward stretch and forward stretch, repeated and repeated until several of our number collapsed and others came near to that condition.

Each day, Monday to Friday, at 9am we paraded at our classroom in the 'Nisi Prius' courtroom, with our instructor awaiting our arrival and ready to pounce on any latecomer, but in our third month he never arrived before 10am. He had previously ensured that we had sufficient writing-up to keep us occupied and had also ordered that all constables with notes completed should study set chapters from our textbooks or continue learning, by rote, the definitions of various offences, in particular those embodied in the Larceny Act, 1916.

After 30 minutes or so had passed, with the unsupervised hour inducing boredom, horseplay commenced. On one fateful day this took the form of paper-ball throwing, leading to the necessity for one of us (Stormy Gale) to climb on to the judge's chair and recover pieces of ammunition.

This had ceased and all was quiet when Charlie stalked in. He was in a black, black humour and we learned that, directly behind and above the said judge's chair, the window illuminated a corridor leading from various offices to the office of the clerk to the Devon County Council and that this high-ranking official had witnessed our classroom activities whilst passing the window. He had reported the matter to Charlie who, I suspect, was actually absent without permission and was positively vengeful. The offenders were weeded out and each awarded a punishment, to write on the back pages of one of their exercise books in fair hand, and a thousand times: "I must not throw paper pills around the classroom". Their books were to be produced for examination three days later.

Several of the older men, Stormy Gale in particular, were upset by this childish imposition (although fully accepting their actions had been infantile), but duly complied. It was just a week later that one of His Majesty's Inspectors of Constabulary arrived. We were immediately issued with our uniforms, having been in casual wear until that day, and paraded in the exercise yard.

After having witnessed our marching, had us produce our accoutrements and spoken a word or two to a few randomly selected men, the H.M.I. decided that he would see samples of our classroom work. He selected four men who were despatched to bring their books from 'The Castle'.

On their return, Charlie officiously took and examined the books from each man in turn, but found Stormy (one of the four men concerned) reluctant to hand over his consignment and whispering that he had not brought his own books as one was half-filled with the "I must not..." penance. As a result, he was sent back to 'The Castle' by a very indignant Charlie and told to "bring back your *own* books". On his return, we were again paraded, the H.M.I. reappeared with the Chief Constable and 'Murphy's Law' immediately came into force. The H.M.I. opened the first book on the pile, belonging to the last man back - Stormy.

For some reason he started reading from the back of the exercise book. He signalled Major Morris to join him and they then read together. The Chief Constable, meanwhile, beckoned Charlie to join them, and so we then had the scenario of two very senior officers, together with a 'lesser light', all reading: "I must not ...".

The H.M.I.'s face reddened, the Chief (usually imperturbable) seemed somewhat put out, whilst our instructor's explanation, although lengthy, did not appear to placate his listeners. They made a most unhappy group, the H.M.I. apparently having completely lost interest in us and the inspection ending with our being summarily dismissed. Probably our behaviour improved during our last weeks of training, but definitely no further 'lines' were inflicted.

A few days later we were given an afternoon's instruction on the martial arts. This had been eagerly looked forward to, and it was a disappointment when we found that there was just one instructor to demonstrate to thirty of us all the facets of defensive holds and grips. The instructor was a Sergeant Hooper of the Exeter city force (father of Chief Superintendent Roy Hooper), kindly loaned to the Devon force for just two hours. Certainly he did his best in the very limited time at his disposal, but it was woefully inadequate in preparing us to deal with the rowdies and drunks that we were to encounter when we finally went out on our beats.

Early in September Charlie again called for volunteers, stressing only the strongest men in our group would fit the bill. Six lucky men were selected, issued with blue overalls and despatched to the railway goods yard adjoining the Central railway station in Queen Street, Exeter, trundling a two-wheeled handcart which had been unearthed from the dark, deep recesses of one of the exercise yard sheds. In the goods yard they were directed to a rail coal wagon containing 15 tons of 'best grade' coal. On their arrival, Constable Hare suddenly appeared and explained that they were to shovel the coal from the wagon into sacks, and weigh them on the scales which had been brought to the wagon by a smiling railway porter.

***The force coal handcart.*** *Recruits were required to collect coal from the railway station for the home and office fires of the senior officers at headquarters. Constable Cyril Luscombe is pictured sitting on the wheel.*

*Mrs C. Luscombe*

The filled sacks were to be loaded onto the handcart and wheeled to the force lorry, parked on the yard roadway. There Constable Hare personally supervised the loading. When he decided, after checking and rechecking his list, that he had sufficient sacks he drove, with his coal-covered crew, to the homes of the Chief Constable and other senior police officers, where the required number of sacks were unloaded and emptied.

The said officers annually purchased a truckload directly from a colliery, in so doing saving an appreciable amount on the normal retailer's delivered-in price (in 1938 this was 1s 7d per hundredweight).

The force lorry had a maximum load weight of 5 tons, requiring the whole operation to be repeated twice more, and it was only after the final delivery had been made that our volunteers were driven back to the exercise yard. There they were still not released from duty as the sacks had to be shaken, folded and stacked in the freshly brushed-out lorry. The vehicle, too, had to be given an exterior cleaning, inspected by Constable Hare, and deemed ready for the next removal. Only then were the volunteers told to return to their lodgings.

***The force removal lorry c1925.***
*Devon & Cornwall Constabulary Museum archives*

[It was in 1920 that the first lorry was acquired by the force, an ex-army, three-tonner, tarpaulin-covered vehicle, which saw service for a number of years, mainly in the removals of men from one county station to another. Removing married men had always occurred in the county and, prior to 1920, had entailed the use of the railway goods departments. It was the responsibility of the policeman to get his family, furniture and effects from the police cottage that he was vacating to the railway goods yard. This inevitably involved the use of the 'ways and means act', the officer being expected to enlist the aid of a friendly disposed farmer to lend a horse and cart to get the furniture to the railway station.

One such removal was that of Constable 223 Thomas James Hawkins, his wife and their five children - two daughters and three sons, 'Jim', 'Bert' and 'Sam', who all became Devon county police officers. The family was moving from Malborough, near Kingsbridge, to Ermington. The constable had got his furniture into the Kingsbridge goods yard and, with his family, took the train to Ivybridge, then to make their own way to Ermington and the empty police cottage. Unfortunately the cottage remained bereft of all furnishings until the arrival of the railway delivery horse-drawn cart some four days later! How the Hawkins family fared in the interim is, unfortunately, not now known, but apparently this was accepted as the norm in the pre-1920 days.]

Removals were part and parcel of life in the Devon Constabulary, being made for many reasons; on promotion was one of the most pleasurable causes, whilst a transfer following a disciplinary charge was one of the worst. In September 1938 the Assistant Chief Constable, Mr F. Hutchings, retired, resulting in the promotion of Superintendent Martin, who moved from Torquay to Exeter. Superintendent Theo Milford moved from Totnes to Torquay, and the chain reaction included promotions to superintendent, chief inspector, inspector and sergeant, all requiring transfers from one constabulary property to another. There were additional moves of constables as a result of the single retirement, and the county lorry was fully engaged conveying the effects of the various officers to different parts of Devon over a period of three weeks.

Each loading and unloading of the furniture and effects was carried out by constables detailed for such duties in the towns or sections involved, their work always being supervised by Constable Hare - a most important man on such occasions! It was expected that he and his assistants would be given a hot meal by the officer's wife, with liquid refreshments also made available. The removals were usually quite successful, damage and breakages being kept to a minimum, with everyone working on the premise of "do as you would be done by" and exercising due care.

Throughout our training period we had been given various tasks, and after we were issued with our uniforms it was considered that we were fit enough to be entrusted with some minor police duties. Nearly all of us were first sent out to do traffic and crowd control work at the Devon and Exeter racecourse, at the top of Haldon Hill. I had a three-hour spell of traffic duty, separating passing-through vehicles from the race-going traffic which had to be directed into the racecourse car parks. At the end of my spell I was a very tired probationer and very relieved to be allowed to walk around the outer perimeter of the course to ensure that no one was gaining entry without paying.

In those days race duty was one of our great pleasures, an opportunity to get away from routine beat duties and to meet other constables. At the Haldon racecourse there would be between 20 and 25 constables on duty, whilst at the Newton Abbot course there were always at least 25 men engaged on traffic and crowd control as well as keeping watchful eyes for pickpockets and the occasional bookie attempting to evade his successful punters. Then there were also racecourses at Totnes, Torquay, Chelson Meadow (just outside the Plymouth city boundary) and Buckfastleigh, requiring the same police cover by the Devon Constabulary.

On the last Saturday in July 1938 Exeter Airport was officially opened and our whole group was allocated duties at Clyst Honiton and at the airport. The highlight of the opening was an aerial display by three of the Royal Air Force front-line aeroplanes - Bristol Gladiators, bi-planes capable of some 230 miles an hour! Their pilots gave a thrilling demonstration of aerobatics to the large and enthusiastic audience before landing and disappearing into the reserved area.

***Exeter Airport contingent July 1938.*** *Standing, left to right: Stan Coldridge, Ron Lee, Bob Southcott, Fred Windeatt, Jack Elliott, Ken Reid, Ken Harvey, Sid Bray, Sid Richards, Frank Harding, Arthur Lemon and Cliff Moore. Seated, left to right: Ben Muckett, Dickie Bennett, Tom Pill, Jack Smith, Ted Trist and Reg Fear.*

*Frank Harding*

Other displays ended and the crowds of pedestrians, cyclists, packed coaches and motor cars were safely seen away from the area before we weary probationary constables assembled in the reception area to await our transport (the county lorry, of course) back to headquarters.

Up to that time we had been unimportant cogs in the machinery that ensured the efficient running of the proceedings of the day, but suddenly we were approached by senior officials and even a superintendent, together with our own inspector. It appeared that a difficulty had arisen; the pilots had received a report that a few miles from the airport, on their homeward flight path, there were adverse flying conditions making it advisable for the Gladiators to remain grounded until the weather improved. This was surprising as we were still enjoying a perfect day, sun shining and not a cloud in the sky. Unfortunately, however, the aircraft were on the 'secret list' and could not be left unguarded. It was wondered, therefore, if we constables would be willing to undertake the important job of guarding the said aircraft until the following morning.

To a man we all agreed and conscientiously stood guard, two men to each 'plane, hour and hour about throughout the evening and the night until relieved by the return of the three pilots at about 10am on Sunday. We watched their departure, all of us knowing that we had been well and truly 'conned'. It was not adverse weather conditions that had delayed their departure but, rather, pressing invitations to share with the council officers and airport officials the evening and night celebrations marking the opening of the airport. Ah well, you live and learn!

# CHAPTER 6
# EX-SERGEANT PHILIP PROWSE - THE STOREMAN

Deep down in the bowels of the headquarters building was the kingdom of ex-Sergeant Philip Prowse, the man in charge of the uniforms for the force, plus a mixture of cleaning materials, paint, furniture, blankets, and even slats for the repair of the wooden blinds fitted in all stations and county-owned properties.

'Uncle Phil' had joined the Devon Constabulary in November 1901 as a third-class constable. At that stage he was a 26 years service man, but at some time in 1928 his service had been extended by a Chief Constable's special order, to 31st July 1931. Just 30 days before this extension had expired he had then been promoted to sergeant, and had served in that rank until September 1934. There was no doubt that his work had been appreciated by his superiors, as he had then continued in a civilian capacity and was destined to carry out identical duties into the war years, in total serving more than 40 years.

Without doubt the most important part of all his domain was the area occupied by returned uniforms. Many a man had endeavoured to wheedle out of Uncle Phil a piece of uniform and had, invariably, received his stock reply: "It's more than me job's worth to let ee' have it. You put in a report me boy, an' us'll see what us can do". On the other hand, a constable who had suffered a genuine misfortune in damaging a piece of uniform (a cigarette burn on a tunic, a barbed-wire tear in a trouser leg or a torn gabardine raincoat caused by a fall from a cycle), which he was loath to 'put on report', could usually find a willing ally in Uncle Phil.

He was the man who ensured that our uniforms fitted well and that we were issued with our full entitlement of every item of equipment, booklets and other papers, including literally dozens of Diseases of Animals Regulations, forms and pamphlets, plus a first-aid pack which consisted of a khaki-coloured linen sealed cover, about 8 x 5cm, containing a bandage, lint and a plaster. The packs were an ex-army issue and bore the date of manufacture - 1918!

The most important item issued was our warrant card, a piece of cardboard marked: 'DEVON CONSTABULARY. Constable...' and bearing a seal over the signature of the Chief Constable. Most of us went to a local luggage retailer and purchased a celluloid-fronted leather address holder, in which to keep the card in clean condition. Dire warnings were given by Charlie as to the fate of anyone having the misfortune to lose his warrant card: possible dismissal was one of the threatened punishments. It may have been because of the stress placed on the importance of the card in those early days that I never learned of a policeman in the Devon force having to report that he had lost his card. Ex-Sergeant Prowse also issued to each of us a suitcase, black in colour, stamped on the inside with 'Devon Constabulary, Constable No...'.

For a reason quite unknown to us, when these cases were returned by a man on retirement, resignation or dismissal, they were destroyed by the ex-sergeant. We were in the exercise yard on one occasion, busily engaged in brushing up the area, when he brought to a corner of the yard five or six of these cases - all in good condition - and proceeded to make a bonfire of them. Two of our group endeavoured to persuade Uncle Phil to let them have a case each, but all to no avail. The cases were officially issued for the conveyance of uniform, official papers and accoutrements, but were woefully inadequate for this purpose - in fact, a police helmet would not fit into them. Several of us paid a visit to Messrs Cummings and bought sturdy trunks for 30 shillings, half a week's wage, but, in fact, an excellent investment outlasting, as they did, our many removals around the county during our service.

In the vital matter of uniforms the force was most generous, the clothing being made of good quality materials, tailored to a high standard, giving excellent protection from the elements and covering every possible requirement of the service.

Our first issue consisted of two helmets, two seven-buttoned high-necked tunics, three pairs of trousers, one overcoat, one gabardine raincoat, waterproof leggings, two capes, a pair of black woollen gloves, two pairs of white cotton gloves, a whistle on a chain, handcuffs and, of course, a truncheon.

Replacements in peacetime were scheduled to be a helmet, tunic, two pairs of trousers and one pair of cotton gloves annually, with a pair of woollen gloves every two years. The overcoat, raincoat, leggings and cape were replaced on the basis of one garment each year over a four-year period. Force orders detailed that the black woollen gloves were to be worn on night duty throughout the year and on day duty from 1st October to 31st March, whilst the white cotton gloves were carried, or worn, on ceremonial occasions and on traffic duty from lst April to 30th September.

Also issued were several booklets laying down exactly what every constable had to possess in the way of underclothing, even to the requirement that he had three pairs of socks and a change of shirt, vest and pants, whilst another booklet detailed how the constable should conduct himself (including the instruction that he was not permitted to take any form of intoxicant on licensed premises within his beat, *whether or not* off duty).

Under the heading 'FACIAL HAIR' was the instruction: "All members of the force are to shave, before going on duty, such portions of the face they are in the habit of shaving, and it is to be distinctly understood that no eccentric peculiarity of beard will be permitted. The sergeants and constables may wear moustaches, but the throat and chin are to be shaved clean, unless otherwise permitted on medical certificate". The instruction was stressed by a further publication that contained the statement: "No eccentricity of beard will be permitted". How these instructions were interpreted in pre-1914 days is not known (a glance at photographs of members of the officers' mess causes one to wonder exactly what would be considered an eccentricity of beard!), but 'facial hair' was very much on the minds of supervisory officers in 1938 and the ensuing years. In fact, I can recall only one bearded constable in the force until the late 1950s. He was stationed at Torquay and had the misfortune to contract facial eczema, making shaving impossible. He was promptly taken off beat patrol duties, put in a back office out of the view of the public and even encouraged to dress in mufti when walking to and from the police station.

During his service with Captain Vyvyan, Uncle Phil had seen the arrival *and* disappearance of some quite 'un-constabulary' uniform styles. In about 1903 the Boer war bush-hat, with clipped up right side brim, had been introduced. Lighter than the police helmet, with its wide brim, it had given better protection from the sun, but been heartily disliked by the constables, attracting, as it had, disparaging remarks until being withdrawn after just a few summer seasons.

Another innovation, and definite departure from the norm, had been the issue of a uniform with trouser legs ending just below the knees and worn with navy blue puttees, made by the Somerset company, *Fox & Co*. Again, they had been most unpopular with the men despite the enthusiasm of that old soldier, Captain Vyvyan. They had been time-consuming to don compared with the putting on of normal trousers, and had not been allowed to be worn when off duty – as nearly every constable had been wont to do with his normal uniform trousers.

Sometime, early in 1940, Reserve Constable Tooze chuckled when relating the details of a memorable pay parade that he had attended when the hated puttees were obligatory wear.

Sergeant (later to be Superintendent) Daddy S. F. Smith had been marching with the rest of the division when one of his puttees had slipped down his calf and ended in an unshapely concertina encasing his ankle, above which was exposed a very white, extremely thin leg. The unpopular garb had disappeared very shortly afterwards.

***Right.*** *Captain H. Vyvyan, the 'old soldier' Chief Constable of the Devon Constabulary from 1903 until 1931.*
*Devon & Cornwall Constabulary Museum archives*

***Left.*** *Constable 111 Reginald Lee, photographed in the late 1920s wearing the unusually distinctive and universally unpopular 'great war' style puttees.*
*Devon & Cornwall Constabulary Museum archives*

***The Devon Constabulary c1905.*** *This photograph shows the 'X' Exeter area division officers wearing their distinctive Boer war style bush or 'slouch' hats.*

*Devon & Cornwall Constabulary Museum archives*

# CHAPTER 7
# PAIGNTON

Throughout our period at New North Road we had been repeatedly told that at the end of our training, and before we were permitted out on a beat, there would be a final examination. Failure to reach a certain mark would result in remaining at headquarters for further instruction with the next intake of recruits. Failure to reach an even lower mark would result in dismissal.

Charlie had also warned us that our probationary period did not end until 31st May 1940. Until that date, when we would again undertake another examination, the failure by anyone to maintain the required standard of good conduct, sobriety and industriousness could, and would, result in dismissal.

Fortunately we all attained the required 'pass' marks and on 24th September 1938 the constables posted to South Devon were taken in the force lorry, firstly to Newton Abbot for Ron Lee and Ben Muckett to alight, and then to Torquay, where the two men for Torquay and I were dropped. The lorry was then driven to the 'F' division's superintendent's house in order to load Mr Martin's furniture.

Needless to say the lorry had to leave New North Road early on such an important mission (the collection of Mr Martin's effects, *not* the delivery of probationers to their stations) and we were at Torquay very shortly after 9am. The two men for Torquay were quickly taken away to commence their first outside duties, leaving me alone and nobody's responsibility as I was en route to Paignton.

It was then that I again experienced the penny-pinching attitude pervading the force. I was to await a means of conveying me the three miles to Paignton. At 3pm, some six hours later, Motor Patrol Constable (subsequently Inspector) 'Len' Rodd was instructed to take post from Torquay to Paignton and so was able to take me and my 'baggage' without any expense being entailed.

Paignton police station, a Victorian brick-faced building in Palace Avenue, was ideally situated to serve the needs of the public; central, fronted by a small park, and within easy walking distance of the railway and bus stations. An imposing arched porchway led directly to the charge-room door or, by turning right two paces in the porch, one reached the stone stairway to the courtroom on the first floor.

The charge-room was furnished with a large desk, behind which stood the duty constable. At his back was the door leading to the office of the sub-inspector and the sergeant, they, unseen, being able to hear all transactions occurring in the charge-room.

From the charge-room a passage led left to the sub-inspector's quarters, the stairway to the single men's dormitories and the prisoners' exercise yard, where the kennels for stray dogs were also situated. Directly ahead from the charge-room were the four police cells.

Above the courtroom and the upstairs rooms of the sub-inspector's quarters were the two dormitories, one with four and the other with five beds. With my arrival all nine beds were taken, the eight other probationers being Edgar Burnell, 'Percy' Evans, 'Ron' Ferris, 'Frank' Holman, 'Larry' Hurrell, 'Ken' Quick, 'Bill' Rice and 'Stan' Thornton.

Situated at the rear of the building were the sergeant's quarters, with a small garden which was partly taken for the sub-inspector's garage. No other officer at Paignton owned a vehicle.

Having dropped my property on the last vacant bed, I paraded before Sub-Inspector Walter Hutchings, a big man and one-time heavyweight boxing champion in the Royal Navy, who gave me fatherly advice - to work with my fellow constables as a team, to give the public due respect at all times, and to comply strictly with orders - before telling me to meet the patrol constable in Torbay Road and work the beat with him until 9.30pm.

As I saluted him and turned to leave, the telephone bell rang. Telling me to wait, the sub-inspector answered the phone, expressed surprise, mentioned he had seen Mr ... earlier that day, promised immediate attention and hung up. Countermanding his earlier instruction, he then told me to: "Go to the mortuary and help Constable Quick with the body of Mr ...".

At the mortuary, situated behind the Palace Avenue Theatre, I found Constable Quick and then, as my first post-training job, assisted in preparing a corpse for the post-mortem examination. Knowing how grass-green I was, Constable Quick kindly suggested that I remained outside whilst he undressed the deceased and did the general preparations, but realising that there would be many such occurrences in my career I declined his offer.

The deceased had owned the Elm Road Garage in the Totnes Road, and a just-married couple had been waiting in his office for their taxi to take them to the railway station en route to their honeymoon. The taxi had arrived, the garage owner had rushed in to the couple, called out: "Your taxi's ...", and collapsed. What effect it had had on their honeymoon arrangements I never knew, but I later found out that the garage was where a 2am point was made. Outside the garage was a swinging sign which, in the winter night winds, creaked most eerily!

Although I was at Paignton for only six months, there were further sudden deaths and post-mortem examinations for me to report on, and the instructions given to me by Constable Quick on that first occasion were invaluable.

Like many other seaside towns, Paignton appeared to have more than its due share of sudden deaths, causing me to wonder why it is that people come away from home, arrive at a pleasant resort, and within a day or so collapse and die. A Dr Reynolds conducted nearly all the post-mortem examinations at Paignton and he explained that the majority of such fatalities were caused by heart failure. Quite often the victims had had sedentary jobs and had come away for a relaxing holiday but, instead, had almost immediately started playing competitive games with their children and other adults, chasing after a ball, tearing down the beach and vigorously diving, swimming and splashing. I checked on the immediate activities prior to fatal collapses of the next fatalities I worked on and found that they had all been so engaged in unaccustomed strenuous activities, fully bearing out Dr Reynolds's opinion.

To work with him was both a privilege and an education. Not only did he explain each incision and operation, but every matter was couched in understandable, non-technical phrases, making the constable's report to His Majesty's Coroner (then Mr Hutchings) much easier.

Apart from his peculiar mode of dress - invariably he arrived at the mortuary in black coat and vest, striped trousers and carpet slippers - Dr Reynolds had another idiosyncrasy; any hour after midnight was his choice of time to make his examinations. After completing the examination and his report, he was wont to leave everything else to the constable, including the stitching together of the chest cavity and the general cleaning up of the examination slab, the floor, the dishes, the instruments and the sinks. After his report was written and 'translated' to the constable, he would walk out, his work completed. Being left alone with the corpse in the silent, very silent building in the 'small hours' could be, and often was, a testing experience.

In 1938 Sub-Inspector Hutchings oft-times laid claim that "Paignton was the fastest growing town in Britain"; each summer it was packed with nearly treble the winter population. The demands of the residents and visitors made police work extremely onerous from May to September and, in retrospect, it is difficult to comprehend how the two supervisory officers, Sub-Inspector Hutchings and Sergeant 'Frank' Newman, coped with all the responsibilities thrust upon them. They covered the 24 hours of each day and the seven days of every week without relief or assistance. No acting ranks were considered necessary, even when either officer was on his weekly, or annual, leave break.

They worked well together, one covering various periods of the day and being responsible for the night hours, whilst the other was early turn, taking all calls requiring his attention from 6am until finishing time, i.e. after the closing times of the public houses - 10pm from 1st October to 30th April and 10.30pm from 1st May to 30th September.

A working day for the constables was eight hours, plus any extra time necessary to clear an enquiry or other duty. A constable was unfortunate if called to a vehicular accident, or any other occurrence, as he was reaching the end of his tour of duty. He merely got on with the job and worked until it was cleared.

Each week consisted of six days duty and one leave day. By working on an eight-day sequence of duty days, constables were able to have a long weekend every six weeks, the period of leave being from after completion of duty at 6pm on the Friday to commencing the tour of nights at 9.30pm on the following Monday. Sundays and bank holidays were normal working days (certainly there was no 'time off in lieu') and such days would usually attract longer hours "in view of the needs of the service".

Annual leave was six days, with any accumulated weekly leave days added to the six days. By applying for annual leave to commence on the day on which the constable was scheduled to commence night duty, and by adding on one or two 'back days', it was possible to extend the leave period to as much as ten days!

A sergeant or constable taking his annual leave or weekly rest day away from his station was required to submit a pass for approval. The annual leave passes were on Devon Constabulary headed forms, whilst the weekly/long weekend passes were typed on the buff wrappers encasing the *Police Gazette* publications which arrived each day, Monday to Friday, and were collected from the railway station. The wrappers were carefully slit open and were large enough to be used for two passes. The format was similar to that of the official annual leave pass, and stated:

*Devon Constabulary, Paignton (or wherever).*

*The bearer, Constable 489 Trist, has permission to pass in plain clothes from Paignton to ..., he having leave of absence from ... am on (date) to ... pm on (date)*

| | | |
|---|---|---|
| *Recommended by* | ..... | *Sergeant* |
| *Passed by* | ..... | *Inspector* |
| *Approved by* | ..... | *Superintendent* |

(Such passes were required to be on the sergeant's desk at least three days before the leave commenced.)

The force housing officer, who was to end his police career as such, was Inspector Frank 'Tiger' Wheeler and he had become one of the most important officers to any constable requiring repairs to his police house. Needless to say, when he made a visit to anyone's quarters he was regaled with tea and cakes and, whilst engaged in consuming the same, was inclined to reminisce about 'the old days'.

One of his stories concerned a leave pass. The then Constable Wheeler was stationed at

Parracombe in the North Devon 'A' division and had submitted his application to 'pass in plain clothes...to Whimple'. Arriving at his parents' home in that village, he was invited by his father to join him on a business call that he had to make in Taunton. Such an offer was too good to miss, involving, as it did, a pleasant car ride and the shops of Taunton!

Whilst Mr Wheeler senior was engaged in his business, the two Mrs Wheelers, with Frank in tow, were engrossed in window and real shopping. However, Frank was not over-interested in the shops and more interested in a man passing in the crowded High Street. He was, yes definitely, he was ..., whose photograph had appeared in a very recent *Police Gazette*. Frank closed in on his quarry, disclosed his identity and arrested the dumbfounded man. Off he then went to the Somerset Constabulary headquarters, where it was confirmed that his prisoner was, indeed, a 'wanted' man.

In due course a letter from the Chief Constable of Somerset to the Devon Chief Constable extolling Frank's dedication and tenacity was passed to his superintendent (Mr Parr). The superintendent called Frank before him and demanded to know what he was doing in Taunton, in another county, when his pass only authorised him to travel to Whimple, in Devon!

Arrangements regarding hours of duty were quite complex. A normal 'day turn' was worked from 9.30am to 1.30pm and from 5.30pm to 9.30pm. Constables also worked a 'late turn' from 6 pm to 2am and a 'night duty' from 9.30pm to 5.30am. A 'relief turn' was worked perhaps twice a week to cover constables enjoying rest days. At Paignton, constables also worked 'split shifts', consisting of an early turn from 5.30am to 9.30am and from 1.30pm to 5.30pm or a day turn from 9am to 1pm and from 2pm to 6pm.

On late and night duty turns the constables were each allowed to return to the station for a 30-minute meal break (times staggered). Such meals invariably consisted of sandwiches and a thermos of tea or coffee, brought from home by married constables or from their boarding houses by the single men. There was no canteen facility at the police station and certainly no oven, gas ring, electric kettle or power point. In Torquay, meal breaks were taken in one of the police boxes on the different beats. The constable telephoned the police station on arrival at the box and again when about to leave. With four patrolling sergeants in Torquay, the length of time spent in a police box was closely supervised.

Paignton was divided into three areas - 'central', comprising the area from Hyde Road in the east to Tweenaway in the west, where there were various timed meetings at points with the Tweenaway constable; 'Preston', which was the area from the Hyde Road traffic lights to the gas works on the dividing line with Torquay, again where points were occasionally made with a Torquay-based constable; and 'Goodrington', a beat covering the area from the Gerston Hotel at the commencement of the Dartmouth Road, Paignton, to the boundary at Churston Ferrers.

When there were shortages of night duty constables, the Goodrington beat was not covered. This occurred, perhaps, on one night in a week, and then the late turn constable would be ordered to go to Goodrington immediately after making his midnight point to check all shops and other vulnerable properties. Each constable was required, physically, to try every shop and office door on his beat, with the points programmed so that a different public house was covered each evening at closing time.

In the event of a shop, office or public house being broken into and not discovered by the night beat man, he was awakened and questioned as to the time of his last checking of the attacked property, what persons he had seen in the vicinity and what vehicle numbers he had noted during his tour of duty.

Another duty of the night constables on the 'central' and Preston beats was switching off the traffic lights immediately after making their midnight points. For the 'central' beat man the lights were situated at the Totnes Road junction with Winner Street, at the Palace Avenue five-way junction encompassing Dartmouth Road, Totnes Road, Torbay Road and the Torquay road, and at the Hyde Road junction with Church Road and the Torquay road, whilst the Preston beat man dealt with the traffic lights at the Seaway Road junction with the Torquay road. These traffic lights were switched on again by the early turn men shortly after 6am. There were no traffic lights on the Goodrington, Churston or Tweenaway beats.

Street lights were controlled by timer switches situated in the bases of the lamp-posts. With just two exceptions, all lights were extinguished at midnight - in the whole of Paignton there were only two lamps burning until dawn, one at the Palace Avenue junction and the other at the Seaway Road junction.

The 'points' mentioned above refer to a system which required all beat constables on the hour on certain beats, and on the half-hour on the remaining beats, to be at a specific place and to remain there for ten minutes. In the police station charge-room, out of sight of the visiting public, was a framed list of these points. The list covered each beat, spaced over eight days, so that a point was not made at the same spot on the same day each week, supposedly to prevent sharp-eyed members of the public noting where policemen were at certain times. Needless to say, this did not prevent householders/shopkeepers and others from knowing that a policeman would be standing outside certain premises at a certain time next Saturday "as he was there this Friday!"

Before leaving the station each constable was required to enter into a rough notebook, not on a scrap of paper or in his official notebook, his points for the duty period, including the date. This precluded use of the excuse that he had written down the wrong point details if he was not at his point at the correct time.

He was required to be at the point unless "necessities of duty prevented his attendance". In such an event the omission had to be entered in the station duty book: "Omitted (time) point at (place) for (reason in full)". Failure to comply with this requirement, or entering "Beat correct" after missing a point, resulted in many constables being charged and fined.

Whilst at Paignton I had a salutary experience as to how this was dealt with. Amongst the single men was a post-probationary constable, Ernest Trump. He was a corpulent, comfortable, happy-go-lucky man, so it was with some surprise that I learned that he had had a quite violent shouting match with Sergeant Newman.

'Ernie' had asked if he could take an extra day's leave at the end of his long weekend. The sergeant had brusquely refused. Had Ernie explained why he so wanted the additional day, the sergeant probably would have replied that as he, unfortunately, had no back days in hand, there was no ordinary means of the request being granted. Instead, Ernie typed an application for an interview with the superintendent, and when the sergeant asked if the matter could be cleared without such action Ernie, now dignity personified, rejected the placatory gesture and insisted that the application be submitted.

That week Ernie was 'nights' on the Goodrington beat, whilst Sergeant Newman was 'early turn', with the sub-inspector making the night points.

He made Ernie's midnight point, which followed the all too familiar pattern:

*Sub-inspector................ "All quiet?"*
*Ernie............................. "All quiet, sir".*
*Sub-inspector................ "Right, put me down as 12.05am, Big Tree, get in...".*

Ernie dutifully got into 'Subbie's' Flying Standard and was driven back to Palace Avenue, where he got out and opened the station's backyard doors and then the garage doors, enabling the car to be garaged without the driver leaving his seat. 'Ernie' then shut the lane gates and the garage doors before following Subbie into the police station, where they checked that there were no matters requiring action.

The constable then left the station to resume his beat and heard the charge-room door being locked behind him. From the park he was able to see lights go on and off, marking Subbie's passage in to his quarters, then to his bedroom and, after an interval, the bedroom light was put out, the officer apparently having gone to bed.

There was a definite rule that when leaving a superior officer the constable never bade him "goodnight", but from what Ernie had witnessed he could be fairly certain that he would not see a supervisory officer again during that tour of duty. He also knew that Sergeant Newman would never commence duty until the night duty men had signed off. Coming off duty at 5.30am, Ernie signed off, entering the point made at 12.05 and "Beat correct", before repairing to his bed.

Later in the day his path crossed that of Subbie, who apparently was a little mixed up about the points that he had made during the previous night's tour of duty. Their conversation went something on the following lines:

*Sub-inspector* ................ *"All quiet last night, Constable Trump?"*
*Ernie* ............................ *"Yes sir, all quiet".*
*Sub-inspector* ................ *"Let me see. I made your 1am point, didn't I?"*
*Ernie* ............................ *"No sir, midnight, Big Tree".*
*Sub-inspector* ................ *"Ah yes. Where was your 1am point?"*
*Ernie* ............................ *"Goodrington caravan site sir".*
*Sub-inspector* ................ *"Where did you make that point?"*
*Ernie* ............................ *"At the main entrance, by the warden's office".*
*Sub-inspector* ................ *"That's where I made it, but you weren't there".*
*Ernie* ............................ *"Oh yes sir. I got there a bit early and I heard someone moving among the caravans, I went to check. I suppose I was back to the point just after 1.15".*
*Sub-inspector* ................ *"That's strange, I waited until 1.20".*
*Ernie* ............................ *"Well it might have been a bit later than I thought".*
*Sub-inspector* ................ *"You DID make the point?"*
*Ernie* ............................ *"Oh yes sir!"*

There the matter seemingly ended, but not so. I was making a point at Preston that afternoon when the sub-inspector drove up. We exchanged the usual formal phrases before he ordered me to get into his car and then drove me to a 24-hour taxi depot at Goodrington. There we saw the proprietor, who stated that he had no knowledge of Constable Trump's movements during the previous night. The usually amiable inspector then became extremely officious, warning the taxi-man that "Harbouring a constable was an offence"(!!), which had the effect of drawing a very reluctant admission that "Constable Trump had looked in to the depot some time after midnight and had had a cup of tea before getting into a parked taxi and going to sleep for a couple of hours". I was instructed to draw a statement to this effect and, on our journey back to my Preston beat, was warned to tell no one of our activities.

Later a worried, no longer happy-go-lucky Ernie admitted his part in the miserable affair, resulting in his 'having the book thrown at him'. "Missing a point without good reason; sleeping whilst on duty; making a false entry in an official document; lying to a superior officer".

He was subsequently fined £5 on each charge (close to seven weeks wages) and reprimanded, all details being entered on his records. Whether his promotion prospects would have been affected will never be known as he failed to take the promotion examination. Needless to say, his transfer out of the 'F' division was made immediately after his appearing before the Assistant Chief Constable.

During the war Ernie served in the R.A.F., attaining the highest non-commissioned rank, that of warrant officer. He returned to the force after demobilisation, but our paths never crossed. He did appear in force orders on one subsequent occasion. During the austere years immediately after the war, when rationing was still in force, there appeared an entry: "A constable serving in the 'A' division was fined and reprimanded for illegally purchasing dairy cream, contrary to ...". That was our Ernie!

In 1938, at the junction of Torbay Road and the Torquay road, stood a branch shop of the Maypole grocery chain. This was one of the points, named on the sheet as 'Maypole Corner', but unofficially known to us all as 'Glanvilles Corner'. This came from the time, prior to traffic lights being installed in 1934, when the five-ways crossing (the Torbay, Dartmouth and Totnes roads, Palace Avenue and the Torquay road) had necessitated the posting of a constable on traffic control. Constable Glanville, then a probationary constable, had been given this duty, standing at the centre point beside a granite-based lamp-post, now long gone. Traffic had gradually increased to its peak shortly before noon and the constable eventually become so frenzied with his signals that he had guided a motorist directly into the lamp-post so that the front wheels of the car had been completely off the roadway. The incident had passed into the folklore of the force, as had many other incidents.

Probably the main cause of such folklore was one 'A.E.M.', Arthur Martin, mentioned previously, the former superintendent at Torquay. Mr Martin had joined the force in 1905 and been later appointed 'sergeant major', the title of the training officer responsible for the transformation of raw recruits on their arrival at New North Road into efficient police officers by the time that they left his charge some three months later.

During his years of training intake after intake he became an authority on evidence and court procedure. He had been promoted to superintendent in 1928, taking charge of the 'C' division at Cullompton, and from his very first appearance in the Cullompton magistrates' court had taken absolute charge.

***Cullompton police station.*** *The former station at Cullompton had the well-known landmark of the 'Devon Constabulary clock' on its upper fascia.*

*'Bill' Newton*

In answer to a point of law presented by a defending solicitor, he was reputed to have replied, without referring to any document: "If Mr .... would care to look at page eight hundred and two of his *Stone's Justices' Manual* he will find that in the fourth paragraph it states..." - quoting the whole paragraph from memory and completely destroying the solicitor's case.

He had introduced monthly 'tea parties' in his division, when all probationary constables had spent an unhappy afternoon being questioned and taken apart on the many facets of the law, evidence and procedure. Just two things had been missing from these parties - any kind of liquid refreshment and the milk of human kindness.

Mr Martin had later transferred to take charge of the 'F' division. His reputation having gone before him, he had immediately been given due respect and deference in the courts and from his officers. All the probationers at Paignton assured me how lucky I had been in arriving on the day that he was leaving the division to take over as Assistant Chief Constable.

Mr Martin built up an aura of fear amongst his subordinates, mainly through harsh criticism of their work or lack of his encyclopaedic knowledge, but with him it certainly was a case of 'do as I say, not as I do'. If he saw a constable with a sweet in his mouth, he would order him to: "Spit it out man, what are you - a baby having to have something to suck?" Yet he would parade in uniform smoking a pipe, going so far as to walk through the Torquay streets and market with his pipe tightly clenched in his mouth.

Another of his idiosyncrasies was rarely to allow a report to pass through his hands without finding some reason to return it with a query. This served to demonstrate his superior knowledge, not only over the reporting officer but also the submitting officers, who made every endeavour to clear any possible reason for the report being so returned. Their method was to find an excuse to return the report for themselves before it reached the superintendent.

When the sergeant read the report it was not to ascertain what it covered, but rather to find some possible omission to enable him to return it to the reporting officer for clarification. In turn, the inspector and the chief inspector would have to show their 'sharp-wittedness' by also returning the report with a query! No matter how penetrating their questions might be, 'A.E.M.' would almost certainly find some point that he required to be cleared, so back through the chain would go the report to the hapless constable.

In their desperate efforts to avoid the mortification of having to return and then resubmit the report, these senior officers occasionally asked questions or wrote submissions that bordered on the ridiculous. Some of their howlers were carved deeply into the woodwork of the police boxes in Torquay. Sentences so carved appeared quite innocuous until one knew their contexts, and there was always someone able to give those!

For example, there had been a number of thefts of produce from a Torquay allotment and finally a constable had caught the offender leaving the allotment at 1am with muddied boots and a sack filled with freshly cut cabbages. Despite the overwhelming evidence, the chief inspector had returned the report with the query: "Did the cabbages fit the stumps?"

***Left.*** *A police box on the sea front at Torquay, c1926.*
*Devon and Cornwall Constabulary Museum archives*

Again, following a road traffic accident, the reporting constable had included the fact that one of the cars was a sports car. The same chief inspector returned the report with the query: "Was the hood up or down?", and on yet another occasion, with another road accident report, in his submission he had written the indisputable truth: "Sir, this accident would not have occurred if both vehicles had been stationary". In the cramped police box, space had also been found to record yet another query by the same officer: "How far did the car travel after it had stopped?" There were many other such tributes to the inquisitive natures of submitting officers, but all were lost when the police boxes were demolished in the early 1950s.

Almost every Sunday shortly after 2pm 'A.E.M.', accompanied by Mrs Martin, the daughter of the one-time Chief Constable of Tiverton Borough, Mr Mercer, would drive from Torquay police station in Market Street and 'visit stations'. His route invariably took him to Paignton via the seafront. If a motor car was found parked anywhere on that roadway between the Pavilion and the Grand Hotel, 'A.E.M.' would telephone from Paignton police station to the Torquay duty sergeant requiring him to explain why the offending vehicle had not been moved on by the seafront patrol constable. Cars were not so numerous in the 1930s but there were quite a number of 'Sunday drivers' who liked to stop and gaze out to sea. Their rapid moving-on often required some quite frantic pedalling by the bicycle-mounted constable, given the task of keeping that piece of road completely clear at that crucial time.

Discipline in the pre-war years was harsh and apparently unfeeling. At Paignton, in 1938, was a constable from one of the 1937 intakes. Shortly after leaving headquarters for his first station he had been obliged to report that his fiancée was pregnant. He was brought before his superintendent and pleaded to be allowed to continue serving in the force, explaining that he had been engaged to marry for some time and would have married had he not been accepted as a recruit to join the force.

Grudgingly, he was permitted to continue his career, but it was stressed that he would have to complete his two years probationary period before he could apply for a married station *and* during that time he would serve as a single man at Paignton, with his wife and baby living in Plymouth.

He was allowed to marry, and then endeavoured to manage the difficult task of serving and boarding at Paignton, whilst supporting a wife and baby elsewhere, on his net weekly wage of under £3.

One of the immediate requirements of a constable at his first station was to acquire a typewriter. The cheapest model was the Remington 'Good Companion' portable, costing nine guineas (£9.45) - over three weeks pay, and far beyond the pocket of our unfortunate probationer. All reports had to be typed in off-duty hours, no time off being allowed for such work or for enquiries, interviews, road measuring etc., which were also carried out in after duty hours. Overtime or typewriter payments were quite unknown. Whenever he had a report to submit he was obliged to beg his colleagues either to type the report for him or to allow him to use their precious machines. None was an expert typist, and when typing for him there was a tendency to ignore errors, the completed work reflecting no credit on the author.

The nine constables in the Paignton single men's quarters shared one bathroom/toilet. Hot water was obtained by inserting pennies into the geyser gas meter. Our man was reduced to trying to extract sufficient gas from the previous user's penny to heat his shaving water. After a few months he found the struggle too much and resigned.

The first weeks out in the cruel, outside world after the security of the training school have a tendency to stand out in one's memory despite being, in truth, quite unremarkable. Other, more interesting incidents, however, came along, each presenting different challenges and, hopefully, from each something was learned for future use. One case, to me, has always had instant recall, and is, perhaps, a good demonstration of how 'Their Worships' in 1938 dealt with an offender with lasting good effect.

A lady reported that her blind mother, who lived alone, was losing small sums of money from her house. Routine questions were asked; "Who visited mother?", "How was the house secured?", "Was it left vacant?", "How often?", "Under what circumstances - workmen visiting, window cleaners or tradesmen?". It was when the question: "Who does her shopping?" was asked and it was learned that it was a 12-year-old boy from two doors away that a solution appeared likely, despite the very strong assurance that: "He is a lovely boy and as honest as the day".

It was with some difficulty that the complainant was persuaded to detail that the 'lovely boy' collected a grocery list from her mother each Friday just after 4pm, did the necessary errand and brought back the groceries by 5pm.

On the following Friday the boy did exactly that and then proceeded to put the groceries away, enquiring where each item went and then placing it as instructed. Sadly, at the same time, he was busily engaged in opening the blind lady's purse and extracting sundry coins from therein. After completing the putting-away exercise he then waited until the now-closed purse was reopened by its owner and was given sixpence (such a coin purchased ten cigarettes in 1938).

The boy then made his farewells and left the house, but had barely reached the garden path when he was in the grip of a large policeman and quickly half-carried to his own house. There, to his mother's horror, the stolen coins were recovered from his pocket. Under caution, his statement, a full admission, was taken down and he and his mother told of the probable future events.

It was then that the incident was dealt with - so differently from how such an offence would be processed today. The offence was committed and detected on the late afternoon of Friday, and on the afternoon of the following Wednesday the boy appeared before magistrates in the Paignton juvenile court.

No probation officer, no psychology tests, no smokescreens or half-veiled suggestions that the boy had been traumatically affected at birth or in his formative years. Instead, he was asked if he understood the charge. He did. Did he admit or deny the offence? He admitted it. He was then told that he had committed a disgraceful breach of trust in stealing from a blind lady. The chairman hoped that he was truly ashamed of his conduct and, when assured by the boy that he was very ashamed, told him that he would receive six strokes of the birch and that it was hoped he would never appear before the court again.

To me, it was then that justice was seen in perfect action. The boy was taken from the courtroom, down the stone steps, through the charge-room and into the cells corridor. In cell number one was Constable 'Ted' Nicholls, 6 feet 2 inches, 16 stone of heavily moustached manhood, standing with feet apart.

"Drop your pants, boy", he instructed, and when this was done he pulled the boy's right shoulder to his right thigh. The one-time Royal Navy heavyweight boxer, now the sub-inspector, then brought up the birch (a handful of hazel twigs, possibly ten in number, each no thicker than an ordinary knitting needle and about 18 inches long) and struck the boy across his bare buttocks.

The blow caused the boy to excrete over the sub-inspector's polished boot. The officer looked down at his soiled footwear, remarked more in sorrow than anger: "You dirty little ..." and administered the remaining five strokes in quick succession. The sobbing boy was quickly cleaned, pants pulled up, and returned, with skin reddened but not broken, to his now also crying mother.

All dealt with efficiently and expeditiously. Today there would be cries of 'brutality', 'unfeeling magistrates' and, most probably, the police would be likened to inhuman, bloodthirsty tyrants, or worse. Certainly there would be strong criticisms of the process of law that afternoon.

There was a sequel which gave me great satisfaction. In February 1953 I returned to Paignton as a patrol sergeant and commenced enjoying the peaceful season before the summer invasion of visitors. When on day duty, with paperwork cleared, I was able to be out making points shortly after 10am and it was my habit to greet any member of the public who glanced my way (unofficially I was nicknamed 'the laughing sergeant').

Walking down Torbay Road, I saw a man approaching whose face was vaguely familiar, and as we passed each other I remarked: "Good morning, lovely morning". Had he merely agreed the matter would have ended there, but, instead, he scowled and increased his pace. Piqued, I turned, overtook him and enquired if I had upset him at some time, as I was sure that I knew him.

He snarled: "I don't know you and I don't want to". I felt that this was unkind to say the least and gave him a closer look before assuring him that I *did* know him and had thought about him many times. This caused him to retort: "You don't know me. How could you?".

With the incident of 14 years before recalled, I answered: "Oh yes I do. You were the last boy in Devon to be birched and I've wondered about you many times, whether you got into any other trouble".

He almost gasped out his reply: "No, never. If I saw a ten bob note in the gutter and you were coming along, I wouldn't touch it!".

Would there now be 'no go' areas in towns, or juveniles terrorising whole districts with house breakings and car thefts, if their local magistracy enjoyed the powers in force in pre-war days? Certainly then no senior police officer confessed that his men were 'powerless' to deal with certain classes of persistent offenders, and throughout my whole career I never met a frustrated or stressed policeman! I have unsuccessfully endeavoured to picture Constable Nicholls being called a 'pig' by one or even a dozen long-haired, scruffy teenagers!

One of the minor pleasures of being on late turn for we ever-hungry probationers was to have a chat with Mike Dimeo, standing, as he had done for the previous 19 years, in his pony-drawn potato chip cart in The Square outside Paignton railway station. From him one could learn of the various misdeeds being perpetrated in the area, and he was also a mine of information concerning the local citizenry, both respectable and otherwise. In addition he would kindly hand out a newspaper-wrapped bag of chips as he was packing up for the night. At around 11pm in the winter months, this gift would be most welcome.

On one occasion I had just received my packet and thrust it under my cape when I saw Sergeant Newman approaching. Hastily bidding Mike "Goodnight", I walked to meet 'Sarge'. After the usual "All quiet?" and my affirmative answer, he decided that we should walk to the seafront, with me very aware that the smell of chips would soon permeate the air with a no longer fragrant scent.

On reaching the front, our walk was stretched to the whole length of the promenade, past the Redcliffe Hotel, and then on to Seaway Road at Preston. We then made a leisurely return journey to the station square, where we parted, me to make my next point still clutching the packet of now cold and inedible chips, whilst the sergeant was en route to the police station, there to share a good laugh at my expense.

At that time there was no question of the high esteem in which members of the force were held by the public. Shortly before Christmas 1938 the 'recreation room' (it was a passageway which held a dartboard) was completely filled with gifts to be shared between the officers, handed in by members of the public to show their appreciation of our efforts on their behalf. I have no idea how the 'goodies' were shared out as I was sent home with influenza on about 20th December, and when I returned on the 27th the recreation room was bare. By the following Christmas the nation had been at war for nearly four months and rationing had begun. Certainly there were no similar demonstrations of appreciation during any of the wartime Christmas seasons, or at any time since.

Early in December 1938 we organised a ball for the force widows and orphans' fund. The owners of the Paignton Deller's Café, in Torbay Road, made the whole of their premises available to the police at no charge. Three Torquay hotel broadcasting orchestras also donated their services; we had one band on the ground floor playing modern ballroom music and another on the first floor rendering old-time music, each in turn being relieved by the third orchestra. The event was a sell-out, raising a goodly sum for the fund.

Paignton was a lucky station for me. Incidents occurred when I was near at hand, experience was gained and valuable lessons learned.

For example, shortly after midnight lights came on in the upper flat above a Torbay shop, while from the flat came screams from two females, a window was violently opened and a nightdress-clad figure climbed out on to the window sill, three flights up. A female in the flat was still screaming while the nightdress-clad female shouted: "Shut up or I'll jump!"

Standing in the street, feeling helpless and hopeless, I pulled out my police whistle and blew it so hard that it drowned the screams from above.

There was then a sudden, deathly silence, broken only by my ordering in what I hoped was a masterful voice: "Get back in the room at once and come down and admit me, *NOW*". Probably I was the most surprised person when the female climbed back into the flat and within a very short time opened the street door to admit me.

In the flat, with window closed, the females wearing coats over their night attire and each trying to out-shout the other, I learned that the girl who had been on the window sill was just 15, an usherette at the Regent Cinema. After the cinema had closed she had been accompanied home by a youth and been found by her mother, shortly after 11pm, kissing in the doorway. The mother had promptly dragged the girl indoors and upstairs.

The girl was illegitimate, causing the mother , who had had a hard struggle over the previous 15 years, to be terrified that her daughter might suffer a similar experience. In their flat she had nagged and nagged until the girl, in desperation, had jumped out of bed, thrown open the window and climbed out on to the sill, uttering her threat to jump.

Taking lengthy statements from each female effectively quietened them, and I left a very subdued pair. Later, the girl appeared at the juvenile court and was kindly, but firmly, advised as to her future conduct. Unofficially, I later learned that one of the lady J.P.s took the trouble to visit the mother and gave her not only excellent advice but also some financial assistance.

The main reason that the court appearance stayed in my memory was that both mother and daughter arrived bareheaded, and were not permitted to enter the courtroom until 'fittingly dressed'. They were loaned headscarves by the sergeant's wife, who else?

The month of March 1939 brought rumours of impending transfers for all of the June 1938 intake. Far-off stations were named, with Barnstaple my apparent destination. This seemed a very long way from my Plymouth home, but that near-angelic lady, Mrs Newman, assured me, ironically as it turned out, that: "Barnstaple is lovely, far better than holes like Honiton".

# CHAPTER 8
# HONITON

Removal orders were circulated and on lst April I moved to Honiton, from the 'F' division to the 'D' (*the dirty 'D'*) division. How the division got this unattractive appellation I have never discovered, though I have questioned everyone who has used it to me as to its origin.

It was a different station indeed to Paignton, where probationers were actively discouraged from being in the charge-room when off duty. At Honiton the three probationers, 'Bert' Wykes, Frank West and I, *had* to be on the station when off duty, manning the telephone and dealing with enquiries. We were also sent out to deal with road traffic difficulties, including vehicular accidents, when off duty. This enabled the beat constable to continue his patrol duties. We were also expected to make ourselves generally useful around the station, which included keeping the lawn at the rear of the station cut with a 12-inch hand machine, the lawn being sufficiently large for the whole division to parade and carry out their drill movements. This work was carried out on any day but Sunday; on that day it was possible to avoid other jobs around the station when off duty, attendance at church or chapel taking precedence over everything but normal duties, both the superintendent and the sergeant being local lay-preachers.

In 1939 the station building front was level with the inner edge of the pavement, the site being immediately in front of the ground on which the present station stands. The building had a centre arch with open driveway to the rear, flanked by offices on either side.

As one entered the arch, on the left-hand side was the charge-office, the sergeant's office - in the occupancy of Sergeant (later Superintendent) James Eddy - a telephone room and the stairs leading to the single men's quarters and a billiard room. On the right-hand side was the superintendent's office (Superintendent James Marshall - 'Jimmy the one') with the divisional office adjoining in the charge of (then) Constable 'Bill' Craddock and his aide, 'Stan' Hoyle.

The proximity of the superintendent's and the divisional office doors to the entrance-way was unfortunate, as time after time members of the public would knock on one or the other of these doors, interrupting the work being done therein. However, on at least one occasion it proved beneficial to the caller. I had reported a motorist for a road traffic offence. Immediately after being reported he had called at the station to produce his driving licence and insurance cover, had been invited to enter when, mistakenly, he had knocked on the superintendent's office door, and had managed to give such a persuasive version of the reason for his being reported that he was cautioned there and then by the superintendent - before I had even typed the report!

The day for the divisional pay parade arrived, with Inspector Holmes from Exmouth and the sergeants from all the sections in attendance; and every constable that could be mustered, most sections being manned by just one constable to cover any emergency call. Leave days had been cancelled to ensure that the maximum number of men would parade to hear the words of wisdom dispensed by the superintendent.

Firstly came drilling, with several constables and two sergeants taking their turn in having the 80 men on parade carrying out various manoeuvres, these being the men who were taking their promotion examination later in the year. Then the superintendent took charge, first ordering us to 'stand easy' and then addressing us. He commenced: "I am worried, very worried (he really did have the appearance of being extremely worried). What is happening with you men today? I am getting your weekly passes for my approval and I note you are putting yourselves down to be absent from your stations from eight in the morning until eleven in the night. What is wrong?

Aren't you happy in your stations? Why else would you want to be away for so long?"

Having set the scene for a miserable parade, he added: "Another thing I have noticed on my visits to some of your stations is that your gardens are not kept up to the standard I expect. At one or two stations I saw torn and tattered notices exhibited on the boards. I tell you it won't do".

Until making points with married constables I had no idea of the size of the gardens to which the superintendent had referred. When it was decided to build a country station, the county negotiated the purchase of a half-acre site and had the constable's house built a few yards back from the road line, with the remainder of the ground situated at the rear of the house. Another feature was the siting of the lavatory as far from the house as possible. An indoor lavatory was unknown and bathrooms did not appear until well into the 1930s, and only then in newly-built police houses.

Later I served with one of the true 'characters' of the force, one 'Bill' Mugridge, constable number 190, and learned from him of his experiences whilst he had been stationed at Membury. Not satisfied with having such an amenity as piped water in his police house, he had made several applications to have a bathroom with indoor lavatory installed. Supporting his applications, he had laboriously prepared plans showing that the huge and underused pantry was sufficiently large to be converted into a water closet and bathroom, but all to no avail.

Months had passed without his applications even being returned to him, and so he had then decided to endeavour to move matters in his own way.

At that time the outside lavatory was situated against the perimeter hedge, the absolute maximum distance from the house. In fact, it was a rather superior edifice as contemporary outside lavatories went, insofar as it had an opening at the rear, adjoining the hedge. It also had a water-butt on one side collecting rainwater from its roof. Users of the lavatory, therefore, had the luxury of having a utensil partly filled with water, and after use of the building the waste matter could be sluiced through the rear aperture and the emptied utensil replenished with water from the butt.

Bill planned for far better things and one morning made it his business to be busy in the garden when the farmer, owner of the adjoining field, came to check his cattle. Leaning on his spade, Bill looked into the far distance as the farmer approached. They exchanged formal pleasantries, but Bill continued to stare, only now at the base of the hedge. The farmer, curiosity aroused, came closer and enquired if something was amiss. Bill explained that he was worried, very worried, that the waste resulting from sundry visits to the lavatory should be seeping into the field. The farmer, used to clearing tons of animal manure year by year, assured him that there was no cause to worry.

Bill refused to be placated, explaining: "Ah, but human waste is a different matter, sir. Where do all these animal diseases come from? How about epizootic lymphatics, foot and mouth and anthrax? Where do they come from? It's always been a mystery". The farmer departed deep in thought and Bill went out on his split tour of duty.

He was at his second point of the tour when his sergeant arrived. Not the usual "All quiet?" but a gasped out statement that the superintendent had received a telephone call from the Chief Constable concerning a complaint made by Mr ..., the neighbouring farmer *and* a member of the Devon County Standing Joint Committee, that his field was being fouled by human excrement. Apparently the superintendent had been extremely put out and had instructed that: "Constable Mugridge should return to his station and remain there until otherwise ordered". In due course the superintendent arrived and, despite the constable's assurances of utter innocence, said: "I see your hand in this Mugridge, and you *won't* get away with it".

However, within a few days builders arrived, and for the next three weeks worked to convert the larder into a bathroom/toilet, almost religiously following Bill's drawings. The Mugridge family, meanwhile, put up with the upheaval and the inevitable dirt, dust and debris carried into the house, their sufferings alleviated, to some degree, by the numerous pots of tea shared with the builders.

At last, conversion completed, plumbing connected, farewells and thanks tendered to the departing workmen and the house cleaned from top to bottom, the family could say 'goodbye' to the garden lavatory and the old metal bath.

On that, what should have been a wonderful, day came an order from headquarters: "Constable Mugridge will remove from Membury to Frogmore on ... 1936, there to be stationed".

At the new station a metal bath was still required for the weekly soak in front of the kitchen range, whilst the garden was a touch longer and the lavatory a yard or so further from the house than at Membury. Furthermore, it lacked the amenities of a water supply, whilst the waste therefrom required disposal in pits dug by the constable.

Bill accepted the removal as all 'part of the job', although he hated being the butt of his colleagues' ribbing.

He had been at Frogmore only a few months when he was called to Croft Farm, West Charleton, in his beat, and found himself at the scene of what, ultimately, was a triple murder and arson.

With no other illumination immediately available, Bill found in his torchlight Mrs Emily Maye and her daughters (Emily Jean aged 28 and Gwenyth aged 25) in different parts of the farmhouse dying from ghastly injuries inflicted by a walling hammer, taken from a cupboard in the kitchen. There were several sites of fire, causing rooms, the stairs and passageways to be smoke-filled. Rushing about the building, finding water and dowsing the flames, Bill then discovered the farmer, Thomas Maye, lying on a smouldering bed with superficial injuries. He was later charged with murder and arson.

At the Devon Assizes the defending barrister savaged Constable Mugridge, playing on the words that Bill had said to Maye when he found him after examining the three terribly injured, dying women. He had asked: "What have you done?", and the barrister asserted and repeated to Bill "Without any evidence whatsoever you made up your mind that my injured client was guilty of murdering his wife and daughters".

Using this as his main plank of defence, freely sprinkled with words and phrases such as "biased", "not a scrap of supporting evidence", "this terribly injured man", "questioned when in a deeply shocked state" etc., the King's Counsel obtained a 'not guilty' verdict from the jury. After his discharge Mr Maye left the Kingsbridge district and emigrated to Australia, where he died.

Bill's version of the events was told when we were serving together at Newton Abbot, and I learned of his many experiences and escapades whilst serving. He was, undoubtedly, a 'character' for whom I had a great respect, so it was with some regret that I learned that he was being transferred yet again, being replaced by one Constable Harold Bastin.

In a lesser way Harold also had a reputation for being a 'card', arising mainly from his activities during his service at Starcross. It appeared that when he went out on his tours of duty he invariably cycled, while from the saddle was suspended an extra large saddlebag. When he left his station the bag was always empty but, on returning at the end of his tour, the bag was invariably filled, sometimes over-filled, with a cabbage or two, a few swedes, perhaps, or some other produce of the land such as a freshly trapped rabbit; on occasion, it was said, a glimpse of pheasant's feathers had also been discerned. A question asked in Starcross hostelries was: "Who is Constable Bastin going to leave his saddlebag to when he retires?"

Whenever a police-owned house was being vacated it was usual for the new occupant to visit and check that all items on the inventory were on the premises and in good order. These included the light fixtures, blinds and noticeboard, down to the 'Devon Constabulary' wooden lettering above the front door. Having satisfactorily disposed of the official check, it was then the time of coming to agreement concerning the unofficial property, a small shed, an apple tree, perhaps, and nearly always the garden produce. It was this episode that usually entailed some haggling between the out-going and in-coming constables before money actually changed hands.

***Devon Constabulary police cottage c1939.***
*The sign above the front doors of the police cottages at that time had a small section where the constable's collar number was inserted, thus showing the identity of the constable stationed there. At other stations, such as divisional headquarters, the title of the rank of the senior officer would be inserted into the sign.*
*Devon & Cornwall Constabulary Museum archives*

In Bill's case he had procured and erected a clothes-line pole as well as planted his spring onions, potatoes and cabbage plants, so looked for a modest repayment for them. Harold, however, explained that he did not agree with such settlements, which left Bill quite disgruntled, he having already visited his next station and paid a small sum for similarly planted produce.

The removals took place and it did seem that Bill had come off worst in the transactions. Later, on arrival at Newton Abbot, Harold plaintively told me that he had found that Bill had sawn off the clothes pole "tight to the ground", had cut the heads off the cabbage plants, "leaving the useless roots in the ground", and dug up the potatoes and spring onions, "leaving the garden in a mess". Perhaps Bill had the last laugh as Harold had no opportunity to cycle around Newton Abbot picking up oddments from friendly farmers.

In those days there was little to lighten the routine of police work, which led, perhaps, to happy acceptance of 'black humour' - by everyone except the recipients! This, however, was nothing new, as had been exemplified in about 1930 by Captain Herbert Vyvyan (Chief Constable from 1907 until his retirement in 1931, at the age of 68).

He had made a point of visiting every division at least once each year, and perhaps a description of one such visit will give an idea of the changed life in the constabulary between then and today.

In about May, a uniformed sergeant left the New North Road headquarters and walked, wheeling a bicycle, to the Central railway station, in Queen Street, Exeter. There he purchased a first-class monthly return ticket to Barnstaple, before taking the bicycle onto the station platform. He called a porter and carefully explained that the bicycle was to be placed in the guard's van of the North Devon train, the said porter to ensure that it was stowed in such a way that it suffered no damage, it being the property of the *Chief Constable of Devon*. At Barnstaple, attired in knickerbocker suit, Captain Vyvyan took possession of the bicycle and cycled around the division, visiting police stations and cottages.

Arriving at one country station, his knock was answered by the constable's wife, who curtsied when he disclosed his identity. He learned that the officer was out on his beat and was invited into the house. Given tea, he discussed the absent officer's career with the wife. Following a set form, he mentioned that the constable had nearly 25 years of service and so could retire the next year. He asked if any plans had been made.

She replied: "Well sir, in all our married life we have never had a seaside posting. What we were hoping was that perhaps our last shift would be to Paignton, Teignmouth or some other seaside town, and then when we retired we could get a house or cottage there and I could take in summer visitors to help out the pension".

The Chief Constable replied: "Seaside station! Ah, yes. I must note that". He duly made a note on the constable's record before departing to cycle on to another station.

Perhaps two or three months later the constable received his removal orders - "Constable ... will remove from ... 'A' division to Holne, 'B' division, there to be stationed." (Holne being situated in the exact centre of Devon, the furthermost station from the sea in the county.) How the headquarters' staff must have enjoyed the chief's little touch of humour!

Captain Vyvyan had introduced country station beat books in 1929, in which the country beat man was called upon to enter details of every matter in his province. These were massive tomes, some 33 x 28 cm and originally consisting of 259 pages with 25 headings under which the constable entered and cross-indexed information concerning:

Accidents
Aliens
Arrested
Summoned & cautioned persons
Complaints
Occurrences suggesting indictable offences
Complaints and occurrences suggesting non-indictable offences
Constables - nominal roll of
Convicts, supervisees & section 7 Prevention of Crimes Act individuals
Cottages occupied by police
Diseases of Animals Acts & Orders
Outbreaks of disease
Explosives - persons authorised to keep

Firearms - holders of certificates etc
Fires - outbreaks of
Gipsies - who frequent beat
Hawkers & pedlars who frequent beat
Licensed premises & clubs
Mentally defective persons, residing in or frequenting beat
Miscellaneous particulars (including owners of vehicles in beat)
Motor char-a-bancs, hackney carriages & trade plate holders
Parishes - particulars of
Police reserve list & special constabulary
Sheep worrying
Suspects & persons of bad character.

Until the beat books were officially withdrawn in 1954 every detail of every occurrence was religiously entered, resulting in the limited number of pages being used up relatively quickly. Supplementary pages were, therefore, inserted into the books.

The books were examined regularly by supervisory officers and duly initialled. Entries were made in off-duty time, but to a newly-arrived constable the information was invaluable. So much so that many beat books were unofficially kept up well into the 1960s by constables who recognised their immense value.

A few beat books are now in the force museum and of great research value, giving, as they do, a chronicle of the duties that constables were engaged upon mainly in pre-war days. (Many entries were allowed to lapse after 1945, gipsies, hawkers and pedlars being no longer worthy of entries, whilst charabancs and other motor vehicles in a beat could not possibly be subject of ever-current details.)

Honiton was a lively town and, being on the direct routes to London and Southampton, had an almost continuous stream of traffic flowing through the main thoroughfare, a road so wide that a street market was held each Saturday without causing any traffic dislocation. The Plymouth to London coaches, the brown and fawn liveried *Highways* and their main rivals, *Royal Blue*, made their first 'comfort' stops from Plymouth and their last from London at Honiton. They used the services of the two main cafes, The Highland Fling and The Carlton, which were situated almost directly opposite one another, on the higher side of the parish church.

Catering activities ceased at The Highland Fling some years ago, but The Carlton, despite several ownership changes, is still a convenient stopping place for through motorists. There were occasions when there were coaches parked outside each establishment without causing any undue difficulties for other traffic. Numbers passing through the town are now greatly reduced thanks to the bypass.

Traffic hold-ups did occur but the causes were far from Honiton. Each Saturday in the summer months vehicles were at a standstill for long periods, stretching from Exeter to Axminster, all owing to the bottleneck at the Exeter swing-bridge.

Honiton constables were on traffic point duty from 8am until after 6pm, both at the Station Road junction in the town centre and at Sidmouth Corner. Without such controls drivers would have found it impossible to emerge from the secondary roads. Even with their efforts, Honiton station would receive frantic calls from Exmouth, Budleigh Salterton and Sidmouth police reporting that lines of traffic stretched from these resorts to Honiton.

**Constable Frank Harding,** directing traffic at Honiton.
Photo courtesy of Frank Harding

The worst hold-up occurred on the Saturday preceding the 1939 August Bank Holiday, when there was a continuous line of vehicles from the Dorset border to the Plymouth side of Ivybridge, 60 miles of frustrated motorists and their hapless passengers! It appeared that almost every car owner in the country had decided to visit the Westcountry, possibly realising that war was almost inevitable and that car driving would then be severely restricted.

When off duty, the single constables at Honiton could occasionally escape office manning and telephone duty by volunteering to act as observers in one of the two motor patrol cars when a crew member was on weekly rest day. The crews at that time were Motor Patrol Constables 'Bill' Kingdom, with Sam Hawkins (who had joined the department and arrived at Honiton on 1st April 1939), and 'Buddy' Willcocks, with Leslie Dart.

The 'concession' was eagerly sought after, despite the constable concerned having to be prepared to miss a meal and leave the patrol car with virtually only a minute or so prior to the deadline for reporting for beat patrol duty.

OFFICIAL INSTRUCTIONS ISSUED BY THE MINISTRY OF HOME SECURITY

# GAS ATTACK

## HOW TO PUT ON YOUR GAS MASK

Always keep your gas mask with you – day and night. Learn to put it on quickly. Practise wearing it.

1. Hold your breath. 2. Hold mask in front of face, with thumbs inside straps.
3. Thrust chin well forward into mask, pull straps over head as far as they will go.
4. Run finger round face-piece taking care head-straps are not twisted.

## IF THE GAS RATTLES SOUND

1. Hold your breath. Put on mask wherever you are. Close window.

2. If out of doors, take off hat, put on your mask. Turn up collar.

3. Put on gloves or keep hands in pockets. Take cover in nearest building.

## IF YOU GET GASSED

*BY VAPOUR GAS*

Keep your gas mask on even if you feel discomfort
If discomfort continues go to First Aid Post

*BY LIQUID or BLISTER GAS*

| 1 | 2 | 3 | 4 |
|---|---|---|---|
| Dab, but *don't rub* the splash with handkerchief. Then destroy handkerchief. | Rub No. 2 Ointment well into place. *(Buy a 6d. jar now from any chemist).* In emergency chemists supply Bleach Cream free. | If you can't get Ointment or Cream within 5 minutes wash place with soap and warm water | Take off at once any garment splashed with gas. |

***Gas attack instructions.*** *Issued by the Ministry of Home Security at the outbreak of war.*
*Devon & Cornwall Constabulary Museum archives*

# CHAPTER 9
# THE DAY WAR BROKE OUT

The 3rd of September 1939 came with the Prime Minister, Neville Chamberlain, addressing the nation over the radio waves, announcing that we were at war with Germany. He detailed the lies, the disregard of treaties and the merciless invasions that Hitler had instigated, and, whilst all of us were extremely worried at the outcome, it seemed that the public fully supported the declaration of war.

The force was on immediate wartime alert and the brief air raid precaution instruction that we had received whilst recruits, from Sergeant 'Sam' Kelly, now became all too relevant. Previously issued steel helmets and service-type gas masks were carried whilst on duty, and at other times were always kept to hand. All leave was cancelled, and for several months police personnel were ordered to report to the police station whenever there was an air raid warning. We remained on the station until the 'all clear' was sounded. In the early days of the war, air raid warnings 'yellow' occurred as many as four or five times daily, resulting in almost continuous attendances at stations. Later, the requirement to report to our stations was reduced to only 'red' (air raid imminent) warnings, which were always subject to the air raid sirens being sounded.

These sirens were fitted on all urban police stations as well as on divisional stations, but in the rural areas details of impending air raids were telephoned to the county beat constable. He then immediately donned his steel helmet, mounted his cycle and rode through his beat either blowing his whistle or furiously twirling his hand-rattle, intermittently shouting: "Take cover, take cover, air raid, air raid".

Trains began arriving at Devon railway stations loaded with hundreds of children, 'evacuees' from urban areas. Voluntary workers had worked desperately hard persuading local householders to billet these bewildered, often frightened, children, some of whom were little more than babies. The first trainloads were dealt with quite quickly, places having already been found for every child, but as more and more children arrived accommodation difficulties arose and some quite unsuitable people were pressed into accepting them. Whilst, on the whole, householders treated their wards with kindness, taking them off on arrival with promises of 'treats' at their new homes, inevitably there were exceptions where children were left in no doubt that they were unwelcome and unwanted.

***Evacuated children** arriving at Torquay railway station at the outbreak of war in 1939. Sergeant 'Harry' Gale, the left one of the two sergeants, is pictured supervising the arrival of these lost and bewildered children.*

*Courtesy of Mr K. E. Gale*

One incident, in Honiton, involved a child under four years of age. Nicely dressed and well-spoken, there was little doubt that she was from a good home and some mother's pride and joy. Like so many arrivals, she was tearful and very frightened as she alighted from the train and became separated from her little group of now familiar children.

The harassed, sorely-pressed billeting officers had allocated the infant to a local spinster. To them she was just the occupier of a Honiton address, but I knew that she was simple-minded, lived in utter squalor and was quite unsuitable to foster anyone's child. She was walking the infant off the station platform when I first saw and stopped them, and she became very agitated when I gently led them back to an official. Fortunately, whilst a decision was being made as to her suitability, her agitation worsened into a screaming rage, with her descending to gutter language and with arms flailing, making it obvious that she was totally unfit to have charge of any young person.

She would probably have been kind to the child, treating her more as a doll or toy, but her changing moods could have been traumatic to her ward. Like so many incidents in a police career, we have no knowledge of the subsequent effect that our actions had on those directly concerned. In the majority of cases we honestly do our best, and can only hope that our decisions are the right ones. On this occasion I like to think that my action, upsetting to the adult, was absolutely right for the child.

The first few days of the war saw the departure of policemen who were service reservists, they being replaced by the recall of recently retired police constables and sergeants. These replacements were great assets to the force, bringing with them their vast experience and utter dependability in all situations. All were men who had joined the police service prior to the 1914-18 war, served in one of the armed services during those calamitous years and returned to complete their 26 years service in the force. I cannot recall one with whom I served, or came into contact with, ever complaining at having, once again, to be working a beat, suffering split turns and night duty, despite being recalled from their well-earned retirement.

***Reserve Constable 'Fred' Connett of Tavistock,*** *pictured in the centre. He is seen here with Inspector 'Jack' Derges, the officer in charge at Tavistock in the 'H' division, along with Constable Arthur Walters of the Whitchurch beat. Constable Connett had served in the Devon Constabulary, also at Whitchurch, subsequently retiring and being replaced by Constable Arthur Walters who is also seen here in uniform, on the left. Constable Connett had volunteered for military service in 1914, being attached to one of the police 'old contemptible' regiments, working with heavy horses at the front, drawing large guns. He eventually succumbed, only a few years after this photograph was taken, to a chest ailment which he contracted as a result of being gassed at Ypres. At the outbreak of the Second World War Constable Connett was still living in retirement at Whitchurch and was recalled for police duty. Such officers, known as the First Police Reserve, wore the uniform of a constable, and carried out identical duties to those of the regular constables; they were also paid.*

*Courtesy of Mr D. Connett*

In addition to these veterans, the force gradually brought in P.W.R.s (police war reserves), mainly local special constables, and later W.A.P.C.s (women's auxiliary police constables), the latter being engaged entirely on office and telephone duties. Although uniformed, they were never called upon to do patrol or traffic duties. The police war reserve officers did identical duties to their 'regular' and 'reserve constable' colleagues. Several remained in the police service long after the war had ended; indeed, at Tiverton Police War Reserve Constable Richard 'Dick' Squires remained as a police constable until well into the 1960s.

***Women's Auxiliary Police Constables, Headquarters, 1944***

*The headquarters contingent of the women's auxiliary police constables, pictured with the Chief Constable, Major Morris, and the Assistant Chief Constable, the legendary A. E. Martin. They are: Standing, left to right: Margaret Carter (her father was a policeman), Rita Joan Summers (later to marry Constable Charles Harris), Rosemary Dalling (she married an American serviceman), Miss Buckingham (her brother was a policeman), June (surname unknown, but she came from Exmouth) and Ida Clemo (she came from Tavistock). Front row, left to right: Kay (surname unknown, but was later dismissed from the service for 'indiscretions' with some American servicemen), Yvonne Parsons (later to marry Constable 'Jimmy' Green), Assistant Chief Constable A.E. Martin, Chief Constable Major Morris MC, Olive Powesland (she was a married lady who worked in the C.I.D. office with Superintendent Harvey) and Mrs Lethbridge (who came from Exeter).*

*Courtesy of Mrs Rita Joan Harris (nee Summers)*

***Above.*** *Members of the Plymouth city women's auxiliary police service at the Greenbank force headquarters (which was subjected to enemy bombardment), a prime target during the blitz on the city.*
***Below.*** *An Exeter city sergeant with a group of Exeter city women's auxiliary police service officers. Affectionately called 'WAPSies' by their male colleagues, they were held in high regard for uncomplainingly and tirelessly working long hours during the blitz on their city.*
*Devon & Cornwall Constabulary Museum archives*

***A senior officer and clerk typist in the control room at force headquarters, Exeter.***
*Devon & Cornwall Constabulary Museum archives*

***Air raid control room at force headquarters, Exeter.***
*Devon & Cornwall Constabulary Museum archives*

My stay at Honiton proved to be of short duration, my transfer to Newton Abbot being caused to a great extent by my own actions and also the pressing need to transfer a man from that station to another. Whatever the cause, it did have a marked effect on the lives of at least four people.

The events that led to me being the 'chosen one' at the Honiton end commenced with the cancellation of rest days and our working seven days a week. We three beat patrol probationers, Bert Wykes, Frank West and I, were found additional odd jobs to engage our 'off-duty' hours.

Being on day turn, 9.30am to 1.30pm and 5.30pm to 9.30pm, I told Sergeant Eddy that the next afternoon, Saturday, I wished to attend the local cinema show. He immediately replied that he required me to man the telephone, but had no answer to my statement that I had carried out this duty every day of that week and that Saturday would my last chance to see the particular film being screened. My promise to inform the cinema usherette where she could locate me in the case of an emergency did not placate the sergeant, but he was obliged to give way, albeit very reluctantly.

Unknown to any of us at Honiton, a much greater drama had occurred at Newton Abbot, causing the heads of several senior officers to be furiously scratched. The main character involved was Constable 227 Charles Young Brown, already a rarity in the force, he being a divorcee bringing up a young daughter. He had divorced his wife for infidelity and been transferred from his country station to Newton Abbot, where he and his daughter were in lodgings.

Off-duty hours were difficult for him, his married colleagues enjoying such periods in their homes, whilst the single men were otherwise engaged and certainly had no wish to be in the company of a much older constable. But night duty turns were probably the most difficult for him. Having put his daughter to bed, he had the evening hours to fill before reporting for duty. His options were few in those pre-television days - either to sit in the lodgings listening to the radio or to go out visiting local hostelries.

He favoured the latter but lack of cash made such excursions beyond his pocket and had already gained him a reputation in the station of being a scrounger. To overcome his money problem he developed what the probationary constables called the 'Brown system'. His method of operation was as follows. He would trawl the Newton Abbot public houses and, on reaching his first port of call, gently push the door open an inch or so and survey the customers within. If he espied a possible victim he quietly walked in and, coming up behind the chosen man, slapped him on the shoulder, at the same time warmly greeting him: "Evening Mr ..." or "Evening (first name, whenever known). Long time since I've had the pleasure of seeing you", plus any other pleasantry he could rattle off in the one breath.

The usually startled recipient of the verbal barrage normally responded, ending with the looked-for "What'll you have?", and Charles Brown, expressing both surprise and pleasure, invariably ended with a request for "a pint of best bitter". As soon as the pint was drawn and in his hand, our man again expressed warm thanks to his benefactor, raised the glass and the pint disappeared in one gulp!

Placing the empty glass on the bar counter, often beside the still partially-filled glass of the dupe, Charles again warmly expressed his gratitude, rounding off with "Got to go now, remember next time it's my round", and then immediately made his departure. On to another hostelry and yet another 'friend', and so on until it was time to return to his lodgings, put on tunic and helmet, pick up his packed meal and walk the 200 yards to the station in order to sign on for duty.

On the fateful night he had been over-successful in his forays, arriving at least pleasantly lubricated; possibly unfit for duty, especially a long night's duty. Recognising his condition, his colleagues stood one either side supporting him whilst orders were read, wrote out his points for the night and shuffled him out of the charge-room and on to his beat, where he was on his own.

Unfortunately he was not sobered up by the early October night air and, when he reached Marks and Spencer's store in Courtenay Street, he either went to try the door and missed the handle or fell against the door, smashing the plate glass and being precipitated into the store. The crash and noise of breaking glass brought police and public running to the spot and there was no way in which his slurred speech and stumbling steps could be covered up.

Normally he would have been suspended and then dismissed, but it was wartime *and* he held the King's Police Medal for gallantry. He had been awarded this medal because 12 years earlier, on the morning of 3rd June 1927, whilst a married man stationed at Whitestone, he had been on the platform of the Central Station, Exeter, on the old Southern Railway, when the station fire alarm bell had begun to ring and smoke been seen billowing out of the restaurant rooms on the upper floor of the building. At that time railway restaurants catered for very large numbers of the public and, at the Central Station, nine catering staff were employed. Most had escaped from the fire but one waitress had reported that the manager, a Mr Smith, was trapped in the blazing restaurant.

P.C. Brown had dashed up the stairs towards the restaurant area but been so overcome by the flames and smoke that he had collapsed, fallen down the stairs and had had to be rescued by members of the Exeter Fire Brigade. He had sustained burns to his hands and face and been rushed to the Devon and Exeter Hospital, where he had received treatment and been detained. (On hearing the fire bell Mr Smith had run into the fire area before retreating to make his escape by another stairway.)

The *Express and Echo* newspaper had reported in detail Constable Brown's brave action for which, in due course, he had received a commendation from the Chief Constable, followed, early in 1928, by the award of the King's Police Medal for gallantry.

Finally, in 1939, the Assistant Chief Constable decided that P.C. Brown should be admonished, fined *and* transferred to a station where he would be subject to strict supervision. With a superintendent (Marshall) and a sergeant (James Eddy) both lay-preachers and strict teetotallers, what better place than Honiton?

The consequent transfer from Honiton lay between the three single men. Which one was it to be? Obviously the man who so recently had shown signs of dissension, if not mutiny! So I was removed to Newton Abbot!

Constable Brown quickly settled in at Honiton and, in due course, prevailed upon the extremely reserved, shy spinster in the post office to marry him. This one-time hard drinker (he had had an earlier punishment for drinking whilst on duty) then retired after 25 years service and he and his wife spent the rest of their working lives abroad, as missionaries.

***Above.*** *War Reserve Constable 192 Henry Lyle of the Exeter City Police, with his distinctive 'WR' on his collar. He served in the war reserve police from 1943 to 1948.*

*Mrs Sylvia Payne*

***Below.*** *Constable Arthur Lemon, photographed outside a heavily-fortified Okehampton police station. As mentioned previously, it was a divisional headquarters and therefore a vulnerable target for enemy bombing raids.*

*Frank Harding*

# CHAPTER 10
# NEWTON ABBOT

I removed by train and at Newton Abbot railway station hired the town porter to take my baggage to the police station in Union Street, at a cost of half a crown .

The only way into the police station was by the constantly-locked charge-room door, reached via a narrow passageway between the building and an outer 'wall' of sandbags, every other ground floor entrance door and window being completely blocked with sandbags. Entry was gained by ringing the doorbell; the charge-room officer checked who wished to enter, then unlocked the door and admitted the person. Later this changed to anyone wishing to enter ringing the bell, when the charge-room constable would pull a string connected to an arm soldered on to the Yale lock button and shout: "Come in".

After Dunkirk, he was armed with a World War I ·45 revolver, which he wore holstered on a Sam Browne belt and strap. No one liked being so equipped as it seemed inappropriate for a policeman to be carrying a gun, and after a few months the holstered gun was usually left on the desk. This led to a near-fatality and an immediate tightening of the system. A constable entered the charge-room and, whilst chatting to the constable in charge, took the revolver from the holster. For some quite unknown reason he touched the trigger, there was a terrifying bang, and Constable Cyril 'Dutchy' Holland shouted: "You've shot me!"

It was true. Dutchy was leaning on his folded arms behind the desk and the revolver bullet passed through his upper right arm. He had been a carpenter before joining the force and had well-developed biceps; the bullet caused a gaping wound, but this healed quite quickly and, apart from the scarring, there was no lasting damage. An inch or so and it would have been a different story!

The constable responsible for the incident was a man previously destined for early promotion, but this promise was blighted by his foolish action - his promotion to sergeant was delayed until after he had served 23 years, and he was to retire in that rank four years later.

Immediately above the charge-room and adjoining telephone room were the single men's dormitories. Each room was completely bare except for a single bed, mattress, bedding and a chair. Along one wall was a line of wall hooks on which to hang uniforms and other outer garments, but there was nothing in which to put footwear (which went under the bed), shirts or underclothing.

Within a few days of taking over the last dormitory I went to Messrs Cross's auction rooms in East Street and obtained a huge chest of drawers for £1. Later I bought a chair, and within a few months all of us had 'furnished' our rooms with sundry pieces. It was fortunate that we did our 'furnishing' at that time. A few months later and prices of second-hand furniture had doubled! None of us put down any floor covering because we were ordered not to do so; the senior officers preferred to see 'snow-white' floorboards (resulting from our weekly scrubbing of them) during their regular inspections of our quarters.

In pre-1939 days one of the strongest crime deterrents was public opinion and condemnation. Woe betide the youngster who had a policeman call at his home, not so much for the offence he was alleged to have committed but on account of the 'disgrace of the police visit'.

For example, my grandparents had a shop in Russell Street, Plymouth, adjoining their landlord's builders' yard. Altering the premises, he had set the entrance door back some 20 feet from the pavement and, on each side of the passageway, had built a narrow showroom window, just wide enough to house examples of the then new-style tiled fireplaces.

A 14-year-old girl, in her first job, passed the show windows and central passageway on her way home and one evening told her parents that a man standing in the passageway had stepped out, flung open his raincoat and been 'rude'. Details were passed to the police, and the girl told to keep to her usual routine. A few nights later as she approached the passageway, her heels making their usual clatter, out stepped a man who threw open the front of his raincoat; in that second a constable, who had been silently following the girl, grabbed the article that was being exhibited.

I have been inclined to consider that the constable lacked intelligence because, as his hand closed over the item, he enquired: "What's this, then?". He really should have known!

The upshot of the matter was that the man, a clerk in the builder's office, appeared before the Plymouth magistrates, was fined and also lost his job. But, to him, the worst punishment was having his name and address, together with full details of his actions, published in the local papers - the *Evening Herald*, the *Western Morning News* and the *Sunday Western Independent*. He lived in the same neighbourhood as my family in Laira, Plymouth, and to my knowledge never ventured out of his house in daylight from that day in 1935, when he was convicted, until I left home in 1938. That was the power of public opinion in those days and why so many offenders made such great efforts to have details of their offences kept out of the newspapers.

The period 1919-1939 was, possibly, also the zenith of public esteem for the police. We enjoyed the confidence of most people, with any call for assistance or information readily answered. Violence was virtually unknown, whilst the use of firearms - even immediately after the 1918 armistice - when so many servicemen brought home 'souvenirs', occurred so infrequently that the incidents were almost always 'front page news'.

Our instructor, Inspector Webber, spoke of a "drunken man lying in the gutter, held down by three men, Starkey, Knight and Ford" (the name of the brewery in Fore Street, Tiverton), and, explaining the importance of maintaining good relations with the public, advised us to "treat the drunk firmly but kindly, so that the public, witnessing your actions, will approve and be supportive".

He also prophesied that our hard-won approval would be lost owing to another trio of men - Austin, Ford and Morris - to wit the manufacturers of the majority of cars on British roads in those days. That has manifestly been proved correct; put a man in a car and his character seems to change from upholder of the law to that of potential lawbreaker. The deterioration of police/public co-operation and respect seems to be in direct proportion to the ever-increasing number of vehicle drivers that there are today.

In charge of the division was Superintendent Francis Coppin, a benign, kindly man, who had joined the force in 1908, had at one time been the county lorry driver and could have retired on full pension in 1934. Instead, he had been promoted to inspector just before his retirement date and then, three years later, had again been promoted, each promotion being a sufficient 'carrot' to persuade him to continue serving.

His second in command was Inspector Hulland, who had removed from Crediton in the big shuffle occasioned by the promotion of 'A.E.M.' in 1938. He was an excellent policeman, but we probationers found him to be of rather uncertain temper and avoided having much contact with him. He was a 'night bird' and made as many points at 3am as he made at 3pm.

One Saturday about noon, early in October 1939, Inspector Hulland picked me up from my beat and took me to Kingskerswell. On the way he explained that there had been a fatality in one of the local quarries. At the quarry, we learned that dumper drivers had been loading their vehicles with recently blasted stone. They were driving the loads to the upper edge of the higher level and dumping the stone over the quarry face for subsequent crushing.

The procedure was to drive the dumpers as close as possible to the top level of the quarry face, slam on the dumper brakes and, at the same time, release the tipping lock. This resulted in the load being tipped while the fierce braking ensured that the dumper was completely emptied.

One driver had misjudged the distance from the edge and, as he tipped his load, the sudden movement of the stone had caused the dumper, load and he himself to go over, crashing to the lower level some 50 feet below. A doctor had already certified that he had died, probably instantaneously, and we were left with the responsibility of arranging the removal of the deceased to the Newton Abbot mortuary and informing the next of kin of the fatality.

As Inspector Hulland was instructing me to obtain details of the man's family, we were approached by a very large man who informed us in no uncertain terms that he did not want the police ("you lot") to frighten the man's widow, adding: "I'm a friend of the family and I'll do it. It'll come better from me". Inspector Hulland accepted the offer but added that I should accompany the man to the house, explaining that details had to be obtained for inclusion in the report to His Majesty's Coroner. This was grudgingly accepted by the 'friend', and we walked off together towards the home of the deceased's widow.

We were only a few yards from the quarry gates when the 'friend' stated that he would like to approach the house on his own, with me out of sight. After he had informed the lady of the tragedy, he would explain that the police required necessary details and would call me. This would prevent her from being too shocked. I agreed.

We had walked on for another short distance when he had another suggestion; perhaps it would be better if I stood on the corner whilst he went to the house. The lady would see me and realise something was wrong, making his task of breaking the news a little easier. Again I agreed.

We reached a turn in the road and he indicated the home of the deceased. I stayed on the corner, as arranged, whilst he strode off towards the house. He had gone perhaps ten paces when he stopped, turned, and walked back to me. Throwing his arms in the air, he said: "I can't do it, mate. You're on your own", and hurriedly made off back towards the quarry. I never saw him again.

The newly-made widow answered my knock on her door, I went through the usual routine of asking to be admitted and requesting her to sit down before informing her that her husband had been involved in an accident at the quarry, and finally told her that her husband was dead, though mercifully without having suffered any pain.

She stared and then calmly said: "He can't be dead, he's going to pick in the apples this afternoon". However, gradually the full impact of my words hit her and she collapsed. A neighbour was called, who comforted and quietened the widow before I took my leave. Such are the jobs that the police have always accepted and which the public take for granted that we do without, presumably, being affected in any way.

Sergeant 'Bill' Lamb was the resident sergeant, a much-respected and liked officer. He had been stationed at headquarters at the time of the murder of Constable Potter and had played a leading role in the arrest of the two offenders.

In charge of the C.I.D. was Detective Sergeant (later Detective Inspector) 'Jack' Vickery, an affable, imperturbable man, who had Detective Constables 'Bill' Carpenter, 'Bill' Harvey, Alfred Abrahams and 'Freddie' Brooks as his aides.

The Air Raid Precautions Department was headed by Sergeant 'Alf' Worden, assisted by Constable Wiltshire - a very handy 'handy-man', who had soldered the latch on the charge-room door Yale lock and was forever preparing models and visual aids for use at A.R.P. lectures together with War Reserve Constable Friskney, who had retired from the Metropolitan Police prior to the outbreak of war and joined the Devon Constabulary in preference to returning to London.

Friskney (we never were on first-name terms with him) had been a sergeant but would not disclose just what he had done in the 'Mets'. His reticence made the matter all the more interesting, and there were many suggestions as to what 'secret' work had engaged him prior to retirement; Flying Squad, Special Branch, Royal Attachment, House of Commons or Downing Street, even down to being in the force band. No matter how we tried to wheedle the true facts, Friskney kept his career details to himself. It was not until after the war that I learned that he had transferred to the Metropolitan Police library shortly after completing his two years probationary period and remained within its hallowed walls until his retirement.

The divisional office was in the charge of Sergeant 'Len' Luxton, his assistant being Constable Arthur Dawe, who, in later years, became a sergeant himself and, after retiring as officer in charge of the Cullompton section, was appointed Deputy Registrar of Marriages for the city of Exeter. Meanwhile, from early 1941, Sergeant Luxton and Constable Dawe were assisted in the divisional office at Newton Abbot by four of the many women auxiliary police constables to join the force, carrying out day duties, these being Dorcas Knight (telephone duties), Mabel Marsh (CID), 'Betsy' Mole (divisional office clerk) and Mrs Smith (telephone duties).

The motor patrol officers were Constables 'Spud' Baker and Arthur Chappell. They were later joined by MPC 'Frank' Zanazzi (Frank had been one of my teachers at my Plymouth school, Mutley College) and his observer, 'Larry' Hurrell. They had a soft-top Ford Prefect, whilst Baker and Chappell shared an Austin 10 saloon. These cars had no radios, flashing lights, sirens or heaters. The tourer, in particular, was a draught-filled refrigerator!

The beat men were 'Bill' Lentle and Stanley Searle, and a number of single constables, 'Len' Blamey, Cyril Holland, Harold Pearce, Kenneth Reid and Sidney Walters. The war reservists just recalled to serve with us were:-

Constable 413 Cotton, who had joined the force in August 1910, served in the army during the First World War, rejoined the police service and served until 1936, when he took his pension to become the Newton Abbot Prevention of Cruelty to Animals inspector. (Newton Abbot has maintained its own P.C.A. for many years, quite independent of the national association, the R.S.P.C.A.)

Constable 87 Loosemoore, who had been appointed in May 1914, joined the army in January 1916 and served until 1919, when he returned to constabulary duties. He had been retired only three months when he was recalled in 1939 and went on to serve until 1945.

Constable 268 Tooze, who had been born in 1878 and become a 'third class' constable (a probationer in today's terms) in 1899. He had then served in the army from 1915 until 1919 before returning to the force and eventually retiring in 1925.

Constable 397 Pook, who had been born in 1888, become a 'third class' constable in 1909, served in the army from 1914 to 1919 and retired from the force in 1938.

Constable 366 Woolland, who was the 'baby' of these men. He had retired from the Kingsteignton beat on 31st May 1939 after serving (with army war service) exactly 26 years, having been appointed on 1st June 1913.

[The war reservists were all good-humoured, tolerant men, who had experienced desperate days, both in the police service and the Great War. All were constables that I was proud to have served with, and from whom we probationers learned so much.

When they had been issued with their first uniforms and accoutrements one item had been a 'bull's eye' lantern. These were oil-burning lamps with a stout clip at the rear for slipping on to the leather belts then worn outside their tunics. On night and late turn duties the constables had invariably worn capes, with the lamp burning and supplying warmth to cold hands under the garment.

As the 'bull's eye' implies, the lamps each had a thick bulbous glass which gave some magnification to the small round wick burning inside. The top had fluted vents connected to a skirt within the body of the lamp. By twisting the lamp top this skirt revolved, completely masking the glass.

At night the constable would come upon a person or matter requiring illumination, and by flicking open his cape and, at the same time deftly twisting the lamp top, he 'flooded' the area with light. At least that was the desired effect!

The fuel for these lamps was the reason for the second portion of the payment drawn by policemen, the 'boot and oil' quarterly allowance of about nine shillings. From the reserve constables' stories no part of the allowance was ever 'wasted' on purchasing such burning oil. Instead, a visit was made to the nearest railway station's store, where a sauce bottle or similar receptacle was kindly filled with the oil used in the lamps at railway signals, level crossings and, in those days, the platform and waiting rooms.

The oil was virtually odourless and smokeless when used with a properly trimmed wick. In fact, some of these reservists seemed regretful that the 'bulls eyes' had been replaced with electric torches!

From these men I learned of the importance of the 'landed gentry of Devon', with country stationed constables being at the beck and call of Lord ..., or the Earl of ..., and heaven help the constable who, it was deemed, had failed to prevent poaching on the land of Sir ... of his pheasants or other game birds. Their commencement pay had been £1.2s per week.]

Also, without exception, the country station constables in the Newton Abbot section were competent, responsible men who took pride in their work and in the uniform that they wore.

'Reg' Vinton was at Kingsteignton, reputedly then the largest village in England with a population of some 3,000. Among the residents were a large number of china clay pitmen, hard working, hard drinking tough men who ensured that 'Reg' had continual demands on his expertise in public relations and diplomacy. In addition, the beat averaged a road accident almost every day of the year, leaving the beat constable no time for hiding near road junctions to pick up 'halt sign' offences and the like.

On Reg's leave periods, weekly and annual, it was necessary for the beat to be covered by a Newton Abbot constable. One such 'relief', in particular, would pick up such minor offences. Reg's attention would be drawn to these 'successes' by Sergeant Lamb (a great 'stirrer' and 'leg puller'), but his replies are unprintable.

Kingskerswell was the domain of Constable Raymond Sanders, affable and quite unflappable, and respected by everyone with whom he had dealings. His reports were so detailed that it was apparent that he had, at one time, suffered at the hands of the querying supervisors in the 'F' division. On one occasion he submitted a report concerning the collapse of an elderly lady in her home, situated in a back road in Kingsteignton. The ambulancemen had had difficulty in locating the address, resulting in some delay in treating the stricken lady.

Raymond glossed over this by reporting: "During the 40 minutes before the arrival of the ambulance, a neighbour, Mrs ... kindly served tea and light refreshments, which was most appreciated by all those waiting".

Another time he was in Newton Abbot charge-room when a special constable enquired who was the operator at Kingskerswell with the 'huge fleet of lorries?' He explained that he had noticed the owner's name on one lorry, 'Max Speed', and caught just the one word 'Kingskerswell' on the lorry door. Raymond painstakingly detailed every quarry and other lorry owners in his beat before giving up.

A week or so later they met again, and, when assured that the last thing the special constable would contemplate was leg-pulling, Raymond kindly instructed him that 'max speed' was a shortened version of maximum speed, which should have been followed by the figure '40' - indicating that the lorry was not permitted to exceed that speed, etc. etc. - all received with rapturous attention by the straight-faced 'special'!

John Body had Ipplepen as his 'patch', which he patrolled with his constant companion, a Jack Russell. The dog helped John in turning out tramps (and courting couples) from barns, outhouses and other such havens and, on one memorable occasion, an escaped convict, who had quickly surrendered when faced with the barking and snarling animal.

John was the senior regular constable in the division, having joined the force in July 1919 shortly after being demobilised at the end of the 1914-18 war.

In the late 1920s he had served several years at Crabtree, between Plymouth and Plympton, where, when off duty, he used to sit in the police cottage watching the horse-drawn 'trains' of china clay pass his window from Lee Moor on their way to the Millbay Docks, as well as the rest of the world pass by. His main interest, however, had been espying passing servicemen - soldiers from Crownhill, sailors from ships berthed in Devonport and Royal Marines from their barracks in Stonehouse. John, and his dog of course, would then immediately confront the uniformed man and ask him to produce his pass. Being unable to do so had meant his instant detention and the inevitable questioning by the appropriate service police. For each such detention John had received one shilling, and claimed that he had made several hundred such arrests.

Shortly before 1945 John applied to retire, despite being in a reserved occupation. His superintendent, Ernest Stone, saw him and, in his usual gruff manner, told him the application had been refused, quite correctly adding: "What's your hurry to leave? Nobody's bothering or chasing you".

He and John had been in the same intake of recruits in 1919, and in their first year of service Constable Stone had had the misfortune to have a prisoner escape whilst in his charge. This would have been at least 25 years earlier, but when John was giving me his version of the interview he ended the diatribe with: "Heh!, he had the record for losing prisoners; I had the record for catching 'em"! The trouble with policemen is that they invariably have exceedingly long memories!

John Gulley at Highweek was yet another conscientious, reliable man, typical of the old school of ever-dependable constables. We probationers owed so much to these stalwarts in our first years of service.

From them I learned of the trials and differences of being a pre-1914 constable as well as in the years 1919 to 1939. Their conditions of service had been abysmal, and there had been no machinery available to improve their lot. It had not been until the editor of the *Police Review* magazine intervened on their behalf by drawing to the attention of Members of Parliament that constables received just pennies over a £1 weekly net pay, with no recognised leave days, that the police had been advised to set up a body to represent them in endeavouring to obtain better conditions. That advice had then seen the birth of the Police Federation, and with it the subsequent improvements in pay and conditions of service.

Constable Stanley Searle was one of the very few married beat patrol constables left at Newton

Abbot and it was he who took me to Elm Road, where I was to board with Constables Reid and Pearce. Our landlady was a Miss Ellis, who had been in service all her adult life until, on the advice of P.C. Searle in 1937, she had rented the Elm Road terraced house and begun boarding single constables. She was a wonderful lady; though suffering dreadfully from arthritis, she kept the little house spotless, in addition to laying a first-class table. She ensured that throughout the leanest of the rationing days we ever-hungry men were amply fed. Constable Searle was a kindly, considerate man in many other ways to that of having helped Miss Ellis to establish herself in Newton Abbot. He also had many tales of his experiences in his early days in the force, one of which particularly still remains in my memory.

Early in his service Stan had come on duty at Torquay at 9am on a sunny Sunday, to be immediately told by his sergeant that there had been a report of a body washed up on Oddicombe beach. With another young constable he was instructed to collect a stretcher from the mortuary, go to Oddicombe, locate the body and stretcher it to the mortuary at Maidenway. Having walked the three miles to the beach, successfully located and loaded the corpse (a man of some 15 stone) and then strapped down the tarpaulin cover of the stretcher, they laboriously picked their way off the beach with their load.

The first short distance walked on the solid pavement was easy compared to the sandy beach, but after a hundred yards or so their wrists and arms began aching and a short halt was necessary. On again, but the distances walked grew ever shorter and the rest breaks ever longer and soon, with the sun beating down and their high-necked heavyweight tunics making them feel as though they were in a Turkish bath, both young men were finding their task getting beyond them.

In those days the first public service omnibuses left the depot in Torquay Road at noon on Sundays. Oddicombe beach was the turning point for vehicles on that service, so it was shortly after 12.15pm that the first vehicle passed them and their load, but going in the wrong direction. A few minutes later the same vehicle overtook them on its return journey to the town centre. The vehicle slowed and then stopped, the driver asking if they wanted a lift. Thankfully they accepted and, carrying the loaded stretcher, entered the otherwise empty bus, carefully manoeuvring their load down the centre aisle until they could each take a front seat with the stretcher between them.

What joy to be relieved of the weight of the loaded stretcher and what luxury being conveyed towards Maidenway on a padded seat!

As the vehicle continued its journey passengers joined them and, horror of horrors, with every pothole covered by the solid-tyred vehicle, an indescribably nauseous smell arose from beneath the stretcher cover. The seats directly behind them had been taken by various passengers who, as the stench assailed their nostrils, moved back to the rearmost seats, some even leaving the bus - possibly because they had reached their desired point of departure, but to 'Stan's' stricken conscience undoubtedly because of the smell.

Finally the constables could no longer bear the tension, or the foul atmosphere permeating the vehicle, and hurriedly left with their 'passenger'. The experience had lent them previously unknown sources of strength and they were able to walk the remaining distance to the mortuary with not too many stops. There they carried out the various post-mortem examination preparations before reporting back to divisional headquarters.

To their relief no complaint had been made concerning their 'improper use of public transport', but for the following week they were in fear and trembling of an irate passenger on the memorable bus journey writing a letter of complaint. Such a letter could have resulted in a sacking, a fine or, at least, a reprimand. Fortunately no complaint was made and their careers continued.

Later, in each mortuary could be found a stretcher-carrier, a platform some 18 inches wide and 54 inches long, suspended between two axled cycle wheels. These made life very much easier for constables sent out to recover corpses, but in a very few years they fell into disuse. Undertakers, realising the potential income to be made from being given responsibility for the funeral arrangements, offered to do the fetching and carrying on behalf of the police.

In December 1939 I had my first experience of being offered a bribe. One night, shortly after midnight, I heard a car being driven in bottom gear along the level road of Queen Street and, as I moved towards the noisy vehicle, I was in time to see it entering the parking space between Newton Abbot railway station and the Railway Hotel. The car hit an advertisement hoarding and its engine stalled. Running to the vehicle, I helped the occupant out of the driving seat. He staggered and more than merely 'smelt of intoxicants', being a perfect example of a person who had been driving under the influence.

When told that he was under arrest, the driver started to cry, saying that he would lose his job. He then pulled his wallet out of his jacket pocket and pushed it towards me saying: "Take it, but please let me go".

At the police station he was examined by a doctor, certified as being 'under the influence of alcohol' and duly charged. I then told Sergeant Lamb that I further wanted to charge the man with attempting to bribe a police officer, recounting the occurrence. Sergeant Lamb, that wise and experienced officer, subsequently looked at me for what seemed a very long time before asking: "Was he too drunk to drive a car?"

"Oh yes, Sarge," I assured him.

"Then he must have been too drunk to know what he was doing when he offered you his wallet: you can't have it both ways!", was his reply. Ah, well - you live and learn!

When I was talking to retired Inspector Arthur Lemon recently, he recalled his one experience of attempted bribery which occurred when he was a probationary constable at Okehampton. Arthur was approached by the owner of a local cafe, who asked if he could mention her premises if he received enquiries regarding a suitable local eating place. Knowing her catering was good and reasonably priced, Arthur said that this would be no trouble. At that, without thanking him, the lady pushed a bar of chocolate into his hand. Quickly returning it to her, Arthur beat a hasty retreat. Over 50 years later he could still recall his 'terror' that someone might have witnessed the incident and reported it to his sergeant.

Food rationing began on 8th January 1940. The first items requiring the use of the coupons in the recently issued ration books were sugar, butter, fats, tea, milk, jam, fish, canned goods, meat, bacon, cheese and sweets. It led to our seeing our first 'spivs', a word then quite unknown to us but later accepted as the name for men who could obtain sundry rationed items 'at a price'. At the Newton Abbot station the single men had already had their first experience of the breed in the guise of Constable 'Happy' Pearce.

One day, at the end of December 1939, we saw that the wall of his bedroom beneath the clothing hooks was lined with dozens of identical brown packages, each labelled 'Lyons Tea, 24 x 1/4 lb' and a description of the tea packets within. 'Happy' explained that he had met the Lyons Tea representative and been told in confidence that tea would be going on ration within a week or so. He had invested over £50 in buying the tea and filling his bedroom with it, looking forward to selling it at a profit when tea became scarce. Although we had never heard the words 'black market', we probationers considered that 'Happy' was entering onto dangerous ground and should certainly be discouraged.

Somehow I was elected to show 'Happy' the error of his ways and, knowing that any appeal to his conscience would have no effect, told him that he was on course to lose money. That ensured his full attention and he listened carefully while I explained that tea deteriorated at an exceedingly fast rate, so that by the time tea was in such short supply that it would command a high price, his stocks would be reduced to useless tea dust. Did he not know that in the past tea had been rushed to this country by the famous sailing ships, the Tea Clippers, the crew of the first to arrive in the London docks sharing small fortunes by cornering the market for fresh tea?

This caused 'Happy' to enquire of other constables (already primed) as to the life expectancy of tea and to him then hurriedly going, in uniform, from shop to shop begging the grocers to relieve him of his stock. How he made out financially we never knew, but his entrepreneurial leanings were definitely dampened.

The Clerk to the Justices at Tiverton was one A.R. Penny, whose initials alone should have caused him to view members of the A.R.P. service favourably, but not so, as the following readers letters column from the *Western Morning News* clearly indicates:

*4th October 1939*

*Sir,*

*Many people will have wished to applaud Colonel Ward for his courageous fight in the county council against the appalling waste of money that is going on under the name of the A.R.P. There may be certain parts of Devon that are susceptible to attack and where it is right to take reasonable precautions but for the vast bulk of Devon - regarded by the government as a safety area - an air raid can only happen by mistake, and is just about as likely as an earthquake. I do hope that those who have come amongst us from danger zones will really feel they are safe in Devon, and that those normally resident here will continue to sleep soundly.*

*Particularly when it comes to paying for all the sandbags, trenches, whole time wardens, firemen and others who are likely to be bored stiff doing nothing for many months to come. I hope the ratepayers will face their privilege gladly.*

*A. Raymond Penny, Tiverton.*

Mr Penny was an excellent solicitor and beyond criticism insofar as his court work was concerned - but events proved him to be a terrible prophet!

Police work now entailed new responsibilities, posting warnings being one of the earliest tasks. Perhaps because it was the first instance of me having to sally forth, armed with paste, brush and notices to post, that I can still recall almost every word of the first of these:

*POLICE NOTICE*
*AIR RAID DANGER*
*CONCEAL YOUR LIGHTS*

1. *All windows, skylights, glass doors etc in private houses, shops, factories and other business premises must from today be completely screened after dusk so that no light is visible from the outside.*
2. *Dark covering must be used, so that the presence of a light within the building cannot be detected.*
3. *ALL illuminated advertisements, signs and external lights of all kinds must be extinguished, except any specially authorised traffic or railway signal lights or other specially exempted lights.*

4. *Lights on all vehicles on roads must be dimmed and screened. The police will issue leaflets describing the requirements.*
*THESE MEASURES ARE NECESSARY FOR YOUR PROTECTION IN CASE OF ATTACK.*

Air raid wardens were also heavily engaged in advising and helping the public concerning lighting regulations, and there is no doubt that their advice concerning 'blacking-out' of windows and other apertures ensured that cities, towns and villages alike became areas of almost total darkness at night. Like the police, their responsibilities increased almost week by week with a proliferation of new regulations but, despite all their efforts and being mainly unpaid volunteers, they were never appreciated by the public.

From 3rd September 1939, for every minute of every day until V.E. Day nearly six years later, the police were responsible for the guarding of key sites and installations. For example, all London to Devonport naval dockyard rail traffic passed through Dainton tunnel, just outside Newton Abbot, and this was designated to be one of literally hundreds of key targets for enemy saboteurs.

Similarly, electricity generating stations, gas works and petroleum storage depots throughout Devon were constantly patrolled by armed constables. As the demands on police personnel grew it was necessary for the regular police to be assisted by members of the special constabulary until, eventually, the 'specials' undertook nearly all the duties of guarding these vital points.

***Special Constable William Stanley Turl.*** *'Stan' was one such special constable who had joined the Devon Constabulary in 1938 and served in the force throughout the years of the Second World War. Stan was a farmer from Aylesbeare, not far from Exeter, and his duties included guarding Fenny Bridges against I.R.A. attack armed only with a whistle and truncheon. What his more modern-day counterparts might make of such a duty remains to be guessed at! Stan's daughter, Ruth, joined the force in 1970, the year before he retired from the 'specials', and took up a position in headquarters, where she now serves as secretary to the Deputy Chief Constable. Between them, Stan and Ruth have notched up over 60 years service to the constabulary.*

*Ruth Simpson*

On one occasion two 'specials' patrolling and guarding the gasometers off The Avenue, Newton Abbot, climbed the inspection ladder to the top of one gas holder. Unfortunately, one of them was able to ascend to the top rim without difficulty but, on glancing down, immediately had an attack of vertigo and became transfixed. He was unable to move either up or down and, desperately gripping the side pieces of the ladder, made it impossible for his companion above him to descend. To them it was a long, long time before their shouts for help were heard and even longer before their plight was understood and the fire service called. There was always a competitive edge between the fire service and the police, so the rescue of the 'specials' was made the most of by the firemen, much to the annoyance of Superintendent Coppin and Bill Copp, their sergeant.

Another duty in which the police were involved was in accompanying ministry men making valuations and compulsory purchases of lorries for the armed services. We visited the yards of hauliers, millers, forestry workers and other professionals with two or more heavy goods vehicles. Those who had purchased new vehicles, realising war was inevitable, were the worst affected. Their new, or nearly new, trucks were eagerly taken over, whilst those with well-worn vehicles were left with their fleets intact.

In the Westcountry, apart from the extra responsibilities we undertook, we had little knowledge of the war during the months from September 1939 to April 1940. So little detail of action was publicised that this period was dubbed the 'phoney war'. This suddenly came to an end when, in April, we were forced to withdraw our troops from Denmark and Norway.

Even this was glossed over in the press and on the radio. (The very limited area receiving the B.B.C. television transmissions had lost their programmes immediately after the declaration of war on September 3rd), so we were totally unprepared for the collapse of the French forces, followed by the over-running of France and the low countries by the Germans in May 1940.

Dunkirk brought home to us that all the confident assurances of an early victory were merely empty propaganda, but even then we had no knowledge of how pathetically unprepared we had been when we had declared war. Our coastline was virtually undefended; for example Dover, where so many of our evacuated troops landed, was guarded by just six 6-inch guns, five 12-pounders, two 9.2 inch guns and two twin 6-pounder guns, a grand total of 15 guns!

The losses before and during the successful evacuation from France of some 400,000 troops were ignored; instead, the whole operation was proclaimed a brilliant achievement. True, it was a superb, possibly unique, operation, but certainly no 'victory'.

The Newton Abbot war reserve constables were men who had rejoined the police service after demobilisation from the 1914-18 war and they were shocked to see the state of the soldiers who began to arrive in the town at the end of May, direct from Dunkirk. Many had no uniforms and the majority had discarded their rifles whilst queuing, sometimes neck-deep in the sea, off the evacuation beaches. Our colleagues expressed utter surprise, always having been told during their war service: "Your rifle is your best friend. Look after it and guard it with your life".

The remnants of the Gloucester Regiment were based in the town immediately after their return from Dunkirk, being billeted in local halls, vacant offices and other properties. One such building was Wolborough Hall in Wolborough Street, adjoining the then Bulpin's Garage. The soldiers housed there, with others scattered throughout the town, were gradually issued with uniforms and equipment, including pre-1918 Lee Enfield ·303 rifles.

The men were subjected to long periods of intense drilling, the market car park being taken over for this purpose. At first this was mainly to keep them occupied and to reassure the civilian population that all was not lost. In a few weeks, however, the soldiers were transformed from an unkempt, bewildered, moaning, near-rabble to a disciplined smart fighting force once again.

New weapons also gradually filtered through, including a number of 'Sten guns'. These did nothing to improve the drilling qualities of the soldiers, looking more like pieces of old tubing welded together than deadly killing machines.

These Sten guns were in very short supply, resulting in only one soldier of those billeted in Wolborough Hall being issued with one. Coming off the drill ground, he put the gun on top of his kit whilst he went to the ablutions. Another soldier picked up the gun to examine it and, possibly because he had never handled such a weapon before, was clumsy in his movements. Somehow his hand brushed against the gun-trigger and a stream of bullets was projected, which cut another soldier virtually in half.

The offending man collapsed, requiring medical treatment, but no treatment was possible for his unfortunate colleague. Men were charged and punishments allotted, but valuable lessons were also learnt, and there were no further shooting incidents involving the 'Gloucesters' during the remainder of their stay in the town.

After Dunkirk the whole of the country was stirred out of its previous cheerful 'everything will be all right' attitude. In addition, enemy aerial attacks became regular features affecting everyone, whilst the night attacks on Plymouth brought home to us just how vulnerable we all were.

***The Plymouth blitz.*** *Officers were drafted in to the city of Plymouth in order to reinforce their hard-pressed colleagues. Here Constables Charles Richards (on the left) and Ira Barrett (centre), of the Cornwall Constabulary, are pictured with a Plymouth city war reserve constable outside a city shop during an air raid. The only illumination used to take this picture was the burning building opposite the officers.*
*Western Morning News*

Appeals went out to the nation for all privately-owned weapons to be brought to police stations to be used 'in the defence of our homeland'. Many strange, even weird, weapons were delivered into our hands. Shotguns, all ancient, were brought in and might have been of some use in a suicide attack on enemy paratroopers; the *Daily Express* had printed a method, with illustrations, as to how a shotgun cartridge with its casing carefully reduced to a single paper thickness could be fired, resulting in a lethal 'bullet' leaving the gun. The fact that such an article was written and published gives an indication of just how desperate the situation was in the immediate 'post-Dunkirk' period. At Newton Abbot the African spears, rusted swords and other 'weapons' (even a boomerang!) merely littered the cell in which the contributions were stored.

# ANTI-PERSONNEL BOMBS ARE BEING USED

On the night of June 13/14 1943 the enemy, in an attack on an East Coast town, used a large number of these bombs along with about 6,000 incendiaries.

**These three photographs show how the anti-personnel ("Butterfly") bomb actually comes down. If in the ceiling of a room, it may explode downwards and sideways with terrific force. Pending disposal of the bomb, the room concerned and those immediately above, below and on either side must be vacated.**

When an attack from the air develops and incendiaries are dropped in numbers, the police and Civil Defence services should use their handlamps freely to detect the presence of any anti-personnel bombs, and the N.F.S. and fireguards may remove the dimming material from their torches.

**EVERY WARDEN SHOULD MAKE HIMSELF FAMILIAR WITH THE INSTRUCTIONS FOR THEIR TREATMENT.**
(C.D. Training Pamphlet No. 1)

NEVER TOUCH AN ANTI-PERSONNEL BOMB IN ANY CIRCUMSTANCES WHATEVER; THEY ARE LIABLE TO EXPLODE AT THE SLIGHTEST CONTACT.

**Bomb has Penetrated Ground—Wings Left Above**

**Bomb Caught in Roof—Looking Upwards**

(8/43) (29558r) Wt. 29463—428 25m 9/43 D.L. G. 373

**Separated Wings**

**Body of Bomb**

**Bomb Detached on Floor of Loft —Wings Left in Roof**

*An anti-personnel bomb warning leaflet. These were distributed to police stations early in the war.*

*Devon & Cornwall Constabulary Museum archives*

B02/4

# DANGER

## SMALL ANTI-PERSONNEL BOMB

**BEWARE** OF THESE BOMBS WHICH ARE VERY DESTRUCTIVE AND ARE MEANT TO DO YOU HARM.

THEY MAY BE FOUND

● – LIKE THIS – OR – LIKE THIS –

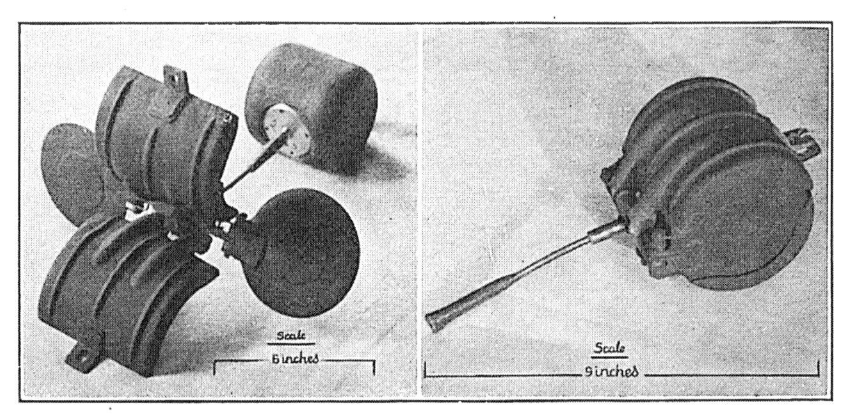


BOMB WITH CASING OPEN — BOMB WITH CASING CLOSED

● IF YOU SEE THEM DO NOT TOUCH, KEEP AWAY AND REPORT THEM TO THE WARDENS OR POLICE

DO NOT TOUCH SUSPICIOUS OBJECTS
REPORT THEM TO WARDENS OR POLICE

*Issued by the Ministry of Home Security*

4/43 (19037) 21682/321 50,000 7/43 K.H.K. Gp. 8/8

*Ministry of Home Security information leaflet concerning small anti-personnel bombs.*
*Devon & Cornwall Constabulary Museum archives*

# CHAPTER 11
# FLYING DUTIES IN THE RAF

All police officers serving after the immediate call-up of 'armed services reservists' in September 1939 were deemed to be in a 'reserved occupation', but from about June 1941 police officers were permitted to volunteer for flying duties as pilots or observers with the Royal Air Force. Six of the single men at Newton Abbot - Cyril Holland, 'Dickie' Pitts, Ken Reid, 'Jack' Stevens (who had taken the place of 'Len' Blamey when he returned to Devonport Dockyard), 'Sid' Walters and I - applied and travelled to one of the colleges at Oxford University for medical examinations and tests.

We all passed the 'medical' but only Pitts and I passed the quite testing educational examination, although I was told that I needed a refresher in geometry before call-up. Richard George 'Dickie' Pitts was later to become a flying officer, and to be awarded the Distinguished Flying Cross.

Superintendent Coppin was relieved to have us all return for duty, albeit with the knowledge that within a short period two of his single men would be leaving.

I began cramming mathematics with boys in the local air training corps. To me they seemed very bright and terribly fit 14 to 16-year-olds, all having a higher standard of geometry than I would ever attain.

Our instructor was the headmaster of Highweek Senior School, Edwin Rogers (father of the later to be famous actor Paul Rogers). The classes were held in Newton Grammar School, and one evening he and I were leaving together, discussing some problem, just as a group of air raid wardens emerged from a school annexe on the opposite side of the road. Apparently they had been receiving instruction on identification of gases, including sniffing various odours said to be identical to war gases. As they emerged into the night air, one warden, female and very attractive, fell to the ground in a faint.

In a trice I crossed the road and rendered first aid until the young lady recovered consciousness. As she refused to have any medical assistance, I was, of course, obliged to ensure that she reached her home safely. This I did, after assuring the other wardens, mainly male, that it was all part of my job. Perhaps it was just that at the time, but the incident was, in due course, to affect the rest of my life.

Shortly afterwards a very perplexed Superintendent Coppin remarked that he just couldn't understand what was happening to his single constables as two seemed to have gone back to their childhood days. One had chicken pox ('Dutchy' Holland) and another had jaundice (me).

While I was still on sick leave my call-up papers arrived, with instructions to report to R.A.F. Air Crew Reception Centre (A.C.R.C.), so ten days later it was out of the sickbed and off to St. John's Wood in London. There, in company with hundreds of 18 to 30-year-old men, I was issued with a uniform and directed to join a group. We were then allocated an unfurnished room in the hitherto luxury flats making up the area opposite London Zoo. The zoo became very much part of our lives for the next few weeks, as we were marched there three times daily for our meals.

Another feature of our training was being marched to certain cafes where it appeared that our N.C.O. was either a part of the family or had a financial interest in the business. The long periods that we spent in these establishments, quaffing cup after cup of tea, hardly contributed to the war effort, but was much easier on our feet!

In due course our group was sent to No. 22 Initial Training Wing (I.T.W.) at Cambridge, where I had the good fortune to be housed in a dormitory in the ancient portals of Magdalen College. Our educational training and drilling was compressed, so much so that just 38 days after reporting for duty at St. Johns Wood the survivors of our group were en route to 'Marshalls', the home of the peacetime university squadrons which had formed the nucleus of the fighter squadrons that beat off the Luftwaffe in the Battle of Britain during the summer of 1941. I had my first flight on the same day, in October 1941, and, horror of horrors, was dreadfully airsick! Further flights resulted in the same malaise, resulting in my being sent for examination by a specialist, Wing Commander Grace.

***Left.*** *Pilot recruit Edward Trist, pictured in a photograph taken on 6th September 1941.*
*Edward Trist*

***Right.*** *Pilot recruit Edward Trist, seen in flying kit, 1941.*
*Edward Trist*

After a 30-minute examination, though I thought it was hours, he grounded me, and in response to my protests explained that the airsickness would slow my reaction and that after an hour or so of flying I would be a 'zombie'. When I had the temerity to say that I wanted to be in fighters, whose flight durations were an hour or less, he lost his patience and barked: "After an hour with an M.E.109 on your tail you wouldn't be capable of taking avoiding action. Besides, it isn't just you - a Spitfire costs nine thousand pounds". How times have changed! £9,000 today would not purchase a modern-day fighter's instrument panel.

That figure was an indication of the rapid rise in prices in wartime Britain. In August 1940 the Exeter evening newspaper, the *Express and Echo*, had started a fund to raise £5,000 to purchase a Spitfire, to be named 'City of Exeter'. £1,000 had been raised in ten days and the target reached in just 20 days. Even so, the newspaper had had cause to warn its readers against 'unofficial collectors'.

Grounded, I persuaded the airfield administration officer to have me in his office until I was fit enough to recommence flying training. After six weeks I travelled to Halton for a further 'medical', this time by a Wing Commander Armstrong. After reading 'Wingco' Grace's report, he gave me the most searching, thorough medical examination that I have ever endured. At the end, although stripped to the waist, I was streaming with perspiration. The result was that I was passed 'fit for all flying duties'.

Elated, I returned to 'Marshalls' and informed my administration officer, a shrewd solicitor in peacetime. He examined both reports and then said: "You know what this is. In civvy street they're both Harley Street specialists and hate each other's guts. Whatever one says, the other will say exactly the opposite".

Flying training resumed and, sadly, so did the airsickness. My new instructor, Sergeant Hardwick, was also a friend and checked with the station medical officer. His reply was succinct - holding my medical file, he said: "Winco Grace - unfit to fly. Winco Armstrong - fit for all flying duties. Me - flight lieutenant - no comment".

He was good enough to arrange that every day I had a large dose of belladonna immediately before flying. This did little for the airsickness but definitely slowed down my reactions, finally resulting in me being grounded by the chief flying instructor - a charming man and a brilliant pilot whom I nearly killed when failing to recover quickly enough whilst in a spin a hundred or so feet from ground level!

***Plymouth bombsite 1941.*** *A young man surveys the debris of a recent air raid on the city.*
*Devon & Cornwall Constabulary Museum archives*

***Plymouth street corner,*** *photographed during the blitz. The sign to the nearest A.R.P. shelter is affixed to the wall of the gutted premises of W. J. Rundle, on the corner of a street in the city centre.*

*Devon & Cornwall Museum archives*

# CHAPTER 12
# RETURN TO THE FORCE

Unable to fly, I was obliged to return to the force and, moreover, to continue in service, as my subsequent efforts to join the army were aborted. Discharged from the R.A.F. on 13th April 1942, I made the journey from Blackpool on the first available train, starting at 6am on the 14th. On the way to Exeter we experienced an air raid and several precautionary stops before I was able to report to the newly-built police headquarters at Middlemoor, on the outskirts of Exeter, at about 9am on the following day.

*An artist's impression of the new headquarters building at Middlemoor, on the outskirts of Exeter city.*
*Devon & Cornwall Constabulary Museum archives*

There, I was seen by the chief clerk, Superintendent Garnish. He examined my discharge certificate, pointed out that I had been discharged two days before and was not at all happy with my explanation of the air raid and other hold-ups causing the train journey to be of over 24 hours duration. He remarked flatly: "You are no longer in the air force but back in the Devon Constabulary. Where were you last stationed?" Having been told "Newton Abbot sir", he instructed me to go to the stores department, pick up my uniform, and await a patrol car to take me to Newton Abbot. This took some time but I eventually arrived at Newton Abbot at about 4pm, to be warmly welcomed back by Superintendent Coppin. He then allowed me to continue my journey to my home, enabling me to pick up boots, clothing and other necessities prior to starting back on the beat at 9am the following day.

Much had changed in my absence. All constables who had been under 25 years of age on 3rd September 1939 had been taken out of their 'reserved occupation' category and were awaiting call-up into the armed services.

Inspector Hulland had been replaced by Inspector Burgess, while the police war reserves had been augmented by three local ex-special constables, Browne, Churchward and Smith.

The main difference was in the considerable ageing of the supervisory officers. Every man, from sergeants to the superintendent, were haggard and toil-worn, due much to the ever-increasing requirement to turn out on every air raid warning, together with the increased responsibilities each had had thrust upon him.

It was at about this time that the requirement to turn out for air raid warnings 'yellow' (enemy aircraft expected) was relaxed. Unfortunately enemy air raids were tending to increase, resulting in the police being on standby duties almost every night, frequently until, with the dawn, came the long-awaited 'all clear' drone on the sirens.

I had been back in 'the job' just a few days and was on night duty when there was an enemy air raid in Newton Abbot in the early morning of 25th April 1942. There were a number of civilian casualties, including three locally-based 'specials'. Area officer Samuel Chetham had taken two of his men, 'Fred' Pearse and 'Jimmy' Scawn, out on patrol. They had reached the junction of East Street and Devon Square when an enemy bomb exploded close to them. The area officer and Mr Pearse were killed, whilst Mr Scawn received severe injuries, including the loss of a hand. The main raid that night had been on Exeter, and the bomb dropped at Newton Abbot had apparently been jettisoned by a returning enemy aircraft. Such is fate.

***Exeter City Police Constable 32 Cole***
*Devon & Cornwall Constabulary Museum archives*

In the early hours of 4th May 1942 there was a further raid on Exeter and, in about one and a half hours, the heart of the city, with one outstanding exception, was destroyed. Whilst almost every shop, office and other building in the city centre was destroyed, Exeter Cathedral was hit by a single 1,000 lb bomb which, although badly damaged the St. James Chapel, left the main building intact. Fortunately many of the cathedral's treasures, including the wonderful stained-glass windows, had been moved out of Exeter to places of safety. An ancient screen received a large proportion of the bomb blast and not even a splinter from the screen was ever found. At this time an autographed copy of Reverend Sabine Baring-Gould's *Onward Christian Soldiers* was on display in the cathedral and was lost. Its rousing tune and uplifting words will continue, as they did in those dark days, to inspire us all.

The May raid resulted in the death of over 150 persons, with 560 seriously injured. Of the 20,000 houses in the city, over 1,500 were completely destroyed and nearly 3,000 others seriously damaged. That the cathedral was saved from destruction was in large measure due to the fact that, from the commencement of hostilities, a rota of 24 volunteer firewatchers were on duty every night patrolling the roof. In the May raid it was estimated that 10,000 incendiary bombs were dropped; they were the main cause of the destruction of property in the city.

Immediately after the bombing, county men were drafted in to assist their city colleagues. For several months after May 1942 the Chief Constable of Exeter, Mr Rowsell, travelled the country lecturing other senior officers, air raid wardens and council authorities concerning the raids and the weaknesses that they had revealed. Apparently there had been a complacent outlook in Exeter and a belief that it would never happen there, as there were no major factories or industrial centres. Certainly the Chief Constable, stressing the destructive power of incendiary devices in words and with photographs, caused the role of fire-watchers to be more sharply defined nationally. For 48 hours no civilians were allowed into the devastated area, but the restrictions were then relaxed, allowing shop owners and their staff to enter properties and begin salvaging any worthwhile stock.

***Exeter blitz.*** *A devastated High Street in Exeter, with St. Stephen's Church tower standing defiantly in the ruins. The church is now situated next to Dingles store in the city centre. The remains of Colsons Haberdashery is also seen in the foreground.*

*Devon & Cornwall Constabulary Museum archives*

One such shop was Messrs Colsons Ltd, a ladies' fashion and drapery emporium situated in the Exeter High Street. Whilst the building had been extensively damaged, later having to be demolished, a large proportion of the stock was possibly saleable as almost every commodity was then in short supply. The staff were engaged in boxing these goods, which were loaded into lorries and brought to Newton Abbot. There, space in a warehouse off Wolborough Street had been cleared to take the goods, and some of the shop girls from Colsons were set to work sorting the articles. My job was to keep traffic flowing past the lorries while they were being unloaded and to ensure that no unauthorised 'assistants' got into the warehouse.

**Exeter bomb site.** *An Exeter City Police inspector and constable, pictured at the top of Paris Street in the city amid the debris of the previous night's air raids.*

*Devon & Cornwall Constabulary Museum archives*

A.R.P./M.4

**MESSAGE FORM**

| Date | Time at which receipt or despatch of message was completed | Telephonist's Initials |
| --- | --- | --- |
| 25. 4. 42 | 04. 23 | HDB |

ADDRESS TO :— Police Control

TEXT OF MESSAGE :—

P.S. 36. Paris Street Incident

2. Dead, number trapped so far about 20 recovered. Soldiers assisting under Sgt Clarke & Bombdier Reason who deserve commendation. We must have something to drink. Four rescue squads are operating. Trapped persons still being found.

M. E.

TIME OF ORIGIN OF MESSAGE :—

ADDRESS FROM

SIGNATURE (of official authorising the despatch of an " out " message). 3

*Hurried messages, written in pencil, were recorded at the police emergency control centres, detailing the scenes of bombs dropped in towns and cities, such as this example relating to a bomb dropped on Paris Street in Exeter city. They convey little of the real horror and trauma that police officers and other emergency service personnel went through at the scene.*

*Devon & Cornwall Constabulary Museum archives.*

Form No. 8.

No. O.B. 16/6.

# EXETER CITY POLICE

*Time* 3.a.m. *Date* Friday January 17th, 1941.

*Subject* Air Raid Damage, Magdalen Road district.

*To the Chief Constable.*

*I beg to report that*

AMBULANCE :
Called
Attended : Yes :
No :
Used: Yes :
No :
Time called ...m
Arrival ...m

on Thursday January 16th, 1941, at 10.48.p.m. four H.E. bombs, each of apparently about 50 kilo, were dropped from enemy aircraft in a residental district of this City, there were no injuries and very little damage caused to property.

Three of the bombs fell at about 15 yard intervals in soft ground, in "Fairpark Gardens", Magdalen Bridge, two of these caused craters measuring about 10' wide and 8' deep, the other struck a main sewer which runs through "Fairpark Gardens", causing a hole in the sewer about 20' x 9',

The other bomb, making the four in all, fell in the front garden of "South Lawn", Magdalen Road, this house is now occupied by the A.T.S. and used as a hostel, about 20' of the front wall of this property was demolished, the explosion also demolished part of the gateway and gate pillar of a house opposite, "North Park West", Magdalen Road. There was also some damage to a glass roof at the side of the house "South Lawn", it is not known by whom this property is owned.

Fairpark Gardens, is in the occupation of Mr. Clarence Hannaford, he resides in a house in the grounds, there were several trees uprooted and one small pane of glass broken in an upstair window of the house.

Slight damage was also caused to No's 10, 13 and 16, Pavilion Place, Magdalen Road, this mainly consisted of small holes in the roofs and ceilings, apparently caused by small pieces of metal or stone being thrown into the air and falling through the roof.

Magdalen Road was blocked at a point just above Fairpark Road, the Road Repair Party were on the scene and cleared the roadway which was opened again to traffic at 2.a.m.

The sewer was left open, the channel was not blocked by the explosion and the sewerage was able to run away causing no inconvenience or danger to anyone. Two P.W.R's were left on the scene all night.

Sidney Geo Collins
Sergeant. No.9.

Supt Brown. Please send Daily Report. Four H.E. in centre of City. fell in gardens, no casualties - damage to sewer. [initials]

C.C.

*Each bomb that was dropped onto a residential area was made the subject of a police report, whether lives were lost as a result or not. This report by Sergeant 6 Collins of the Exeter City Police fortunately relates to a damage-only incident in Magdalen Road in the city.*

*Devon & Cornwall Constabulary Museum archives*

At the end of the afternoon vans had come to collect the shop girls to take them back to Exeter, and it was then that I noticed that several of the young ladies were apparently bulkier than when they had earlier entered the warehouse. I therefore stopped the van and instructed the driver to go to the police station, where W.A.P.C. Mabel Marsh found that each of the shop girls had donned sundry articles from the salvaged stock. There was much crying and wailing from the girls, who were finally charged and bailed before being allowed to return to their homes.

Later they appeared before the Newton Abbot magistrates, Superintendent Coppin's opening remark being: "Your worships, the defendants appearing before you are charged with offences for which I could ask for the ultimate penalty. They have pleaded guilty to stealing the articles before you but the charge could, instead, have been one of looting. Whilst I take a most serious view of the offences, I am only going so far as to ask you to take into consideration that the articles had, just hours earlier, been salvaged from a shop virtually destroyed by enemy action...".

Certainly it was Superintendent Coppin's day, but whether the shop-girl defendants realised that his reference to 'the ultimate penalty' was to the death sentence is not known. Whatever they made of his submission, it is quite likely that they will never have offended again; if still alive, they must, I am sure, still vividly recall their morning in the Newton Abbot court.

In Union Street, Newton Abbot, there was a long-established saddlers shop owned by the Coombes family. The daughter of the proprietors was known as 'Princess BaBa', the 'BaBa' being from her babyhood days and the 'Princess' from her marriage to an Egyptian, reputedly of royal blood, whilst he had been a student at Seale Hayne College. She had gone to Egypt with her husband after his agricultural course ended but had returned to Newton Abbot shortly afterwards and never rejoined her husband. Nor was he ever known to have revisited Newton Abbot. The lady was blonde and, to my eyes, rather overweight, though others might have considered her 'cuddly'. She was certainly never short of male company.

While I was on duty one evening, I turned into Union Street and was confronted by a totally unscreened upstairs front window above the saddlers shop. Dashing to the side door, I pummelled it loudly, which caused the light to be put out, and shortly afterwards 'Princess BaBa' came to the door apologising profusely for the offence.

Her statement had to be recorded and the window checked, so rather reluctantly she invited me into a room, with a properly blacked-out window and in which was a Polish army officer. She explained that she had been showing her friend some of her paintings and had rushed into the front room to fetch some further examples. Hurrying back out of the room, she had inadvertently left the light on, totally forgetting that blackout frames had not been fitted to the windows.

Later she was summonsed to appear at the magistrates' court, where I gave evidence. The magistrates, faced with a lengthy case list, had appeared a trifle listless until I reached the point where I reported that the defendant had been showing her friend some of her paintings. At this point the chairman stopped me, asking me to repeat what the defendant had been doing.

"She had been showing her friend her paintings and had rushed into the front room to fetch other examples, your worship", I replied. "Ah, thank you officer", said the chairman, "She wasn't showing her friend her etchings, then?", he enquired.

"No, she definitely said it was her paintings, sir", I replied. "Thank you, please proceed", he instructed. For some reason the whole bench appeared to have lost their previously listless attitude and were all smiling.

A few months later I was on day duty in Courtenay Street, Newton Abbot, when two German twin-engined bombers appeared at less than 50 feet above the clock tower, just about 100 feet above ground level. Their starboard wings dipped, and almost immediately there were two loud explosions: the roadway and buildings shuddered and a black cloud filled the sky at the far end of Queen Street. I found myself running into and down Queen Street, where, at the lower end, a cloud of dust and debris was hovering over the railway station.

The station contained dreadful sights, the afternoon train from Plymouth having received a direct hit. One carriage was just a mass of twisted metal, and on entering the one adjoining (appearing from the outside to be comparatively undamaged) I found a scene of utter carnage. Several bodies, literally blown to pieces, were amongst the wreckage. Hearing a groan and searching for the source, I found a young man lying on the floor of one compartment with the back of his skull missing, blood and brain oozing from the ghastly wound. My 1918-issue first aid pack was hastily ripped open and the sterile bandage used to cover the wound.

After propping him up, I found two other bodies before dashing from the carriage to get help for the still breathing man. His compartment was next to the carriage's lavatory, the door of which had been blown off its hinges. The paper towel dispenser had also been torn off the wall by the blast and was lying on the floor. Beside it were four pennies. Somehow I saw and recorded the whole scene as I ran from the carriage.

Within a few moments I returned with an ambulance man, only to find that the young man was dead. As we lifted his body and carried it onto the station platform, we again passed the lavatory. I saw the shattered door and the towel dispenser on the floor *but the four pennies were gone.* In that scene of horror, destruction and death, someone had seen fit to stop and pick up and steal the 4d!

That scene has stayed in my memory for over 50 years. What manner of man could have been responsible? Was he haunted forever after by recollections of his action?

While I was still at Newton Abbot, one morning at nine o'clock a lady told me that she had not seen her neighbour that day, adding that she was mentioning it because he was a police pensioner by whose movements "you could set your watch". He was a widower, occupying rooms behind shop premises at the lower end of Queen Street. His normal regime, which involved rising at 6am, collecting his newspaper at 7am and taking his daily constitutional at 8am, had not been followed on this particular day, and this departure from routine had been sufficient to cause an early alarm to be raised.

As knocking at his door brought no response, I obtained permission to force the door; then finding an awful scene. The old man suffered from crippling rheumatism, and for some years had slept in his kitchen in a high wooden chair in front of his kitchen range. Apparently, during the night, he had experienced a seizure or heart attack sufficiently violent to cause him to rise out of his chair and then collapse head first onto the range. I was dealing with this tragic incident when Constable Ken Reid came into the kitchen shortly after 10pm, and the following conversation ensued:

*Ken* ............................... *"I'm taking on this job".*
*Me*................................ *"Why? How am I so lucky?"*
*Ken* ............................... *"You're shifted".*
*Me*................................ *"Shifted? Where?"*
*Ken* ............................... *"Morebath".*
*Me*................................ *"Morebath! Where's Morebath?"*
*Ken* ............................... *"The other side of Bampton".*
*Me*................................ *"Where's Bampton?"*
*Ken* ............................... *"The other side of Tiverton - and you'd better get a move on, as you've got to catch the 12 o'clock train".*

At the police station I learned that there was an outbreak of foot and mouth disease in the Bampton section and I was to be transferred to Morebath (which had never had a constable, being in the Shillingford beat) for "as long as required". I was obliged to pack my gear and break the news to Miss Ellis that her lodger would not be in for lunch that day, or for some considerable time. Unfortunately she would receive no payment for the period of my absence. In turn, she had to get together the remains of my week's rations - butter, margarine, sugar, meat and fat - together with my ration book, for me to take to wherever I might be lodging in Morebath.

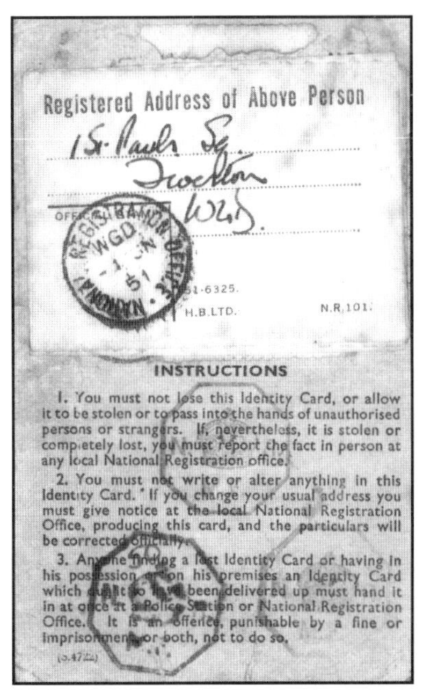

Registered Address of Above Person

15 St. Pauls Sq.

Tiverton

N.R.101.

INSTRUCTIONS

1. You must not lose this Identity Card, or allow it to be stolen or to pass into the hands of unauthorised persons or strangers. If, nevertheless, it is stolen or completely lost, you must report the fact in person at any local National Registration office.

2. You must not write or alter anything in this Identity Card. If you change your usual address you must give notice at the local National Registration Office, producing this card, and the particulars will be corrected officially.

3. Anyone finding a lost Identity Card or having in his possession or upon his premises an Identity Card which ought to have been delivered up must hand it in at once at a Police Station or National Registration Office. It is an offence, punishable by a fine or imprisonment or both, not to do so.

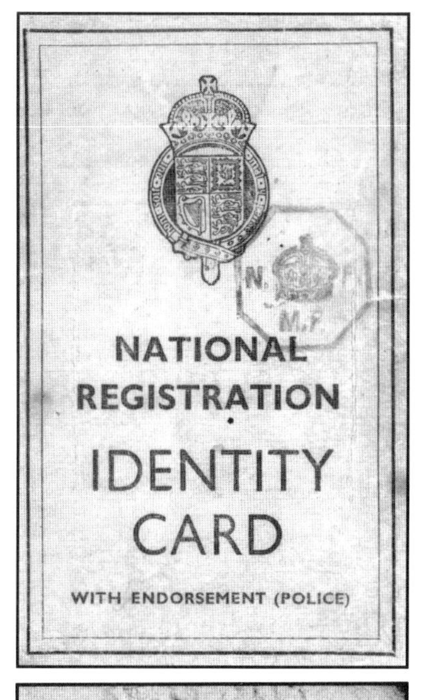

NATIONAL REGISTRATION

IDENTITY CARD

WITH ENDORSEMENT (POLICE)

***Police identity card.***

*The National Identity Card with police endorsement belonging to Constable Ted Trist, issued to him shortly after returning to the force following his brief spell in the R.A.F.*

*Note that the Assistant Chief Constable who had signed the card was none other than 'A.E.M.' Martin himself!*

*Edward Trist*

CLASS CODE A

WEA 93354 ---

TRIST. Irvin Edward.

PHOTOGRAPH OF HOLDER

HOLDER'S— Signature

Visible Distinguishing Marks Mole left cheek.

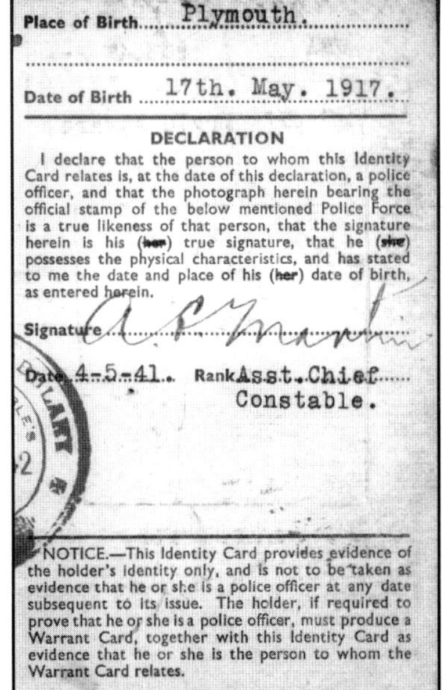

Place of Birth Plymouth.

Date of Birth 17th. May. 1917.

DECLARATION

I declare that the person to whom this Identity Card relates is, at the date of this declaration, a police officer, and that the photograph herein bearing the official stamp of the below mentioned Police Force is a true likeness of that person, that the signature herein is his (her) true signature, that he (she) possesses the physical characteristics, and has stated to me the date and place of his (her) date of birth, as entered herein.

Signature

Date 4-5-41. Rank Asst. Chief Constable.

NOTICE.—This Identity Card provides evidence of the holder's identity only, and is not to be taken as evidence that he or she is a police officer at any date subsequent to its issue. The holder, if required to prove that he or she is a police officer, must produce a Warrant Card, together with this Identity Card as evidence that he or she is the person to whom the Warrant Card relates.

***Foot and mouth outbreak.*** *Constable 'Tiny' Turner mans a stirrup pump whilst Constable Hancox sprays the wheels of a vehicle which has entered a farm where an outbreak of foot and mouth disease has occurred.*

*Devon & Cornwall Constabulary Museum archives*

# CHAPTER 13
# FOOT AND MOUTH DISEASE AT MOREBATH

On arriving at Bampton I was met by the sergeant, Alexander Macrae, and driven the three miles to Morebath, where, for the following four weeks, I and another 'transferee', 'Bert' Hookins, were to control the area. This entailed prohibition of animal movements, disinfection of access points, vehicles and footwear of all authorised persons entering, and such other matters as the Ministry required police to control at these types of incidents during the 1940s.

***Sergeant Macrae,*** *along with Constable Maurice Haysom of the nearby Oakford beat, pictured at Bampton just above the railway station bridge. Note the cycle lamp which has had regulation guards fitted to prevent the light being seen by enemy aircraft.*

*Irene Haysom*

From the sergeant we received but a single directive - to cover Morebath outbreaks 24 hours a day and seven days a week until further notice. He kindly allowed the two of us to arrange our duties to suit ourselves, as long as we always provided proper cover. Could we ask for anything fairer than that? It is unnecessary to mention that neither Bert nor I received a penny for the 36 extra hours we worked during each of the weeks that we were joint 'chief constables' of Morebath, nor was any time off in lieu ever given! The reason we were subject to 'transfers' to a non-existent station was to avoid the force having to pay us each 3s 6d per day subsistence. That was a scheme formulated by a member (or members) of the clerical staff who, of course, were never called upon to carry out anything other than clerical duties.

Fortunately Bert and I worked well together. We lodged with a wonderful couple, Mr and Mrs 'Percy' Soper, in an aptly-named 'Rose Cottage' on the Morebath Estate. The weather was superb and, whilst it was heartbreaking to see apparently healthy herds being put down because they had been in contact with infected cattle, we had to accept the veterinarians' claims that that was the only way to eradicate the disease.

Whether these Ministry 'experts' were correct is, perhaps, open to debate, for local farmers assured me that their fathers had experienced outbreaks of the disease and had immediately treated their whole herds by encasing each animal's feet in Stockholm tar. The cattle had lost weight and condition but, because they had been unable to transfer the disease from their hooves by licking, their mouths had not been affected, thus enabling them to eat without discomfort. The farmers claimed that the animals had made full recoveries in due course.

In those stringent meat-rationing days it was terrible to see the slaughtered animals being tipped into deep pits, covered with lime and then buried. In normal times the carcases would have been incinerated, but that was not possible while the blackout regulations were being so strictly enforced. After just over four weeks the disease was deemed to have been eradicated in the Morebath district and we constables were able to return to our stations and to normal duties, but not for long it seemed...!

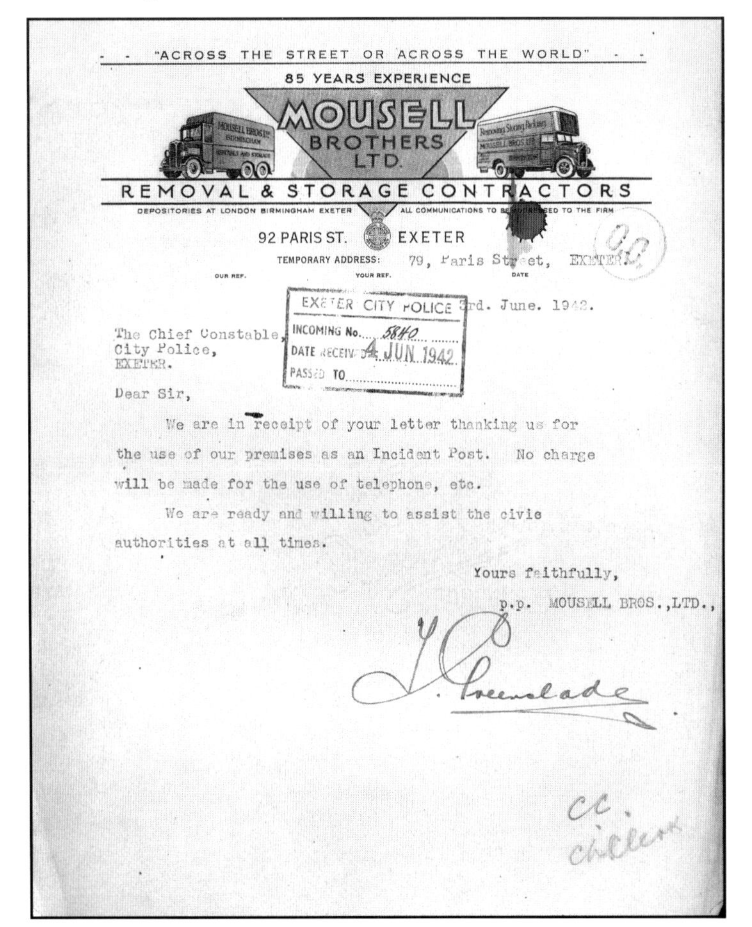
"ACROSS THE STREET OR ACROSS THE WORLD"

85 YEARS EXPERIENCE

MOUSELL BROTHERS LTD.

REMOVAL & STORAGE CONTRACTORS

DEPOSITORIES AT LONDON BIRMINGHAM EXETER — ALL COMMUNICATIONS TO BE ADDRESSED TO THE FIRM

92 PARIS ST. EXETER

TEMPORARY ADDRESS: 79, Paris Street, EXETER.

OUR REF. YOUR REF. DATE

EXETER CITY POLICE
INCOMING No. 5840
DATE RECEIVED 4 JUN 1942
PASSED TO

3rd. June. 1942.

The Chief Constable,
City Police,
EXETER.

Dear Sir,

We are in receipt of your letter thanking us for the use of our premises as an Incident Post. No charge will be made for the use of telephone, etc.

We are ready and willing to assist the civic authorities at all times.

Yours faithfully,
p.p. MOUSELL BROS.,LTD.,

*Numerous buildings were taken over by the police as incident posts during periods of wartime emergencies. As can be seen from this letter, the never-failing support that the public offered the police was always given gladly.*

*Devon & Cornwall Constabulary Museum archives*

# CHAPTER 14
# THE PLYMOUTH AIR RAIDS

Between the Morebath and Culm Valley (see next chapter) foot and mouth outbreaks we were kept informed by the wireless of the city of Plymouth suffering almost continuous enemy night air raids, and it seemed that a number of Devon Constabulary men were being drafted in to help their hard-pressed Plymouth City Police colleagues. As a single man I was naturally regarded as a very mobile commodity, and it was only a matter of time before I received the orders to once again remove from my 'normal duties' to go in support of the Plymouth officers. Many large buildings in the city were commandeered as temporary accommodation for officers from forces all over the Westcountry, who were brought in to assist. The Royal Eye Infirmary was one such building where young men of the Cornwall Constabulary were billeted. As one of the draftees, I had been on duty for 12 hours on one day and, when relieved, instead of having to sleep on a concrete floor in one of the barracks where we Devon men were housed, I was able to go to my mother's house in Darwin Crescent, Laira, on the outskirts of Plymouth. We had just started our meal when the sirens announced yet another air raid so, with plates in our hands, we dashed to the family Morrison shelter, there to await the 'all clear' siren.

***Bombed dwelling during the blitz on Plymouth.***
*Devon & Cornwall Constabulary Museum archives*

Hours went by with regular 'crumps' and ground shudders telling us that bombs were exploding close to our shelter. Then there was an horrific whistling sound and an explosion which caused our shelter to shake and rattle, while articles fell all around us. When we had recovered and taken stock, we found that we were unhurt and undamaged but could do nothing but wait until daylight before venturing out to check if our home was still standing.

After an interminable wait came the first light and the 'all clear', allowing us to creep out to find that our next door neighbour's bungalow had received a direct hit and was totally destroyed. Fortunately, like us, the members of the family had been in their Morrison shelter and, whilst suffering the loss of home and possessions, were physically unharmed.

Later that morning, when reporting for duty, I found that whole areas of central Plymouth had been razed to the ground. Streets that I had known all my life had literally disappeared - Basket Street, Bedford Street, Whimple Street, George Street - along with their shops, restaurants and banks. Where were they? My short, but eventful, period in the city has stayed in my memory since those dark days. I became disorientated, and so shattering was the experience that the new Plymouth has never felt the same to me. A fresh order came and I was to return to my former duties back in rural Devon, this time at Hemyock, in the east of the county.

***The Plymouth blitz.*** *A lone Plymouth city constable stands in Craigmore Avenue in the Stoke area of the city, inspecting the devastation caused by the previous night's bombing raid on the area.*

*Devon & Cornwall Constabulary Museum archives*

*Another Plymouth street scene, pictured at the height of the blitz on the city.*
*Devon & Cornwall Constabulary Museum archives*

# NOTICE
# TO HOUSEHOLDERS.

---

Following the recent air raid incident in your district, you are advised

**TO BOIL ALL DRINKING WATER**

until such time as the Local Authority is satisfied as to the condition of the water mains.

A general warning to this effect appeared in the local Press on 4th July, 1940.

G. B. PAGE,

*Medical Officer of Health,*
*Exeter.*

Bartlett & Son, Printers, Chapel Street.

*Notices to the residents of areas which had suffered from air raids instructed the public to boil all drinking water as a matter of precaution, to prevent the outbreak of disease. Such handbills, and also loudspeaker announcements, were frequent at such times.*

*Devon & Cornwall Constabulary Museum archives*

# CHAPTER 15
# RETURN TO RURAL POLICING

I immediately slipped back into the routine of the country policeman again when I transferred to Hemyock, to assist in their, much larger, outbreak of foot and mouth disease. The sheer size of the area affected made it necessary for many more police to be drafted to the Cullompton section than had been the case in the Bampton section, mentioned previously.

The supply of single constables ran out, requiring the 'transfer' of married men from country stations. This presented difficulties for the authorities; if a married man was to be transferred, how could this be effected without also moving his wife and family? This problem was overcome by introducing a system of 'temporary transfers' which enabled the constable to be temporarily transferred while his family was 'allowed' to remain in police quarters (the country station) during the period of the temporary transfer. (Undoubtedly another brainchild of the headquarters clerical staff!) The Culm Valley outbreak was a major disaster for many farmers in that area. They had to witness the putting down of herds which they had spent years, even decades, in building up. Compensation was not over-generous but certainly, for many farmers, no compensation could recompense them for the loss of animals on which they had lavished so much effort and work.

On one farm where I was on control duties the farmer became so distraught that, on a pretext, I entered the house and persuaded his wife to let me take possession of his shotgun. Several years later, when I was in the C.I.D. in Tiverton, I met him again. He confessed that he had raged at his wife for handing over the gun *but* admitted that at the time he would have used it on himself if it had been to hand.

In the intervening years he had rebuilt his herd and had, hesitatingly, to admit that it was even better stock than that which had been slaughtered, including, as it did, several local and Devon County Show prizewinners. Haltingly, he expressed thanks for my action.

One morning, when off duty, I visited a farm where I had been on duty when the herd had been destroyed. The farmhouse was occupied by the farm manager, Mr Richards, and his wife. We were standing in the kitchen looking out at the hill leading to the centre of Hemyock when a runaway horse, pulling a cart, passed the window. We ran to the door in time to see the cart driver thrown off and crash head first onto the roadway. On reaching him, we found that he was dead, his neck broken and skull smashed.

The horse had run less than 30 yards beyond the body before stopping and beginning to munch green stuff from the hedge. What had caused it to take fright we could not tell, but this was the only time in my career when I actually witnessed the whole scenario of a sudden death.

'Reg' Stokes was the Hemyock constable, already fully engaged with all the additional traffic and work that the building of Dunkeswell airfield had brought to his 'patch'. The workforce included several hundred imported labourers and a number of local boys. The innate honesty of these boys sorely tried the airfield contractors.

On starting work at the site all workmen were kitted out with overalls, protective clothing and rubber boots. Whilst the boys took great care of these (to them) scarce items, the outsiders made regular calls for replacements of 'lost' gear.

The work was on a 'cost-plus' contract, so the higher the expenses the greater the payments claimed by the contractors, resulting in their not being over-zealous in checking if the claims were genuine. I do not know whether the Devon boys eventually gravitated to their workmates' level, but the 'system' certainly invited dishonesty.

On one occasion, when I was out in Hemyock with Reg and the area officer of the 'specials' (Stanley Wide, owner of the Hemyock central garage) covering the boundaries of the foot and mouth outbreaks, I was diverted by one of their exchanges:

*Reg* ............................... *"Do you know what day it is Stan?"*
*Stan* .............................. *"Thursday".*
*Reg* ............................... *"Ah yes, but what date is it?"*
*Stan* .............................. *"Thursday the 16th".*
*Reg* ............................... *"Yes, but what's special about it?"*
*Me* ............................... *"Please, Reg, please tell us what you're driving at".*
*Reg* ............................... *"Well, it was on the 16th, exactly a year ago, that 'the' bomb fell".*
*Me* ............................... *"You had a bomb on Hemyock? Where?"*
*Reg* ............................... *"Stan and me'll show you".*

They then walked me across several fields and showed me a crater where an enemy aircraft had dropped a bomb which, mercifully, had hurt no one or caused any real damage.

After all that I had so recently witnessed in Plymouth, Hemyock's bomb was quite an anti-climax, but it brought home to me just how chance plays so large a part in our lives. If that bomb had been jettisoned a fraction of a second earlier the whole of Hemyock could have been destroyed.

Weeks passed. Then, with the foot and mouth outbreak finally being contained, the Hemyock area again resumed being a mere beat station and Reg Stokes saw 'his men' return to their own stations.

A few weeks later, in August 1942, I returned to Newton Abbot, and on routine beat duties again. One day I came off duty to find the station in a state of turmoil - due to the activities of Constable John Howard Stevens, one of the young men who had joined the force during my service at Paignton in 1938. 'Jack' Stevens was a big north-countryman, with the accent and aggressive mode of speech of his kin.

Apparently a uniformed visitor had called, introduced himself to the charge-room constable, and had been left whilst the officer dashed to inform Superintendent Coppin, who was in his upstairs office.

Between his departure and his return with the superintendent, Jack had rung the doorbell and been admitted by the telephonist stationed in the adjoining office.

Addressing the superintendent, the now irate visitor asked: "What is happening in your station, Mr. Coppin? I was awaiting your arrival when this constable was admitted. First he totally ignored me, then he commenced writing in that book (a beat book), turned towards me and said: "How do. Nice day", before putting the book back on the desk. When I asked him if that was his usual way of addressing one of His Majesty's Inspectors of Constabulary, he looked at me *and laughed*!"

Jack, now standing rigidly to attention, attempted to apologise, but his blurted-out explanation did nothing to improve the shining hour. His words: "I'm sorry, sir, I thought you were a St. John's ambulanceman" did nothing to alleviate the situation!

Superintendent Coppin snapped out: "Constable Stevens, pick up your beat, I will deal with you later", before asking the seething H.M.I. to accompany him to his office.

A week or so later Jack was transferred to the Holne beat on Dartmoor, remaining there, I believe, until his untimely death in 1961.

# CHAPTER 16
# MORETONHAMPSTEAD AND DARTMOOR

Although I had only returned to Newton in August 1942, I was not allowed to remain there long. Orders arrived for me to transfer to Moretonhampstead on 24th December 1942. Miss Ellis, my landlady, cried but assured me: "You won't go there without having your Christmas dinner. I'll see to that". So we had our meal on Christmas Eve, prior to my departure to join Sergeant Hedley Blamey at Moretonhampstead (known locally as just 'Moreton').

***King George VI.*** *The King arriving at Moretonhampstead railway station in the Royal Train prior to continuing to Princetown by car. Constable Clements of Moretonhampstead station is pictured, in uniform, on the left.*

Devon & Cornwall Constabulary Museum archives

Sergeant Blamey and I had served together at Honiton prior to his removal to Torquay as acting sergeant in August 1939. His forte had been the finding of vehicles with defective tyres and he had rarely missed a Honiton court, almost always having had one or two of these offences to report. Before joining the force he had been an aircraftsman in the peacetime R.A.F., and later became the force training officer at headquarters.

His pride and joy was his daughter, Heather, who married after the war and moved to Rhodesia. Later she achieved international status, representing that country in either the Commonwealth Games or the Olympics. Shortly after his retirement Hedley was involved in a car crash at Clyst St. Mary, sustaining fatal injuries.

The reason for my transfer to the Moreton section was to take the places of Constables Owen Osborne and William Taylor, called to serve in the Royal Navy and army respectively. At that time the section also had two police war reserve constables (William Johnson and Lester Trump), and attached to it were the 'country' stations - Chagford, with Constable Tucker, Dunsford, with Constable Nunn, Tedburn St. Mary, with Constable Tonkin, and Lustleigh, with Constable George Henry Skinner. George, in fact, had only taken over the Lustleigh beat during 1941, having previously been stationed at Dartmouth, and, although it is now over 50 years ago since he died, in 1946, his family still well remember the kindness and support that they received from the force at that sad time. His widow was even found a job in the pay department, serving under 'Tiger' Wheeler, which supported her pension.

Sergeant Blamey had found me excellent lodgings with a Mr and Mrs Underhill. Mr Underhill was a retired master builder who, in the early 1930s, had been unemployed until he and two other Moreton builders obtained employment in Dartmoor Prison, at Princetown. Mr Underhill explained to me that this had required them to get to their workplace six days a week and to work a ten hour day before returning home to Moreton. As they had had no means of transport, they had walked the 15 miles each way in all the changeable weather experienced on that all too often bleak moor.

In the mornings they did not wait at a Moreton point for one another, having an arrangement whereby the first arriving at a certain gateway would place a stone on the hinge post before walking on at a steady pace. The second to arrive would then place another stone on the post before proceeding at a faster pace, whilst the last man would take the stones off the post and half-trot until catching up with his workmates.

The lodgings were excellent, our rations being augmented by a plentiful supply of rabbits, produce from Mr Underhill's garden and allotment, and by the once-yearly demise of a pig reared on kitchen waste collected locally, which enabled us first to enjoy some delicious home-made hogs puddings and other strange (to me) delicacies, before enjoying home-reared pork and bacon: rich fare indeed after the scrimping and scraping experienced previously (and also later) in order to eke out wartime rations!

On weekly leave days I would cycle from Moreton to Plymouth, on one memorable journey coming off my bicycle four times on the icy hills between Moreton and Bovey Tracey. On another leave day I arrived back in Moreton after 11pm, ready for bed, only to learn that a prisoner had escaped from Dartmoor. So, without more ado, I had to change into uniform and go out to man a point until relieved the following morning.

Escapes from Dartmoor were fairly frequent occurrences. A working party of prisoners would leave the prison in the charge of one warder, who would march them to the work area, sometimes two or three miles from the prison, and set them to their allotted tasks. After an hour or so, two or three convicts would ease themselves away from the main group and, whilst the others distracted the attention of the warder, would slip away. When they were missed, the warder would then attempt to round up the remaining convicts, who suddenly became 'deaf' and quite unable to understand his instructions. As a result, there would be a general state of confusion for a while until, eventually, some order had been restored and the men instructed to 'quick march'. Even then they walked as slowly as they dared, giving the escapees as much time as possible before the alarm could be raised.

With no radio or other means of communication, the warder was reduced to regularly blowing his whistle and repeatedly exhorting his charges to hurry up. Often the escapees would gain as much as two hours of freedom before the authorities could even begin to search for them. By the time that the police were able to man checkpoints, at least four hours would have elapsed.

However, despite there being so many factors working against the men being found quickly and detained, in wartime the police had one advantage - the absence of household or beacon lights for the escapees to use as 'fixes'. As they were obliged to steer clear of roads and to try and cross the moor half running in the darkness, they tended to go around in circles until completely lost and demoralised. Often they were almost grateful to be picked up and taken back 'inside'. On one occasion two escapees were out for three days before being arrested just five miles from the prison. Their claim that they had walked many, many miles was supported by the condition of their boots and clothing.

***Prison escape check point.*** *Constable Sid Pollard of Roborough station and a prison warder stop and search a vehicle during a prison escape.*

*Mrs Jean Creber*

For the police, these escapes represented yet another task to be undertaken by an undermanned and much overworked team. Crossroads had to be covered so that the prison was ringed, and tours of duty were 'eight hours at a designated checkpoint, eight hours off'. However, unfortunately the 'eight off' included the time that the patrol car crew took to collect up to three men from three scattered points and to drive them back to their respective stations. Then, less than seven hours later, another motor patrol crew went through the same procedure in reverse. This reduced the 'off ' period to some six hours only, during which time we had to have supper (no matter what the time of day), undress, wash, sleep, rise, wash and shave, dress, have breakfast and be ready and waiting for the patrol car.

On one occasion, whilst stationed at Newton Abbot after being at the North Bovey checkpoint until 8am, I arrived back at Newton Abbot at 9am only to be told that the Chief Constable, Major Morris, would be inspecting all available men at the Ambulance Hall in East Street at noon. So, two hours later, it was a case of out of bed to shave, polish boots and ensure that my helmet and uniform were spotless. Then, immediately after the parade, it was back to change into the number 2 uniform and a hurried meal before dashing to meet the patrol car in order to be back at North Bovey by 2pm. This was on the third day of an escape, so at the inspection we were a tired-looking group. In fairness, Major Morris looked even more weary than we did; unknown to us he was a sick man, literally working himself to death.

***The Chief Constable, Major Morris,*** *in the centre, with senior officers of North Devon. On the right is also pictured the Assistant Chief Constable, 'A.E.M.' Martin.*

*Devon & Cornwall Constabulary Museum archives*

Some convict escapes offered occasional moments of glory. One such escape involved three convicts getting off the moor before breaking into a garage containing a car. The owner had laid up the car 'for the duration' in 1939, before the 'Immobilisation of Vehicles Order' had come into effect post-Dunkirk, and it had not occurred to him that he should have rendered the vehicle inoperative. As a result, the convicts had been able to start the car and, in some triumph, had driven off into the night *but* with side and headlights totally unscreened.

Within minutes alarms were sounded and two motor patrol crews were quickly in pursuit, despite being severely handicapped as a result of having their car lamps legally screened to emit mere pinpoints of light. Nevertheless, they succeeded in forcing the stolen car off the road at Drumbridges, near Newton Abbot. The convicts then ran into the nearby thick woodland, chased by Constables Owen Osborne and Cyril Holland who had been at the Drumbridges checkpoint. Owen grabbed one convict and Cyril 'bagged' another, whilst the third just gave himself up.

Everyone was surprised and delighted, as the convicts had enjoyed a very easy passage; not for them nights of lying out on open ground in pouring rain, trying to locate and avoid checkpoints. Instead, they had merely run a few miles, broken in and stolen a car, ridden in comfort until the chase and abandonment of the car and then, after just a few minutes, had virtually given themselves up. We learned later that when they were returned to Dartmoor Prison, their fellow inmates rapturously cheered them as returning heroes.

Probably more important to them was the fact that all their tobacco debts were rendered void by their escape. These debts resulted from convicts accepting one or more cigarettes from one of the 'tobacco barons', who were active in all H.M. prisons. The cigarettes so obtained were subject to repayment within a week, 'with interest'. As interest rates were 100% per week, this meant that for one cigarette obtained two had to be repaid. On inability to repay, after another week four were demanded, and so on. This would finally result in physical violence being inflicted on the debtor if he was obliged to admit that he could not settle his debt. His only way to avoid such retribution was to escape. This foul practice was finally broken when prisoners were allowed to work at paid tasks in prison and to purchase tobacco with their earnings.

The chasing and arrest of escaped prisoners were always minor triumphs for the officers concerned, but on many occasions we also managed to find some humour in the incidents. There was never any dark side to the matter; no convict offered resistance, and certainly no violence was involved when he was cornered and apprehended. Usually the escapee was only too glad to be picked up, and his subsequent treatment by the police prior to being handed over to the prison authorities sometimes bordered on the ludicrous. Invariably, within moments of being arrested, the convict would be given a cigarette before being almost tenderly placed in a car and taken to the nearest station boasting cells. There he would be given a hot meal; no matter how miserly were the food rations at the time, somehow an egg and at least a couple of bacon rashers would be found, together with fried potatoes and bread with a scraping of butter or margarine. He would also be plied with scalding hot tea and enough sugar to satisfy even the most sweet-toothed escapee.

Probably the most isolated route off Dartmoor was the unclassified road from Princetown to Hexworthy and Holne into Ashburton, then even narrower and more winding than today. It was one of the most favoured lines of escape for convicts, and led to members of the Ashburton section frequently being the 'detainers' of would-be escapers. I heard details of two such incidents from the then sectional sergeant, later chief inspector, 'Reg' Perryman.

The constable at the Holne checkpoint had learned that a stranger had been seen near the Holne rectory and the sergeant, with every man that he could muster, began an immediate search of the area. The rector was abroad and the properly-secured rectory showed no signs of having been tampered with. The search area was, therefore, widened to adjoining woodland and overgrown gorse land, aided by a police dog in the charge of its handler, P.C. 'Bert' Townsend. The dog showed great interest in some piles of straw but, after a very short time, came away and could not be coaxed to them again.

To the 'expert' this suggested that the convict had been near the straw piles but had left them before the police arrived. It was, therefore, decided to let the dog have its head, and it responded by going off at a great pace, closely followed by its handler and the constables.

It was at this moment that other matters required the immediate attention of the sergeant; a long deferred call of nature could no longer be ignored. Taking advantage of the solitude and seclusion of a high hedgerow, he experienced that unique relief that follows too long a period of repression of a very natural requirement.

Apart from a very minor rustling of the disturbed hedge growth, all was silent until, from one of the straw piles, a man arose. For a moment both he and the sergeant viewed one another in utter astonishment before the convict, for it was he, took to his heels and disappeared into the thick undergrowth.

***Constable Reg Perryman,** pictured second from the left. With him, on the left, is Motor Patrol Constable Larry Hurrell, along with Constables George Rodd (next to Reg) and Pat Henley, on the right of the group. George Rodd had joined the Devon Constabulary as a war reserve constable and had then transferred into the 'regulars'.*

*Larry Hurrell*

Shrill whistle blowing and loud shouts from the sergeant brought his constables, the dog and its handler running, and the search was renewed. The undergrowth was so thick that the searchers could find no trace of their quarry, whilst the dog appeared to be quite happy to run from one uniformed officer to another, setting up a furious barking each time it reached a constable.

Climbing a tree growing in the hedge, Sergeant Perryman was able to see the undergrowth swaying some 100 yards away, indicating that a hidden body was crawling away from the rectory courtyard area. Guiding the constables by shouts and gesticulations, he quickly had the convict flushed out and arrested. Then followed the usual routine - friendly smiles, an offered and accepted cigarette and a pleasant car ride to Ashburton police station, where a huge meal, cooked by Mrs Perryman, was wolfed down by the extremely hungry man.

Warm and comfortably replete, the convict then confessed how terrified he had been when the police dog had nuzzled the straw pile where he had been hiding. He had been utterly astonished when the dog had licked his hand, and when he had gently said: "Nice dog, good dog", it had reacted by backing out of the straw and disappearing from his sight.

Holne featured in yet another Dartmoor escape when a convict broke into a workman's hut on the bank of the reservoir, donned overalls and found a bicycle, both items left there conveniently (for him) by the workmen. With his prison garb now hidden and a roadworthy bicycle to ride, it is understandable if he thought that everything was going his way. So he happily cycled off and, seeing a constable at the Holne crossroads checkpoint, who could blame him for thinking that his cheery "Good morning" would be sufficient to get him past that officer?

It was then that his luck ran out, firstly in his trying to ignore the Constable's signal to stop and, secondly, in that the constable concerned was one P.C. Norman, a Paignton lad that I had helped enrol in the force who was a very fit athlete.

The convict cycled off as fast as he could but P.C. Norman also had a cycle to hand and his speed was much too great for the convict, who realised that he was being overtaken, threw down the cycle and took to the fields. At that point the matter became a case of 'no competition', the escapee being grounded by a rugby tackle worthy of Twickenham after only a few yards.

Once again a cigarette was offered by a happy, smiling constable, a car ride was taken to Ashburton police station and a more than ample meal was cooked by Mrs Perryman. One of a very few unchanging things in an ever-changing world!

Duties at Moretonhampstead mainly involved enforcing the lighting regulations and all the other wartime regulations and orders seemingly introduced almost daily, and also ensuring that unattended vehicles were immobilised (usually by removing the rotor arm from the distributor). Crime was negligible with so many men away in the services, and with road traffic much reduced there were very few vehicular accidents or offences. Nonetheless, transgressions did occur and were detected, resulting in my attendance at the monthly sessions held at the Moretonhampstead magistrates' court.

It was at these 'Petty Sessions Courts' that I gave evidence to magistrates chaired by Sir Henry Slessor, a one-time high court judge in India. Sir Henry was one of a group of retired colonial judges who occupied and graced the office of 'Chairman of the Devon Quarter Sessions' over a long period and who protected the citizens of Devon by their attitudes to miscreants found guilty in their court. The chairmen that I knew and admired were Sir Archibald Bodkin, Sir Leonard Costello, Sir Henry Slessor and Sir Douglas McNair.

I was a witness in a case at the quarter sessions before Sir Leonard when he had just received notification from the Home Office that all His Majesty's prisons were full and that persons pleading, or found, guilty were to be made subject to 'binding over orders' (ordered to 'keep the peace' for a specified period). If the offender was again found guilty within the period of the order, he would be brought back before the 'binding over' court and sentenced for the original offence.

Sir Leonard showed his utter distaste for such a procedure by issuing the order, through clenched teeth and launching into a frightening diatribe as to just how lengthy a sentence the offender would receive for any transgression during the period of the order. On one occasion I heard him address a prisoner: "At these sessions I have warned offenders time and time again that if they appear before me and are proved guilty they can expect no mercy. You have come to

Devon and committed housebreakings, for which you will go to prison for ... years". This attitude was matched by that of Sir Archibald, and I truly believe that they discouraged many criminals from venturing into Devon to practise their 'trade'.

I remember being present on the first occasion when Sir Douglas McNair sat on the Crediton bench. He was welcomed by the chairman and then invited "in view of your vast experience in the high courts of India" to be chairman. His polite refusal overcome, he took the chair and the first case was called, that of a local farm labourer accused of 'riding his cycle during the hours of darkness without a red light showing to the rear'. The brief evidence was heard and then Sir Douglas addressed the defendant: "I take a most serious view of this type of offence. Not only do you endanger yourself but you put other road users at risk also. A motorist coming upon you could well take avoiding action and damage his vehicle, possibly being himself injured or injuring other road users. For that reason I am going to make an example of you and hope that other cyclists will take heed and not be as foolhardy as you have been".

By this time the defendant was visibly shaking in the box. Sir Douglas continued: "You will therefore be fined a shilling".

In India the fine of a shilling might well have been 'an example' to the offender, but it certainly did not cover the cost of processing the summons in this country. In fact Mr Pope, the magistrates' clerk, half turned towards the bench and was about to speak, only to change his mind. Instead, in honeyed tones, he then asked the by now very relieved defendant whether he would pay immediately or: "Do you ask for time to pay?". Assured that immediate payment would be made, without a change of expression Mr Pope told his clerk to accept the money.

At a subsequent Crediton magistrates' court, Sir Douglas was presiding when a motor patrol constable was relating the facts concerning a motorist having contravened a one-way order in force on the higher side of the bridge at Copplestone, on the Barnstaple road. The officer was detailing, at the breakneck speed peculiar to members of the motor patrol department, that he had been proceeding towards Barnstaple and had turned right at the bridge. On entering the road, he had found that a car was approaching him in contravention of the order. "Stop, officer, stop", came an instruction from Sir Douglas. "Are you saying that the car was being driven towards the bridge on the higher road?". "Yes your worship", was the patrol officer's immediate reply. "But that is what I have always done", said Sir Douglas. "I think it would be better if I were to stand down on this case". This was an indication of his total honesty, and I am sure that he never repeated that particular manoeuvre.

One windy March afternoon Sergeant Blamey found me in The Square and told me that a fire had been reported in the charcoal works, some three miles out of the town. As a result of the war there were no imports of charcoal and, as it was used as the filtering agent in all service-type gas masks, the local works was playing a vital part in meeting this demand for charcoal.

As the firing of a maroon to call the local men to the fire station had been banned, it was necessary for them to be individually informed. Sergeant Blamey went to the local pharmacy and called Mr Rihll, whilst I hurried to call another fireman from his workplace. Each of us then called another man and eventually eight of us hurried to the fire station, where the local fire chief, Mr Coldridge, had driven the fire engine into the roadway and was impatiently awaiting the arrival of his crew.

Whilst trotting to the fire station with one of the firemen I learned, as we ran, that: "It's a pity our Leyland is away for its annual overhaul as all we've got is an old Merryweather". However, on seeing that machine standing outside the fire station with its brasses and paintwork gleaming I saw little reason, at first, for anyone to regret its substitution for the regular engine.

*The Merryweather fire engine.*

*Mr Sidney Wooton*

Once aboard the fire engine we set off and proceeded through Pound Street at what, to me, seemed a rather slow speed. Gear changing revealed that the vehicle was of pre-synchromesh vintage but, having reached the top of the slope by the library, it still came as a shock when the driver came to a virtual stop and engaged bottom gear, with weird noises emanating from the box, before we moved down the hill towards the old swimming pool. As the firemen appeared to accept as normal their travelling at about four miles an hour, I did not venture to ask the reason.

By the pool we began the long ascent up to the moor and, as we reached the rather sharp dog-leg turn on the hill, all the firemen with the exception of the driver and Mr Coldridge leapt off. Following suit, I found that the men had all run to the rear of the engine, where one of them had lifted a heavy swivel-jointed steel bar from its retaining hook and had dropped the pointed end onto the roadway. It was explained to me that this was a precaution in case the fire engine started to run back down the hill.

All now became clear. Not only was the vehicle grossly underpowered, but it also lacked efficient brakes. This was shocking as the manufacturers, Merryweather, had supplied fire-fighting equipment to British fire services for decades. Although the company manufactured the finest water pumps in the world, their vehicles had not been updated to modern standards. This became immediately apparent when Mr Coldridge exhorted us all from his front seat to: "Push lads, and put your backs into it!" Push we did, assisting the labouring engine until it reached a less steep part of the hill, where we could all jump aboard and resume our positions on the port and starboard sides.

With the hill surmounted, and seeing a long level road ahead, the driver went through all his gears, and soon we were reaching perhaps 20 miles an hour and making real progress towards the fire. However, the wind was blowing at gale force into our faces and suddenly whipped the cap off the head of Mr Coldridge, obliging the driver to apply the brakes and slow to walking pace, in order to allow one of the firemen to run back, retrieve the cap and return it to its owner.

On we went again, the headwind making it seem that we were travelling at quite a high speed, when, unfortunately, it now whisked the driver's cap from his head. Again he slammed on his brakes so that another fireman could jump down, run back, pick up the offending headwear and hand it back to him.

By now there was a certain tenseness in the air and we had only proceeded a few hundred yards further when Mr Coldridge, undoubtedly after due consideration, announced that if anyone else's cap should come off we wouldn't stop to pick it up. This edict had the desired effect: caps were either pressed even more tightly onto their owners' heads or were taken off, while I surreptitiously checked my helmet's chinstrap.

Like all good things, our headlong pace had to come to an end some time. We had now reached the top of a steep hill so, once again, the driver engaged bottom gear to enable us to drop down to the charcoal works at walking speed. At the entrance was the owner, who had suffered a disastrous fire at the works just 18 months earlier. His opening words to us were: "Where the ... hell have you been? The ... place could have burnt to the ground by this time".

Considering our endeavours and experiences this did seem a little unkind, but the firemen accepted the hostile greeting without replying. We then learned that the fire had already gone out; without any outside assistance, it had just given up and not even a wisp of smoke could be found coming from the site of the fire. It appeared that a spark from the charcoal-making bins had landed in one of the building's rain-chutes, igniting the collection of twigs and seedlings lying therein. Although the fire had been a very minor one, in view of his previous experience the works owner had rightly telephoned for the fire brigade. In the event, however, all our efforts had proved unnecessary.

Mr Coldridge now got down from the fire engine, called for a ladder to be placed against the offending chute and climbed up to examine the charred twigs and to announce that all was safe. It was at this moment that a fire tender and crew arrived from the Bovey Tracey fire station as back-up. Their fire chief alighted and, after a discussion with Mr Coldridge, also mounted the ladder to reach the conclusion that the fire had, indeed, definitely subsided.

At this point the works owner reappeared carrying a tray of mugs of tea. The firemen surrounded him and were about to relieve him of his load when a car appeared from behind the two fire engines, driven by a divisional commander from the Torquay fire station. Men came to attention, salutes were exchanged between the newcomer and the two fire chiefs, and explanations made. Could the mugs of tea now be drunk? Well, no, not at least until the divisional commander had also climbed the ladder and checked that there was no danger of the chute's debris reigniting.

Satisfied, he joined his fellow officers, accepted a mug and, after consuming the contents, instructed the Bovey Tracey chief to take his crewmen back to their station. Graciously I was permitted to return to Moretonhampstead on the Bovey vehicle, being back there in a matter of minutes. When typing a report of the incident I confined myself to the barest details, reporting that the call-out had been made 'with good intent'. It had been a small incident, but never will I forget the words of the Moreton fire chief, Mr Coldridge: "If anyone else's cap..."!

Sergeant Blamey lived on the Moreton station with his wife and daughter. As he was always prepared to answer the telephone and be responsible for the office coverage, the three constables were required only for the early, day and night turns. This allowed ample time off and enabled me to have a certain amount of courting time, though even so a difficulty arose from a rule that, even when off duty, a constable was not allowed to be absent from his beat area without written permission.

The object of my affection was the manageress of a Newton Abbot shop, who was also an air raid warden. Her free time was limited to after shop closing hours and such time as she was not on A.R.P. duties but, as is usual, ways are found to overcome such difficulties. When on early or night turn I was able to meet this young lady at Moreton, after she had travelled on the last (6.30pm) bus from Newton Abbot. Unfortunately it was also the last bus from Moreton back to Newton Abbot, so our time together was limited to the waiting time at Moreton (mere minutes) or, if I cycled towards Bovey Tracey as far as I was able to travel before meeting the bus, the longer the time we were able to spend together before the bus returned to that spot.

One evening, as I was cycling towards Bovey Tracey with my head down and travelling as quickly as I could, I met Sergeant Blamey driving towards me. I had no alternative but to continue my journey and keep my tryst. Cycling back, more slowly up the hills, gave me time to consider my position and the possible repercussions of 'being absent from station'. There was nothing for it but to make a clean breast of the matter so, on seeing the sergeant, I asked him if he had seen me cycling past him earlier that evening. He said that he had not recognised me, but heard me to the end of my explanations before remarking: "And very nice, too". Much to my relief that was the end of the matter, but from that time on I made a point of mentioning my excursions, which invariably received his approval.

Perhaps Moretonhampstead as a station was too good to be true because after I had been there just seven months removal orders arrived, in July 1943, and I was transferred yet again, this time to Highweek, a married man's station on the outskirts of Newton Abbot.

From..........

No. of Pigeons..........

NATIONAL PIGEON SERVICE

LIVE PIGEONS

NOT FOR LIBERATION

To..........

..........

Destination Station..........

Company..........

Authorized for Transit to above address :—

*Signed*..........

SECRETARY, NATIONAL PIGEON SERVICE COMMITTEE,
22, CLARENCE STREET, GLOUCESTER.

Railway Stamps to be affixed here.

*The National Pigeon Service and its gallant birds played an important wartime role, especially in the recovery of airmen who had been forced to ditch in the sea. These small birds saved countless lives during hostilities.*

*Devon & Cornwall Constabulary Museum archives*

THIS COSTUME MAY BE COMFORTABLE FOR THE GARDEN ON A SULTRY DAY · · ·
WHILE THIS MAY GUARANTEE COMFORT IN COLD WEATHER · · ·
THIS IS POSSIBLY NOT TOO BAD FOR GOLF · · ·
AND THIS MIGHT PASS AT SOME POINT TO POINT MEETINGS BUT CERTAINLY NOT AT MANY OF THEM · · ·
THERE IS NO EXCUSE FOR THIS AT ANY TIME EVEN IF YOU HAVE BEEN SURPRISED BY THE SIREN!
IT MUST BE CLEARLY UNDERSTOOD THAT UNIFORM MUST BE WORN WHEN ON DUTY!
CHARLES LANE VICARY 1941
Sc 2874.
To MAJOR L.H.MORRIS M.C. CHIEF CONSTABLE OF DEVON
A HUMBLE ACKNOWLEDGEMENT OF HIS UNFAILING COURTESY TO ALL "SPECIALS".

# CHAPTER 17
# HIGHWEEK

In January 1943 the Tiverton borough force became part of the Devon Constabulary, but not until the Chief Constable of the borough, Benjamin Mervyn Beynon, a Welshman, had extracted the maximum benefits from the county authority, both on his own behalf and that of three of his men.

Mr Beynon received the salary of an inspector, but was able to augment this with payments for being the chief of the borough fire service as well as with fees for being shops inspector and inspector of weights and measures. He had just ten men under his command, two sergeants and eight constables, several being men who had transferred to the borough after training and serving in other forces. They were all policemen/firemen and, to a man, elected to remain where they were, continuing their service and living in their own homes in the borough.

Just prior to the amalgamation,, Mr Beynon had appointed his clerk constable, Sidney Badcock, to be temporary sergeant and Constable Cyril Richards to be the first detective constable in the history of the borough force. He also insisted that his senior sergeant, Sergeant Galpin, be promoted to inspector. Mr Beynon himself was appointed superintendent, and part of the agreement was that the 'C' division headquarters should remove from Cullompton to the old borough police station in St. Andrew Street, Tiverton.

Possibly during the honeymoon period of the transaction it did not occur to the Devon negotiators just how much was being gained by Mr Beynon in the horse-trading. It was not until the 'marriage' was some months old that the Devon authorities awoke to the true state of affairs, and then damage-reduction operations commenced immediately with the detective constable being told that if he wished to retain his appointment he would have to leave Tiverton. He agreed, and removed to Torquay, later being promoted to sergeant and then inspector.

Temporary Sergeant Badcock was also given the same choice - remove or revert - and he, too, elected to move. But where, with police accommodation everywhere filled? The solution was to move Constable Gulley from Highweek and for the Badcock family to occupy the police house, with Temporary Sergeant Badcock working in Newton Abbot on patrol duties in tandem with Sergeant Lamb.

All that was then required was to find a single constable to work the Highweek country station, so I was moved, being told that I could occupy my old dormitory in the Union Street police station until I could find lodgings in Highweek. For several weeks I did this, whilst regularly calling on householders to enquire if they could offer me a billet. With everyone endeavouring to augment their meagre wartime food rations, the last person most households wanted was a constable lodger, who would become privy to their activities. However, finally, the Highweek coalman and taxi proprietor, Mr Hutchings, agreed to take me on the understanding that I should endeavour to find other accommodation as soon as possible.

Police work was extremely difficult at the time and, with shortages of men in Newton Abbot, I found myself continually being called to do beat work there. This became so bad that in a stretch of seventeen weeks, I had some thirteen weeks and five days night duty in the town. Demands were also made on me to cover all complaints, road traffic accidents and crime enquiries in the Highweek beat. It therefore came as no surprise when Mrs Hutchings said that she could no longer accommodate me as she had to work full-time on the business accounts, in addition to taking orders for coal and for taxi work. When giving me notice she explained that, in view of the telephone ringing almost continuously and her anxiety of my being disturbed, she found it all too much for her. So, with some regrets, I returned to my old quarters once again.

During my first weeks back in the Newton Abbot area a deep depression had settled over the station. It appeared that Inspector Burgess was leaving and another inspector would shortly be arriving. Several of the older men seemed quite distressed at the forthcoming change, in particular Sergeant Lamb, who had lost his usually jocular disposition.

When the new inspector arrived I found it difficult to believe that he could have cast such a dark shadow over the station. Short, very rotund, a smile for everyone, he appeared to be the very model of the laughing policeman. However, later I learned that he and Sergeant Lamb had served together at headquarters, where the then Constable Donald 'Bucky' Buckingham, a probationer, had earned a reputation for tale-bearing to senior officers. One such incident had involved Clerk Constable Lamb, who had threatened the recruit with physical violence if the offence was ever repeated, to wit that he would be the recipient of a 'thick ear'. He was quite sure that the newly arriving inspector would not have forgotten or forgiven the incident.

On the Highweek beat one day I had occasion to see Mrs Hutchings and learned that the 'nice inspector' had taken it upon himself to ignore the details in my report and personally called on her to check if she had any complaint to make against her one-time lodger. I do not know whether he had been disappointed or delighted to hear that she had no complaint, but apparently he had then been obliged to listen politely whilst she extolled my virtues at some length and expressed her regrets at not being able to continue being my landlady. In hindsight, I suspect he was definitely disappointed.

The Highweek beat was always demanding as not only did the felons and petty criminals of Newton Abbot journey out into the surrounding country to commit offences, but Seale Hayne College has always housed a large group of healthy, over-active agricultural students who, with all the japes and fun of their *rag weeks*, regularly managed to cause mayhem in the district. A victory on the rugby field could also almost guarantee that there would be damage or minor vandalism in the beat.

My predecessor, John Gulley, had been an ideal man for the beat; calm and quiet in all circumstances, he had the knack of clearing up matters efficiently to the satisfaction of everyone. On the other hand, unhappily, I appeared to be continually upsetting my inspector. My reports were never quite right in his eyes and my phraseology definitely caused him distress.

For example, one day when on duty in Newton Abbot market, a successful bidder reported to me that when he had gone to collect the four hens that he had purchased, they had disappeared. I went to the auctioneer, Mrs Hussey of *Hussey and Company*, who was filling her husband's post whilst he was serving in the army, to get any information that she might have. Market days are always harassing times for all the workers involved, not least the auctioneers - and I got short shrift from the lady who, if she did not actually use the words 'get lost', more or less told me that she could not be bothered with such a trifling matter. Being lumbered with an undetected crime report (a form number 41, which, incidentally is still a crime report form to this day!) perhaps coloured my account, in which I mentioned that I had received a brusque reply from Mrs Hussey when I had asked for information. The report was duly returned for continuation of enquiries and with the 'brusque' heavily encircled.

A week or so later, when off duty, I received a call that an unidentified aeroplane had landed in a field at Sandford Orleigh in the Highweek beat. I dashed on my bicycle to the field, there to find a fire engine with crew, an ambulance with driver and attendant, Inspector Buckingham with his car and accompanied by Sergeant Lamb, Detective Sergeant Vickery, who had brought Sergeant Worden and Detective Constable Harvey in his car, a motor patrol car and crew, and a handful of civilians, including the man who had reported the incident.

From him I learned that a uniformed man, complete with canvas holdall, had climbed out of the plane and had walked briskly out of the field, making off in the direction of Newton Abbot. The plane, described as 'quite small', had been turned in the field and then flown off in an easterly direction. There being nothing to see or do in the field, everyone else made his departure, leaving me in splendid isolation and with Inspector Buckingham's instruction: "Find out what happened and get your report in as soon as possible" ringing in my ears.

I went into Newton Abbot, first calling at the Globe Hotel on the corner of Bank Street and Courtenay Street. My enquiry of the reception clerk: "What guests have arrived in the last hour?" received the reply: "Only one, a Major Ballard of the American Army".

My knock on this guest's door was answered by a big, friendly U.S. army major. Apparently quite unsurprised by my call, he greeted me: "Hi, what can I do for you?".

In the bedroom, I asked: "Did you come by plane and land in a field just outside the town?". To my delight, he replied: "Oh sure. My buddy, Major ... flew me over in a spotter kite. Nothing wrong is there?".

We parted on most friendly terms, and in my report concerning the major's query I typed: "I explained the *furore* his unofficial landing had caused". I completed my report on the same day and handed it in when I arrived for night duty in Newton Abbot at 9.30pm. I was off duty at 5.30am and still in bed when, at about noon, Sergeant Badcock awakened me. He explained that Inspector Buckingham had sent my report back for retyping as it had to go to the American authorities and he wouldn't send it with the word '*furore*' in it, saying that he didn't know what they would think of us by suggesting that the landing had caused an uproar.

By this time fully awakened, I told the sergeant that I would not retype the report; if having a fire crew, an ambulance crew, a motor patrol crew, an inspector, three sergeants and other policemen and all the excited civilians assembled in the field had not been a furore, then what was? Sid looked at me quite sadly, remarking: "I knew you'd be awkward, so I've typed it again for you. Come on sign it or I'll be in trouble with Bucky ".

At the next pay parade dear old Superintendent Coppin cleared his throat before saying: "I've had some reports recently with fancy words in them. I don't like fancy words, so don't use them". Once again the inspector had 'done me down'.

Over a short period I had a run of luck with arrests, resulting in there having to be a number of special courts to deal with the offenders. Superintendent Coppin had occasion to remark to the inspector: "Another special court and Constable Trist again. This is the fourth in two weeks. He's having more arrests than anyone".

The immediate reply was: "Yes, what a pity he's so headstrong". One of his astute ways of putting me down was always to refer to me as 'young Trist', suggesting, as it did, that there was plenty of time before considering me for any appointment. Probably I had brought this criticism upon myself, being no actor and showing far too readily my distaste of some habits or actions of others.

Inspector Buckingham was a man with a gargantuan appetite and was wont to walk in upon the late and night turn constables whilst they were eating their suppers, remarking on what a splendid meal he had just eaten before returning to the station. With rationing so tight, our suppers were usually much bread with very little filling, our cheese ration being just two ounces per week, while cooked meats had almost completely disappeared. Apparently Mrs Buckingham was a luckier shopper than most housewives at that time.

On one occasion, immediately after remarking how well he had dined, he sent the telephonist to

Holland's fish and chip shop, just below the station in Union Street, for a pound's worth of chips. For comparison, my pay in 1943 was just £4.2s a week. Whilst the price of potato chips had greatly increased from the charges made by Mike Dimeo in my Paignton days, £1 still bought a large quantity. The telephonist duly returned with a very large, newspaper-wrapped bag of chips, which the inspector consumed whilst walking about the telephone and charge-rooms. Quite possibly my face showed disapproval of this piggishness and he caught sight of my expression. Whatever was the cause, there was always a barely concealed mutual dislike between us.

Later he was my chief inspector when I was patrol sergeant at Paignton. He was promoted to superintendent in 1954, to take charge of the Tiverton division. There, the special constabulary held a dinner each year and, in his first year, Superintendent Buckingham was the principal guest. It was the usual lavish spread, but it was noticeable just how generous were the portions laid before him. With the main course, there was a succession of special constables spooning out to him: "A few more potatoes, 'Super'?", "More meat, 'Super'?" - as several slices were added to his already well-filled plate. "More greens?", and so on and on. Once the main course was over the sweets were taken around and, whatever he had selected as his first choice, the 'specials' were not happy until he had sampled each of the several other confections. Always their offers were smilingly accepted and at the apparent end of the meal, with his complexion assuming a ruddy hue, he sat back, apparently well and truly replete.

It was then that a special constable, standing in the entrance way, placed a trumpet to his lips and blew a fanfare, ushering in Special Sergeant Govier, a Westexe baker, bearing aloft a serving dish on which lay a huge two-feet long pasty. Placing the dish before the superintendent, the sergeant, amidst cheers and clappings, challenged the guest: "Let's see you eat that lot then, 'Super'!". Apparently not the least surprised, or put out, the superintendent took up knife and fork and ate and ate his way through the pasty, not having to declare himself defeated until all was consumed except for one small end piece of pastry. It was little wonder that this 5 feet 8 inches tall man tipped the scales at well over 20 stone!

At the end of 1943, in addition to the normal Highweek residents, I had two camps of American soldiers. One camp, of some 3,000 coloured conscripts, was set in the cleared woodland area which is now the Heathfield industrial estate, whilst in the grounds of Stover House (now a boarding school for young ladies), on the east side of the Newton Abbot golf course, there were over 3,500 white U.S. soldiers. For someone such as I, brought up in rural Devon, I couldn't help but wonder why the white and black servicemen, brothers-in-arms together and fighting on the same side, had to be segregated. Such is the injustice of man. These men were undergoing concentrated training in preparation for the long-awaited invasion of the occupied countries of Europe.

There has always been harsh, perhaps exaggerated, criticism of these visiting troops, but there was little one could say against the conduct of the near 7,000 men in my beat. There had been trouble between the members of the two camps when they first arrived, but this had quickly been stopped by making Newton Abbot 'off-limits', alternate days to each camp. On some occasions there would be a slight hiccup when a member of the camp banned that day from the town arrived back from a course, or from leave. His appearance on the streets of Newton Abbot would result in him being chased and, if caught, beaten up by members of the other camp. Quite quickly this danger was identified and, with typical American efficiency, leave and other rotas were rearranged to stop the trouble.

The policing of the town by the U.S. military police played no little part in ensuring the lawfulness of their men. A woman could walk through the town at any hour of the day or night without the slightest fear of even being 'wolf-whistled', and certainly there was no danger of molestation.

With access to hitherto impossible sources to obtain articles like nylons and chocolate from their 'P.X.', their equivalent to the British 'NAAFI', the American soldiers had no need to recourse to violence to obtain sexual favours as there were all too many local ladies ready and willing to make themselves available! The use of some of these 'ladies' rather indicated that some of the soldiers were not over-critical.

Just at the entrance to East Street there was a dirty, dilapidated second-hand shop, now long gone. The site now forms part of Messrs Austins' store. Above the shop were rooms occupied by three sisters, all of them very much in keeping with the premises. The ugliest (should I say the least attractive?) of the sisters 'rejoiced' in the nickname of 'Fourpence', apparently this being the price she charged her 'clients' for whatever she did. However sparse her customers may have been prior to the arrival of the Americans, from that time until their departure 'Fourpence' was in constant demand.

On one occasion I had to see the colonel commanding the Stover House camp, where, at the lower end of the grounds, the Newton Abbot to Moretonhampstead 'express' train passed by on its journeys. I told the colonel that if his men did not stop their practice of putting stones on the railway line there would be a train derailment. He looked at me in total bewilderment, exclaiming: "Everyone back home puts rocks on the line. Don't you do that here?". Patiently I assured him that nobody but nobody did that in this country and would he please put a stop to it before there was an accident and possible fatalities. I did point out that in the States the locomotives were much bigger and much heavier, and that this, possibly, made it safer to put objects on the line, but that we just did not have such 'magnificent steam monsters' over here. Put to him that way, he assured me that the activity would stop, and stop it did!

Within a few days of the first troops arriving in the district I was called out to deal with a sudden death. An American private had been returning to his camp some time between 11pm and midnight and had used, as a short cut, the area which had once housed the Bradley Mills, off Bradley Lane. The soldier, hurrying in the dark, had been traversing the one-time floor of one of the demolished buildings. Originally the floor surface had been composed of six feet square flagstones, many of which had been stolen to be used elsewhere. He had stepped from one flagstone onto an area where a flagstone had been removed and left a gaping pit. He had then fallen forward, his neck striking the edge of the next stone, and the blow had rendered him unconscious; apparently, with his body suspended across the cavity, he had choked to death.

U.S. military personnel in the form of a major, a sergeant and two military policemen ('Snowballs', as they were known with their glossy white helmets) joined me on the enquiry using two of their jeeps - the first of these later-to-be-proved versatile machines that we had seen. Having gone to the mortuary, then in Halcyon Road, to view the body, we were about to go to the mills when I saw Superintendent Coppin approaching. I asked the driver to stop, explaining that it was my superintendent and that I had better report what I was doing.

The jeep stopped and I introduced Mr Coppin to the major before detailing our activities. However, Superintendent Coppin showed only polite interest to my explanation, his mind apparently being elsewhere, but then he plaintively said: "I've never ridden in a jeep". I, in turn, then asked the major if he would please give my senior officer a lift back to the police station, which he said he would gladly do, and so we duly drove a highly delighted superintendent back to Union Street before resuming our enquiries.

[Just before the end of 1943, after some 35 years' service, Superintendent Coppin resigned. He had been a '26 year man', so had faithfully and well served the force for more than nine years after he could have retired. In effect, this meant that having secured his pension in 1934, for the ensuing years he had been working for one third of his salary. His successor was Superintendent Ernest John Stone, who moved from Middlemoor, where, from 1939, he had been in charge of the air raid precautions department. At his first parade in the 'E' division he had every available man parade, and in his address began by assuring us that, whilst he knew we expected him to introduce changes, this would not be the case. In fact, everything would continue exactly as in Superintendent Coppin's years of command. For the next half-hour he then laid out what he expected of us, involving many, many changes. His was a very different regime from that of Frank Coppin, with tighter discipline, but providing a man did his best on whatever task he was assigned there were no complaints or criticisms from the new superintendent.]

At the post-mortem examination, carried out by an Exeter pathologist, the small mortuary was over-filled. In addition to the pathologist and his assistant (me), there was the major (who, I then learned, was a doctor), a captain of their military investigation branch, a sergeant of their military police, plus Detective Sergeant Vickery and Sergeant Lamb.

The dead soldier had been an 18-year-old conscript, and the reason for the large U.S. military presence was that he was one of the first American soldiers to die overseas. Every such man was covered by a 10,000 dollar insurance, payable on his death to his family, *provided* that his death had not been caused by, nor was due to, any unlawful act. Had it been found that he had been drunk at the time of his fall, or if the accident had occurred after midnight (the time that he had to be back in camp), when he would have been deemed absent without leave, then the insurance cover would automatically have been invalidated. The post-mortem findings were that he had died at some time prior to midnight and, whilst he had drunk a small quantity of beer, had not been intoxicated. The death was very much a test case, and the findings were a great relief to the soldiers present.

Over the months to May 1944, the roads were constantly thronged with (to us) huge American lorries, weapon carriers, tanks and amphibious vehicles, making it obvious that the invasion day was near. Rumours were rife and military manoeuvres were so frequent that in the end most people just gave up guessing, accepting that it would be 'some day, soon'.

The 6th of June 1944 soon came; when 'D-Day one' *did* actually occur, it took practically everyone by surprise. On the day before all was calm and apparently normal in my two camps. Then, overnight, every man and every piece of equipment and machinery just vanished. We had come to know and accept the American systems and 'know-how'. They were so laid back, so apparently casual, their marching was a joke, and their lack of military 'spit and polish' made their parades seem more like social gatherings than discipline-building exercises *but* they got things done. Their solutions to problems sometimes appeared to be ridiculous, but they worked. For example, during their pre-invasion practices in the South Hams district they had to move their massive vehicles along narrow lanes and negotiate tight bends. The British army had been obliged to take long, circuitous alternative routes when they came to such bends, but the Americans merely threw a few gallons of engine oil onto the road surface and push-pulled the vehicles round in their own length. We never really learned how they left our shores with their allies so quietly on that fateful night, and this was yet another tribute to their efficiency.

The war years were testing times for everyone working in the police service, but some men stood out from the norm by displaying dedication far beyond the 'call of duty'. Without doubt one of these men was Sergeant 284 Alfred Mock, whose story I shall now relate.

Born in 1893, his tenacity was first displayed when he walked to London from his North Devon home in order to join the Coldstream Guards. At that time he was aged just 18 and soon proved to be an outstanding soldier, being selected three times to be escort for the Colour at the annual Trooping the Colour ceremony. After completing his service he left the army to join the Exeter City Police.

In August 1914, with the outbreak of war, he was recalled by the army, and became a member of the British Expeditionary Force, sneeringly referred to by the Kaiser as the 'contemptible little army'. He suffered all the hardships and horror of trench warfare, serving with distinction until 1919, when he returned to the Exeter police force.

In the following year he transferred to the Devon Constabulary, later being promoted, and in 1933 was posted as officer in charge of the Brixham station, living with his family on the station. Like many of his contemporaries, his experiences, his time and his skills were fully utilised, resulting in him rarely being out of uniform. With his serving constables, aided by the recalled war reserves, and the contingents of special constables (for whom he had the highest regard), Sergeant Mock covered a vital area containing fuel installations, torpedo boat yards and other potential targets for the enemy.

***Above. 'Old Contemptible and Yeoman of England', Guardsman Alfred Mock.***

***Right. Constable Mock*** *of the Exeter City Police.*
*Courtesy of 'Frank' Mock*

Following Dunkirk, he recruited and registered suitable men for the Local Defence Volunteers (L.D.V.), then just a token force pathetically 'armed' with truncheons (a lucky few carried their own, or a borrowed, shotgun) and with their only uniform being an L.D.V. armband.

It was at this time that Sergeant Mock received a message: "Possible enemy invasion within 12 hours". He entered in the station log: "Firearm drawn to repel invasion", and, armed with a 1914 .45 revolver, jocularly remarked to his son: "If they do land, my filing system will baffle 'em".

The war years demanded the shouldering of ever-increasing responsibilities, and, with Brixham a designated restricted area with masses of troops contained therein, rumours were rife. It was at this crucial time that Sergeant Mock learned that, in nearby Churston, American troops were gambling, using French bank notes. He realised that this could only mean that the long-awaited invasion day was imminent. Fearing the possible infiltration into the village by 'fifth columnists', Sergeant Mock took it upon himself to close Churston, keeping villagers 'out of circulation' with their vital information.

A memory that remained with him for the rest of his life was the night on which he and his son stood on an ordinarily isolated crossroads as numerous, probably thousands of, invasion troops passed them en route to the landing craft, waiting to take them across the Channel to take part in one of the greatest invasions in the history of warfare.

Standing with memories of his own soldiering days, the suffering, the loss of comrades etched in his mind, he knew only too well what lay ahead of the marching men. To them, with husky voice, he repeatedly said: "Good luck boys". From some groups there was no reply; from others he received assurances: "We'll finish the job this time, Sarge".

Fearing the toll that would be taken from these men before they did 'finish the job', he unashamedly shed silent tears in the darkness of the night. It was to the 'Sergeant Mocks' that the Devon Constabulary owed so much. Their strength and unassuming leadership, welded by their years in the trenches, set a shining example to both their junior and senior officers alike. I well remember Sergeant Mock of Brixham at our divisional pay parades when I was a probationer at Paignton in 1938. My everlasting memory of him was that he was ever-smiling and jocular.

***Sergeant Alfred Mock**, seated with his staff at Brixham station. Standing, left to right: Constable Knowles, War Reserve Constable Emmett and Constable Banks (an ex-Grenadier Guardsman).*

*'Frank' Mock*

After some weeks of working the Highweek beat from Newton Abbot I found lodgings with another family named Hutchings, who farmed Littlejoy Farm on the Ipplepen backroad from Highweek. I quickly found out that the farm name was appropriate, the farmer and the two daughters living at home all being dominated by Mrs Hutchings, a lady of some 17 stone, whose obesity caused her much unhappiness - which she inflicted upon everyone about her.

It was a move made in desperation, pressures being placed upon me to "find somewhere in your beat to lodge", and in a very short time I realised just how inconvenient the move was to be. No telephone, no running water, oil lamps, and a state of isolation made for a spartan life, and most difficult for any communications and other police requirements to reach me. In fact, I had to visit the Badcocks' house on each tour of duty to ensure that there were no outstanding matters requiring attention.

Fortunately, the Badcock family were quite happy to take messages and to assist in every way. Sid Badcock was an ex-guardsman, extremely easygoing and co-operative, whilst Mrs Badcock was a very pleasant lady, her only grumble being at their having been obliged to: "leave Tivvy". They had two children: Wendy, then aged about 7, a lovely little girl who later married a Devon county constable, and a two-year-old son, Melvyn, who was later to join the force and eventually retire as superintendent when serving at Newton Abbot.

Near Littlejoy Farm were two cottages occupied by a gypsy-like family named Browning. The grandparents occupied one cottage, whilst their daughter in-law, along with her six or seven young children, lived in the other. I cannot recall ever seeing Mr Browning junior. The eldest boys were continually in minor troubles, requiring fairly frequent police visits to their cottage.

On occasions, when making such a visit, and at other times when cycling to and from my lodgings, I would notice that Newton Abbot ladies from a higher social class were at the cottage. Often, after such visits, Mrs Browning, or one or other of her children, would appear in fresh clothing, quite inappropriate for their way of living amidst dirt, unwashed crocks and with an earth closet. It was apparent that the ladies were not visiting the cottage as a charitable exercise, but for the purpose of buying the family's clothing coupons.

Enquiries resulted in the subsequent appearance of a number of the ladies, with Mrs Browning, at the Newton Abbot magistrates' court for clothing coupon offences - despite the quite frantic efforts of some of them to avoid being summonsed. It all seems quite petty now, but in those rationing days it was essential that the limited supplies of items should be shared fairly; the flaunting of the regulations by a wealthy few made a mockery of the system. The coupon purchasers were fined quite heavily, but Mrs Browning was given a stern warning before being fined a nominal sum.

Finally I was offered lodgings by a local garage owner called 'Les' Rowe, who was also a sergeant in the special constabulary. He and his family lived just two doors from the Highweek police house, so the move was not only to a more pleasant atmosphere but was also so much more convenient. With such a beneficial change, all seemed to be going well for me until a single constable was required at Dawlish. Such men had become extremely scarce. Apparently there were just two to choose from, one being me and the other being Constable 'Jack' Ewart Crapp, but as Jack's parents lived at Dawlish the 'inevitable' happened. In July 1944 I moved to Dawlish, there to be stationed.

Before I leave Highweek there is another matter concerning the Newton Abbot area that I ought to record. The town was 'railway orientated', with over 1,200 local men employed by the G.W.R., 'God's Wonderful Railway', on the station and in its many departments. With drivers and firemen coming off duty at all hours, they were a source of much useful information as they knew almost every 'local petty criminal' and his reputation. Also, there were the 'knockers-up', young men just embarking on their railway careers, who had the responsibility of ensuring that the footplate men and the guards were awakened whenever they were on night call. Such night work often started at most unsocial hours - 2, 3 and 4am.

The 'knockers' cycled around the town equipped with a pole with a ferruled end. On arriving at the house of one of the railwaymen to be called, and finding no sign of movement within, the 'knocker-up' tapped the bedroom window with the ferrule until the blackout curtain was pulled back and he was assured that the man was fully awake. It was not an arduous job but the 'samaritan', endeavouring to ensure that the night train ran with its full complement of crew, was often assailed with a torrent of abuse for 'waking the missus' or 'the kids' or 'the baby' or, on occasions, all three.

Whilst the 'knockers-up' were an unloved group by their rail peers, to us beat men they were a wonderful source of information. Silently cycling through practically every street in Newton Abbot, they frequently saw night travellers laden with suspicious-looking items, or a stranger leaving a house or store. If the night duty constable was fortunate enough to meet a 'knocker-up' and able to act quickly on some such nugget of information, a nice pick-up could result in his spending the last hours of the duty in the warm police station instead of remaining out in the bitterly cold night air. It was, indeed, under such circumstances as these that the matter referred to above had first come to light, and which I shall now describe.

Early in 1940 a young Newton Abbot man named Slocombe was called up, but found that life in the army was not to his liking. He deserted, was picked up from his home and placed in the army detention rooms, a requisitioned house in East Street. This had been converted by merely putting bolts on the outside of each detention room door and lacing barbed wire across the window exteriors.

Very promptly Private Slocombe found a way of squeezing out through the barbed wire and disappeared. Searches of his home in Prospect Terrace brought no useful result and, as time passed, other more pressing matters caused his desertion to be almost forgotten. Then, from railwaymen, including the 'knockers-up', came reports that Slocombe had been seen creeping along Queen Street, near Madge Mellor's, or that he had been seen in other parts of the town at different hours of the night.

On each occasion that a report of a sighting was received the No.2 night constable would find his mate on No.1 beat. While he quickly went to the front door, the other hid close to Slocombe's back door. Then the pantomime commenced. Loud, insistent bangs on the front door had no apparent effect on the house's occupants, whilst the adjoining, and their immediate, neighbours were sufficiently disturbed to come to their doors or to peer out from their unlit bedrooms.

After a long, long time an upstairs window of the Slocombe's house would be opened and 'Mother' Slocombe would querulously croak: "What do you want? What are you waking me up for, this time of the night?". "Police here, Mrs Slocombe. Come down and open up", would be the retort. Further protests and grumbles ensued but finally, after perhaps another ten minutes, the three bolts were drawn, the lock key turned and the door opened an inch or so before allowing entry to be gained. Every room, and the roof space, was searched, each of our moves being the subject of complaint, but all without any sign of the missing soldier. Much to our annoyance, we then had to admit defeat and make as dignified an exit as was possible, the harridan, meanwhile, screeching her low opinion not only of us, but also of the listening neighbours and Newton Abbot citizens in general.

Fifteen years later an old lady that I knew purchased the house and invited me to inspect it before she embarked upon a complete renovation of the property. She was despairingly showing me the dreadful state of the kitchen (a leak in the pipe to the sink tap had allowed water to run down the interior wall for so long that the floorboards were spongy rotten, making portions of the floor dangerous to walk upon) when, lifting the filthy piece of linoleum to trace how far the floorboards would have to be replaced, I found a trapdoor. All then became clear - the deserter had been living with his mother from the day of his escape from army custody until at least 1943. Whenever the police had visited the house the lengthy delay in opening up had been to give him time, literally, to 'go to ground'!

Opening the trapdoor and peering down, the first item that I saw was the frame of a motorcycle, minus its engine, gears and number plates, quite possibly a stolen machine stripped of parts which had been sold during the war years. Dropping through the trap door, I found that it was possible to travel the whole length of one side of Prospect Terrace - from No.1 to No.47! The occupants of the other houses would not have slept soundly had they known this fact. It is doubtful that any other house in the street had a similar trapdoor facility, so unlawful entry had not been possible, but Master Slocombe had probably spent many hours in hiding underneath the houses, listening to the conversations of his neighbours. Two things are certain; he had never heard any good of himself expressed by any of those good folk, but how he must have laughed at our efforts to arrest him! In 'the job' it has always been a comforting thought to know that you can't win 'em all!

# CHAPTER 18
# DAWLISH

The police station at Dawlish was large enough to provide living accommodation for the sergeant (Sidney Stephens) and his wife as well as two single men's dormitories on the upper floor. However, when I arrived there I was told that I had the use of both rooms and that it had been arranged for me to take my meals with a Mrs Davies in Regent Street, an excellent arrangement whereby I was accepted as 'one of the family'.

The beat was covered by two 'regular' constables, one being 'Len' Doble and the other, up until my arrival, being C. J. 'Buck' Taylor, who had been transferred to police the Denbury area. There were also two war reserve constables (Luxton and Andrews) attached to the Dawlish section, and the outlying rural area was covered by the three country stations at Exminster, Kenton and Starcross. Constable Edgar Manley had, at one time, been the beat man at Kenton, and it was whilst he had been stationed there during some of the war years that an incident had occurred which had caused quite a stir at the time, but one which, no doubt, was repeated in rural areas the country over. His report on the matter, though, makes most interesting reading:

*Kenton Station 'E' Division* *Date: 12th July 1941*
*Report to Superintendent F. Coppin*
*From Constable 230 E. Manley*

*Subject: Enemy Aircraft (H.E 111.) shot down and destroyed by fire, at Big Ringsdon Field, Helwell Farm, Kenton, at about 1.20am on 9th July 1941.*

*Sir,*

*I have to report that an enemy aircraft, a Heinkel 111, twin engined bomber, crashed in Big Ringsdon Field, Helwell Farm, Kenton, at about 1.20am on Wednesday the 9th inst., undoubtedly through being engaged by one of our night fighter aircraft.*

*The machine was entirely burnt out, and three of the crew of four, which manned the machine, were either killed during the engagement, or burnt to death. Their bodies being found in a very charred condition, in the wreckage of the aircraft.*

*The fourth member of the German crew (Leutnant Anton Engelhart) the pilot, baled out, and came down by parachute, and was taken prisoner.*

*On the date in question, I was on duty at Kenton Hill, Kenton, in the vicinity of my house, owing to the fact that an alert was in operation. Several enemy aircraft were heard at different times, in the locality, and at about 1.15am I heard cannon fire from one of our fighter patrols, and shortly after, what appeared to be a ball of fire, appeared in the direction of Exminster. It grew in intensity as it proceeded in a southerly direction, and suddenly seemed to drop almost vertically to the ground, but owing to the intervening hill I was unable to determine its exact location but formed an opinion that it was on the borders of Kenton and Kenn Parishes. The reflection of flame from the burning plane illuminated a large area, and I immediately proceeded in that direction to obtain definite information of its location to enable me to inform Sergeant Stephens. On reaching the Devon Arms, Kenton, I saw Mr George Wills, the licensee, who offered to take me in his car.*

*On reaching the junction of Church Street and High Street, Kenton, I met Home Guardsmen George Stoneman and Victor Bult, escorting a German airman in the direction of the police house. This being the pilot, who had baled out and landed on a hedge of a market garden at the junction of High Street and Chiverstone Lane, Kenton, and who had been taken into custody by Stoneman.*

*The airman was immediately disarmed in the car and taken to the police house, where, I immediately searched him to prevent him destroying anything which might be useful to the intelligence departments of this country, the particulars of which are stated later in this report. Then, leaving the prisoner in my kitchen, in the charge of Special Constable Colin Wood and Home Guardsmen Stoneman and Bult, I telephoned the facts to Sergeant Stephens of Dawlish, who arrived shortly after accompanied by War Reserve Constable Luxton, and Messrs Draper and Davis, members of the Dawlish special constabulary.*

*In the meantime, Special Sergeant Wood and Special Constable Pitt had been detailed to locate the aircraft, and Special Constable Gardener, to guard the spot where the enemy pilot had landed, and had left his parachute.*

*The prisoner had badly scorched arms and face and received medical attention from Dr. J.H. Iles of Starcross. I remained with the prisoner until the arrival of Sergeant Stephens and upon his arrival, I informed him of the action taken up to that time. Shortly after leaving my station, in the first instance, when I left to locate the plane and prior to me returning with the prisoner, Special Constable Burrington, of Helwell Farm, Kenton, telephoned my station and informed my wife, that the plane had crashed in a field known as Big Ringsdon, on his farm, and stated that he was proceeding there to carry out what duties he was able to.*

*On the arrival of Sergeant Stephens, I gave him such particulars as I had been able to obtain, and on his instructions I accompanied War Reserve Constable Luxton and Special Constable Wood to the scene of the crashed plane, where they had been detailed for duty. We were taken there by car through the courtesy of Mr Wills of the Devon Arms, Kenton.*

*On arrival there, I found Special Sergeant Wood and Special Constables Pitt and Burrington on duty. The wreckage of the plane was burning furiously, but it was impossible to get very close to the machine. Members of the Kenton Home Guard, and Air Raid Wardens were also in attendance, as were members of the Dawlish Auxiliary Fire Service.*

*Air Raid Warden Philip Soper of Kenton, informed me that the body of one of the crew could be seen in the rear part of the machine but that it had been impossible to remove it owing to the intense heat and the fact that ammunition had been exploding. I examined the wreckage as far as possible but was unable to see any trace of other bodies, and in accordance with instructions, when leaving I returned to my station, taking with me Special Constable Wood, who I considered would be of more assistance at my station in view of the number of special constables already on duty at the wrecked plane. On the return journey I stopped at the point where the pilot landed, and collected the parachute, as a number of civilians had collected there and Special Constable Gardener was having some difficulty keeping them away from the parachute. I detailed Special Constable Gardener to maintain a guard on the spot and prevent the public from souvenir hunting, and search the surrounding ground with a view to collecting any matter which the pilot might have endeavoured to dispose of. In view of the fact that the pilot had been taken into custody as soon as he had released his parachute, I did not consider he had had sufficient time to dispose of anything.*

*Upon arrival at my station I found that Superintendent Coppin had arrived, and also had Constable Beare of Starcross with him. The injured pilot had received medical attention and arrangements had been made for his removal to the military wings of the Devon Mental Hospital, Exminster where he was taken by car by Sergeant Stephens accompanied by Constable Beare.*

*Divisional office had been kept informed of all the facts and information which were obtained, and the R.A.F. Intelligence Department had been informed.*

*Upon the departure of the prisoner to hospital, Special Constable Wood was left at my station whilst I accompanied Superintendent Coppin to the scene of the burning plane. On arrival there I found that the fire was greatly subdued, and whilst searching around the debris, I found another body in a charred state lying between the two engines. I then returned to my station with Superintendent Coppin, and on reaching there found that Sergeant Rowe and Constable Willoughby of Chudleigh, had arrived there.*

*Every effort had been made to ascertain how many were in the crew of the plane, as I had been unable to get this information from the pilot, owing to his inability to speak or understand English, but from what appeared to be a pilots log sheet taken from him during my search of his garments, on which was an entry 'Persononzahl 3', an opinion was formed that it consisted of three.*

*The wreckage was positioned in a field known as Clarkes Field, Chiverstone Farm, Kenton, a military guard was requested from the Buffs regiment stationed at Dawlish Warren, and took over the guard of the wreckage. A police guard was also maintained.*

*When searched, the following property was found on the pilot:-*

*Pilots log sheet. Wrist watch. Identity Disk No. 53578 over 689. Identity certificate (Ausweis). Envelope containing French currency to the value of 685 francs, consisting of bank notes for the following amounts: one for 500 francs, one for 100 francs, one for 50 francs, three for 20 francs, one for 10 francs, one for 5 francs. Also a 'Nederlands' bank note to the value of 10 guilder. A tin containing 6 tablets. Various pages of coupons. Wallet engraved with the words 'Soldbuck, Personalausweis Luftwaffe. Surmounted with an Eagle on a Swastika in gold' Packet of cigarettes, box of matches. Gold chain and key. Automatic pistol with spare magazine. Holster and belt. Gloves. Signalling lamp. Flying suit. Life jacket.*

*When taken into custody by Home Guardsman Stoneman, the pilot had lost one of his flying boots, and during a search for this, later in the day, I found a sheet of paper in a crumpled condition, near where he had landed. This is attached and appears to be a meteorological report. I understand that the boot was found and handed to R.A.F. officers, who visited the scene, but I have been unable to ascertain who the officers were.*

*At about 7am on the 9th inst. Flight Lt. Segnor, interrogation officer of H.Q. 19 Group, Mount Wise, Plymouth, and Flight Lt. Brown, Mechanical Inspector of crashed aircraft called at this station and were conducted to the wreckage, which they thoroughly inspected in the presence of Sergeant Stephens and myself, after which Flight Lt. Segnor accompanied me to my station and inspected the property which I had taken from the prisoner, certain articles of which he took possession of and gave a receipt for (receipt attached).*

*Flight Lt. Segnor dwelt at length with the pilots log sheet, which he informed me was most valuable in assisting him with his enquiries and with the interrogation of the prisoner and other prisoners who he had to interview. He informed me that it was a very rare occurrence to obtain possession of this document and expressed his deep appreciation of the action taken by the police and others concerned in preventing the destruction of the document. Flight Lt. Segnor informed me that it revealed facts which had been suspected for some time, but which could not be definitely established until he obtained possession of the paper in question. He informed me that he was able to state the 'Staffell' to which the machine was attached, from where it had come to where it was destined and to where it would return. He later again accompanied Sergeant Stephens and myself to the wreckage and thence to Ash Farm, Kenton, to confer again with Flight Lt. Brown who had visited the above mentioned farm as I have received a telephone communication to the effect that bombs had been dropped near the farmhouse just prior to the plane crashing. (See separate report.)*

*Before leaving Flight Lt Segnor asked me whether I could recall much of what I had seen in respect to the machine being engaged by one of our night fighters. I explained that a short burst of cannon fire was heard but I was unable to see anything of this. The enemy plane then appeared to turn west, circle around by the foot of Haldon Hill towards Exminster, where it started to glow like a ball of fire in the sky. The glow increased until it became a blaze, it was then travelling in a southerly direction, and when it reached a point almost due west from my house it dropped almost vertically to the ground.*

*Flight Lt. Segnor thanked me for the information and again expressed deep appreciation for the assistance rendered by the police, stating that his duties had been rendered very light through their co-operation. The markings on the plane, in addition to the Swastika and black cross were:- '5J +GR'. and the number of the plane was 3983.*

*Flight Lt Segnor made arrangements with the adjutant at the Exeter airport for the removal of the bodies of the dead airmen, and these were removed by an R.A.F ambulance at 3.30pm on the 9th inst. He also made arrangements for a military guard to guard the prisoner at Exminster Hospital, to relieve the police of that duty.*

*The three bodies were found in the following positions: No 1. Apparently a rear gunner, about midway between the main structure of the main planes wings and where the tail had broken off. No 2. Apparently the radio operator / navigator. Immediately forward of the main plane structure. No 3. Bomb aimer, was lying forward between the engines. The plane was facing south east.*

*A police guard had been maintained on the wreckage, which had all been removed with the exception of the engines, which are being removed and the site being cleared up, tomorrow the 13th inst.*

*The parachute used by the pilot, another found about 200 yards from the plane, together with the pilot's flying suit, flying helmet, lifejacket, automatic pistol, holster, belt and 11 rounds of ammunition, electric lamp and pair of gloves, were taken possession by Sergeant Hill, 67 Maintenance Unit R.A.F. Taunton, and receipt (attached) obtained for it.*

*Receipts for property, meteorological report and memorandum and copy of pilot's log sheet are attached.*

*Sir,*

*I consider the action and promptitude of Home Guardsman Stoneman is worthy of recognition, and his prompt capture of the prisoner undoubtedly prevented the prisoner from destroying very valuable matter and also saved considerable police time.*

*The position of the wreckage on Flight Lt Segnor's map was V.T. 3705.*

*(Signed)* **Edgar Manley**
*Constable No. 230*

As a coastal town, Dawlish had, in 1941, been designated a 'protected area', entry to which was forbidden without a permit. This resulted in the town being extremely quiet, the only 'outsiders' being railway employees who were sent from all parts of England for up to three weeks stay at their convalescent home.

The beaches were allegedly mined as well as being criss-crossed with anti-invasion barbed-wire barricades. Many of these defences had been hastily erected in mid-1940, immediately after Dunkirk, using whatever materials were to hand. Four years later everything was encrusted with rust, making the whole seascape dreary and uninviting.

With the exception of an outdoor bowls rink in the Lawn Park, sporting and social activities were virtually non-existent. There was a local cinema, but its small seating capacity made screening anything other than second-run films uneconomic.

Bowls was an obsession of both the sergeant and P.C. Doble, so that much of my duty time was spent manning the office whilst they were engaged in matches. (Len was later to receive his 'County badge', in 1947, and become County Singles Champion the following year before going on to become the honorary treasurer of the Devon County Bowls Association, from 1979 to 1993. For many years Len was also a regular member of the Devon Middleton Cup team and was generally considered unlucky not to have been selected to play for his country.)

After the responsibilities of the Highweek beat and the additional duties that I had had to carry out at Newton Abbot, working at Dawlish was a pleasure and delight. Patrolling the town was never over-demanding, crime was almost non-existent, traffic was light and accidents few. Whilst there were always blackout and other minor offences to deal with, it was never over-taxing. In hindsight, the months that I spent at Dawlish were amongst the most enjoyable of my service.

Quite unexpectedly, an order was issued from Middlemoor that a promotion examination would be held on a specified date just six weeks later. Through my contact with the Badcock family, I knew that the examination had to be held to honour an agreement that Sergeant Galpin of the old Tiverton borough force should be promoted. With no such rank in the borough there had been no reason or opportunity for him to take the inspectors' examination up to that time.

Possibly it was considered by the authorities at Middlemoor that the very limited notice given would cause many constables and sergeants to decide against entering. If so, they must have been surprised at an entry of well over a hundred candidates.

At Dawlish, I dusted off *Moriarty*, the *Police Constable's Guide to his Daily Work* and other text books so as to enable me to spend every possible moment endeavouring to recall all the details of acts, regulations and orders that might figure in the questions set for us in the forthcoming examination. One evening Sergeant Stephens came into the office to find me deeply engrossed in one of the books and commented: "If you don't put that ... book down, you'll have your ... brains coming out of the back of your ... head!".

The appointed day came, an intended inspection by the Chief Constable before the examination requiring me to take the 8am train in order to ensure that I reached Middlemoor in time. On leaving St. David's Station I found that Exeter, due to the vast increase of wartime industrialisation in the city, was fogbound with a thick pea-souper, the like of which had not been experienced in the Westcountry in living memory. As a result, traffic was at a standstill and not a bus or taxi was to be found. I had no alternative but to get to Middlemoor on foot, which I did, running, trotting and walking in my 'number one' high-necked tunic uniform, finally reaching Middlemoor after the inspection had been made and the examination already started.

The invigilator in charge of the examination room was my former sergeant from my Honiton days, now an inspector, James Eddy. After hearing my explanation and seeing my perspiring state, he found me a seat, table and papers, and allowed me to start writing.

After about ten or fifteen minutes I found the room so unbearably hot that I had to signal to be escorted from the room by an invigilating assistant and taken to the toilet, whereupon I was violently ill. After washing my face with cold water, I was accompanied back to continue my writing only to find half an hour later that the previous events needed to be re-enacted. At the time I had not even completed the first paper, but thereafter there were no further interruptions.

When the results were published only Sergeant Galpin had passed the examination for inspector and just two candidates had succeeded in passing the examination for sergeant, both having required passes in either one or two subjects because they had already been successful in the remainder in pre-war examinations. In my case I failed in two subjects, 'Evidence and Procedure' and 'General Knowledge', which was a pleasant surprise under the circumstances of the day.

Promotion examinations were an entirely local affair, the questions normally being set by the force training officer, but during the war years that post did not exist: I suspect that the Assistant Chief Constable was the author and person responsible for all aspects of the examination arrangements, apart from the actual invigilation. Papers were also marked by senior officers stationed at headquarters, no outside body or person being involved. Each candidate was allocated a number but, as the marking officers knew the handwriting of men who had served with them, this concession to anonymity was more of a gesture than a reality.

Back in Dawlish and on day duty, I was awakened one morning at about 2am by Special Sergeant Davis, owner of the pharmacy facing The Lawn, who was doing his tour of duty of manning the office during the night. Constable George Lidstone, stationed at Kenton after having replaced Edgar Manley, had had an urgent message which he had said: "Must be passed to a 'regular' ".

Putting on a coat over my pyjamas, I came downstairs to the phone to learn from George that he was dealing with the sudden death of a naval petty officer who had been struck by a train on the stretch of line between Powderham and Starcross. He had found the man's pay book amongst the scattered remains and had been shocked when he rang the Dawlish station to find that the man who answered the telephone (Special Sergeant Davis) was the dead man's father. It was left to me to tell him, when both he and another special sergeant, Charles Sampson, were waiting in eager anticipation of being told some confidential police matter.

Muttering that I had heard some extremely bad news, I left the two specials and went to my bedroom to get dressed. Returning to the office, I asked them both to sit down and then told them the dreadful news.

Special Sergeant Davis was stunned. His son had been on leave, only having left home the previous evening en route to, and apparently quite happy to be returning to, Devonport and his ship. There had been no inkling that anything was wrong and, as far as his father knew, everything was going well with his son's war-service career.

I explained that I had dressed so that I could take over the remainder of his duty turn, enabling him to go home. "No, I'll stay", he replied. "At least then my wife will have a good night's sleep - probably the last for a long, long time". So we remained together until the arrival of the early turn man, when we broke up, he to go home to his wife....

Strangely, it had been only a month or so previously that the other special sergeant, 'Charlie' Sampson, the local bookmaker, had also experienced the trauma of a sudden death in his family. Again, I had been involved, having been called to the Dawlish railway station, where an elderly man had been struck by a train.

It was a tragic occurrence as the engine of a train moving at not more than two miles an hour, before coming to a halt at the station, had collided with a man who had been standing at the far end of the platform, where it slopes down to ground level. The disastrous effect of what can have been no more than a nudge from the engine was difficult for me to accept, or understand, until I learned that the force of the blow the man had received was calculated in foot-pounds per second, the figure being arrived at by multiplying the total weight of the train by its speed at the moment of impact.

Witnesses stated that he had been at the spot for several minutes, moving just as the front of the engine had nearly reached the point level with him. Perhaps it was an effect of the close proximity of the engine or possibly its emission of a cloud of steam from its escape valve, but he had slipped and fallen directly in front of the engine, and been killed instantly. A shower of rain shortly before the incident had caused the sloping part of the platform beyond the platform roofing to become wet and, possibly, slippery. These facts were presented at the inquest and, taking them into account, H.M. Coroner gave a verdict of 'accidental death'.

This verdict scotched rumours circulating in Dawlish that the old man had been involved in a row with his son-in-law, Charlie Sampson, on the morning of his death.

While on duty with him, I learned of Charlie's career and, whilst initially it seemed rather questionable, it certainly was by sheer hard work and astuteness that he had become a wealthy man. His mother, a widow, had delivered newspapers and as soon as Charlie had been old enough he had first assisted her and then acquired a round of his own.

One means of augmenting one's wages for paper deliveries was to act as a bookie's runner. This was an offence under the 1906 Street Betting Act, carrying a penalty for the first conviction of £10, for the second of £20, whilst a third conviction rendered the offender liable to a fine of £50 or six months imprisonment. However, these daunting penalties had had little effect on people like Charlie and his mother, who had regularly taken bets from their customers, delivering them with the stake money to the local licensed bookmaker.

One morning Charlie had told his mother that a customer had given him a bet of £1 on a certain horse. Mrs Sampson had been delighted, the commission on such a stake being two shillings, until Charlie had told her that he was going to "stick with the bet", that is hold onto the £1 in the hope that the horse did not win. When his mother had told him that he could go to prison for doing such a thing, Charlie had assured her that the horse wouldn't win "even if the others only had three legs". His mother had remained unconvinced and had been near to hysterics.

At the time Charlie did 'stick'; the horse 'also ran', and with the £1 capital Charlie started his own bookmaking career, at first acting 'rather close to the wind' but becoming a licensed bookmaker as soon as he had reached the minimum age for registration. In direct contradiction of the adage that 'cheats never prosper', he had never looked back and by the mid 1930s had purchased land on the Warren Road, where he had had three houses built. The three dwellings - a double-fronted centre house, which he occupied, and single-fronted houses on either side, which he let to tenants - were always referred to by the locals as 'Mugs Row'.

The early months of 1945 came and it was apparent that the war against Germany was nearing its end. Victory was no longer in doubt, only when it would be achieved, and everybody began discussing what would happen when the 'boys come home'.

An antiques dealer named Eugene Ervine had taken an empty shop at the lower end of The Brunswick, then at the unfashionable side of The Lawn. As he was a newcomer to the town, there was a certain amount of resentment that he would take business away from some returning local serviceman. This reached such a pitch that the landlords of the shop, the Dawlish Council, had to place restrictions on the nature and extent of his transactions. He was allowed to purchase items for onward sale elsewhere but not to sell in Dawlish itself. Complaints then began to be made that he was not complying with these tenancy conditions, and P.C. Doble was given the task of keeping the shop under observation, recording movements taking place there.

Len spent a couple of weeks on this observation duty, sitting in a shelter on The Lawn busily writing copious notes. Whether Mr Ervine was aware of Len's presence or his purpose in spending so many hours in the shelter is not known, but the notes so industriously written were nothing to do with Mr Ervine or any other local matter. Len was, in fact, writing details of his 'system' for placing bets on greyhounds running on the four Devon tracks: Beacon Park, Plymouth; the Half Way at Kingskerswell; and the County Ground and Marsh Barton at Exeter.

Apparently the same dogs ran on all four tracks but under different names so that 'Happy Jack' at the Plymouth track could well be 'Wild Boy' at Kingskerswell, and two other names when running at the Exeter tracks. The 'system', so painstakingly collated by Len, was to associate four names with each greyhound, then to enter the times that it took to cover certain distances at each track and its place in each race. Len assured me that, with his records complete, he would be able to place winning bets based on the true form of each dog.

Charlie Sampson was non-committal as to whether Len was onto such a dead certainty and as to whether I should accept an invitation to 'invest' in forays against the bookmaking profession. He replied: "If you want a bet I hope you will give me your business and I hope you have a winner or two *but* if at the end of the year you are showing a profit and I'm showing a loss, I shall want to know the reason why".

In short, his view was that in the long run the punter can never win, so I didn't take up Len's offer and, as I moved shortly afterwards, I never knew whether his 'system' did, in fact, work. But I can say that Len never made enough from his 'system' to be able to drive around in a Rolls Royce, though my successor in Dawlish did exactly that. He acquired a Rolls, circa 1928, and, when not tinkering with its engine or cleaning it in his off-duty time, was even known to drive it. However, as petrol was strictly rationed and the car did only about eight miles to the gallon, it must have been extremely expensive motoring.

One of my last enquiries in Dawlish was in response to a complaint from a smallholder at Dawlish Warren that six of his ducks had been stolen. At that time there were just six or seven houses in that area. The complainant had a piece of unkempt, overgrown land mainly covered with couch grass. Otherwise there was nothing but wasteland stretching from the few houses to the seashore. Apparently no one had yet seen the potential of the area or, if they had, certainly taken no action. The changes at The Warren since 1945 have been almost unbelievable but, sadly, much of the development has done nothing to enhance the district.

Going from house to house in the course of my enquiries was not unduly arduous, but nor was it at all rewarding so far as solving the 'crime' was concerned, until I called at one of the last dwellings in the area, where my knock was answered by a Chinese national. His lack of English being matched only by my ignorance of Cantonese led me to believe at first that my enquiry had reached an impasse until the man's employer appeared. Then, to my delight, I learned that the Chinaman had, indeed, seen the six ducks and had actually watched them take off and fly to 'who-knows-where'. From his wild gesticulations it was apparent that they had disappeared far away beyond the blue horizon.

I took a statement from the very pleasant employer, detailing the employee's version and certifying that it was a true translation. Back at the station, I typed the report confidently expecting Superintendent Stone to decide that there had been 'no crime', the next best thing to a detection.

Though my description of the man's torrent of words, accompanied by his frantic arm waving, had been more than sufficient to persuade me that the birds were probably living life to the full in some far distant place, not so for the superintendent. Clearly he had doubts, as back came the report for "further enquiries to be made".

A week or so later, with the undetected crime complaint still on my hands, I visited The Warren again, more as a gesture than with any expectation of clearing the matter up. There I met a man carrying a shotgun, for which, at my request, he produced a game licence.

He was delighted to talk about the sport and, in particular, his successes. These included the recent bagging of six wild duck on The Warren sand dunes. It was clear that he had no idea that he had shot domestic poultry and, when he learned that the date on which the ducks had disappeared coincided with his 'successful' day's shooting, he agreed to accompany me to the home of the smallholder, made humble apologies and paid the loser's much-inflated value of the birds, since, if not unique, they were apparently very dear to *his* heart.

*Superintendent 'Ernie' Stone, (pictured on the far left without a cap), with army personnel who had recovered an unexploded German bomb in the South Hams area.*

*Devon & Cornwall Constabulary Museum archives*

*Officers of the Plymouth City Police seen marching down North Hill, Plymouth, passing the public library and museum buildings, during a 'wings for victory' parade. Above, are the 'regular' and 'war reserve' male officers, and below are the ladies of the 'women's auxiliary police service'.*

*Devon & Cornwall Constabulary Museum archives*

# CHAPTER 19
# TEIGNMOUTH

Another move, this time involving only a one station train journey. At Teignmouth station I borrowed one of the railway porter's hand trolleys and pushed it, fully laden with my kit, while dressed in my police uniform, the 200 yards to the police station in Station Road.

There I met yet another sergeant, Wilfred Martin. He took me to the single men's dormitories, where I learned that P.C. 'Bob' Pillar was occupying the other bedroom. Bob had been stationed at Yarcombe when I arrived at Honiton in 1939 and we had made the occasional point together. I had then been told by Sergeant Eddy that Mrs Pillar was "quite unsuitable to be a policeman's wife, always wanting to be away from her husband and leaving him to fend for himself".

By 1945 she and Bob had divorced and, since becoming a 'single' man, he had started a lucrative sideline repairing radio sets. Although self-taught, he had become a skilled radio mechanic and, as many household sets were over ten years old while, because of the war, the remainder must all have rendered at least six years sterling service, his expertise was in great demand in Teignmouth. However, the 'business' was carried out very discreetly, there being a 'Force Order' that no member of the Devon Constabulary was to be engaged in any other employment. (That prohibition, incidentally, survives to this day.) What would have happened if it had come to the notice of the superintendent or of Mr Martin at Middlemoor is difficult to imagine unless, of course, either had had a radio needing attention. The same rule applied to the wives of police officers, and it was not until late in 1948 that a blind eye was turned to the fact that wives were being gainfully employed in shops and offices.

With my possessions having been stowed away, Sergeant Martin gave me a conducted tour of the town, detailing the difficult areas and the various points on the different beats.

The following day he was on leave, the station being left in the charge of the section's senior constable, 'Tom' Prior, stationed at Shaldon. I came on duty at 9.30am to find four 'P's (Constables Perryman, Phillips, Pillar and Prior) having a heated discussion. Apparently a call had come in from the Royal Hotel - in those days the premier hotel in the area (later a home for mentally-disturbed people and then an empty shell serving as a blot on the whole seafront and a desolate monument to the entrepreneurial world, but now converted to most pleasant retirement flats) - that a guest had registered but did not appear to have any valid documents authorising him to be in the still-prohibited area.

Each of the constables was giving his reason for not going to deal with the matter, such comments floating around as "I've got two crime complaints", "I'm dealing with a careless driving *and* a road traffic accident" and "I've got three reports outstanding and sarge says...". Realising that the charge office was no place for me, I eased myself out into the street and disappeared. Apparently someone in the office suddenly remembered the newly-arrived constable and, when it was discovered he was not to be found, all became extremely critical of their new colleague. An hour or so later I returned, enabling a now highly indignant Tom to demand to know where I had been. When I said that I had been down to the Royal Hotel and was reporting the man for four offences, he was somewhat taken aback, finding it hard to accept that anyone should go out on an enquiry without first being ordered to do so.

Police work in Teignmouth was quite demanding. With a good number of trawlermen in the town, nightly free fights could almost be guaranteed in one bar or another, whilst the dances in the London Hotel required a hired constable to be in attendance at every 'hop'. Certainly one never suffered from boredom.

Cases started to come my way - a housebreaking, a burglary and then a rape in my first four weeks at the new station - during which time I was still returning to give evidence at the Dawlish magistrates' court.

For my first return there I was instructed to await the arrival of Superintendent Stone from Newton Abbot, who would take me to Dawlish. The superintendent arrived and I saluted the seated figure, wishing him a good morning. He replied "Get in" and then drove me to Dawlish without another word passing between us. This was in direct contrast with his actions when we arrived at the courthouse and he espied the magistrates' clerk, Mr Gordon McMurtrie, about to enter the building. Heaving himself out of his Austin 16, his face red with exertion but wreathed in a broad smile, he hailed the clerk and hurried to join him, after which they walked into the court together, the superintendent talking animatedly. Whatever the subject, it caused both speaker and listener to burst into peals of laughter. Later our return journey was again made in complete silence, Ernest Stone merely emitting a grunt when, on leaving his car, I thanked him.

A day or so later was V.E. Day and, like most other cities, towns, villages and hamlets, Teignmouth was suddenly bedecked with flags, bunting and streamers. Parties were organised in practically every street, quantities of food and drink almost miraculously being found to keep everyone fed and happy. People danced in the highways, drinks were offered to, and accepted by, strangers. There was a wonderful upsurge of spirits in citizens; men, women and children alike, who had endured nearly six years of shortages and, in many instances, survived enemy bombing and/or suffered agony and despair through the loss of loved ones.

A few days later the two cinemas in Teignmouth, the Riviera and the Carlton, featured a newsreel (they shared the same edition, the projectionist having to run from his cinema to collect the spool of film from the 'rival' cinema before each screening). The cinema house lights had to be put on and all persons under the age of 16 escorted from the building, though assured that they would be readmitted after the news had been screened.

The Gaumont British News on this occasion fully justified their proud caption: *"Presenting the Truth to the Free Peoples of the World"*, by showing film of men, women and children held in the prisons known as concentration camps, places which had names hitherto quite unknown to us, such as Belsen and Auschwitz. The inmates were walking skeletons - that is those amongst them with sufficient strength even to stumble around the prison areas. Others lay in helpless groups, too ill to have any hope of survival despite the care and attention that they received from their liberators, the Allied Forces.

The sight of those pathetic figures on the cinema screens brought home to many of us how fortunate we had been that Hitler had been thwarted in his plan to invade Britain, baulked by the few miles of water separating us from Europe and by the defence provided by our airmen in the summer of 1940. After Dunkirk the Luftwaffe had begun a systematic programme of bombing British airfields, and had the attacks continued for a very few more weeks the R.A.F. planes would have had no bases from which to fly, with the inevitable outcome that the enemy would have invaded in their own chosen time, secure from any air attacks and their forces protected by German aircraft.

Our prime minister, Winston Churchill, had ordered the bombing and destruction of Dresden, a German cathedral town, although in truth it had no military or armaments centre to justify such an attack. This had caused Hitler to override his chiefs of staff and their quite correct strategies by ordering 'revenge' attacks to be made on English cathedral cities which, though disastrous to those cities such as Coventry, Bath and Exeter, had saved our remaining airfields from being bombed out of existence. From them, our Spitfire and Hurricane aircraft had been able to remain operational and succeeded in defending the country - but it had been a very close call!

From that day in September 1940, when our newspapers had carried headlines that our pilots had destroyed 187 enemy aircraft raiding Britain in the daylight hours of the previous day (a false figure, but in wartime the truth is always the first casualty), we had experienced the turn-around - the defeat of the Luftwaffe, the arrival of the Americans, the invasion of Europe and, at long last, 'Victory in Europe'.

There was then an immediate repeal of much of the emergency legislation; street lights came on again, cars travelled with unscreened headlamps, shops could have illuminated window displays (though limited by the need to conserve electricity, which was still vitally necessary), whilst household windows were quickly cleared of their protective strips of adhesive paper and had their blackout frames dismantled.

However, rationing continued, with everything in short supply, though wherever possible the government allowed easements so that on one glorious occasion even bananas appeared in almost every greengrocer's shop. Many children attending primary school had never seen and had certainly never peeled or tasted a banana. The fruit had just disappeared before the end of 1939.

Having been accepted by the other constables and become nicely absorbed into the routine at Teignmouth, I had hoped that I was to enjoy a lengthy period of service in the town. But not so, for after just ten weeks another removal order arrived. A day or so later and I was again awaiting the arrival of Superintendent Stone to take me, for the third time, to the Dawlish court. His car drew up, I opened the front passenger door and, as I climbed into the car, without any preliminaries and unable to contain my pent-up anger, I literally shouted at him: "They are shifting me to Bampton after just ten weeks here. Can you tell me what's going on?".

*A young wartime constable, seen on his motorcycle with regulation guarded headlamp.*

*John Russell*

For the first time in the two years that I had served under 'Ernie' Stone I got a reply that was longer than two words and did not contain a single grunt. Instead, he uttered a whole sentence, words that have remained with me to this day: "Yes. I can't understand them sending a keen young chap like you to a place like Bampton".

Then, presumably regretting such uncharacteristic openness when addressing a subordinate, he lapsed into his usual uncommunicative state for the remainder of the journey. But the damage had been done; Superintendent Ernest John Stone had actually been surprised into stating that one of his constables was a "keen young chap!".

In all, I received 19 commendations during my police career, amongst others from my Chief Constable, from an assize judge, from Sir Leonard Costello at the quarter sessions and from three petty sessions magistrates, but to hear such words of praise from the very lips of Superintendent Stone - well, that was quite something!

*Senior police and military officers met frequently at police headquarters, Exeter, to discuss service co-ordination and the initiation of civil emergency regulations. The important co-operation between the civil and military authorities was the eventual reason why the smaller borough police forces, such as Tiverton and Penzance, were amalgamated into their respective county forces, in order to have fewer civil police forces that the military had to deal with.*

*Devon & Cornwall Constabulary Museum archives*

*Inspector J. C. Eddy (front row, second from the right) seen with officers outside Sidmouth police station during the war years. The rear rank consist mainly of war reserve constables who were brought out of retirement and back into uniform for the duration of the war.*

*Devon & Cornwall Constabulary Museum archives*

Tel. No.:

Any reply to this letter should be addressed to:—
THE DIVISIONAL OFFICER,
and the following reference quoted: SFW/YAH/B/1/47/4

Your reference.

NATIONAL FIRE SERVICE
No. 19 AREA
"B" DIVISION HEADQUARTERS
"CROSSMEAD"
DUNSFORD ROAD
EXETER

EXETER CITY POLICE
INCOMING No. 4447
DATE RECEIVED 28 APR 1942
PASSED TO

27th April, 1942

The Chief Constable.
City Police Office,
EXETER.

Dear Mr Rowsell,

With reference to the very busy time we have all experienced during the last few days, I feel I cannot let this opportunity pass without expressing to you my heartiest appreciation of the assistance and co-operation given to the Fire Service by members of your Police Force and the wardens services.

During the period on Friday last when many fires were being dealt with in the Newtown district, I was more than surprised at the manner and eagerness displayed by all personnel in their desire to help with the work of extinguishing the fires, and I would add that some of the fires they tackled with stirrup pumps receives from me my fullest admiration.

The task set for my own men and myself was without a doubt made so very much easier through the help and grand work of the part of yours.

Thanking you,

Yours sincerely,

S.F. Willey.

Divisional Officer.

Ack. Many thanks
Draft heading for DDRS? request.

*Notwithstanding how over-stretched the emergency services were during the busy periods of the blitzes, courtesy and letters of appreciation such as the above were commonplace when thanks were due.*

*Devon & Cornwall Constabulary Museum archives*

# CHAPTER 20
# BAMPTON

Yet again I packed my trunk, gathering my bits and pieces together for conveyance with me to the railway station, this time by Sergeant Martin in his car, and was off to another station. Changing at St. Davids, Exeter, I went down platform one to the branchline platform for the 'Dulverton Express', a little tanker train scheduled to stop at every halt between Exeter and Dulverton.

At Bampton Sergeant Macrae was awaiting my arrival to drive me to the police station and to my quarters in the single men's dormitory above the charge-room/office. This was an eye-opener, a doorway from the ground floor passageway led up a semi-spiral wooden scrubbed stairway to a room in which there was one iron bed - and that was it! The stairs led directly into the room; there was no door, just one and a half paces from the bedside and there was the top stair. Heaven help any constable with sleepwalking propensities!

Sergeant Macrae helped carry my luggage to the room and, on me asking where I should keep my uniform, shirts, underwear and the like, simply indicated the quite wide window sill.

He left me, but returned shortly afterwards bearing a wooden tablet, roughly in the shape of a table tennis bat with a large hole at the top of the handle. This was to enable the tablet to be hung in the station office. The sergeant presented it to me with a request that I sign the yellowed sheet of paper stuck thereon. This sheet was to the effect that I had received: one bed, iron; three blankets, woollen; four sheets, cotton; two pillows; three pillowcases, cotton; one bedside table, wooden; one chair, wooden; and one set of window blinds, wooden. All these items in good, serviceable condition.

My pointing out that there was no chair, no bedside table or any blinds to the window appeared to cause a minor hiccup. The sergeant cleared his throat before replying: "Ah yes. They had to be burnt; they had woodworm".

He finally admitted that this had occurred a long time previously, and, apparently, my predecessors had quite happily signed for the non-existent pieces of furniture. I duly signed after Sergeant Macrae had meticulously drawn lines deleting the three items, and, at my suggestion, recorded that they had been "destroyed, woodworm infested".

[The chest of drawers that I had purchased in 1939 was still in my old dormitory at Newton Abbot. My report requesting that it should be collected and brought to Bampton when a removal would allow this to be done 'without cost to the force' was apparently approved, as some weeks later the county lorry brought it to Bampton.]

The sergeant then escorted me downstairs and introduced me to his wife, a very pleasant, rather nervous lady, and her sister, who lived with them, before taking me out on the main street and to my new eating place.

This was with a Mr and Mrs Gibbings; he ran the adjoining butcher's shop whilst she catered for passing traffic with light teas. Mr Gibbings was a delightful man, full of jokey anecdotes and *savoir faire*, with a tendency to slip out of his shop at odd times when Mrs Gibbings was engaged in order to pay lightning visits to The Castle pub, almost opposite his butchery. Mrs Gibbings, on the other hand, was dignity personified, all four feet ten of her, with an affected accent one could 'cut with a knife'.

Sergeant Macrae, having made the introductions, withdrew; the Gibbings' then immediately enquired if I drove and, having been assured that I did, asked if I would be willing to make the Friday deliveries of meat to their country customers. They told me that Constables Brooks and Cheek had each assisted them in this way with the full approval of the sergeant. Later, Sergeant Macrae agreed that he had no objection to my being absent from the station to help them, he considering it was part of the 'war effort'. So, every Friday after lunch I dashed off in the Gibbings' very decrepit Ford delivery van and called at all the nearby villages and hamlets, dropping off the previously ordered parcels of meat. Certainly it was a good way to learn the local geography and to meet the villagers. In the van I carried a gallon of oil. It was fortunate that engine oil was not rationed, as was petrol, for the old engine burned, or lost, as much oil as it consumed petrol on the round.

The whole range of duties, way of living and relationship with the resident sergeant was entirely different to anything that I had previously experienced. Duties were best described as 'elastic'. There were the inevitable 'fatigues' each Saturday morning, except when I was on weekend leave, when they were done on the Friday. Out on the street shortly after 8am, Mondays to Fridays, I saw the children across the main road near the school, repeating the duty at noon, 1.15pm and 3.45pm.

Having seen the children into school, I went to breakfast, prepared and served by Mrs Gibbings. On most mornings she would breakfast with me; I would have cereal and several rounds of bread with my ration of butter/margarine (two ounces of each per week), while 'Mrs G', sadly watching me, would eat just a single thin half round of toast. On several occasions, unable to bear witnessing my almost voracious clearing of the food, she said: "You eat too much; nearly everybody eats too much. I know, I used to be a nurse".

One morning, leaving the house after breakfast to resume my beat patrol, I realised that I had left without my white gloves. Returning, I entered the dining room to find Mrs Gibbings still at the breakfast table, busily engaged in clearing a plate of fried bread, bacon and egg. Apparently her small portion of toast, eaten in my presence, had merely been an appetiser preparing her for the good things to come after my departure. The episode had one very good effect - there were no further references to anyone's appetite!

Unless there was an enquiry or other duty, after seeing the children into school for their afternoon session, I was off duty until they came out at 3.45pm, afterwards patrolling Bampton before going to tea at 5pm. Then, from 6pm to 9.45pm, I manned the office before again patrolling and making the 10pm or 10.30pm point at one of the four public houses in Bampton. It was usual for Sergeant Macrae to make this point.

If all was quiet we returned to the police station together and I signed off at llpm. My average daily hours of duty were in the region of eleven; I can't help but wonder what present-day constables might make of such a situation.

A few days after my arrival the sectional pay parade came, with all members of the section, with one exception, attending in good time prior to the arrival of Superintendent Reginald Annett with the divisional clerk, Sergeant Alway. Having been sent to lunch shortly after lpm and told to be back by 2pm, I did just that, only to find the superintendent had already arrived and had the whole section standing to attention. He demanded to know why I was late on parade. I apologised and explained that I had been instructed to parade at 2pm and it was not quite that hour.

He gave me a very hard stare, looked at his watch and stated: "I make it well after two. What time do you make it, sergeant?", this question being directed to the clerk-sergeant.
He duly replied: "Just after two, sir".

It appeared that I was a doomed man, late on duty *and* daring to suggest that this was not the case. A pantomime then commenced, Constable Bill Mudge, stationed at Yeo Mills, dragging out his pocket watch (totally ignoring the fact that we were all at attention) and shaking his head slowly and deliberately.

Sergeant Macrae looked at his wristwatch, stepped to the office table and lifted the telephone. Bampton was on a manually-operated exchange and "Number please" was clearly heard by all in the room. "May I have the Greenwich time please?", replied Sergeant Macrae. "The time now is one fifty eight" came clearly from the operator, and Sergeant Macrae replaced the receiver back on its hook on the old-style 'candlestick' telephone before stepping back from the table.

A moment of silence followed before the superintendent said: "It appears my watch is fast and you were not late *but* it is usual *and* I expect my officers to parade at least ten minutes before parade time. Bear that in mind in future".

After the parade and the departure of the superintendent and his clerk there was a certain levity amongst the constables. Sergeant Macrae had left the office and, from the constables, I gathered that the sergeant had scored a minor victory over the superintendent.

It was beyond me at the time; probably I was too relieved at having come out of the matter unscathed, but later I learned of the barely-concealed mutual dislike between Superintendent Annett and Sergeant Macrae. They had been in the same intake to the force in 1922, and been housed in the single constables' quarters at New North Road. One night there had been some horseplay in the dormitory, with Reg Annett picking up fellow-recruits and throwing them onto their bunks.

He had tried to do this to P.C. Macrae, a man of similar build (both being over 6 feet 2 inches tall with matching physiques), but Macrae had just taken his discharge from the merchant navy and had not only been able to resist Annett's attack but had also reversed roles and thrown his adversary onto *his* bunk. Apparently Annett had never forgotten or forgiven the incident, and it was seldom that the Bampton section was not the subject of his criticism of some matter or another.

On my first leave day I discovered that it was a simple matter to leave Bampton; there was an early branchline train to Exeter and a choice of through trains to either Newton Abbot or Plymouth. The return journey, again, was well served to Exeter, but there was no service from Exeter to Bampton in the late evening. There seemed to be no alternative other than to buy some sort of transport, but in 1945 this was next to impossible. Enquiries throughout the district brought this home to me very quickly, and I was left considering what appeared to be the only option - cycling the near 30 miles to Exeter, and finding somewhere where I could leave the machine safely before collecting it again late at night and cycling back to Bampton.

Fortunately I met John Baker, owner of the Shillingford Road garage, just outside Bampton. He was later to become a prominent racehorse trainer, as well as running a prosperous timber merchants' business. John promised to 'scout around' for me, and in a week or so came back from the wilds of Exmoor with a Rudge 500 Ulster motorcycle, a powerful beast of a machine but, at that time, in a dreadful condition.

It appeared that it had belonged to a Somerset rabbit-trapper who had returned home one day late in 1939, announced that he was joining the army and had pushed the Rudge into an old, leaky shed, where it had remained for nearly six years. When put into the shed it had been caked with mud, and this had resulted in the mudguards having rusted to a state beyond repair.

Nevertheless, I bought the machine for £30, while a letter to Claude Rye resulted in a pair of very rough ex-War Department mudguards being obtained, complete with camouflage paint, apparently applied with a ladle. Having beaten them into shape to fit the Rudge, I took them to Tiverton to a local paint-sprayer, 'Dick' Dart, who agreed to strip the offending paint and respray in "a couple of weeks".

When I telephoned a fortnight later there appeared to be some hesitation before Dick replied "they were not quite ready" and that he would telephone when they could be collected. The message duly came, I collected the pristine mudguards and fitted them onto the motorcycle. It was not until two or three years later that I learned from Dick that he had had a clean up of his workshop and my mudguards had been thrown out. After my call he had despatched two of his staff to the local refuse tip to recover them!

I was never happy on the machine and was later able to purchase a 1929 Austin 7 from the Holcombe Rogus postman. It had a gravity-feed petrol tank, and a stop for anything longer than a few minutes necessitated opening up the bonnet and switching off the supply to the carburettor or it would leak the tank dry.

Life at Bampton became much more pleasant after I had the means to leave the place on my days off. Also, through his efforts on my behalf, John and I became friends, a friendship which lasted until his death in 1995.

A week or so after my arrival in Bampton, 'V.J. Day' was celebrated throughout the British Empire, America, and in the many other countries which had been overrun by either the German or the Japanese forces during the war. After 'V.E. Day' the allies had been faced with the problem of how to defeat the fanatical Japanese. It had been anticipated that the cost in human lives would be almost unbearable, with every Japanese soldier apparently willing, even wishing, to die for his Emperor. Instead, there had been bombs dropped on just two cities in Japan and surrender terms had been swiftly agreed. It is hard today to even try to describe the relief and jubilation that everyone felt. Nearly six years of war and then this wonderful, almost unbelievable, ending.

Once again there were celebrations everywhere. Funds were raised for the events and for 'the boys returning from the war'. Bampton was no different from any other place in the United Kingdom, with the flags once again flying, church bells being rung and food being found from heaven knows where to ensure that there were parties for the children and adults alike. There was dancing in the streets and seemingly inexhaustible supplies of beer suddenly becoming available.

The chairman of Bampton Parish Council was one George Davey, the local blacksmith. He had headed committees and events to raise funds for the local men returning home after serving in the armed forces. A goodly sum had been raised and a deputation of the demobilised men approached Mr Davey asking when there was to be a share-out of the fund monies. His reply was to the point, if not diplomatic, when he informed the enquirers: "If you think that we are going to share out the money for you lot to p... it up against the wall, you can think again. We'll buy something useful that will benefit everybody".

There was grumbling, talk of 'our money' and a lot of hot air about 'little Hitlers' but, in due course, a piece of land was purchased and converted into a sports ground, with a football pitch. Over 50 years have passed since the purchase, and the pitch is still the home ground for the Bampton football team, with a play area for children.

The previous constable to me at Bampton was Montague 'Monty' Brooks, who had joined the force in October 1938 and served as a single constable in various stations prior to successfully applying to join the R.A.F.V.R. as a trainee pilot in 1941, when his police service had still been a reserved occupation. Unfortunately, he had failed to make the grade, been 'grounded' and obliged to return to the force. That was in about November 1942.

During the year that he had been away from the Devon Constabulary, Monty had married his fiancée of long standing. On his return he had been called before 'A.E.M.', the Assistant Chief Constable, who had had no time for any of the young constables whom he considered had 'deserted' the force when volunteering for service as pilots or observers in the R.A.F. The interview had been an unhappy one for Monty, and had gone something along the lines of:

| | |
|---|---|
| *A.E.M.* ............................ | *"Constable, I understand that you are now married".* |
| *Monty* ............................ | *"Yes, sir".* |
| *A.E.M.* ............................ | *"Did you obtain the Chief Constable's permission to marry?"* |
| *Monty* ............................ | *"Well, no sir. I was in the R.A.F. and I didn't know I had to ask permission".* |
| *A.E.M.* ............................ | *"Indeed you did. As you now see, you are back in the police force and you have taken yourself a wife without permission. There are no married stations available and as far as the force is concerned you are still a single man".* |
| *Monty* ............................ | *"I really am sorry sir, but in the Air Force there was always the chance I would be killed and so we married".* |
| *A.E.M.* ............................ | *"Well, that was your decision and it was the wrong one. You will serve as a single constable until the Chief Constable sees fit to approve your marriage and you are given married quarters. Where is you wife living?"* |
| *Monty* ............................ | *"Great Torrington, sir. She is employed in the Ministry of Food office".* |

At the time Monty was then sent to Torquay but, as all the single men's quarters had been taken over as offices for the special constabulary and the air raid warden's department, he had to find outside board and lodgings. He was still officially a single man, with the opportunity of travelling to see his wife restricted by the much-reduced public transport services to his long weekend, occurring every sixth week.

Air raid warnings occurred almost nightly and all police personnel had to report to the divisional office, there remaining until the 'all clear' was sounded. Monty's undoubtedly long-awaited weekend eventually came. His duty finished at 6pm on the Friday *but* his pass showed him as having leave "to pass in plain clothes from Torquay to Torrington from 8am on Saturday ..., he having leave of absence until ...pm on Monday ...".

That Friday night there was an air raid warning 'red' and the Torquay-based off-duty police officers arrived at the police station, occupying themselves with various things in different parts of the station. Some congregated in the billiard room, watching and remarking on the skill or otherwise (depending on his rank) of the players, others got in odd corners and played cards, whilst a very few might even have cleared some backlog of work.

On the following morning Chief Inspector Annett enquired if anyone had seen Constable Brooks during the night's standby. Getting only negative replies, he instructed that P.C. Brooks be fetched from his lodgings, only then learning that Brooks was on weekend leave. The instruction was changed to reporting before the chief inspector immediately upon his return.

Back in Torquay, Monty was soon made aware of the interest being shown in his movements on the Friday night so he was ready with his explanation when standing at attention before the redoubtable Chief Inspector Annett. He explained that for some time he had been suffering from severe headaches and insomnia. In consequence he had taken two aspirins before going to bed on the Friday evening. These had caused him to sleep through the sounding of the air raid sirens and he had left the following morning on leave. Every effort was made to break down his explanation, but he stuck to his story and the matter was finally, apparently, left in abeyance.

For several years it had been the practice to carry one officer at Torquay as an acting sergeant. Chief Inspector Annett had the chosen man into his office and stated that he had a job for him to do before he recommended him for substantive rank. He was to 'befriend' Constable Brooks and get him to admit that he had missed the air raid warning turnout because he had already left Torquay for Torrington. The acting sergeant duly did this and, by using a lot of "understanding why you did it" and "I don't blame you, you had done your day's duty", etc. etc., finally got Monty to admit his absence without leave.

Whether the 'acting' did become 'sergeant' as a result is not known, but Monty was charged with the offences of 'failing to carry out required standing orders' *and* 'making false statements to a superior officer', resulting in him being fined, reprimanded and transferred. His departure from Bampton in June 1945 had possibly marked the end of his single constable status. If so, he had been given a two-and-a-half-year 'sentence' for failing to ask permission to marry!

[The force had always imposed the requirement to make a formal written request for 'permission to marry'. The original request required details of the lady, name, date of birth, address, work, parents' names and occupations, to which the applicant usually added how long he had been courting her, together with anything else that he thought might expedite the granting of the desired permission. The application invariably resulted in the constable's sergeant or inspector making direct enquiries concerning the suitability of the lady.

In the main the system worked well but, on occasions, bias could result in an unfair observation being made. For example, in about 1937, a constable stationed at Torquay submitted his application. He had completed his probationary period, done quite well in the examination after his two weeks return to headquarters and had a good record of arrests and submissions of process reports.

As was usually the case, policemen being extremely good pickers, his fiancée was an attractive young lady, intelligent and with an excellent background and character. It seemed approval was a mere formality and that the couple would, in due course, have been allocated a married station.

Unfortunately the inspector given the task of checking out the suitability of the young lady was the proud father of a daughter; she was the apple of his eye, but to her contemporaries a rather ordinary, even plain, girl. Following excursions to the Spa Ballroom at Torquay, she would return home and, in reply to her father's fond question as to the success of her evening, complain that it had not been good, adding that the evening had been spent mostly standing, a 'wallflower', unwanted by the male dancers, and watching Constable ...'s girl almost being besieged by admirers in the absence of her constable fiancé.

When compiling his report the inspector stated that this young lady "was a flibbertigibbet kind of girl", a "known flirt" and, in his opinion, unsuitable to be the wife of a policeman. Apparently the powers at headquarters in the 1930s knew what a 'flibbertigibbet kind of girl' was and the application was not granted. Faced with this quite unfair decision, the constable resigned and the force lost an excellent police officer in the process.

There were many such refusals due to personality clashes and other circumstances before the 'system' ended on 31st December 1947. I am definite about the date as some time in that month, stationed at Tiverton, I applied to marry. The lady whose hand I sought lived in Newton Abbot, and Inspector Buckingham undertook the task of checking upon her suitability.

Shortly before Christmas I was instructed to parade before the Chief Constable, Colonel Ranulph Bacon, who told me: "I have had a report from Inspector Buckingham concerning your application to marry. Of course you can marry, and good luck to you both". With the report in his hand, he added: "I didn't know this rubbish was still going on. You might like to know that I have issued an order that no such applications will be required from the New Year onwards". Assuming that there were no other applications in the 'pipe line' at that time, it is most probable that my wife was the last person to be so vetted in the Devon Constabulary.]

***The senior officers mess - 1947.***

*Standing, left to right: Superintendents Jack Roper ('C' division), Edgar Eddy ('G'), Ernest Tothill ('B'), James Eddy (chief clerk), Harry Langman ('H') and William Doney (Traffic). Seated, left to right: Superintendents William Harvey (CID) and William Johnson ('D'), Percy Melhuish (Assistant Chief Constable), Ranulph Bacon (Chief Constable) and Superintendents Archibald West ('A'), Ernest Stone ('E') and Walter Hutchings ('F').*

*Devon & Cornwall Constabulary Museum archives*

Back in Bampton in 1945, police work continued in its usual way with beat patrols, complaints, enquiries and minor thefts, plus all the transit of animal regulations *and* the one day of the year when Bampton came alive - Pony Fair Day. This event, held on the last Thursday in October, drew to the small market town, in addition to fair lovers, every gipsy and layabout from miles around. The four licensed premises were open all day and did a roaring trade.

The top of the town, within a hundred yards of the police station, was fenced off with hurdles and, by 8am, filled with moorland ponies. They varied from foals only weeks old to shaggy old animals who looked so ancient and poor that the R.S.P.C.A. inspectors were continually climbing into the enclosure to make hurried decisions as to whether they were fit to be auctioned.

The main street had cheapjack stalls on either side and, with the crowds thronging the remainder of the roadway and the pavements, vehicles were practically at a standstill. Every now and then a fight would break out, mainly between rival groups of gipsies. One fight which I broke up was between an enraged, drunken, giant gipsy smashing into a much smaller man, totally ignoring the fact that the man was carrying a few-weeks-old baby in his arms.

Probably because October 1945 saw the first pony fair after the war, it was said to have attracted a record crowd. Certainly the debris littering the streets the following morning supported this view, but the auctioneers and the pony sellers were unhappy men. Shortages of feedstuffs and stabling facilities made it impractical for many people attending to buy a pony, so prices were ludicrously low. Hundreds of ponies failed to attract a bid, whilst most others were withdrawn when bids as low as a pound were made. A few, though, were even sold at this price!

By now I had been fortunate to have had several clear-ups of crimes and successfully dealt with other complaints in the district. Having caught the man who had been obtaining cigarettes from the Central Garage slot machine with nicely turned pieces of flatiron, I was talking to the garage owner when he remarked: "You're a very good policeman but you'll never be the policeman that P.C. Cheek was".

Being somewhat 'nettled', I enquired what was so outstanding about the said P.C. Cheek and learned that on a typical Bampton Fair day it had poured with rain throughout the morning and into the afternoon and that the pubs had become so full of customers that it had been impossible to get inside the doors, let alone obtain a drink. The crowds, drenched and despondent, had then begun to disperse and later, at the railway station, the 'down' platform had become tightly packed with dispirited Exonians awaiting the arrival of their train to Exeter. The 'up' platform, too, had become fairly full when, onto it, had strolled P.C. Cheek, secure against the rain with waterproof leggings and cape. He had then come to a halt, turned left to survey the crowd opposite and, without change of expression, had suddenly shot his head forward, propelling his helmet into the air. Shooting out his wellington-clad foot, he had then caught the helmet and, with a deft flick of the foot, shot it into the air again and back onto his head, producing a loud round of cheers and applause from an appreciative audience. P.C. Cheek, meanwhile, had solemnly bowed, turned and departed, leaving behind him a crowd no longer full of their personal miseries but emitting a hum of remarks. I agreed with the garage owner that P.C. Cheek was in a different league to me!

The constables in the Bampton section were 'Lou' Cann at Shillingford (later succeeded by Ernie Tucker), Bill Mudge at Yeo Mills, 'Jack' Westlake at Holcombe Rogus and Maurice Haysom at Oakford. Constable Haysom had a succession of sick leave as he suffered from some painful condition in his spine and leg. Each period resulted in me having to cover his beat, which entailed me cycling up the hill out of Bampton, down the hill to the Black Cat cafe and across Oakford Bridge before the very long climb to the village.

***Constable Maurice Haysom**, pictured outside the Oakford police house with his wife Irene on 23rd August 1938.*
*Mrs Irene Haysom*

Maurice was eventually transferred to Torquay on medical grounds, but there were murmurings amongst his erstwhile colleagues that he had 'swung the lead' and wasn't as bad as he had 'made out'. I was one of the men who assisted in loading the county lorry with his effects, and, to me, he did seem to have a very bad limp. It was not until much later that I learned that his alleged exaggerated leg disorder had finally been cleared - by Maurice being discharged on medical grounds, he having arthritis in the lumbar spine, together with fibrositis of the leg and back muscles.

Maurice was confined to a wheelchair for the last six years of his life. There was little charity shown in the Devon Constabulary in those days.

Whilst patrolling in Bampton one day in early 1946 I was approached by a couple. The man enquired the way to Oakford and, after being given directions, introduced himself as "Constable Stamp, taking over the Oakford beat". He was a little taken aback when I immediately asked: "Are you healthy?". He assured me that he was, and I explained my delight and relief at not being called again to face those Oakford hills.

We became good friends, which lasted throughout our periods of service and long into our retirement. 'Ken' Stamp never achieved promotion, which he deservedly earned by always being a hard-working, conscientious constable. This was probably due to a snap judgement passed on him by his inspector at their first meeting after his arrival at Oakford. The inspector's opening remarks included: "I hope you aren't one of those eight hours a day men we're getting now", to which Ken assured him he was not, but perhaps inadvisedly adding: "If I can get my work done in eight hours then I will, sir". That was enough for the inspector who, on his return to Tiverton, reported Ken as being "Another eight hours a day man and a bit of a troublemaker", all without any basis of fact. Promotion chances could be, and often were, blighted by such unfair judgements and utterances!

The cause of Inspector Hockin's remark was the almost revolutionary introduction of overtime cards. Until 1946 there had never been any question of entitlement to either payment or time off in lieu of payment for hours worked over the forty-eight per week. At Bampton the workload remained unchanged and Sergeant Macrae was regularly obliged to sign my card showing an average of eighteen hours per week overtime worked. Having accumulated over a hundred hours overtime in six or seven weeks, my tentative suggestion that I might take an additional leave day on my long weekend was accepted by the worthy sergeant with: "I don't see why not. Put in for it".

Possibly the additional day on the leave pass was not noticed when being signed by Inspector Hockin and Superintendent Annett, for it was returned to Bampton without comment. Deducting the eight hours off the card had little effect; in fact, the gross total had increased by the end of the week, so the taking of an additional day's leave was repeated a couple of weeks later and yet again after a short period. Then someone at Tiverton finally realised what was occurring, causing questions to be asked of Sergeant Macrae. His report blandly pointed out that the station had always required the working of weekly hours in excess of 48 by the single constable and that the introduction of overtime cards had merely highlighted this fact. He rubbed salt into the wound by pointing out that he had repeatedly asked for an additional constable to be posted to the section, but without result.

[Undoubtedly the overtime cards caused difficulties throughout the county. Their introduction was effected by Major Morris, the Chief Constable, as one of his many practical orders to improve the lot of serving officers. At the time he was a very sick man and it must have been one of the last orders for which he was directly responsible. Certainly it was not an order which 'A.E.M.', the Assistant Chief Constable, would ever have suggested or contemplated.

Major Morris died in November 1946, when the Devon Constabulary lost a very great, humane and efficient chief officer. He had been appointed in 1931, whilst serving as governor of Dartmoor Prison, and had worked tirelessly in his efforts to improve the lot of his officers. He had always been hampered by the lack of finances and the frugal outlook of some of the members of the Standing Joint Committees in the 1930s, which frustrated many of his forward-looking plans.

Despite the tightness of the budgets within which he had worked, he had managed to get a number of well-designed police houses built, all with bathrooms and indoor toilet facilities. They were a monument to Major Morris, but were all disposed of when the policing of the county changed radically in later years.]

Two comparatively minor matters occurred in the 'C' division about the time of the death of the Chief Constable, Major Morris, both of which affected me. The division had 'Jack' Hurley as its C.I.D. officer, an excellent detective constable covering the large area of the division from the Somerset border to Pinhoe and Cowley Bridge, where the Exeter city force line ended.

In Newport Street, Tiverton, stood the old drill hall which, many years before 1946, had been converted into the 'Electric Cinema'. The entrance was glass fronted, and inside was a kiosk forming an island in which sat an attractive blonde cashier issuing tickets to patrons. One of the films currently being shown on the cinema circuits was *Dillinger*, detailing the life of the one-time American 'public enemy No.1'. From being an immensely rich racketeer, Dillinger had been reduced to petty crime, but was fatally shot when robbing the cashier in a New York cinema kiosk, pictured as almost identical to the kiosk in the 'Electric', in Tiverton. One evening a vet's car was stolen in Exeter, and on the same evening two men entered the foyer of the 'Electric' and held up the cashier with a gun, stealing the evening's takings before making their getaway. Jack Hurley's enquiries led him to Exeter, where he linked the theft of the car with the hold-up in Tiverton, the weapon used being the vet's humane killer, later found in the recovered car.

An Exeter detective constable had been assigned to assist Detective Constable Hurley in his enquiries within the city, resulting in their tracing and arresting two young men for the offences, they having 'copy-catted' the episode in the film. It could well have been a coincidence but the Exeter detective was promoted immediately after the arrest of the men, and Jack Hurley considered that his own work should similarly have been recognised. He applied to see 'A.E.M.', then Acting Chief Constable, and although told that his good record would, in due course, result in promotion, he was not placated and submitted his resignation. He joined the probation service, in which he served until his retirement. I truly regretted his departure, he having assisted and impressed me in interrogations of suspects during my service at Bampton.

At the same time my mounting hours of overtime were being considered at Tiverton and a simple solution found; I was transferred to Tiverton and there issued with a new, empty overtime card, the old card being cancelled by my removal!

*A 'Major Morris' police house, now seen all over the county of Devon and particularly in villages and rural locations. With an identical design of country beat stations the constable knew that his carpets and curtains would fit his new station upon removal. These stations had either a small office situated under the stairs or a larger room attached to the side of the house, as seen here. They remain standing as a fitting monument to a popular Chief Constable.*

*Devon & Cornwall Constabulary Museum archives*

*Constable 'Harry' Fice inspecting the documents of a motorist who had been stopped at a prison escape check point on the eastern side of Dartmoor, using the vehicle headlights for illumination. The other constable is armed with a revolver, which was not uncommon at times when dangerous prisoners had made a bid for freedom. This photograph was taken in the early 1930s.*

*David German*

# CHAPTER 21
# TIVERTON

I arrived at Tiverton early in December 1946, when 'Harry' Fice, the section sergeant, explained that he had found difficulty in securing lodgings for me; there were no single men's quarters in the police station, but Constable Ivor Perryman had agreed to have me as his lodger.

I was taken to Constable Perryman's house in Barrington Street, where I met Mrs Perryman, a charming lady, very pregnant and with a two-year-old daughter.

Ivor was a difficult landlord, having severe changes of mood that varied from over-friendliness to refusing to speak and muttering to himself. He later resigned from the force, moved to Newton Abbot, where he worked in a furniture shop, and finally committed suicide by hanging himself in the shop storeroom.

On Christmas Eve I returned to my lodgings from duty to find Mrs Perryman sitting on the stairs, crying bitterly. Her pregnancy had caused her some difficulty in moving up and down stairs, which she overcame by sitting on a stair tread and easing her body up or down to the next tread with a sliding motion. The cause of her tears was that she was unable to move out of the house and when she had asked her husband to purchase the rations and something for the Christmas dinner, he had replied: "That is the woman's job; never in the history of man has he been expected to do the shopping!".

I was able to hurry around and get the rations of fats, sugar, tea and so forth, but at the butcher's shop there was nothing. By frantically telephoning Johnny Baker at Bampton, I succeeded in getting a very poor specimen of fowl, so that we did have a Christmas dinner. By this time Ivor was affability itself, but I had decided that it was time for me to move out.

Some of the personnel at Tiverton were Superintendent Reginald Annett, Inspector Herbert Hockin, Sergeant Harry Fice, Clerk Sergeant Roy Acton and Constable Ivor Perryman, all Devon Constabulary men, and also one-time 'Tiverton borough men' - Constables Arthur Chidgey, 'Jack' Squires and William 'Bill' Stuckey and War Reserve Constables 'Ted' Howe and Richard 'Dick' Squire. Another war reserve constable, 'Les' Clapp, had resigned shortly before my arrival.

To the surprise of everyone on the station, an order was issued from headquarters at Middlemoor that fatigues would, in future, be carried out by civilian labour. As a result, Sergeant Fice obtained the services of a local window cleaner, one William Dicker, who was well known for dashing around the borough pushing a bicycle with his right hand whilst propelling a two-wheeled cart, complete with ladder, bucket of water and cleaning cloths, with his left hand. To see him engaged in this manoeuvre up the steepest piece of Angel Hill caused surprise and wonderment amongst passers-by.

Mr Dicker quickly settled into the routine of the station cleaning and, in addition to relieving the constables of such work, took it upon himself to polish a sand-filled zinc bucket until it shone like silver. This bucket held back a never-closed door at the entrance to the station and its condition drew complimentary remarks from visiting members of the public. However, one day someone moved the bucket and looked behind the door. The whole space between the door and the wall was filled with cobwebs, being some three inches thick at the door jamb!

For some the borough was (and had been) a difficult place to police, it being considered necessary to avoid upsetting the more important locals. Knowing no one, however, I had no such inhibitions and found Tiverton a happy hunting ground. On my second day on the beat I found a car parked in the centre of Bampton Street, even though both sides of the street were clear of vehicles. When the lady driver returned she explained that there had been post office vans parked outside the post office and that she had double parked beside them. Apparently the postmen had emerged from the post office, driven off in their respective vans and left her car as I had found it.

She was surprised when told that she would be reported, and later in the day her father, the squire of Calverleigh (just outside Tiverton), visited the police station complaining that "These new constables don't know me or my daughter!". In the event, his visit achieved the desired result so far as he was concerned; the daughter was merely cautioned.

The police station was situated in St. Andrews Street, the beginning of the street being level with the town hall. One December evening there was a car parked with headlights on full beam and with the offside rear projecting several feet into the street from the pavement, a particularly bad piece of thoughtless parking. Knowing Superintendent Annett would pass the vehicle en route to the station *and* enquire who was on the main street beat, I stayed near at hand and duly reported the lady driver for the several minor offences.

Her husband wrote to the superintendent explaining that his wife had been attending the prize-giving evening of a local private school, held in the town hall, and had inadvertently left her car headlights on. He more or less suggested that it was a pity the reporting constable did not have something better to do other than reporting such a minor matter, but graciously added that the officer had somewhat redeemed himself by pushing the vehicle, with its flat battery, to the top of Angel Hill, thereby enabling his wife to start the car on its run down the hill.

Somewhat put out by the tone of the letter and by the fact that the superintendent had again merely endorsed my report "record as cautioned", I enquired of Tiverton constables who the writer, Mr Osmond, was. I got a lot of 'flak' from Bill Stuckey and other constables, being told that "Mr Osmond is very highly considered in the borough; he's Sir John's (Heathcoat Amory Bt.) bailiff *and* the president of Tiverton Rugby Club".

[Years later, following a complaint from the Knightshayes estate office, I made enquiries which resulted in Osmond being jailed for three years for offences involving the theft of several thousand pounds from Sir John. The case attracted great interest in the borough and was the cause of the Tiverton Borough quarter sessions being reopened after a lapse of many years. This entailed the appointment of a chairman of the sessions, one Mr Heathcoat-Williams K.C.

Osmond served his sentence and, again, it was a case of the offender returning to his old haunts. I had occasion to visit a local master builder's office and was confronted by Osmond. We passed the usual social remarks before I saw the builder on my business. He was apologetic about employing Osmond, but I pointed out that the man had paid his debt to society and, hopefully, had learnt his lesson. He promised to keep a close eye on his employee and not put undue temptation in his way.

Some time after this discussion, when I had left Tiverton, the builder reported that some National Health stamp money had been embezzled. Osmond was seen and admitted responsibility but, before the date on which he was due to appear in court arrived, he committed suicide.]

Following the resignation of Jack Hurley, his successor, Detective Constable Alfred Abrahams, arrived from Newton Abbot. He quickly found out that the sheer size of the division made it impossible for him to cover all crime enquiries, and made an official request for an aide. The outcome was that I found myself working in the C.I.D., but for a short time it was a most unsatisfactory arrangement. Whenever there was a shortage of uniformed constables for any duty, races, agricultural show or even fetes, I was ordered to parade in uniform in order to fill the gap.

After about six months of this on-off-on working 'Alf' Abrahams was promoted to detective sergeant and I was appointed detective constable. The police station had been the old Tiverton prison and we occupied two of the cells on the first floor, but had to share the telephone in Alf's office. This was inconvenient and so we decided to cut an opening in the dividing wall. This proved a tougher job than we had envisaged, the wall being some 15 inches thick. Before joining the 'force', Alf had been a carpenter and he made a frame and sliding door to fill the cavity.

In the February of 1947 applicants for the post of Chief Constable of the Devon Constabulary had been interviewed to succeed the late Major Morris. There had been almost 100 applicants for this 'plum post', finally whittled down to just twelve men invited to attend for interview by the Devon Standing Joint Committee. No doubt all twelve were excellent police officers, one being Detective Superintendent William Harvey of the Devon force, but it was apparent that one man was special insofar that a motor patrol car was despatched to collect him as he disembarked at Southampton Docks. The ten 'outside forces' applicants were offered no such facility, being obliged to make their own way to Exeter for their interviews.

The odds-on favourite, Colonel Ranulph Bacon, was duly selected. He took over office two months later and immediately there were dramatic changes with the sweeping-away of antiquated repressive rules which, hitherto, had been frequently used to discipline men quite unfairly. A simple example was the rule that a constable could not "imbibe liquor in licensed premises on his own beat at any time". Supervisory officers had caused many, many officers to be the subjects of reports and punishments for contravention of that order.

Shortly after Colonel Bacon took charge he received a report from a superintendent that Constable ... was not only partaking of strong liquor (a glass of beer) in The Red Cow, Honiton, *but* was also playing for that pub's darts team. Across the bottom of the report the Chief Constable had written in his large, florid hand: "If Constable ... has an off-duty drink in the Red Cow, I expect it is because he is thirsty. If he plays in their darts team I hope he gets double top. R. R. M. Bacon, Chief Constable". Those few words virtually ended the previously prevalent hypocrisy that the force was manned by teetotallers.

If this requires further clarification another incident hopefully seals the matter completely. Outside the main entrance of the headquarters building at Middlemoor (yes, in 1947 there was just the single administrative building) a drayman one day halted his loaded vehicle. He entered the building little knowing that it housed a group of estimable, good-living, chapel-going, teetotal senior officers (with one or two exceptions, of course), very aware of their responsibilities in keeping the Devon Constabulary pure and unsullied by the demon drink.

The drayman's statement that he had brought "the beer ordered yesterday" caused the guard duty constable to hasten to inform the sergeant who, in turn, hurried to more senior officers until the clerk superintendent, James Eddy, dashed from his office to assure the now perplexed drayman that no such order had emanated from Middlemoor - perhaps from the city police office but certainly not from the county force - and, furthermore, the superintendent would be obliged if the drayman would remove his vehicle from the premises. Even the production of a delivery note had no effect on that officer.

He assured the man: "There is no liquor on any Devon police station and there *never* will be".

I can still picture my old sergeant of Honiton days, then a chapel circuit lay-preacher, Superintendent James Eddy, resolutely standing, barring the way and pointing (if not actually declaiming): "Get thee hence and never darken this door again".

It was at this moment that the Chief Constable ran down the stairs and greeted the drayman: "Oh, good man, you've brought our beer". He then turned to the transfixed Superintendent Eddy remarking: "Thought we'd make use of the old shooting range in the basement. Going to set up a bar there, so the chaps can get a drink when they come off duty. Good idea, don't you think, superintendent?". That poor man stuttered: "Oh. Oh yes, sir", but, in fairness to his memory, he was one of the few members of the headquarters staff who never visited the new facility, not even when 'Rasher' himself was there.

That conversion of a redundant area into a bar at headquarters was the first of many bars set up in county police stations, and it was not long afterwards that Superintendent Annett drew upon all competent labourers in his division to build a bar in the Tiverton station billiard room. We were all press-ganged in to do the work, the main architect and skilled carpenter being Constable 'Ern' Edworthy, who was stationed at Bickleigh. Prior to joining the force he had been a cabinet maker and joiner and did some most creditable work. The result was a really first-class bar/lounge. When the bar was finally completed, everyone but everyone - serving police, 'specials' and their ladies - frequented it, sharing some very pleasant social evenings.

Although prices were kept low, we began to accumulate quite a large credit balance for future use, which, when remarked upon to 'Reg' Annett, drew a reply: "If you think we're going to build up reserves for our successors to p... against a wall, you're mistaken. We're going to spend it. We'll have a dinner!"

This we did, dining at Clapps' Cafe in Gold Street, Tiverton, where the manageress, Miss McPhail, put up a splendid meal after it had been explained that the dinner was for "blooming big policemen with blooming big appetites"! The event was the first of a series of 'C' division police annual dinners and marked yet another change in our social climate, so markedly different from the pre-Colonel Bacon days.

Colonel Bacon had a phenomenal memory, not only for the important matters expected of chief officers but also for the minutiae that makes up the lives of us ordinary mortals. He knew the name of every serving officer, and when he met any of them on his frequent journeys through the county he would enquire of the man's family, recalling that a child had been ill or some other detail that had affected the man or his family. The result was that when they parted the constable felt elated and all the better for their meeting!

Having settled into the C.I.D., my next ambition was to marry. There was one difficulty; the police had no accommodation available in Tiverton (if I moved from the borough it would probably entail returning to uniformed duties). The situation appeared hopeless; certainly enquiries of colleagues and every other possible source all resulted in negative answers, that is until I learned that there was a vacant flat over a lock-up shop in Gold Street.

The reason it was not occupied was that the shop owner, Mr Carl Bending, was employing a shop manager who had no wish to leave one of the recently built 'prefabs' that he was renting from the council. These metal-walled, two-bedroomed homes were packed with such amenities as built-in wardrobes and refrigerators, making them then quite revolutionary and ultra-modern. They were delivered onto sites in pre-pack form, another innovation, and took less than a week to be ready for occupation. They were planned to fill the urgent post-war need for houses and it was intended they should be replaced after 20 years with traditional houses. Many were still occupied 50 years after erection!

One Thursday afternoon, half-day for Tiverton shops, I was walking with my fiancée in Bampton Street when I told her to cross the road, adding: "I want to speak to a man but take no notice of what I say". We crossed and I spoke to the approaching man, saying: "Good afternoon, Mr Bending. May I introduce my fiancée".

Carl immediately doffed his cap, remarking how pleased he was to meet the young lady, before being taken completely aback by my next sentence. Turning to her I said: "This is Mr Carl Bending, dear. He's the man who is stopping us from getting married".

Ignoring Carl's stuttered question: "What do you mean, Mr Trist?", I explained: "Mr Bending has an empty flat above his shop but won't let it, because the only way to it is through the shop. If he would let it to us, then we could get married".

Mary was as shocked as was poor Carl, a true gentleman of the old school. He glanced at Mary, gave me a hard look and then said: "I think you had better come and see me in the morning". This I did, apologising for my desperate measure, and we took over the flat following our marriage in January 1948.

[During my time at Tiverton we managed to top the 1947 detected percentage of reported crimes for the county, and repeated this success every year until I left the division early in 1953.

The Assistant Chief Constable, Arthur Martin, retired at the end of October 1947 after over 42 years service in the Devon Constabulary. He and his wife moved to North Devon, living with Mrs Martin's father, Mr Mercer, one-time Chief Constable of Tiverton Borough. I had a fantasy of the two old gentlemen interminably arguing on some abstruse point of law, never quite coming to blows but undoubtedly having strong differences of opinion.]

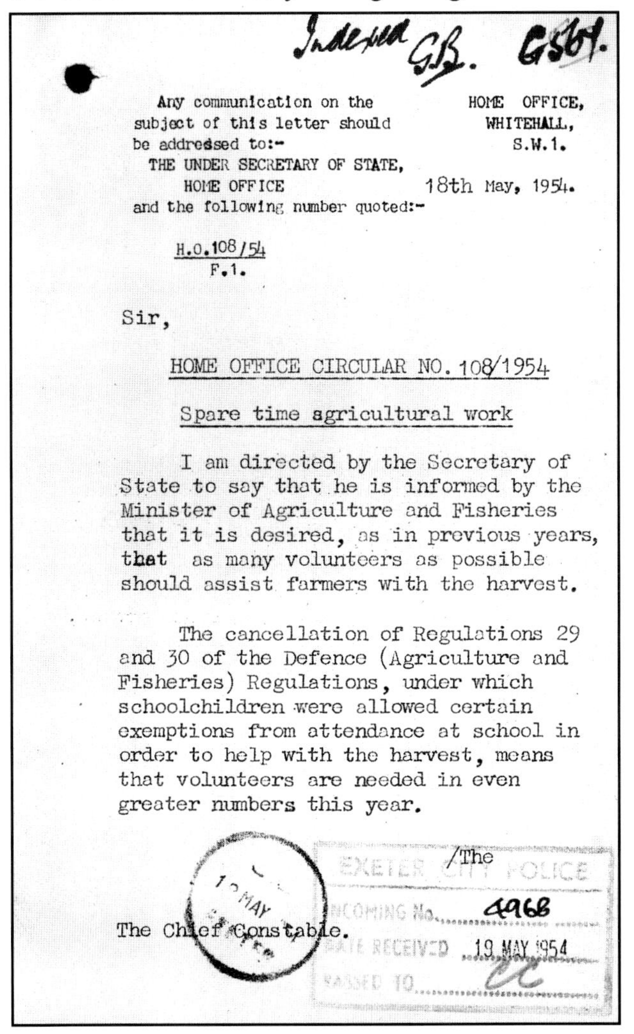

Indexed G.B. G561.

Any communication on the subject of this letter should be addressed to:- THE UNDER SECRETARY OF STATE, HOME OFFICE and the following number quoted:-

HOME OFFICE, WHITEHALL, S.W.1.

18th May, 1954.

H.O.108/54
F.1.

Sir,

HOME OFFICE CIRCULAR NO. 108/1954

Spare time agricultural work

I am directed by the Secretary of State to say that he is informed by the Minister of Agriculture and Fisheries that it is desired, as in previous years, that as many volunteers as possible should assist farmers with the harvest.

The cancellation of Regulations 29 and 30 of the Defence (Agriculture and Fisheries) Regulations, under which schoolchildren were allowed certain exemptions from attendance at school in order to help with the harvest, means that volunteers are needed in even greater numbers this year.

/The

The Chief Constable.

EXETER CITY POLICE
INCOMING No. 4968
DATE RECEIVED 19 MAY 1954
PASSED TO CC

*The post-war years were difficult times and communities rallied around to help at important occasions, such as the harvest in rural areas. The previous strictly complied-with regulations relating to police officers taking part in other gainful employment were relaxed in respect to casual agricultural labouring. This letter from the Home Office clearly shows how conditions in service were becoming more liberal. Spare-time agricultural work remained one of the few activities that police officers were permitted to indulge in for many years without risk of disciplinary action being taken.*

*Devon & Cornwall Constabulary Museum archives*

***'C' division Tiverton, photographed in the grounds of the rectory of St. Andrew's in about September 1950.***

*Rear row, left to right: Constables Jack Squires (formerly of the old Tiverton Borough Police), Prinn, Wilmot (I can't recall his forename now, but he later became a superintendent), Gilling, Powell-Chandler, Gordon Daniels, Dale, Ken Naylor, Ivor Perryman, Ken Maunder ( he was stationed at Oakford at that time and played rugby for Devon), Easterbrook, Levett, George Webber and Swift, and Motor Patrol Constable Horace Grose.*
*Centre row, left to right: Constable Bert Hawkins, Motor Patrol Constables Frank Zanazzi, Banjo Bennett and Lou Woodgates, Constables Bill Tucker (he also became a superintendent), Clifford Moore (joined 1938 with me), Cuttle, Ern Tucker, Gerry Simmonds, Bill Stuckey (of the old Tiverton force), Ern Edworthy, Stan Marshall, Harry Williams and Dick Squires (of the old Tiverton force; he was a war reserve constable at this time but later became a regular constable).*
*Front row seated, left to right: Civilian Clerk Anne Easterbrook, Acting Det. Constable Dennis Moss, Sgt. Bill Bond (he was later appointed superintendent at Okehampton, but died the day before he took over command there), Sgt. Fawden, Sgt. Phillips, Insp. Philip Adlam, Supt. Reginald Annett, Insp. Herbert Hockin, Sgt. Jack Southcott (he also later became a superintendent), Sgt. Len Rodd , Clerk Sgt. Roy Acton (later to become a chief superintendent), Acting Detective Sgt. Ted Trist and C.I.D. Civilian Clerk Joyce Myres.*
*(Missing from the group were Sgt. Macrae, Constable Arthur Chidgey (of the old Tiverton force) and War Reserve Constable Ted Howe (also of the old Tiverton force).*

*Photo courtesy of Edward Trist*
*(With thanks to Roy Acton's memory for names)*

# CHAPTER 22
# THE WIVES

In the eight Devon County divisions in 1938 there were 158 'country' stations, all manned by married constables. To the villagers in each of the parishes on his beat, the man was not 'the constable' but 'our constable'. Likewise the police house was 'our police station' due, in the main, to the rapport and respect established between the parishioners, the policeman *and* his wife. Whilst the wives of a few officers have been briefly mentioned, it would be wrong not to give a much fuller account of the contribution made by country station wives to the efficient and thrifty day-to-day running of the force.

In the years between the formation of the Devon Constabulary in 1856 until well after the first policewomen were employed in 1946, the wives of constables and sergeants were called upon to carry out multifarious duties in support of their husbands. After the lady had been the subject of her fiancé constable's application to marry, been vetted and found 'suitable to be the wife of a police officer', married and the couple had been allocated a 'country station', *then* she was obliged to agree to a number of conditions. These included her discontinuing and not taking up paid employment, assisting her husband in carrying out his constabulary duties and maintaining the condition of the police house to a satisfactory standard, subject to periodical inspections by supervisory officers. Whilst this never occurred in the force during, or after, the tenure of Major Morris, tales were told by senior constables of visits made to their cottages/houses by inspectors, superintendents and even Captain Vyvyan, the Chief Constable, and every room being inspected. Such inspections entailed not merely perfunctory standing in the doorway of rooms and glancing therein; the inspecting officer had been known to open the kitchen range door to scrutinise the interior and even peer into cupboards and the pantry!

The assistance that the wife was called upon to undertake mainly entailed unpaid duties. These included taking telephone messages, both from police and public, dealing with calls at the house by persons requiring the issue of permits for the movement of animals (particularly onerous during periods of outbreaks of swine fever or foot and mouth disease), accepting and issuing vehicle cleansing notices for conveyance of sheep and cattle to or from markets, and taking brief details concerning road accidents, any of the numerous complaints made to the police, and every other facet of rural policing, whenever the spouse was out on his beat. Each matter had to be correctly recorded, with sufficient detail so as to enable the police officer to clear on his return at the end of his tour, unless, of course, the matter was of such urgency (which she had to decide) to require either the constable to be located or details to be passed to sectional, sub-divisional or divisional office for actioning. Decisions as to the necessity to call the fire brigade or ambulance were also her responsibility in the absence of her husband (the '999' emergency call system did not come into operation until 1951).

Prior to the general installation of telephones in the country police cottages/houses, the wife was expected to use her ingenuity in locating the constable out on his beat. She had details of his hourly points and was expected to find, and persuade, a passing cyclist, a tradesman's van driver or other trustworthy person to acquaint the constable of the matter requiring his attention.

Paid duties included the feeding of prisoners, acting as police matron on escort duty with female prisoners (which could entail travelling with her husband to any part of Britain where a 'wanted female' had been detained on behalf of the Devon Constabulary), taking statements from females in cases of alleged sexual offences and the searching of female prisoners and suspects. But no policeman's wife ever made a fortune out of the services that she carried out on behalf of the force!

Supplying meals for prisoners held in police cells usually fell to the lot of the wife of the resident sergeant and, up to the 1950s, the claims that she was entitled to make were - breakfast 1s 3d, dinner (the word 'lunch' had not entered the official vocabulary at that time) 1s 7d and tea 1 shilling.

For being present whilst the relevant facts were obtained in an indecent exposure complaint at Chudleigh in 1942 and then taking a statement from a young girl, a process which took several hours, the 'police matron', Mrs Nancy Hurrell, then very recently married to Larry Hurrell, was promised payment of five shillings. However, the payment was never made, the section sergeant (Rowe) either having failed to submit a report requesting the payment or it was overlooked at headquarters. Certainly Mrs Hurrell did not have the temerity to enquire why the promised sum was not forthcoming. The five shillings then owed to Nancy, if paid now with compound interest, might, perhaps, come close to the current cost of taking a statement in a similar case!

It is interesting to consider the treatment of ladies when they became the wives of policemen.

When Larry applied to marry early in 1942, with over four years service, his application was approved only after Nancy had been vetted, entailing not only enquiries as to her suitability but also as to the good character and good name of her family *and* her associates. The couple were told, however, that there was no vacant police property, so finding accommodation in Chudleigh was their responsibility. A local war reserve constable rented them a very run-down cottage, which, from 1939, had been used as a waste-paper store. It was rat-infested and in such poor condition that after just a few weeks the Hurrells were obliged to move out, being taken in by a fellow constable, Freddie Brooks, and his wife, Gladys. They remained with them until Larry was called up to serve in the armed forces. Nancy then moved back to her home town, Barnstaple, and by a strange twist of fate was almost immediately given permission to occupy a police cottage. This was no sudden rush of generosity or benevolence by the force, but to avoid the property being requisitioned by the local authority.

After the war the Hurrells occupied the house until 1949, and sometime during this period Nancy was again called upon to be 'Matron', taking charge of a young woman with, allegedly, suicidal tendencies. The responsibility of ensuring that the woman did no harm to herself stretched over several hours, a quite difficult and harrowing experience. Once again the magic sum of five shillings was to be Nancy's payment and yet again the payment was never received!

Mrs Marie Reid, widow of ex-Inspector Ken Reid, also experienced the 'vetting' procedure, and after their marriage the Reids had a stay in Marie's home town. Thanks to her local connections they were fortunate enough to locate and rent a flat in Queen Street, Newton Abbot. Although their stay was one of only a few months duration, on several occasions Marie was called upon to be the police escort of women prisoners. Her 'duties' included collecting the women from the police cells, walking them from the Union Street police station to the court in Courtenay Street, there standing 'guard' over them waiting for their cases to be called, and then being 'in the box' during the hearing. On some occasions, when a woman was sentenced to imprisonment, she also had to accompany her back to the police cells and remain in the station until the prisoner was collected, or again escort her, this time from the station to Exeter Prison, in a patrol car.

The payment for police matron duty periods was five shillings for four to eight hours and two shillings and sixpence for under four hours.

One woman, a Molly Cleave, sought for offences at Newton Abbot, was arrested in Grimsby. It fell to the lot of Constable Reid and Marie to travel by train to Grimsby in order to collect the prisoner and bring her to Newton Abbot. This entailed spending over 19 hours travelling in wartime discomfort, with part of the time in the blackout, for total remuneration of £l: in fairness, £l had a very different value from today's coin. With this 'fortune', Marie was able to purchase a length of material and make herself a dress. Ken's salary was under £200 a year at that time.

When Ken was transferred to Clyst Honiton, late in 1941, it was to a police house with a well and hand-pump situated in the backyard, necessitating every drop of water, required for whatever household need, to be pumped into containers and carried into the house. A kitchen range was the sole method of cooking and of the heating of domestic water. Baths were taken in the kitchen in a zinc bungalow bath brought indoors for the occasion. The bath was the property of the Reids.

In the open backyard there was a brick-framed copper. Washdays required a fire to be lit under this copper, already filled with well water, and in due course the washing was boiled. When such tasks coincided with wet days, life was an utter misery, firstly getting the fire lit, then having the job of carrying the boiled clothes indoors for hand-rinsing, and then finding a place to keep the items until they could be hung out to dry. The Clyst Honiton police house did have gas lighting downstairs, but no such amenity upstairs.

Constable 261 'Percy' Richards had joined the force in 1946 and was serving at Torquay when, having been engaged for a considerable time, he made an application to marry. After the usual checking, permission was given for the couple to marry, but only on the understanding that it was their responsibility to find suitable accommodation, there being no police house available. They married on 9th December 1947, although at the time they had only the chance of renting a single room in a Torquay boarding house. Then, very shortly before Christmas, they found a two-roomed flat at Paignton.

The authorities transferred Constable Richards from Torquay to Paignton on Christmas Day 1947, kindly suggesting that they would find it easier to move their effects on that day when there would be minimal traffic. The flat was not a satisfactory arrangement and Superintendent 'Bert' Roper went to great lengths to obtain the lease of one of the then very new prefabricated houses on a Torquay council estate. The Richards were delighted with the move and had a luxurious three years in the all-electric prefab, with its built-in refrigerator and wardrobe, prior to them being transferred to Hartland.

The luxuries enjoyed at Torquay were sadly lacking in the Hartland house, although it did have an upstairs bathroom. Water was pumped indoors from a well in the yard, but later this supply was found to be unfit for drinking and mains water was piped into the kitchen. Beside the kitchen sink, a hand rotary pump was fitted, water was heated in the adjoining copper boiler and then pumped upstairs into the bath. Although they had a happy stay at Hartland, the amenities of 'their' prefab were sorely missed.

In 1949, when I was stationed at Tiverton, information came to hand that a 15-year-old girl was pregnant in one of the outlying villages, necessitating enquiries being made. For some long forgotten reason no policewoman was available to accompany me on the enquiry, so my wife was 'elected' police matron. Our visit to the girl's home was a new experience for 'the matron'. The girl, her mother and her grandmother, all of farming stock, left us in no doubt that the matter was merely a case of "doin' what comes nat'rally" and should have been of no interest to the police or any other 'outsider'. It was a long interview, with the girl shedding many tears, before the matron elicited the events leading to the girl's condition. It was an extremely tired matron who left the farmhouse kitchen with me hours later, with those events fully recorded.

An ex-Barnardo's boy, then aged 23, had been employed on the farm for some five or six years and had started taking the girl to the cinema after her schooldays ended. Their weekly excursions to the nearest town boasting a cinema were by bicycle and, on their homeward journey after the show, they were wont to break the journey with a period of courtship in one of the many fields on their route. There was little doubt that, apart from her age, she was no 'victim'. The co-author of the girl's condition was creditably remorseful, frankly admitting his responsibility.

In due course he made his appearance at the assize court and pleaded 'guilty' to the charge 'that he had carnal knowledge of a girl aged 15 years', contrary to Section 5 of the Criminal Law Amendment Act 1885, as amended. The learned judge accepted my statement that the defendant was of previously excellent character, hard-working and intended to marry the girl immediately after her 16th birthday, and made a probation order which resulted in the man being instantly released.

The aftermath was a good example of rural reasoning: "What's done, is done". The child, a bouncing boy, was born. The couple had a village church wedding, the radiant bride dressed in white, and with the baby, the whole village and my wife in attendance. Over nearly 50 years, commencing with the girl bride bringing her son into our flat for necessary nappy changes, and leaving him whilst she did her weekly shopping, we have seen another seven children bless the marriage, have attended christenings, then marriages, followed by the arrival of grandchildren, not to mention one or two divorces, without a single family member ever coming to the adverse notice of the police. The 'girl' and her husband have been wonderful parents, and are held in high esteem in the village where she was born and where they still live.

During our service years in Tiverton my wife, Mary, was 'matron' on many occasions, some experiences still being recalled with a shudder, in particular taking two young women, convicted for shoplifting, to Exeter Prison. En route she received violent elbow digs in her ribs and kicks in the legs whilst sitting between them in the police car. However, as covertly as the kicks had been administered, she retaliated with as good as she had received. In addition, she left them in no doubt that a few words passed to the prison wardresses on their arrival would make their prison stay a very unhappy time for them. She then had no further trouble, they having no idea of how minimal is police influence within prisons.

Probably neither girl was as unhappy as was the matron when she emerged from the prison, having experienced, for the first time, the trauma of the prison's doors slamming shut and keys being turned behind her, as she progressed through the building with her wards, as well as seeing babies, born in the prison hospital, lying in their cots, and realising that one of her recent charges would be in prison when her child was born.

Having married her police constable and the couple having been allocated a country police station, the newly-wedded lady more often than not found further surprises awaiting her. Constables, in their early years in the job, were invariably urban-based, where, in many cases, they duly met, courted and married winsome maids who knew little or nothing of rural life.

Brought up in, if not born into, an environment with electric lighting, gas for cooking, running water in the house feeding the services of the kitchen, bathroom and lavatory, and so much taken for granted, it was literally a culture shock for such young ladies to find none of these amenities available in her new home. Instead, they usually found a cottage standing alone and aloof with the nearest neighbour some hundreds of yards away, such being the siting of police country houses. The only water supply would be a handpump over the well situated in the yard at the rear of the house and, as was the experience of the Reids, there would be no gas or electricity, lighting being by oil lamps which might have been purchased from the outgoing constable if he was removing to a town station. Otherwise a hurried visit to the nearest ironmongers to buy paraffin, a can to contain it, and the lamp would be necessary. Whilst in the shop perhaps it would also be expedient to obtain a supply of candles, not forgetting a holder for them. The delightful aluminium lightweight saucepans, so carefully selected in the blissful pre-marriage days, would hardly be durable enough for using on an open fire, or even on the kitchen range, black iron pans being so much more suitable and durable.

Probably it would not be until the couple returned to their home that they would realize that, with a privy over 30 yards away at the far end of the garden, the procurement of a chamber pot might also have been advisable. Undoubtedly, the lack of a bathroom and other rudimentary toilet facilities was a great shock to newly-wedded wives, and even their husbands were known to be affected on occasions.

In 1949 or 1950 I met Colonel Bacon, the Chief Constable, who enquired if I had settled in to my Tiverton flat. Assured all was well, he then shot at me: "Trist, what do you shave with?". At that time I was the proud possessor of a Rolls razor, probably the noisiest piece of shaving equipment ever made. He then explained that the Widecombe constable had applied for a transfer on the grounds that there was no electricity in the police house, making it impossible for him to use his electric razor! Whether the application was granted was not known to me, but later I learned the identity of the applicant, one Constable Roger Birch, later to be Sir Roger, the Chief Constable of Sussex. Could that application in his first country station have drawn the Chief's attention to the man and led to early recognition of his worth?

Possibly it led senior officers at headquarters to consider that it was time to assess how the lot of country station wives could be improved. It may have been merely a coincidence, but in 1952 the handpump standing beside the kitchen sink in the Clyst St. Mary police house was made redundant, a mains water supply being piped in! Certainly it had a happier result than when Constable Mugridge had endeavoured to improve the amenities of a country station. Different times and very different attitudes of senior officers, it seems.

Shortly after our daughter was born in Tiverton Hospital there was a complaint of thefts from one of the hospital wards. I arrested a nurse and it fell to the lot of my wife to search the young woman - much to her distress, as the nurse had been most kind and attentive during the birth of our child. Later my wife told me that throughout the search she was hoping that she would not find the stolen money, sparing no thought for me being left with an undetected crime, and was saddened when she found the marked notes in the nurse's shoe.

Another series of thefts, this time from the Belmont Hospital in Tiverton, resulted in the arrest of a ward cleaner. She was placed in police cells and, as Sergeant Roy Acton was on leave, there arose the problem of feeding her. This was overcome by me taking the prisoner to my flat, where she had lunch with us. Afterwards she wiped the dishes that my wife had washed, before we returned to the police station. Apart from the recording "Prisoner taken from police cell by D.C. Trist at 1pm. Prisoner returned to police cell at 2pm", there was no difficulty over this unorthodox 'supplying of meal to prisoner'.

In the afternoon my wife went shopping and, whilst walking on one side of Fore Street, was halted by a call from the opposite side of the road from P.C. Bill Stuckey: "Mary, I want you". With passersby interestedly watching to whom the call had been made, the 6 feet 8 inches tall Bill Stuckey sauntered across to Mary, stating: "You had a visitor today, didn't you?". Nonplussed for a moment, Mary echoed: "Visitor?" and, as realisation dawned: "Oh, you mean Ted's prisoner. Yes I did, I had to feed her".

"Ah-h-h, but did you know she's a convicted prostitute?", enquired my 'friend' Bill.

There was a rapid exchange of questions from Mary and statements from Bill before the lady, shopping completely forgotten, turned and hurried back to the flat, where every dish that the prisoner could have touched was rewashed.

On another occasion, whilst driving from Tiverton to Exeter, my wife, baby and I came upon Motor Patrol Constables Horace Grose and 'Banjo' Bennett standing by their Wolseley with two gypsy women. Their discussion appeared to be rather heated, with the women emphasising their remarks with much waving of arms and head shakings. Apparently the constables were very relieved to see a familiar Ford Anglia number LTA 55 approaching, and signalled us to stop.

Despite frequent interruptions from the women, it was quickly explained that a complaint had been received from a Stoke Canon housewife that a banknote which she had placed under empty milk bottles on her doorstep had been stolen, and it was known that the gypsies had called at neighbouring houses offering clothes-pegs for sale. The women were seen by the constables as they were leaving the village, but were denying all knowledge of the missing note, so: "Would Mrs Trist search them, please?". The women had previously invited the constables to carry out this task, but they had thought it expedient to refuse their offers.

Such was the co-operation enjoyed by the police with the public in general, that at the first house at which we called the housewife immediately agreed to allow her 'front room' to be used for the searches. Leaving me literally, and actually, 'holding the baby', my wife first took the younger woman into the room and began a search of the unpleasantly odorous female, finding that she had no money whatsoever in the two overcoats, three woollen jumpers, skirt and underclothing in which she was attired.

The second woman, Mrs Harvey, a locally very well-known gypsy, with her plaited hair forming 'earphones' on either side of her head, was then similarly dealt with. Apparently she had also not had access to any washing facilities for some time, her unstockinged feet being hidden under a coating of dirt and her body odour causing the matron to hold her breath.

Realizing how important it was to find the banknote, the matron checked not only pockets, but also the lining and seams of the woman's overcoat. Finding nothing, she then carried out an inspection of the woman's skirt and woollen jumpers with equal thoroughness but, disappointingly, the filthy garments also had to be declared 'clean'. It was then found that the gypsy had nothing beneath her jumpers and skirt, she quickly explaining: "I come out in a hurry this mornin' me dear and forgot to put on me knickers".

With nothing found, no witnesses, and their 'outraged' assertions of innocence ringing in our ears: "We gypsies always get blamed" and other variations on that theme, we were, regretfully, obliged to release the women. They then scuttled off towards Stoke Woods, leaving me with an undetected crime complaint and the feeling that, after dark, the women would be returning to the area to pick up the banknote from its hiding place! The motor patrol officers drove off, with an "over to you" attitude as far as the paperwork was concerned, whilst we continued on our journey with my ears burning from my lady's unanswerable query: "Can't you even have a day off without getting involved in police work?". In those days there was little chance of this, especially in the C.I.D. If a complaint was received, immediate action was expected, even demanded, no matter how trifling the complaint or how late the hour.

In the period from the 1930s to the late 1960s C.I.D. hours were 9am to 9pm apart from meal breaks, with quite regular calls after 9pm being taken as the norm. In 1948, just married, my wife was only too happy to accompany me on observation duty night after night, rather than be left alone in our flat. On at least two occasions 'we' made arrests because the offender either did not see us or thought that we were a courting couple far too busily engaged in our own affairs to be interested in his activities.

Another frustration frequently endured by policemen's wives was spoilt meals. Having cooked a mouthwatering dish and heard nothing to the contrary, expecting the hungry man to present himself at the normal time, it was with growing exasperation that the wife kept the food hot - sometimes for hours - before learning that he was miles away dealing with an accident, or following a lead in some enquiry or other. Inevitably, when the husband did put in an appearance, in addition to the dried-up dish put before him there was an added, unwanted, course of 'tongue-pie'.

Like most of my colleagues, I became quite expert in excusing failures to inform the lady of a possible late appearance but, on one occasion no matter how many words of explanation, and assurances that "it would not occur again", were proffered, nothing soothed the ruffled feelings of my wife. This was when our 3-month-old daughter was found to be marked with a mass of flea bites, she having shared her cot with 'livestock' unwittingly brought into our flat when I returned from spending nights in a rag and scrap metal store which had twice been broken into.

The store was managed by a father and his son, a young man who had been terribly treated by the Japanese in one of their prisoner-of-war camps. Malnutrition in captivity had caused his eye nerves to wither so that he was almost blind. His father was a cripple, and the thought that some miserable petty thief had robbed the pathetic pair made me determined to catch him. It was for this reason that I spent many nights in the store, and acted as a carrier to the fleas, which did not bite me and made my 'crime' all the worse in my wife's eyes. (Sadly the identity of the thief was never known.) If ever a man was in the 'doghouse' it was me over this incident, which, quite unreasonably I considered, was liable to be resurrected whenever my shortcomings were being listed.

In general, it is to be hoped that not too many policemen's wives had such an experience, though most of them must have had an unpleasant incident which has remained in their memories long into their retirement years.

In the pre-war years such facilities as central heating and/or a drying room were unknown, probably unthought of, and so another of the tribulations suffered for being a policeman's wife was having to contend with rain-soaked uniforms. November, December and January were the dreaded months, but in 'Devon glorious Devon, where it rains six days out of seven', heavy and prolonged rainfalls seemingly happened all the year round, especially when the escape of convicts from Dartmoor Prison demanded constables being posted on various open moorland crossroads for up to eight-hour stints all around the clock.

On his return home the constable's dripping garments were first put out in the shed, before being brought indoors and draped over kitchen chairs placed around the front of the kitchen range. As the garments dried the kitchen became damper and damper, but this was accepted as part of the job.

Certainly it was a hard life, full of petty restrictions which were sometimes worsened by overbearing superior officers, but all these ladies seemingly accepted their lot philosophically and with good humour. Of the ladies spoken to concerning their recollections whilst being part of the force, not one expressed any bitterness or regrets. Perhaps the old 'vetting' system did have its good points, or could it be that those then young constables were, as already mentioned, extremely good pickers?

"Bless you, ladies, and thank you for your unfailing support in those pre-war and immediate post-war days. Life would have been so much harder without you, your good humour and acceptance of the status-quo!".

## "Bless you ladies, and thank you".

*(The marriage of Constable Frank Burrows and Miss Milly Blee at Paignton, 1932)*
*Photo courtesy of Mrs Gillian Lugg*

# CHAPTER 23
# IN CONCLUSION

Over 60 years have passed since our intake first entered the uninviting portals of the Devon Constabulary headquarters in New North Road, Exeter, and became the newest members of the 'force family'.

Most of us had little, or no, idea of what lay ahead of us and to several the drilling, the office fatigues and the initial introduction to those most serious crimes, such as buggery and bestiality, contained in the Offences Against the Person Act 1861, came as a shock.

With the ending of our training period and our arrival at our first stations, our lives really changed. From being the drudges and dogsbodies of everyone in headquarters, by simply donning a uniform with a rather peculiar headgear and venturing out onto the street, we were transformed into persons whose advice was sought and whose directions were followed! Members of the public appeared to accept that we were the fount of all (well, nearly all) knowledge, gladly seeking information or meekly accepting the advice that we tendered, while the simple lifting of an arm with hand outstretched was sufficient to cause a car, or even a line of cars, to be halted.

Inwardly, we were all too aware of just how little we knew and so the changes brought no pomposity or, hopefully, any overweening sense of self-importance. Fortunately, any probationer developing such leanings was quickly brought to his senses by his supervisory officers and fellow constables.

There was nothing quite so salutary in bringing us to our proper level than our first days out on the beat alone, or being confronted with a problem whilst on 'nights'. At such times we were little better equipped than our original predecessors of 1856. True we had electric torches in place of the 'bulls-eye' oil lamps with their flickering beams, and somewhere not far distant was a telephone that could be used to summon assistance. Our helmets, though, probably gave no greater protection than the tarred and varnished top hats worn in the 19th century. Our truncheons were a comfort to feel nestling against one's thigh, but could be a useless accoutrement against a surprise attack by a felon armed with a stout walking stick, a jemmy or a pickaxe handle, and whilst the whistle chain was decorative, who was to answer the whistle, when blown? In town stations the nearest night duty colleague could be a mile or more away, trudging his beat and unaware of any incident occurring, even in an adjoining street, whilst in the country beats the constable and the shotgun-armed night poacher could well be the only persons abroad in the small hours after midnight.

Certainly the introduction of personal radios has dramatically improved contact systems between police officers but sadly, through the eyes of a policeman who retired almost 40 years ago, it seems that the intervening years have also seen the relationships between police and public deteriorate in an inverse proportion to the improvement in our means of communication.

In the 1930s radio, even the local radio station, had little airtime to spare for police matters, whilst television was so limited in pre-1946 days as to be virtually non-existent. However, we enjoyed good relations through press coverage, especially with the staff of the local newspapers. The local papers very much depended on police-orientated reports - petty sessions, juvenile and matrimonial court cases - to fill their columns, and much was made of little to this end. On one occasion the front page headlines of the *Dawlish Gazette* were: *"POLICE CHIEF WORRIED AT HUGE DRUNKENNESS INCREASE AT DAWLISH"*. Readers found that at the Brewster Sessions the police superintendent had reported that 'Their Worships' had dealt with 19 cases of drunkenness in the previous 12 months, against just 13 cases the year before: "An increase of almost 50%, causing great concern to me and the police in general".

Details of every case heard in the local court could be found in the paper, whilst *the* reporter made at least one visit a day to the police station. Such was the public interest in the activities of 'their' police in pre-war days.

*The first television programme of any consequence featuring the police was 'Dixon of Dock Green'. The 'star' was one Jack Warner as Constable George Dixon, a character portrayed as the very epitome of sagacity and honesty. That the public accepted P.C. Dixon as a role model and a typical policeman yet again indicates the esteem in which the police were held, even in the 1950s. Despite the programme being based on the Metropolitan Police, a Devon Constabulary constable, Horace 'Benjy' Benjafield, wrote to the BBC congratulating them on the first episode but listing the many mistakes that he had noticed. As a result, Benjy became the official police technical adviser for the subsequent episodes in the first series.*

*Photograph courtesy of the B.B.C.*

Current factual television programmes on police work reflect credit on the police for their efforts to maintain law and order but, unfortunately, these are far outnumbered by police drama series in which sex, general salaciousness, corruption and overbearing superior officers predominate. One from my generation of policemen can't help but feel that these programmes distort the true state of affairs for the sake of excitement and do nothing but harm to the police service, being insulting to the vast majority of men and women who served, and are serving, conscientiously and honestly in our police forces. Certainly television has done few favours to the police service and has miserably failed to project a true picture of the debt owed to its members by the public in general.

Having perused the previous pages and, hopefully, gathered what police officers contended with in the past, you must now be the judge of whether 'the old days were the best days', and be able to answer the query expressed in the first paragraph of my preface to these random recollections.

For myself, I would not have missed the experiences or the camaraderie that we shared - not even for the greater monetary rewards that I might have obtained in another vocation. In those days to be in the police was to be a member of a family, a close-knit family who, when the need arose, stood together and finally overcame the difficulties, frustrations and even down-right bloody-mindedness that we experienced throughout our service.

On retirement I received £687 10s 7d per year pension, and now, 60 years on, consider that I am making a small profit over my superannuation payments. Oh, happy days!

Early in 1988, as the 50th anniversary of the 1st June 1938 intake of Devon Constabulary recruits approached, I wrote to those 'survivors' in the Exeter area and enquired if they would be interested in having a reunion to mark that, to us, eventful day. Nearly all replied expressing support, and I found myself with the job of tracing the rest of our group. This was simple with those who were in receipt of police pensions, but several seemed to have disappeared without trace.

To my surprise, I learned from headquarters that no other intake had ever organised a reunion, but the then Chief Constable, Mr Donald Elliott, replied to my rather tentative enquiry of whether we could visit headquarters at Middlemoor, by saying that both he and Mrs Elliott, with as many chief officers and their wives as possible "would be present on the memorable occasion".

He was as good as his word, even arranging for the attendance of the force photographer and the press, which certainly made a day to remember for our wives and the thirteen of us able to attend.

The event was a great success, commencing with coffee and refreshments at Middlemoor, before we left for lunch at the Tudor House at Exeter, followed by a conducted tour and, later, refreshments at the ancient Tucker Hall, before ending our (what I considered would be) last group meeting.

However, in 1992 reminders came from many of my erstwhile colleagues that June 1993 would be our 55th anniversary and what did I intend to do about it? My reply, in a word "nothing", was ignored! With some trepidation I wrote to Mr John Evans, the Chief Constable, asking if we could again use Middlemoor as our base, and received his reply: "Delighted".

There were just eight, of the original 30, able to attend; others were missing due to illness and holiday commitments. The Chief Constable had kindly arranged for early coffee, to have the bar open, and for our group to use the officers' mess for luncheon. On his instruction his (then) staff officer, Chief Inspector Liam McGrath, had arranged a programme of visits to departments that had not even existed in our service years. We were astonished at the many changes which had come about since our retirement; it seemed that we had served in a positively prehistoric age!

Once again we made our farewells, knowing that it was our last group reunion.

The end of 1997 came, and once again enquiries from Cliff Moore and Stan Ledbrook, to the effect that "Surely we could not ignore our diamond jubilee?".

Off went letters to the now very few, and to my dismay I received some very sad replies indicating that the intervening five years had been quite unkind to many of us. Some were confined to wheelchairs, others had suffered crippling strokes, whilst Alzheimer's and Parkinson's diseases had also taken their toll. To each writer I sent suitable, though inadequate, replies. Very reluctantly I wrote to Mr Evans, and yet again received his encouraging affirmative reply that his current staff officer, Chief Inspector Steven Swani, would make all the necessary arrangements.

With just seven of us attending, and only Ron Lee, Ben Muckett and me blessed to still have our Aimee, Joyce and Mary to accompany us, brought home to me just how fortunate we were.

Once again we had a memorable welcome from senior officers, led by Assistant Chief Constable Alan Street, refreshments on arrival, access to the bar, a beautiful lunch (made even more appetising as it was paid for by the Chief Constable) and then visits to the new firing range (with the armed Range Rovers in attendance), where we actually handled guns, each of which cost more than our individual *first five* years gross pay! In addition, we were treated to a wonderful show by members of the dog section (bringing "Ooos" and "Aahs" from the ladies) and a visit to the helicopter (which was called out just as the few of us were about to take an unofficial trip in it. You just can't win 'em all).

With the day rounded off with tea and cakes, we departed on our homeward ways, the others having my words ringing in their ears: "No matter what you write, telephone or say to me - this is the last reunion I am organising!".

Thank you Mr Elliott and Sir John Evans for three truly memorable days, and for your assurances: "You are still part of the police family, and always will be".

With the single exception of a reunion by the first intake of police cadets (held after our 1988 reunion), no other intake in this force has ever enjoyed such an experience. I am sure that you other pensioners just cannot realise what you missed!

At the time of compiling this book, of the June 1938 intake just six of us remain - Stan Ledbrook, Ron Lee, Arthur Lemon, Cliff Moore, Ben Muckett, and myself.

Browsing through these pages, examining the photographs and recalling certain incidents in my career, some never to be committed to print, I reflect on my words at the beginning: "Were we so fortunate?" and "Was life so enjoyable?". The answer must lie with you, the reader, but I look back with memories, possibly sentimentally tinged rosy-hued, and consider that my police service years were spent in the golden age of policing; a period when we had the acme of public respect and support. How fortunate we were to have had that experience, possibly never to be equalled by our successors.

***The 1st June 1988 reunion (50th anniversary).***

*From left to right: Rev Bill Lewis, Assistant Chief Constable Brian Eastwood, Ronald Lee, Richard Bennett, Mr Hollins - the Force Administration Officer, Edward Trist, Sidney Richards, Stanley Powell, Assistant Chief Constable Brian Phillips, Stanley Ledbrook, Frank Harding, Benjamin Muckett, Arthur Lemon, Tom Pill, Clifford Moore, Leslie Evans and The Chief Constable, Donald Elliott.*

*Photo courtesy of the Express & Echo Newspapers*

**The 1st June 1993 reunion (55th anniversary).**

*Standing, left to right: Chief Superintendent 'Bob' Ball, Richard Bennett, Clifford Moore, Stanley Powell, Edward Trist, Sidney Richards, Arthur Lemon, Ronald Lee, Stanley Ledbrook and Chief Inspector McGrath. Seated, left to right: Mrs Winifred Moore, Mrs Kathleen Richards, Mrs 'Hetty' Powell, Assistant Chief Constable Brian Eastwood, Deputy Chief Constable Keith Portlock, Mrs Mary Trist, Mrs 'Nan' Harding (the widow of Frank), Mrs Aimee Lee and Mrs Molly Ledbrook.*

*Courtesy of Devon & Cornwall Constabulary photographic department*

**The 1st June 1998 reunion (Diamond Jubilee).**

*Standing, left to right: a lady representative from the force welfare department, the son of Les Evans, Stanley Ledbrook, Clifford Moore, Edward Trist, Benjamin Muckett, Assistant Chief Constable Alan Street, Ronald Lee, Leslie Evans, Arthur Lemon, the Force Chaplain, Christopher Powell of the Police Federation office and John Medland, Force Welfare Officer. Seated, left to right: the daughters of Stan Ledbrook and Cliff Moore, Mrs Joyce Muckett, Mrs Nan Harding (widow of Frank), Mrs Aimee Lee, the daughter of Arthur Lemon and Mrs Mary Trist.*

*Courtesy of Devon & Cornwall Constabulary photographic department*

# INDEX


'A' Division 27, 30, 67, 163
Abrahams, Det. Const. Alfred 81, 166, 167
Acton, Clerk Sergeant Roy 165, 170, 175
Adlam, Inspector Philip 170
Aircraft crashes 104, 137-140
Air Raid Wardens 137-140
Air Raids 19, 71, 76, 90, 95-99, 109-112, 134
Annett, Inspector R. 154, 157, 162, 166, 168
Anti Personnel Bombs 90-91
Anzio 19
Armstrong, Wing Commander 95
A.R.P. 27, 81, 87, 96
Arromanches 25
Ashburton 35, 123, 125
Austin 10 patrol cars 82

'B' Division 30, 67, 163
Bacon, Colonel Ranulph (Chief Constable of Devon) 158, 159, 167, 175
Badcock, Melvyn 134
Badcock, 'Sid' (Tiverton police) 14, 127, 129, 134, 141
Badcock, Wendy 134
Baker, M.P.C. 'Spud' 82
Bampton 27, 31, 105, 107, 149, 153-164
Banks, Leslie 18, 19, 20
Barnstaple 19, 22, 24, 27, 30, 62, 67
Bastin, Harold 65, 66
'Battle of Britain' 94, 158
Beat Books 67-68, 114
Bennett, M.P.C. 'Banjo' 170
Bennett, Richard 'Dickie' 19, 46, 182, 184
Beynon, Mervyn (Chief Constable of Tiverton police) 14, 127
Bickleigh 24, 31, 35
Birching, (punishment) 60
Blamey, Constable 'Len' 82, 93
Blamey, Sergeant Hedley 115, 116, 122, 125
Blitzes 24, 74, 95, 100, 102, 109, 111, 148
Body, Constable John 83, 84
Bond, Sergeant 'Bill' 170
Booth, Evangeline Miss 32
Botheras, Ronald 13
Bray, Sidney 18, 19, 20, 46
Brixham 27, 31, 133-134
Brooks, 'Freddie' 15, 81
Brooks, Montague 'Monty' 156, 157, 158
Buckingham, Inspector Donald 'Bucky' 128, 129, 130, 158
Burgess, Inspector 97, 128
Burnell, Edgar 15, 51
Burrington, Special Constable 137-140

'C' Division 31, 57, 127, 159, 162, 168, 170
Carlton Cinema, Teignmouth 148
Carpenter, Det. Const. 'Bill' 81
Castle, Rougemont 13, 18, 23, 37, 42
Chamberlain, Prime Minister Neville 71
Cheek, 'Bill' 15, 153, 160
Chidgey, Arthur (Tiverton police) 14, 165, 170
Christophers, Alfred 18, 19, 20
Churchill, Prime Minister Winston 148
Churchward, War Reserve Constable 97
Clapp, War Reserve Constable 'Les' 165
Clements, Constable 115
Climo, Sergeant 24, 30
Coal, deliveries of 42-44
Coldridge, Fire Chief 122-125
Coldridge, 'Stan' 18, 19, 20, 46
Collar numbers 14, 35
Connett, Constable 'Fred' 72
Coppin, Superintendent Francis 31, 36, 80, 89, 93, 97, 103, 114, 129, 131, 132, 137-140
Costello, Sir Leonard 121, 122, 149
Cowling, 'Don' 15
Crapp, Constable 'Jack' Ewart 135
Croft Farm, West Charleton, murder at 61
Crownhill police station 11, 35, 36
Cullompton 31, 57, 81, 113, 127

'D' Day 26, 132, 133
'D' Division 27, 31, 63, 159
Dale, Constable 170
Daniels, Gordon 170
Dart, 'Dick' 155, 156
Dartmoor Prison 36, 116, 119, 162
Dartmouth 26, 29, 35, 116
Dawlish 22, 27, 31, 135, 137-146
Dawlish Warren 139, 144, 145
Dimeo, 'Mike' 61
Distinguished Flying Cross 93
Doble, Constable 'Len' 137, 141, 144

# INDEX


Doney, William 19, 159
Drew, Chief Inspector 31
Dunkeswell Airfield 113
Dunkirk 79, 89, 90, 118, 133, 141, 148

'E' Division 19, 31, 159
Eddy, Edgar (Superintendent) 11, 159
Eddy, James 63, 76, 78, 141, 147, 151, 159, 167
Edwards, Stanley 13, 14, 18, 20
Edworthy, Constable 'Ern' 168, 170
Elizabeth, Princess 29
Elizabeth, Queen 29
Ellicombe J.P., Colonel 13, 14,
Elliott, Donald (Chief Constable) 181, 182
Elliott, John 18, 19, 20, 46
Engelhart, Leutnant Anton 137-140
Evacuees 71
Evans, Leslie 19, 20, 182, 184
Evans, Sir John (Chief Constable) 7, 8, 182
Exeter Airport 26, 45, 46
Exeter City Police 12, 15, 29, 78, 98, 132, 163
Exeter Prison 6, 27, 37, 174
Exmouth 22, 31, 68

'F' Division 26, 30, 38, 51, 58, 63, 83, 159
Fear, Reginald 18, 19, 20, 46
Fenny Bridges 87
Fice, 'Harry' 168, 169
Firebrace, William 12, 18, 20
Fire Brigade 122-125, 128, 137-140, 152
First Police Reserve 72
Flying Fortress Aircraft 22
Foot and Mouth Disease 105-108, 113
Ford Prefect Patrol Cars 82
Friskney, War Reserve Constable 82

'G' Division 27, 32, 159
Gale, Eric Francis 'Stormy' 20, 21, 42, 43
Gale, Sergeant 'Harry' 71
Galpin, Sergeant 'Frank' (Tiverton police) 14, 127, 141, 142
Gardener, Special Constable 137-140
Gas Masks 28, 32, 159
Gloucester Regiment 89
Great War (1914-18) 72, 82, 83
Green, Constable 'Jimmy' 73
Greenwood, Colonel (Chief Constable) 23, 24
Grenadier Guards 19
Grose, M.P.C. Horace 170, 176
Gulley, Constable John 84, 127, 128

'H' Division 35, 36, 72, 159
Halifax Bombers 27
Harding, 'Frank' (Devon Constabulary) 14, 20, 21, 27, 28, 46, 68, 78, 182, 183
Harding, 'Frank' (Tiverton police) 14
Harding, 'Nan' 183, 184
Hardwell, Rupert 15
Hare, Ralph 39-46
Harris, Constable Charles 73
Harvey, Det. Const. 'Bill' 81, 128
Harvey, Kenneth 18, 20, 22, 38, 46
Harvey, Supt. William 19, 31, 32, 73, 159, 167
Hawkins, 'Bert' 45, 170
Hawkins, 'Sam' 45, 69
Hawkins, Thomas 45
Haysom, Irene 8, 166
Haysom, Maurice 107, 160, 161
Hemyock 27, 31, 110, 113, 114
Highweek 27, 31, 84, 125, 127-130, 141
Hockin, Inspector Herbert 162, 165
Holland, Cyril 'Duchy' 79, 82, 93, 119
Holmes, Inspector R. 31, 63, 160
Holne 35, 58, 114, 119, 121
Home Guard 137-140
Honiton 22, 31, 63-70, 72, 76, 115, 141, 167
Hookins, 'Bert' 107, 108
Howe, War Reserve Constable 'Ted' 165, 170
Hulland, Inspector R. 31, 80, 88, 97
Hurley, Det. Const. 'Jack' 169, 163, 166
Hurrell, 'Larry' 8, 51, 82, 124, 172
Hurrell, Nancy 8, 15, 176
Hutchings, Frederick 12, 29, 30, 45
Hutchings, Sub-Insp. Walter 31, 51, 52, 159

I.R.A. 87
Identity Cards 36, 105
Indecent Exposure 79

Japanese Prisoners of War 177
Jewell, Sergeant 'Josh' 36
Johnson, Inspector W. 30, 159

Johnson, War Reserve Constable William 116

Kelly, Sergeant 'Sam' 71
Kenton 31, 137
King George VI 29, 115
Kings Police Medal 77, 78
Kingskerswell 31, 88
Kingsteignton 19, 31, 82, 83
Knight, W.A.P.C. Dorcas 82

Lamb, Sergeant 'Bill' 81, 83, 127, 128, 132
Land, Sergeant 'Bill' (Tiverton police) 14
Langman, 'Harry' 19, 159
Ledbrook, Molly 183
Ledbrook, 'Stan' 18, 20, 22, 181-184
Lee, Aimee 181, 183, 184
Lee, Ronald 18, 22, 46, 51, 181-184
Lemon, Arthur 22, 23, 46, 78, 82, 182-184
Lethbridge, Mrs. 73
Levett, Constable 170
Lewis, 'Bill' 22, 23, 182
Lidstone, Special Constable 133
Lorry, Force removal 44, 51, 161
Luftwaffe 26, 94, 137-140, 148, 149
Luscombe, Cyril 35, 41, 43
Luscombe, John 35
Lustleigh 31, 116
Luxton, Special Constable 137-140
Lyle, War Reserve Constable 78

Macrae, Sergeant Alexander 107, 153-155, 162
Manley, Constable Edgar 137-140
Marshall, Superintendent J. 31, 63, 78
Martin, Sergeant Wilfred 147, 153
Martin, Superintendent A.E. 17, 19, 31, 37, 45, 51, 57, 73, 80, 118, 156, 157, 162, 169
Maunder, Constable 'Ken' 170
McNair, Sir Douglas 121, 122
Melhuish, Superintendent P. 30, 159
Mercer, (Chief Constable of Tiverton) 59, 169
Merryweather Fire Engine 122-125
Metropolitan Police 26, 42, 81
Milford, Superintendent T. 32, 45
Mock, Sergeant Alfred 133-134
Mont Le Grand, Exeter 30
Moore, Clifford 24, 46, 170, 181-184
Moore, Winifred 183
Morebath 27, 104, 105, 107-109
Moretonhampstead 26, 27, 115-126, 131
Morris MC, Major (Chief Constable) 28, 30, 43, 73, 122, 126, 162, 163, 171
Morrison Shelter 107, 106
Moss, Acting Det. Const. Dennis 170
Muckett, 'Ben' 20, 24, 25, 46, 51, 181, 182, 184
Muckett, Joyce 184
Mugridge, Constable 'Bill' 64, 66
Mutiny, H. M. Prison Dartmoor 36

National Fire Service 152
Naylor, Constable 'Ken' 170
New North Road, Exeter (Headquarters) 12
Newman, Sergeant 'Frank' 52, 55, 61
Newton Abbot 16, 22-27, 76-81, 93, 97-99, 103, 104, 127-130, 134, 141, 155
Newton Abbot Railway Station 79
Nichols, Constable 'Ted' 60, 61
'Nisi Prius' Court 13, 18, 37, 42

Oakford 31, 107, 160, 170
Okehampton Police Station 21-23, 30, 78
'Old Contemptibles' 72, 132
Osborne, Owen 116, 119
Ottery St. Mary 24, 25, 31

Paignton 19, 24-27, 51-62, 63, 130, 133, 173
Parr, Superintendent E. 30, 54
Parsons, Yvonne 73
Pay 37, 38, 130
Pay Parades 48, 133
Penzance Borough Police 13, 40, 150
Perryman, Chief Insp. 'Reg' 8, 119, 120, 147
Perryman, Ivor 165, 170
Pill, Superintendent Morley 25
Pill, 'Tom' 18, 25, 26, 38, 46, 182
Plymouth City Police 15, 29, 36, 74, 109, 146
Points 52, 55
Pollard, Constable 'Sid' 29, 117
Potter, Constable 40, 81
Powell, Stanley 12, 18, 182, 183
Prison Escapes 116-121, 164
Prowse, Philip 47-50
Puttees 48

# INDEX

Queen Elizabeth 29
Quick, 'Ken' 51, 52

R.A.F. 23, 27, 45, 57, 93-95, 97, 139, 156
R.S.P.C.A. 24, 82
Rationing 86, 105, 135, 149
Reid, Kenneth 25, 26, 46, 82, 85, 93, 104, 172, 173, 175
Reid, Marie 8, 26, 172, 173, 175
Richards, Cyril (Tiverton police) 13, 127
Richards, Kathleen 183
Richards, Sidney 26, 46, 182, 183
Roper, George 35
Roper, Superintendent 'Jack' 159
Rose, 'Percy' Norman 18, 20, 26
Rowe, Special Constable 'Les' 135
Rowsell, (Chief Constable of Exeter) 98

Salter, Chief Superintendent J. 30
Sanders, Constable Raymond 83
Searle, Constable 'Stanley' 82, 84
Sidmouth 24, 25, 31, 68, 151
Simpson, Ruth 88
Smith, Richard 'Jack' 11, 13, 18, 26
Smith, Superintendent 'Daddy' 35, 36, 49
Soper, Air Raid Warden Philip 137-140
Southcott, Ernest 'Bob' 18, 26, 27, 46
Southcott, Superintendent 'Jack' 27, 170
Special Constabulary 87, 97, 114, 126, 137-140
Spitfire Aircraft 94, 148
Squires, 'Jack' (Tiverton police) 14, 165, 170
Squires, War Reserve Constable 'Dick' 73, 170
Starcross 31, 65, 137
Sten Guns 89
Stephens, Sergeant Sidney 137-140
Stokes, 'Reg' 113, 114
Stone, Inspector Ernest 31, 84, 132, 145, 148, 159
Stoneman, Home Guardsman 137-140
Stuckey, 'Bill' (Tiverton police) 14, 165, 170
Summers, W.A.P.C. Rita Joan 69

Tavistock 22, 35
Teignmouth 27, 31, 67, 147-152
Tiverton 24, 27, 113, 127, 130, 158, 165-171
Tiverton Borough Police 13-15, 29, 40, 127, 141, 150, 165, 169, 170
Torquay 24-26, 45-51, 58, 84, 115, 154, 161
Totnes 19, 32-36
Traffic Department 19, 27, 69, 117, 128, 170
Training 37, 38
Trist, Mary 27, 168, 169, 175, 176, 181-184
Trooping the Colour 132
Trump, War Reserve Constable Lester 116
Tucker, Constable 'Ernie' 160, 170
Turl, Special Constable Stanley 88
Turner, Constable 'Tiny' 106

U.S. Forces 19, 20, 129-134, 149
Unexploded Bomb 145
Uniform, issue of 47
Unilateral Parking 16, 17
Unoccupied properties (checking of) 15, 16,

V.E. Day 148, 156
V.J. Day 156
Vickery, Det. Sgt. 'Jack' 81, 128, 132
Vinton, Constable 'Reg' 83
Vyvyan, Capt. (Chief Constable) 48, 49, 67, 171

W.A.P.C.s 72-74, 82, 103, 146
Walters, War Reserve Constable Arthur 72
War Reserve Police 72, 81, 97, 116, 146, 170
Warrant Cards 47
Webber, Inspector 'Charlie' 13, 14, 15, 20, 23, 29, 37, 38, 41, 42, 43, 51, 80
West, 'Frank' 20, 27, 63, 76
Westlake, 'Jack' 160
Wheeler, Inspector Frank 'Tiger' 53, 116
Widecombe-in-the-Moor 35, 175
Willcocks, 'Buddy' 69
Williams, Sergeant 'Frank' 14
Windeatt, Frederick 18, 20, 26, 27, 46
Wings for Victory Parade 146
Wives 171-178
Worden, Sergeant 'Alf' 81, 128
Wykes, 'Bert' 63, 76

Yarcombe 31, 147
Yeo Mills 31, 154, 165
Ypres 72

Zanazzi, M.P.C. 'Frank' 82, 170